THE
BADGER
RIOT

THE

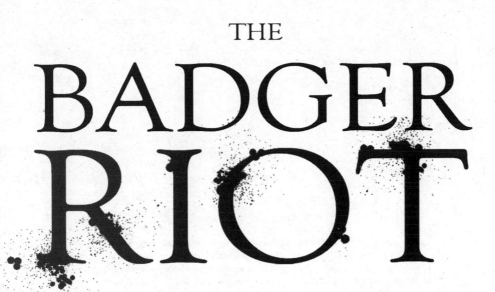

BADGER
RIOT

J. A. RICKETTS

FLANKER PRESS LTD.
ST. JOHN'S
2008

Library and Archives Canada Cataloguing in Publication

Ricketts, J. A. (Judy Ada), 1944-
  The Badger riot / J.A. Ricketts.

ISBN 978-1-897317-32-7

I. Title.

PS8635.I355B33 2008   C813'.6   C2008-904360-X

PRINTED IN CANADA

This book is printed on Ancient Forest Friendly paper that is acid-free,
100% post-consumer recycled, and processed chlorine-free.

Cover Design: Adam Freake

FLANKER PRESS
PO BOX 2522, STATION C
ST. JOHN'S, NL, CANADA
TOLL FREE: 1-866-739-4420
WWW.FLANKERPRESS.COM

13 12 11 10 09   4 5 6 7 8 9 10

We acknowledge the financial support of the Government of Canada through the Book Publishing Industry
Development Program (BPIDP) for our publishing activities; the Canada Council for the Arts which last
year invested $20.1 million in writing and publishing throughout Canada; the Government of
Newfoundland and Labrador, Department of Tourism, Culture and Recreation.

For the people of Badger
and the loggers of Newfoundland

"We was only loggers."
Unknown

Characters

JENNIE SULLIVAN
Eldest daughter of Ned Sullivan, river driver, and his wife Bridey.

VERN CRAWFORD
Taxi operator. Wife Millie, and their only child, Melanie.

RALPH DRUM
Mi'kmaq, logger and union coordinator.

TOM HILLIER
*Woodsman. Son of Albert Hillier, Badger station master,
and his wife Suze.*

ANNIE DRUM
Ralph Drum's mother. Healer and midwife.

PETER DRUM
Ralph Drum's grandfather. Patriarch of the Mi'kmaq community.

ROD ANDERSON
Woods contractor. Wife Ruth, and daughter Audrey.

ALF ELLIOTT
Telegraph operator. Wife Mary, children Amanda, David and Thomas.

PASTOR DAMIAN GENGE
Pentecostal preacher.

FATHER KEVIN MURPHY
Roman Catholic priest.

CECIL NIPPARD
A scab worker. Sister Emily.

BILL HATCHER
Rod Anderson's foreman and good friend.

CONSTABLE RICHARD FAGAN
Newfoundland Constabulary based in St. John's.

LEVI AND BECKY ABERNATHY
Foster parents of Constable Richard Fagan.

These characters are fictitious. Any resemblance to people living or dead is coincidental. H. Landon Ladd, Joseph R. Smallwood, and Constable William Moss are key historical figures.

Prologue

Autumn sun glinted on the surface of a wide, swift-running river. The sky was deep, clear end-of-summer blue. Close to the shore, alders bent toward the burbling water, as if the sound pleased them. Under his smooth, tanned skin, the muscles of the young Beothuk's arms bunched as he paddled his provision-laden moon-shaped birchbark canoe down the river he knew as Running Water. His brothers followed in two more canoes, each as burdened as his own.

The summer had been dry and the small river was shallow in places, difficult to navigate. The young man continued to paddle confident and sure, knowing just where the rocks were. Up ahead was the junction where Running Water ran into Big River. As he approached the larger river he paused to rest, letting the canoe drift with the current.

Summer on the coast had ended and the Beothuks were moving inland for the winter, following rivers and lakes that their ancestors had followed for generations. The rest of his family had gone ahead. Their harvest from the coastal waters was loaded aboard many canoes, and they would first make camp where the three rivers met. At this river junction, the families of the People gathered to renew old ties, exchange stories and hear the spirits speak, as children born during the past year were given their names high atop the Great Mound. As the turning-of-the-leaves season progressed, the people would continue farther into the interior to their winter homes on the shores of the Great Spirit Lake.

Angling his canoe to the right against the swift-running current, the Beothuk entered onto Big River. In a few minutes he would join his wife and young children. The current was strong, and he bent his head and dug the paddle of his canoe deep into the dark flowing waters. A few powerful strokes against the current of Big River brought another waterway into view: gentle Red Stream that sprung from high on the plateaus. Big River had its beginning far into the centre of the island where the Earth Mother was hidden. It was She who gave the People the heart gift of red ochre to cover their bodies from their naming times until their dying times.

There they were, the People of the tribes, their many canoes hauled up near the tall pine trees that guarded the River Spirit.

Beaching on the riverbank, the young Beothuk jumped out. He turned his head to see his brothers close behind, coming ashore as well. People were running to welcome them. Happy to be there at last, he looked up to the Great Mound, green and alive in the sunlight. Around its base the Beothuk families were busy erecting their mamateeks.

John Drum's snowshoes crunched on the frost-filled snow as he plodded his way down the bank of the frozen river. As a Mi'kmaq trapper, he knew the path well for upriver were his trapping grounds, where fox, beaver, muskrat and caribou were plentiful. Once, the land all around had been Beothuk country, but with the white man's coming, things had changed. Beothuk ways to the coast had been cut off, and they had been forced to live inland year-round. Now the Beothuk were no more, but their spirits could still be felt, John thought, especially atop the round hill near the river.

John's people had originally come to this large island from the lands far to the west and northwest. At first they kept to the island's west coast, but their quest for furs caused them to spread farther inland. Thirty years ago, John and his brothers and cousins had come here with their families and settled. It was a good place. Their band had about fifty family members. They lived closely, depending on each other to survive the harsh winters. John was their chief.

White man called this river Badger Brook. It ran south and emptied into the great Exploits River waterway. Little Red Indian River, springing from high elevations to the southwest, joined the Exploits here too. The rushing waters, once joined, surged their way north to the Bay of Exploits and the Atlantic Ocean. These names were all white man's names. No doubt the Beothuk had called them something else.

John continued walking effortlessly in his snowshoes until he came to the spit of land that they called Beothuk Point. John could see the remains of the Beothuk firepits, still visible among the grass and bushes. Here was the convergence of the three rivers. This was a good place, a powerful place.

⚯

Clacking on the narrow-gauge railway, the train's wheels carried an unceasing sound that was mind-numbing to the passengers on board. Outside, trees and bogs rushed past in the evening light. The couplings protested – clank, clunk, squeal, bang – as the engine dragged the passenger units uphill and down. As the big diesel, pulling ten coach cars, snaked around a long bend, the engineer blew his lonely whistle into the stillness of the landscape.

Many miles up ahead lay Badger Station. A large wooden building with a ticket office, spacious waiting room and an area to store freight, the station was a busy place. It served a key role as the main access terminal not only for Badger but also for communities in Green Bay and Halls Bay.

A platform separated the station from the track and on this frosty winter evening many people stood waiting for the train. The arrival of the Express, as it was commonly called, was a daily social event for many of the townspeople, even in winter. It was an excuse to go and see who was boarding and see if any strangers were getting off. Young women would don their bandanas, apply their lipstick and walk arm in arm up the road to stand on the platform, to eye each other and to be eyed.

Among those waiting was Ralph Drum puffing on a cigarette and leaning against the freight platform, his black hair brushing the collar of his dun-coloured coat. Of medium height, his slight stature belied the strength of his sinewy frame. He moved with a natural grace, which was the reason he had easily earned a job as a driver when the logs were on the river. Most striking about Ralph were his dark, almost black eyes set wide in his angular face. His light brown skin was clean-shaven. As he stood there he noticed some of the girls looking at him out of the corners of their eyes. He raised his hand and tipped his salt-and-pepper cap to those he knew.

Ralph gazed east along the track stretching toward the trestle. He was waiting for the arrival of the train that today would be carrying with it recruits for the International Woodworkers of America, the new loggers' union. A few weeks ago the union had called a strike against the Anglo-Newfoundland Development Company, a pulp and paper conglomerate whose owners were English.

The union had rented an empty house, owned by Mrs. Noel, over on Church Road, as a lodging place for the strikers from out of town. Ralph's instructions were to take the incoming men over there and bed them down.

Ralph flicked his cigarette down onto the snow by the tracks where it fizzled briefly. His mind drifted back to his old grandfather who used to tell him about the time when the railway was laid across the bogs, through the thick forests and over the high plateaus. A river of iron, he said, a pathway to a different world.

Grandfather's memory was long and there were many evenings when Ralph sat beside the old man and listened to his stories. Grandfather told him that before the railway came, even before the white man, his ancestor, a Mi'kmaq trapper, came to Badger Brook from the western part of the island. His name was John Drum and, followed by his brothers and cousins, he became the first chief. There was a time when they shared this area with a few remaining Beothuk. Ralph's grandfather, who said he had been born somewhere around 1859, told him that *his* father, Michael, had remembered the sad, dispossessed people as the remains of a once proud and handsome race.

It was said that John took a Beothuk woman into the family. *Beothuk blood runs through us, my son,* Grandfather had said, and there was pride in his voice.

Why are you proud of that, Grandfather? young Ralph had wanted to know.

Because the Beothuk was a strong Indian, Grandfather had answered. *A smart, strong Indian.*

The sound of the train's whistle interrupted Ralph's thoughts. The train thundered over the trestle spanning Badger River and pulled up in front of the station platform. Huge and invincible, the large locomotive came to rest. The small crowd on the platform turned expectantly, subconsciously sniffing the peculiar grease-steam-toilet smell that only trains had, and that evoked a sense of faraway places. The doors of the passenger cars flew back and about fifty people climbed down, most of them loggers who had joined the new union. They had come from points east, having made their way in to the train stations from various bays and coves. They had answered a call, and knew they had ahead of them many long cold hours on a picket line in mid-winter. Ralph stepped forward and, raising his normally soft voice, called out to assemble the men.

Part I

WHERE THREE RIVERS MEET

1

During the night the river water had risen high enough to come in over the floor. When Bridey Sullivan swung her legs out of bed they landed in the ice-cold wetness.

"Ned," she screamed. "Get up! We're going to drown!"

Ned Sullivan shot up in bed, all sleep immediately gone from his eyes. His first instinct was to panic, but he took one look at Bridey's terrified face and quickly found an inner reserve of strength. Ned was like that. Whenever there was a crisis, with the family or in his job on the drive, people said you could count on him to be calm in the middle of the storm. He tried to shush his wife, but she continued to scream. "What are we going to do Ned? Jesus, Mary and Joseph, we're trapped here, Ned," she shrieked.

"Calm down Bridey, it's going to be all right. These houses are built for this kind of thing." Ned got up and waded in bare feet through three inches of water to find his goat rubbers over by the door. He sat down on a chair by the table and pulled them on over his feet, his toes already turning blue.

Ned went to the window and looked out to see water surrounding his house. The scene was something he had never witnessed before and could never have imagined. During the night the mighty Exploits River, known to locals simply as "the River," had overflowed its banks. Gone was the roadway, the fences just showing their top posts. Cut off by flood waters, every house looked like an island unto itself, one isolated from the other. He could see a small boat and a couple of canoes bobbing on the water as they took residents to dry land.

Bridey splashed through the water, screaming even louder, "Oh my Sacred Heart of Jesus, Ned. My trunk, my trunk! Help me."

He tore his eyes away from the flood scene and turned to see Bridey, her nightgown trailing in the water, tears streaming down her face. She was trying to drag a big old leather trunk over to the bed. As he sloshed toward her, Bridey's nightgown became tangled around her legs and down she went, sending up a splash. He reached out to help her up, but she pushed him away screaming, "Never mind me, get the trunk up out of the water!"

Not wanting to make the bed wet, Ned grabbed the precious trunk and hoisted it up onto the kitchen table. Bridey had brought the trunk all the way from Stock Cove, and it held heirlooms and years of memories. She had been collecting things for it ever since she was a young girl. It meant the world to her and Ned knew it.

There was a bang on the door, but first Ned wrapped Bridey in a blanket and settled her back on the bed. He kissed the top of her head and her sobs subsided as he moved to the door. He pulled it open, sending a little wave of muddy brown water in over the kitchen floor.

Outside, two men were looking up at Ned from a canoe at his doorstep. One of them had pounded on Ned's door with his paddle. Already aboard were Mrs. Pike and her five-year-old daughter. Her scared face peered up at him from under a thick woollen cap. Paddling the canoe was Mr. Peter Drum and his son Louis – two Mi'kmaq men. They looked strong and capable and instinctively Ned felt he could trust them. Old man Drum spoke out of one side of his mouth, the other side full of a large wad of chewing tobacco.

"Morning, Ned. Well b'y, the shaggin' River is up again. No one expected it this year. You ever see the like? Some state, isn't it?" He sized up the watery scene as he spat a stream of brown baccy juice over the side of the canoe.

"Well sir, I'm some glad to see you fellas this morning. My

missus is having a fit in there. Can you load her aboard your canoe and take her up to dry ground?"

"Yes, b'y, that's what we're here for. We're the rescue party." Young Louis rolled his eyes and smirked.

In the front of the canoe the Pike child started to wail. "I'm scared, Mommy, I want to go home."

Ned looked back to Peter Drum and asked him to wait a couple of minutes. As he returned to Bridey he could hear Mrs. Pike trying to calm the youngster.

He found his wife dressed and no longer crying, but the distress and shock was evident in her face as he lowered her into the canoe. She was still fretting about the trunk, but Peter Drum told her that the water would never go as high as the kitchen table and, in fact, would soon start to recede, as the dynamiters were at work down-stream.

As the little canoe pulled away Bridey realized that Ned wasn't aboard. "Ned, Ned," she cried, "come with me!"

"Don't worry, my duckie," Ned called back. "I'll be along later. I'm going to see if I can help out. Another pair of strong hands won't go astray in Badger this day."

☙

In 1925, Ned Sullivan had come to Badger seeking work in the lumberwoods. During the months working with the A.N.D. Company, he came to like the growing Company town with its hustle and bustle, its access to services and, especially, the camaraderie among its people. When he came down out of the woods he would often climb the round hill that overlooked the River and a great sense of peace and belonging would steal over him.

Originally, Ned's plan was like that of the other men: to go back to his home in Stock Cove, Bonavista Bay, when the time came to fish again. But gradually he began to dream a different dream on those long evenings up on the hill. Life inland had begun to appeal to him, and the longing to be on the salt water that seized so many men who came into the woods from the outports was fading for him.

Ned was a quick and lively fellow who caught on fast. In the first year he was a cutter. But the working life of a riverman caught his fancy, and he sought a coveted spot on the drive. There were various trades in the logging industry, but the river drivers were considered the elite. This job wasn't for everyone. It required a certain daring and a devil-may-care attitude. And that described young Ned Sullivan.

Ned started as an oarsman on the riverboats at a wage of twenty-five cents an hour. In later years he would tell his son about the fourteen-foot ash oars and how hard they were on the hands. Until they were toughened up, every evening the oarsmen would have to grease their palms with fatback pork.

Later, when Ned got to know the runs on various parts of the rivers, for twenty-seven cents an hour he did the log dance of a driver, his nimble feet defying gravity. He proved to be outstanding as he flicked from log to log like a ballet dancer. A few years later, perhaps because Ned was the best at what he did or perhaps because of his Irish luck, he became drive boss, responsible for the entire operation.

Ned and Bridey had been married for three years and still the couple had no children. Ned was constantly trying to persuade Bridey to move inland, describing Badger as a fine place to live, with a bright future. So, although it meant leaving her family behind, Bridey pulled up roots and moved to Badger in the fall of 1927 to be near her husband.

The young couple rented a small, two-bedroom house down by the River. The rent was cheap, and when spring came they found out why. Every year, extreme cold temperatures caused the ice in the River to wharf up. Having no other place to go, the water rose up over the banks and into the town of Badger. Some years the ice was worse than others, and 1928 was a bad one. Most houses had already been raised up a few feet to try to avoid the flooding, but that winter had been particularly cold and the ice was thick.

The flat land near the River had flooded first, and the day before, Bridey had stood in her doorway watching with alarm as the water rose. Being from Bonavista Bay, she had never seen a flood before, but Ned kept assuring her that the house was high enough and the water would not come up over the steps. But he'd been wrong, and now she was in a canoe headed to dry ground.

That evening Ned met up with Bridey, and along with the other displaced people, they spent the night sitting in the waiting room of the railway station. This was the Sullivans' first experience with the floods that the native Badgerites endured so stoically.

Strategically placed dynamite did its job and next morning the water had gone down. There wasn't too much damage done to the little house, but Bridey was not content to stay there any longer.

"Ned," she said, "I can't live here like this. I can hardly sleep for worry that the house is going to flood again. Every morning when I puts my feet to the canvas I swear I can still feel that cold water." She shivered as she said this, although they were sitting in the kitchen and the wood stove was blasting them with heat to dry up the damp floor.

Ned agreed with her and started the search for another place to live.

He found a house for sale Up the Track, the name given to the railway track area at the west end of Badger going up toward the Gaff Topsails. The land started to rise there, on its thirty-eight-mile ascent to the top of the Topsails plateau. Neighbours told Ned that the flood water never reached in that far, so his Bridey and her trunk would be safe. In time they got used to the trains that ran by on the track just twenty feet from their door. Bridey didn't care if the whistle of the train coming down the grade at all hours in the night woke her from sleep as long as she wasn't waking to water on her floor.

The house had been built by one of the train conductors who was being transferred to Bishops Falls and was looking to get it off his hands. It was a white-clapboard two-storey with four bedrooms upstairs. The kitchen was large and heated by a wood stove, with a grate cut in the ceiling to allow the heat to go upstairs. Off the kitchen were a parlour and another bedroom. Bridey liked the house immediately and they soon moved in. To be extra sure, she had Ned bring the trunk upstairs and put in the largest room, which was to be their bedroom.

As the summer was drawing to a close, Bridey became pregnant. They had just about given up thinking they would ever have a child, and Ned credited their move to the new house as to what did the trick. Their first child, Assumpta Jennifer, was born in May of 1929.

The Mi'kmaq midwife, Missus Annie Drum, brought her into the world. "Well, Missus Sullivan, your first child has a caul over her face."

Bridey was exhausted from straining and pushing. "What? Is she all right?"

"She's wonderful, my dear. A lovely little redhead, she is. Don't worry; I'll pass her to you when I get her cleaned up. I s'pose you knows, do you, that a caul is a rare thing? Children born with it are special. Out of all my twenty-two children, only one had a caul, my little Ralphie. His grandfather said he might become a chief one of these days."

The midwife gave Bridey the caul and told her to dry it and keep it for the little girl. It would bring her luck, she said.

The name Assumpta didn't seem to suit the little girl with her bright copper hair, clear white skin, and green eyes. Everyone called her Jennie. There was a presence about her. She had a way of standing with her sturdy little legs planted apart, her eyes flashing, ready to take on anyone who crossed her and aroused her fiery temper.

The priest was offended that her parents weren't using the name Assumpta. After all, wasn't he the one who'd picked it out when the godparents had brought her to be baptized? "For a child to be named after the Assumption of the Blessed Virgin Mary into Heaven is an honour beyond compare," he said.

Bridey was secretly resentful that parents weren't allowed to be present at the baptism of children, and also that the priest had changed her baby's name from Jennifer to Assumpta Jennifer. She didn't give a fig what he said about the name Assumpta, but she obediently answered, "Yes, Father," and went off home, calling her sweet little girl Jennie.

After Jennie was born, Phonse came exactly nine months later. Then every year came another, until there were eleven. The last pregnancy, a set of twins, caused complications and Bridey nearly bled to death. Even Missus Annie, the midwife, was worried and sent for the A.N.D. Company doctor.

The only birth control that Bridey knew was to "pull out." The priest said that birth control was sinful, although the rhythm method was allowed. Bridey couldn't get the hang of it. She was always so busy that she'd forget to count up the days and, besides, Ned would be impatient with her if she turned away from him in bed. What could she do?

Bridey's friend, Missus Crawford, was the kind of woman who knew a bit about everything. She and her husband and their little boy, Vern, had moved down from Buchans Junction a few years ago. Mr. Crawford worked as a sectionman on the railway, travelling up and down the tracks on a speeder to check the tracks for washouts and breaks. Missus Crawford had quickly integrated herself into the town and soon knew much more than Bridey did about the various residents.

After she recovered from the twins' birth, Bridey confided to Missus Crawford that the doctor had told her that having another baby would kill her.

"Look, maid," said practical Missus Crawford, "you has to do something. It is a bigger sin for you to die and leave eleven young children. Some things are better left to women to decide, rather than priests."

"So what will I do?" she ventured timidly. "I can't turn Ned away."

"My dear," whispered her friend, "don't you know about the things that women inserts into themselves?"

Bridey shook her head.

"Well, for one thing, there's the penny. Put it up just before; leave it there for twenty-four hours after. Same thing with a bit of muslin or cheesecloth soaked in vinegar."

"How . . . how do I get it . . . up?"

"Jest the length of your forefinger, maid," she tittered. "The man does the rest and he don't even know he's doing it."

Bridey was too shy to ask Missus Crawford if she herself used the pennies and the vinegar or the rhythm method or the "pull-out." The Crawfords only had little Vern, so she probably did.

In the Sullivan bed, Ned was none the wiser.

2

The first time Rod Anderson went with his father to negotiate a contract with the A.N.D. Company was an eye-opener for the young man. Eli Anderson was a woods contractor. The Company had already approved Rod to take over from the old man when he retired.

The Company manager at that time was Mr. Hughie Cole. They said he ruled Badger with an iron fist. He planked the contract down on his desk. "Now, Mr. Anderson, there it is. It's changed a bit. Profits are down, sir. Profits are down. We're looking for five thousand cords from you this year."

Eli picked up the contract and read it. "You want an extra thousand cords for the same amount of money?"

"You have good cutting areas, Anderson. The swampers have been in and have your roads cut through for you. You should have no complaints." Mr. Cole had steely, cold-grey eyes, and when he fixed them on a person there was no compromise.

"Can you give me a few minutes to go over this with my son, Mr. Cole? It is part of his training, you know."

"Sure, sure, I'll leave you to it. Don't be too long. I'm a busy man."

Hunched over the paper, shoulder to shoulder, the Andersons scrutinized the contract together. The two men looked very much alike, although they were unable to see the resemblance themselves. Both were big, barrel-chested men, with thick heads of sandy-coloured hair. Both faces were square with cleft chins and keen green eyes.

The A.N.D. Company had it all spelled out. The contractor's responsibility was to cut a specified number of cords and see that the wood was on the riverbanks for the spring drive.

During that time, the onus was on the Andersons to organize the cut, to hire, shelter and feed the loggers, and to see to the keeping of the time sheets that tracked the number of cords each logger cut and the wages due him. All the food supplies and equipment specified in the agreement had to be bought from the Company stores at Company prices. The scalers came through every two weeks and scaled the cords.

The Company's responsibility was to supply and pay the scalers and to pay the loggers directly from its pay office. At the end of the season, when the contractor's expenses and the men's wages were taken out, what was left was the contractor's profit. As a dutiful son, Rod listened to his father's explanations.

Rod heard Mr. Cole's voice as he came back into the room. "What about it, young fella? Meets with your approval, does it?"

"Yes sir," he replied, and his father signed up for another year. Rod couldn't help thinking that if his brother Melvin were here he'd be sitting on the same chair instead of him and enjoying every minute of this, his whole being concentrated on the prospect of cutting the wood, managing the camp, making a profit.

Life sure has a way of taking strange turns, Rod thought glumly.

Melvin was two years older than Rod, tall, dark and slight like their mother. It had been assumed that he would take over from the old man. From the time they were kids, their father had always drilled this into them. "Melvin is going to step into my logans when I gives it up," he'd say. "And what are we going to get for you to do, Rod, me son?"

But Rod didn't know. He thought he might just follow along behind Melvin and the old man. Then, the summer he was thirteen and Melvin fifteen, their father took them to visit his brother, Aaron, in Port aux Basques. Aaron was purser aboard the SS *Caribou* that steamed between Newfoundland and Canada.

The family took the train from Badger, up over the Topsails – Main, Mizzen and Gaff – through to Howley, Deer Lake and Corner Brook, and then on over to Port aux Basques. The train trip was a wonder of wonders for the two young boys. As the train rattled along, they raced from one end of her to the other, pretending to be conductors.

During their stay in Port aux Basques, Uncle Aaron was called back to work on his ship. He asked the boys if they'd like to go with him across to North Sydney for the night. Melvin and Rod were beside themselves with excitement.

Melvin was sick all the way over and on the way back. He allowed that he never wanted to see a drop of salt water again. Rod, however, fell in love. As the handsome new SS *Caribou* plowed through the waves, he felt an excitement like never before. His uncle recognized it, being the same way himself. It was a love for the sea. Rod left poor Melvin groaning in the bunk and dogged his uncle throughout the ship, exhilarated by the thought of the deep wild ocean beneath his feet, revelling in the feel of his body adjusting to its rhythm.

"You have a sailor there, Eli," Uncle Aaron exclaimed when they got back. "Rod, my boy, if you wants to come over in the summer, I'll find you a spot on one of the boats fishing out of the Bay of Islands. You'll know after that if you really wants to be on the water or not."

Eli was a bit taken aback. He'd never expected to have his youngest son take to the sea, but now he supposed that it made sense – two brothers, each taking different paths, as he and Aaron had done years ago.

Melvin went into the camps with his father every chance he got, apprenticing to step into the contractor's job. In the beginning he worked as water boy, carrying drinking water to the men. Another summer he was a cookee. After that he became a cutter. He loved the woods life as his brother loved the sea.

Rod worked the first summer on the fishing boats. The next summer, when he was fifteen, his uncle got him on the *Caribou* as a cabin boy. Rod knew that he had found his place in the world at last. Let Pop and Melvin have the Badger woods.

It was the winter of 1931. Rod was in the middle of grade eleven and Melvin, who had finished two years earlier, was working full-time with his father. Christmas was coming up. School was closed and Eli and Melvin had come down from the camp for the holidays.

Eli had the gout. He sat by the kitchen stove with his foot propped up on a pillow. "Boys, I needs you fellas to go in over the ridge and haul out them sticks we cut last summer. We'll get them sawed up over Christmas and have firewood enough for most of the winter."

The boys were all for it. Men and boys alike looked forward to a trip in the woods for firewood. They'd take the horse and slide, food for a boil-up and, early in the morning, off they would go. Melvin and Rod went to bed with their plans in place for the next day.

But in the morning, Rod was sick. He had a cold on his chest and was running a fever. His mother made him stay in bed with a mustard plaster on his chest.

"That's all right, Pop," Melvin said. "Sure there's nothing to that. I'll go in by myself. I don't have any cutting to do, just load the few logs and come on back."

His father wasn't so sure. "No b'y, I'll go with you. Let me try and get me boot on over me gouty old foot."

But the boot wouldn't go on. The minute the leather touched the toe, the searing pain almost sent the old man through the ceiling.

Though his parents weren't keen on his going, Melvin set out alone. To people born and raised in the woods towns, safety was bred into them. They took care how to chop a tree so the axe never cut into their foot, how to stand aside as the tree fell, and mark their way in the forest so as not to get lost. This little jaunt was without danger. The trees were cut. It was only load them on and come back.

The sticks of wood were in over the ridge, two miles west in on a woods road. It was almost noon on a nice sunny day when Melvin got there. He was in no hurry. The horse, a Newfoundland pony, was sure and steady. He'd get the wood, be home before dark and be down by Coleman's Restaurant later to meet his girlfriend. All was right with the world.

At home, Rod's cough got worse and his fever climbed higher. Around midday, his mother sent Eli to fetch the doctor. His father cut the toe out of his rubber boot, so that his swollen toe was sticking out, and walked down the road to find help for his son.

Lying in bed, burning up with a temperature of 105°F on the mercury thermometer, Rod tossed the covers off and shouted. His mother sat beside him, trying to keep a cold cloth on his forehead. There was a pan of water on the little table by his bed that his mother was using to wring out the cloth. His arm struck out blindly and sent it crashing to the floor.

In his delirium, Rod thought he heard Melvin's shout, the horse's whinny, and a crash. He cried out, "No, Melvin, no!" But there was only silence and blackness. Rod's fevered brain had had enough and he lapsed into unconsciousness.

He awoke to the sound of men's voices. His mother was still with him, and his father and the doctor were standing at the foot of the bed. "You have a sick young man there, Mr. Anderson. His temperature is what concerns me. I'll give you some medicine to help bring it down. Keep him calm and rested for the next few days."

Rod struggled to get up. "Pop," he wheezed. "Have to go and help Melv. Melv's in trouble." He flopped back on the pillow as blackness closed over him once more.

When he awoke, wrung out with sweat, daylight was streaming in through the lace curtains. The wind buffeted the house from outside but underneath the sound he could hear someone sobbing. His chest hurt when he drew his breath, but the pain in his head was not quite as bad as before. His throat was raw, his voice hoarse.

"Hello? Mom? Pop? Hello?"

He heard movements and his mother and father came into the room. When he saw their faces, Rod knew something was terribly wrong. What was it? He remembered from his delirium images of his brother crying out.

"Where's Melv? Something happened to Melv." The pain was coming back into his head.

His mother sat on the bed and took his hand. His father turned away and stood looking out the window. He sighed and cleared his throat. "Take it easy, my son. Take it easy. You've been pretty sick you know, though it seems you've turned the corner now."

"Pop . . . please," Rod whispered hoarsely. "I'm fine. Just tell me." He lay back on the pillow.

Turning away from the window and toward his son, Eli's face looked like it had aged twenty years. He approached the bed and said softly, "I think we should wait awhile till you're feeling a bit better. First have a drop of warm broth your mother made for you. It will help build back your strength."

Rod closed his eyes and dutifully submitted to the ministrations of his mother, but after a couple of sips his head fell back and he motioned that he'd had enough. His mother was fussing over him, straightening out the blankets, when Rod saw tears dropping down on the coverlet. She was crying quietly. He reached out and stilled his mother's hand.

The silence in the room was broken only by the wind against the house. "Tell me," Rod said.

Eli sat in the chair across the room and spoke without looking toward him. "Well, my son, Melvin's had a terrible accident. Terrible."

"Oh yes, my son. Terrible," his mother wailed.

"Something happened with the horse, we thinks," Eli said. "She came back home with her traces broke off, no slide and no Melvin. We set out to look for him. We went up the track and in the little road. Not very far in, we come upon the sled, up against a tree. We could see how the horse must have gone, hooked the sled into the tree and the traces came loose." The old man stopped. Eyes closed, Rod could hear his father's ragged breath and knew he was crying.

"We went farther in. Every few feet we'd see wood scattered on the ground, and then we saw a big pile of wood. Oh my . . . and then we found his body."

His wife's sobbing grew worse as Eli continued. "The men pieced it together, what they think must have happened. They figure he piled too much wood on the slide, and struck a fair-sized rock covered in snow that caused the wood to come forward. This must have startled the horse and jerked Melvin off the slide. His foot caught in something, maybe the wippletree, because we could see by the smear of blood across the snow that the horse dragged him a nice ways with wood falling all over him, before his boot came off and his foot came free."

Rod closed his eyes. He could clearly visualize his brother's foot caught in the wippletree, the swinging bar through which the traces were fastened. He knew that was what had happened. He heard his father get up out of the chair and come over to stand by his bed. "I thinks that every bone in his body is broke, my son. Every bone."

"And his poor face," moaned his mother. "His poor face is so bad to look at."

Rod could hold it in no longer. He howled his grief to the ceiling, a long, drawn-out cry from deep inside him. His brother, on whom his father had pinned his hopes and dreams to succeed him, was gone. Rod knew that Melvin's accident had changed all their lives forever.

They buried Melvin two days before Christmas. It was so cold that the gravediggers had a fire burning on the plot for two days to thaw out the ground.

Rod still wasn't well enough to go. He was weak and shaky, and his fever kept coming back in the evenings, although not as high as in the beginning. His father asked Rod's friend Bill Hatcher, who lived over the back fence, to come and sit while they went to the funeral.

Christmas that year wasn't celebrated at the Anderson's house. Friends came by with kindness and support. The family received them and spoke thanks of appreciation. But when they were alone as a family, they became withdrawn and could offer each other no comfort.

Rod went back to school in February and his father opened his camp and called in his men to get ready for the haul-off. Life started to pick up its rhythm again. But it was a different rhythm. Grief lay over the house like a blanket, smothering every bit of happiness and joy there was to be had.

3

When little red-haired Jennie Sullivan was old enough to go to school, her classmates were Vern Crawford and Ralph Drum. Every morning they would meet and walk to school together.

Jennie loved school and loved the nuns. She thought that when she grew up she might be a nun. That was until one day in grade five. It was early in the school year, and one morning she was writing on her new school scribbler: "ASSUMPTA JENNIFER SULLIVAN, UP THE TRACK, BADGER, N.F.L.D."

Sister Augusta was walking by her desk and stopped. "Who told you that Up the Track was an address?"

Confused, Jennie looked up at her and said, "No one, Sister."

The nun looked down her nose and tut-tutted. "Ignorant girl. There's no such place." She smartly rapped Jennie across the knuckles with her ruler. Jennie was devastated and never again viewed the nuns in the same light.

Jennie, Vern and Ralph went through school together right to grades ten and eleven. Vern was sandy-haired and small, with a constantly runny nose. As he grew older, the runny nose stopped, but Vern was still small. Missus Crawford told Bridey Sullivan that she'd caught him smoking when he was five years old and she thought that was what stunted his growth. Jennie grew tall, taller than Vern, Ralph and all her classmates. In this she and her brother Phonse, who was also tall, turned after Ned, their Pap.

Ralph was Mi'kmaq. One time Phonse told Jennie that white

17

people were afraid of the Mi'kmaq. As she grew up, she'd hear phrases like "never trust an Indian" and "never turn your back on an Indian." Jennie couldn't understand why the Mi'kmaq were treated badly by many white people. Her own family didn't seem to share that view. Maybe it was because of the relationship Mam had with Ralph's mother, Missus Annie, who had delivered all of Mam's children. After ten years of baring her private parts to the Mi'kmaq woman, Mam probably felt a kinship with her. Little Ralph had often followed along behind his mother, playing out around the door with the Sullivan children while Annie Drum went and busied herself with the birthings. Ralph and Phonse were buddies. Phonse was a bit younger than Ralph and seemed to hero-worship him. The two boys were in and out of the house all the time.

One time Missus Crawford had a birthday party for Vern. Jennie told Vern that he should ask Ralph. Vern was somewhat in awe of Jennie's bossy ways, and he agreed without question. Poor Missus Crawford: she hadn't realized that some parents would take it as an insult to have an Indian in the room. So, to please the grown-ups, she told Ralph to sit in a corner and wouldn't let him play any games. It cut into Jennie's heart to see it. When the time came to eat, she took her food and some for Ralph and went and sat by him.

✗

As a member of a small Mi'kmaq community, Ralph's life, growing up among the white, race-conscious people of Badger in the 1930s and '40s wasn't easy. There were the A.N.D. Company personnel and their families – the contractors, scalers, drivers – and then there were the Mi'kmaq. Somewhere in between were the merchants, the doctor, the postmaster, the Newfoundland Ranger, the telegraph operator, and the Newfoundland Railway workers. Two or three of the merchants were Jewish who, while friendly to everyone because of their businesses, usually socialized among themselves.

Ralph recognized at an early age that the high-toned A.N.D. Company families were only too glad to get him to saw up firewood, cleave splits, shovel snow and pay him a quarter for it, but never invite him into their houses. "Here, young fella, have a glass of syrup and a sweet biscuit. No, no, don't come in. I'll pass it out to you." *Just as though I was a dog,* thought Ralph.

Then he was invited to Vern's birthday party. He knew Vern never saw any difference in himself and Ralph, but the grown-ups certainly did. Ralph was made to feel like an outcast because he was Mi'kmaq.

Ralph never forgot what young Jennie Sullivan did that day. They had known each other since they were about four years old when they played in the mud together. To him she was just another silly girl, but after Vern's birthday party he saw her differently.

Jennie was the same age as the two boys, and even at eleven she was tall and beautiful. Ralph, on the edge of puberty and full of his grandfather's stories, thought she looked as a Beothuk woman would look. Her skin was light with a sprinkling of freckles, but he imagined a Beothuk's to be darker. Or maybe it wasn't. Grandfather said the Beothuks smeared so much red ochre on themselves that no one really knew how light or how dark their skin was anyway.

At the party, Jennie got two plates of potted meat sandwiches and snowballs and two glasses of Purity syrup and came to sit beside him. She passed him one of the plates and a glass. "Here, Ralph. What odds about that crowd over at the table. Let's eat over here."

As they ate, she chatted to him about school. Ralph was awestruck by her. She wore a green dress that showed off her long red hair. He was afraid to look at her straight-on, but, out of the corner of his eye he could see that she had bumps where her breasts would be one day. She smelled good too. Clean and sunshiny, like the wind in summer.

Vern had to stay at the table where the parents and the other kids were. Ralph saw Vern looking at them and knew he was wondering what they were saying to each other. People said Jennie and Vern Crawford would marry when they grew up. Both families were Catholic and the parents were friends. But Ralph thought that Jennie deserved a manlier fellow than Vern.

Not long after the party, Vern came across some comic books. He and Ralph went up back of the big hill to have a read. There was this great one called Wonder Woman and her friend Marya, an eight-foot-tall Mexican mountain girl whom Wonder Woman called little Marya. They were from a tribe of women known as the Amazons. Ralph liked the shape of the comic book women. They had nice rounded thighs and great breasts. He told Vern that Wonder Woman and Marya reminded him of Jennie.

Vern looked at Ralph as if he were crazy. "Ya think so? Jennie's awful fat, ya know." Vern obviously didn't see Jennie as Ralph saw her. She wasn't fat; she was an Amazon, his Amazon Beothuk Woman.

As they grew into teenagers Ralph gradually noticed himself thinking of Jennie more and more, especially when he was up on the hill, lying back, puffing on a cigarette and gazing at the clouds. Or down by the River watching the cable boat spinning across, or in bed, before he went to sleep and, then, in his dreams. Everywhere. But Jennie never knew. And Ralph never wanted her to know.

Vern and Jennie went out together every now and then. There would sometimes be a dance in the town hall for the young people. At the dance, the guys would stand around the sides watching the girls, trying to get up nerve enough to ask for a dance. Ralph would not let his eyes drift too often to Jennie. He thought she looked some nice. Her dress was green, again, but more grown-up now. It was straight and tight, showing the shape of her. The wide collar went right over her shoulders.

The gramophone was playing a song by Hank Snow, Vern's favourite singer. Vern asked Jennie to dance. They looked somewhat odd together, with Vern barely coming up to her shoulder. Ralph stood on the sidelines watching them, listening to Hank Snow singing through his nose, *"Now and then there's a fool such as I am over you,"* wishing it was he holding Jennie in his arms, thinking that the song suited him perfectly and that he really was a fool for loving this young white woman.

Suddenly, Jennie hauled off and gave Vern a big smack in the side of his head and stalked away.

Vern made for the door. Ralph looked back to check on Jennie but a gaggle of girls had encircled her. He followed after Vern and found him outside leaning against the side of the building. In the cool night air he lit up a cigarette. Ralph did too. He'd been smoking since he was ten; Vern always bragged that he'd smoked at five.

"Lord Jesus Christ! What'd she do that for? I was being as nice as I could be to her!" He nursed the side of his face.

"C'mon, Vern, you had to say something she didn't like." Ralph flicked the ash off his cigarette as he saw the men do. He thought he was getting pretty good at doing it too. At sixteen, with his hair slicked back with the Brylcreem and a cigarette in his lips, Ralph thought himself pretty cool.

"Well, I was trying to help her, see."

"Help Jennie? Vern, b'y, if there was ever a girl that didn't need any help, it's Jennie."

"Yes she do. She's too big. I couldn't get my arms around her. I told her that she should go on a diet."

His words made Ralph suck in a lungful of smoke the wrong way and he started to cough. Before he could recover some more boys piled out of the hall. They spied him and Vern. Walt Hatcher, loudest mouth in town, jeered, "Haw haw, Vernie got smacked by a gir-ril. Haw haw, Vernie."

That was the breaking point for Vern. He rammed into Walt, knocking him down. Walt was bigger and stronger and he quickly took control by flipping Vern onto his back in the mud and straddling him. He pinned his two arms up over his head. "Whassamatter, Vernie? Trying to fight a man and you can't fight a girl? No good, Vernie. Go home to mommy."

As if adding an exclamation point, Walt punched Vern in the stomach. He got up and looked over at Ralph. "Better look after Vernie, Ralph. He can't look after hisself." Hooting with laughter, Walt and his buddies humped on up the road.

Ralph went over and offered an arm to Vern to haul him up out of the muck. He was too pissed off to accept help at this point and climbed to his feet on his own. "Mind yer own fuckin' business, Ralph," he said as he hauled his coat around him and stumbled off.

⌀

Jennie, Vern and Ralph attended the Catholic school, while Tom Hillier went to the Protestant. Consequently, although she'd known Tom all her life, Jennie didn't really *know* him. The Hilliers lived at least a mile or two from the Sullivans, in on Halls Bay Road, the highway going toward Springdale. Tom's father was the station master, while Jennie's Pap was drive boss. Although they lived in the same small town and the Sullivans and the Hilliers said hello if they passed each other on the street, they never mixed or visited each other, or had anything in common. Religion dominated all social events, friendships, courtships, and business. Catholic youngsters tended to play with Catholics and Protestant youngsters with Protestants.

Tom's family was Pentecostal. The Pentecostals had built a big church, the biggest one in Badger, at the end of Church Road. Many Anglicans had converted and Tom's parents were among them. Later, when the highway went through to Millertown and Buchans, this church would sit at a crossroads, a crossroads that would come to bear the stamp of history.

As teenagers, Tom and Jennie used to see each other around and she always felt drawn toward him, perhaps because he was so big and tall, perhaps because of the way he loped around in those big black boots, or perhaps because of his kind grey eyes, that seemed to stray to Jennie whenever they were near each other. Jennie told herself there was no use in pining after a Protestant who lived in on Halls Bay Road, and Tom thought there was no use of him wanting a Catholic girl who lived Up the Track.

All along, the Sullivans and the Crawfords kept hoping that Jennie and Vern would marry when they grew up. Two Catholics, no cross-religion marriage; the families loved the thought of it.

Well, I tried, Jennie thought. *God knows I really tried to like Vern, but there was something shifty and slick about him. The first time he tried to kiss me his lips were so wet and his mouth so full of spit that I nearly threw up.*

And another time, at a teenage dance when she was sixteen, growing tall and large and Vern staying short and small, he had the friggin' nerve to say, "You're getting too big to put my arms around, Jennie. You needs to go on diet."

She had smacked him hard for that remark and wouldn't speak to him for months. *Dumb-arse*, she thought savagely. *He didn't even have a clue why I smacked him. Sacred Heart! Some guys are some stunned!*

But it was hard for her not to keep noticing Tom Hillier. First of all, as he grew tall Jennie had to look up at him. Sometimes she made a point of "accidentally" standing near him if they were hanging out by the train station or standing in line at the chip stand where a paper cone of hot chips cost ten cents. One evening he bought one for her.

"Here," he said shyly, "have one on me."

It made Jennie's heart do a flip when he looked down at her. She took it. She would've taken a cone full of coal at that moment, so glad was she that it had come from Tom's hands.

But besides his height, Jennie saw that Tom was a good-hearted person. He'd go out of his way for anyone. Jennie used to stray over to the field by the River to see him play a game of rounders with the boys. She knew that Tom noticed her, but she pretended not to see him, in the fashion of girls and women when they are attracted to someone, but not being too forward about it.

One evening, as she stood on the sidelines, Jennie was concentrating on Tom as he loped across the field when, not paying attention to who was hitting the ball, something smacked her in the head. Jennie knew no more.

When she came around, the first thing she saw was a pair of grey eyes looking into hers. They were Tom Hillier's and he had his arm under her shoulders. The crowd had gathered around, everyone offering their advice.

"Geez, Jennie maid, you coulda been killed."

"Didn't you see the friggin' ball?"

"Keep her still, don't move her."

"Here's my handkerchief. I wetted it in the River. Put it on her forehead."

Tom told them all to move back a bit and asked Jennie if she could stand up. Oooh, she was so dizzy. She fell against him, discovering, even in her dizziness, that her head just fit into the curve of his chest. "I'm going to take her home, guys. Go on back to your game without me," he yelled. With that he lifted Jennie effortlessly into his arms and walked across the road.

The players drifted back to the field, all except Phonse, who tagged along saying, "If Jennie arrives home in that state without me, Mam will give me the sharp edge of her tongue for not looking after me sister."

Jennie, whose head was swimming from the crack of the heavy leather ball, thought she had died and gone to heaven. Nestled in Tom's strong arms, leaning against his chest, she could hear the thudding of his heart as he walked. Every now and then he would look down at her and she could feel his breath on her cheek. When they arrived, Mam was in a fuss. She settled Jennie on the daybed and got a cold face cloth for the bump on her temple. Tom and Phonse stood by uncertainly.

"Well, young Tom Hillier," said Mam, as she surveyed him, "you've grown into quite a big boy." Bridey was no fool. She'd seen the way Tom had been looking at Jennie as he walked in the door with her, and the way her daughter's eyes were looking up into his. But Tom was a Protestant. This would not do, not do at all.

"I'm almost seventeen now, Mrs. Sullivan," Tom answered.

"Well, thanks for helping Jennie home today, but it weren't necessary." She turned to her son. "I s'pose you could've done it yourself, Phonse, and not have taken Tom away from his game."

"Aw, Mam, she's me sister. I wudn't going to lug her all the way up the track. Besides, she's too heavy for me, sure."

Tom said, "It was no trouble at all for me, missus."

Mam looked at him and heaved a sigh. "No, I don't suppose it was."

Throughout the conversation Jennie kept her eyes closed. She knew it was because Tom was Protestant that Mam was behaving like this. If Ralph or Vern had helped her home, she'd be getting a glass of syrup and a bit of cake for them. She didn't offer Tom anything. And that wasn't like her mother.

"I'd better go," Tom said. "Take care of yourself, Jennie."

She opened her eyes. The room was spinning a bit. "Tom, thanks for helping me."

He met her eyes and they looked at each other for a long moment. He smiled, and then gave her a wink and bounded out over the front step. Despite her pounding head, Jennie couldn't help but smile too. She knew there'd be other meetings – without Mam.

4

Rod Anderson received a letter from his Uncle Aaron advising him to be ready to join him on the gulf ferry, the SS *Caribou,* on the first of July. He showed the letter to his father.

"So Rod, my son, I'm not going to ask you if you wants to go, 'cause I know you do. All I'm going to say is you're all I have left now. The woods contractor job is a good one and you could get used to it, you know."

Rod felt his heart sink at his father's words. Ever since Melvin had died, he'd known that this day was coming. He'd just refused to believe it. Who could blame his poor father? How could he leave him? The old man was looking at him, beseeching.

"Yes Pop, I know you need me. I'll stay with you."

That night he dreamed again. He was at the seashore; the tide was going out, and out, and out. As it did, tall spruce trees grew up where the sand was. When he awoke, Rod lay still, thinking bitterly that if there was ever a dream that was significant, this was it. He could see the pattern of the days and years to come. He was dreading it. Hating it.

That summer Rod started in the woods with his father. He had written his grade eleven exams, passed tolerably well, and his father thought it was good enough for him to manage the contracting business. It was more than *he'd* started with, he said. Rod was now a man, seventeen years old, and working as a full-time logger.

As they worked side by side, Rod watched his father closely to see where he cut corners to increase his profits. The only way Rod could make sense of it was that a woods contractor was like being a private businessman in that you had some control over your expenses. But that wasn't quite right either, because in another way, the A.N.D. Company was in command of the operation to the extent that sometimes the contractor felt as though he was no different from the loggers.

The Anderson camp, considered a prime spot, was closest to Badger: across the River and in through the forest on a woods road about twenty-five miles up on Sandy Lake. The camp held a crew of forty men who were fed whatever was available in foodstuffs, by a cook and cookee. White navy beans were the staple food: boiled, baked or fried. This, coupled with white bread, strong tea and molasses buns, day after day, breakfast and supper, was far from being nourishing, even though it filled their bellies. All the camps were the same. The Company kept everything on a tight rein.

The bunks were infested with bedbugs and lice. The only heat came from a converted oil drum. The men had only cold water to wash in. Most never washed at all. It was 1933 and camp life had not come forward in the almost thirty years that the A.N.D. Company had been harvesting pulpwood.

Eli and Rod Anderson had never seen anything different. Woods camps were expected to provide only the barest essentials. The men didn't come in to them to work as loggers expecting luxuries and fine accommodations. They never considered change, and for sure the Company didn't.

One evening, in early summer, Rod took his fishing pole and went over to Drum's Pond, not far from the camp. Trout were a good supplement to the beans diet, but it was hard to get free time to sit by a pond and fish. He cast out his line and sat quietly gazing at the still pond water, so different from the ocean that was always alive with motion. Sometimes Rod even envied the River, making its way unhindered to the sea, while he was forever stuck inland among the trees. Such foolish thoughts only depressed him, but sometimes he got so caught up in his own private misery and anger that he couldn't help himself.

Rod glanced to his left and noticed a man sitting no more than three feet away. It was Peter Drum. Rod had not heard him come up, but that didn't surprise him. He knew the Indians moved through the forest like shadows. He had grown up knowing the Mi'kmaq people. Many of them were trappers and guides; some were loggers.

The old man took out his pipe and filled it with tobacco, all the while watching Rod.

"Good evening, sir," Rod ventured.

Peter struck a match, applied the flame to the tobacco, and puffed until the pipe was lit. "Do you smoke, young man?"

"Uh . . . no, not very much."

"Would you like to draw on my pipe? I would be honoured if you would."

Rod was embarrassed. What could he say without sounding rude? He took the pipe and drew in tentatively, expecting it to be horrible tasting.

It wasn't. Rod felt pleasantly surprised. He took another draw, deeper into his lungs. Time slowed down. *What does the old Indian have in this tobacco?* He looked at Peter Drum through the haze of smoke. The old man was smiling.

"Sleep now, young man. I am giving you a spirit guide. When you awaken, it will be the first sound you hear. Let it guide you and soothe you through rough times."

It seemed to Rod that it was Melvin sitting on the bank next to him. Melvin, whole and well. "Rod," he said, "you are thinking that being in the logging camp is the worst thing that could've happened to you. But it's not. In a few years the ship that you would've gone to sea on, the *Caribou,* will sink. You're not meant to go that way, brother. Do your best with father. I'll be around. You'll know when you hear this sound."

Rod came awake suddenly. He was alone on the bank. His fishing pole had fallen over the bank into the water. There was no Indian and no pipe. The lonely, echoing call of a loon came over the pond, sounding near and far away at the same time, as loon trills do.

Maybe the loon was his spirit guide, sent to him by his brother. When he was younger, he'd heard the Mi'kmaq boys talk about spirit guides in animal form. They said it could be the bear, otter, fox, crow, hawk or other beings in the animal world. Who was to say that the loon wasn't there for Rod?

He certainly would never tell anyone about this experience. Every white person he knew would laugh at him and he'd never live it down. Serious sober Rod believing in such things? Never.

Rod kept the incident close to his heart. Whether it was all a dream or not, it comforted him, just as the Indian man had said it would. Over the years, when the going got rough, when Rod thought he couldn't stand another minute of life in the woods camp, he would slip off alone, to a pond or to the River and listen for the call of the loon. Most times it would come, sounding lonely and lost. But Rod privately considered it a connection with his long-dead brother and it helped him continue on with his life.

✄

When he turned twenty, four years after Melvin died, Rod got married. Eli had been encouraging him to get a woman for the past three years. Rod's mother had lived only a year past Melvin. One day, in high summer, she collapsed while pinning clothes on the clothesline. The doctor said that a blood vessel had burst in her brain.

Rod and his father lived on alone, spending more and more time in the camp, and the house took on a neglected air. "Rod, me son," said his father one day as they sat down to burnt meat and salty potatoes, "I thinks 'tis time you found a woman. Ain't you got your eye on anyone around here?"

Rod looked at his father. The old man was past fifty now and the hard life he had lived was catching up with him. He was constantly bothered with gout, arthritis and digestive problems. He kept saying he'd retire soon, any day now, but, season after season he went into the woods again.

Rod still carried deep resentment inside him: against the old man; against Melvin his deceased brother; against every tree in the forest; against the River. He was a bitter young man whose love for the ocean had been cut off too early in his life. To his credit, he worked steadily and never once spoke out his feelings to his father. But buried emotions have a way of coming to the surface, and Rod was known among his peers as being somewhat moody and morose.

"Yes, Pop, I dare say I do need a woman. I haven't found one that suits me, though. There's no one hereabouts and I never go anywhere to meet anyone else."

"I'm sorry that I keeps you so close to me, my son. I knows you should mix with your friends more. Bill Hatcher and them goes to the hockey games down to Grand Falls and up to Buchans. Why don't you go along with them sometime?"

So Rod did. He went up to Buchans with a group of Badger boys. They caught the train to Millertown Junction and then took the branch into Buchans. The Grand Falls team was on the same train. It was mid-winter, but snow and cold didn't bother hot-blooded young men. As the rum bottle was passed around, it didn't take long for Rod to enter into the spirit of the trip and have a good time.

That was the night he met Ruth Ricketts. It was the foolishest thing, but fate can be like that.

The Buchans hockey rink was a converted ore shed with balconies built around for people to sit on. All of Buchans seemed to be there, plus many Grand Falls, Millertown and Badger fans. That night Buchans beat Grand Falls. The Buchans fans went wild. The Badger boys were naturally rooting for Buchans as there was always a certain animosity between Grand Falls and Badger. Many Badger people thought that the mill workers of Grand Falls considered themselves a cut above the loggers of Badger who cut the pulpwood that gave the mill workers their jobs.

After the game, two young men got into a scrap. Rod never found out what it was about, but next thing he knew, guys were punching guys. Women were squealing. The Badger boys were in the thick of it, loving a good fight. Rod was holding his own until someone hit him in the head and knocked him down. Other bodies piled up on top of him and Rod was almost squashed.

Just then, the police came. They broke up the fight and sent everyone in different directions. A Buchans fellow helped Rod up on his feet. "Jeez, b'y, you don't look too good!"

Rod had a cut over his eye and blood was running down the side of his face.

"Come on over with me. I'll get someone to put a bandage on it for you." He headed off out on the road with Rod in tow. Bill Hatcher and the Badger boys were nowhere to be seen.

"So, you're from Badger are you? Do you know the Sullivans? Yeah? Well, Ned Sullivan is my father's cousin. I'm Will Ricketts."

"Oh, pleased to meet you," Rod answered. "I'm Rod Anderson."

Will took Rod home and introduced him to his family. "Well folks, look what I found under a heap of Grand Falls fighters – a feller from Badger. Rod, meet my Mom, Dad and my sister Ruth."

During the year of 1934, the trains between Buchans and Badger became old friends to Rod and Ruth as they courted. Being male and thus having more freedom, Rod could grab a freight train whenever he chose and get dropped off at Millertown Junction, where he was guaranteed to hitch a ride to Buchans. But Ruth, being female, could only come down to Badger on the passenger train. While there, she would stay with the Sullivans, who promised to see that she was properly chaperoned.

Eli Anderson was somewhat bothered that the Ricketts were Catholics, but Rod, hot-to-trot for this young woman, didn't let religion get in his way. Ruth, in love and starry-eyed for Rod, didn't care either. Her parents said that as long as she got married in her own church they would allow the marriage.

They were married in 1935 at the Catholic Church in Buchans. Bill Hatcher was Rod's best man. They all trundled up on the train: Eli, a couple of his contractor friends and their wives, the Sullivans and the Elliotts. Rod had invited the Drum family with their accordions, guitars and fiddles. The Crawfords came along as well. They were originally from Buchans Junction, and dropped off their son, six-year-old Vern, to stay the night with relatives.

The newlyweds settled down in the old Anderson house that soon took on a brighter air as Ruth began to set the stamp of her laughing, cheerful personality on it. Her father's house in Buchans had a proper bathroom, so Rod installed one for her, on the ground floor off the kitchen where the old pantry used to be.

Ruth cared for Eli as if he were her own father. The old man was a bit gruff with her at first, but you couldn't stay gruff around Ruth for long and, after a couple of months, he warmed to her good cooking, her cleanliness and her comforting ways. This was probably due in large part to her successful treating of his gout. In autumn, Ruth would pick gallons of wild cherries that grew in profusion along the banks of the Little Red Indian River. These she would steep, strain through cheesecloth, and bottle. Eli drank the result three times a day all through the winter and spring. When Rod asked her how she'd come upon that cure, she said that she'd gone to Annie Drum for advice. *How come Pop and me never thought of that?* Rod wondered.

5

It took a few days for the goose egg on Jennie Sullivan's head to disappear and then she was out and about once more, looking for any excuse to meet up with Tom. It was easy to find him in the small town. She would often walk down to the chip stand or to Coleman's Restaurant, and if he wasn't in either of those places she would find him over by the town hall. There were always friends about, and she could usually find some reason to stand close to him.

"How you feeling Jennie?" he asked when she joined them that first evening.

"Oh don't you worry about me, Tom Hillier," Jennie laughed up at him. "Sure it was only a little ball and I am made of sterner stuff than that!"

Ralph and Vern were standing nearby and Ralph knew that Jennie was right: it would take more than a ball to hurt his Amazon Beothuk Woman. All the same, he wasn't too sure about the way Jennie was looking up at Tom. Maybe a lot more had come of that accident than he wished.

Vern knew right away that it was a sure thing between Jennie and Tom, especially with them bantering back and forth all the time. Jennie loved to tease Tom and, when she flirted, her quick tongue and saucy manner were at their best. Tom danced around her like a young rooster until both Vern and Ralph were fair sick of them.

Jennie was dying for Tom to ask her to go for a walk down by the River in the dark of a summer evening as other couples did. But he didn't. Religion again, she supposed.

That fall, they returned to school for their last year. Jennie, Ralph and Vern went back with the nuns while Tom attended the amalgamated school. Although his school was only up the road, it was a sad fact for Jennie that the two religions kept all their activities apart.

In the spring of 1946, before he finished his grade eleven, Tom up and quit school. When Jennie heard this, she just had to talk to him. That Friday night was cold and raining and she figured the best place to find him would be up to Coleman's Restaurant. Sure enough, when she went in he was sitting at one of the tables eating chips with a few of the boys.

With Jennie Sullivan there were no back doors. She marched up to the table and tapped Tom on the shoulder. "I heard from Phonse that you up and quit school. What'd you do a thing like that for, Tom? Sure, you know how important education is, especially in this day and age."

Tom stood up and took her by the arm and walked away from the table.

"Yes, Jennie, and it's nice to see you again too." He smiled into her eyes and she realized how abrupt she'd been. "Listen, I've learned all I need to know," he continued, "and besides, them seats are just too small for me. I asked the principal if I could use a table and chair, but he asked me if I thought I was the teacher, because students have to sit in desks and only teachers got tables and chairs." Tom laughed. "Don't worry about me. I am going to work and start making some money. I already got meself a job!"

"What do you mean, a job? Are you going away?" Jennie felt her stomach knot and Tom saw her eyes open wide with alarm.

"Oh, don't worry," Tom repeated. "I got a job up in the woods camps. Rod Anderson has hired me on. He says I have to start as a helper to the cook, but if I work hard – and I will – he'll promote me to cutter. I'm leaving first thing tomorrow morning to go across the River."

Jennie told him she wished he'd stay in school, but, before she had a chance to say much more, Ralph and Vern came in. Tom disappeared out the door with his Protestant buddies. Jennie sighed as she sat in a booth with Ralph and Vern, who were both talking excitedly about all the men that were being hired. It wasn't long before she excused herself, saying she had to be getting home. In truth, she was feeling more than a little depressed. As she dashed home in the rain she realized she wasn't as upset over Tom's quitting school as she was over the fact that she wouldn't see him as often. He was stepping from the world of a schoolboy into a man's world up in the lumberwoods, away from Badger.

Next week at school there were more than a few empty desks as she looked around the room. This was a familiar scene in Badger. Every spring, when the camps started hiring, a lot of the boys got itchy feet. Among the empty seats were Ralph's and Vern's. That evening at home, Phonse was onto Mam and Pap to let him go too, but Pap told him to wait for another year or so and he'd get him a job on the drive. Phonse was somewhat pacified, especially when Pap started talking about how the men who were trained to be river drivers were a notch above the cutters. They spent the whole evening, and many after that, talking about how Phonse would start off as an oarsman. Pap emphasized all the time the importance of working hard, just as he had done himself. Especially in the beginning, when you wanted to get promoted.

Jennie kept on and wrote her Council of Higher Education exams in grade eleven. She matriculated, and could have gone on to higher learning but her thoughts were not on education. They were on seeing Tom Hillier when he came down off Sandy, as he was sure to do every Saturday evening.

Because she was so focused on Tom, Jennie told her parents that she loved Badger and didn't want to go away to find work. Pap went to Mr. Plotsky to see about a job for her in The American Bargain Store. Selling goods from a wagon, Mr. Plotsky's father had come to Badger in 1904, when it was still called Badger Brook. Jennie always wondered why Polish Jews would come all the way to this remote spot, buried in the interior of Newfoundland. She thought they must have been brave people.

She liked the store. It had high ceilings with big lazy fans that stirred the air, keeping the shop cool and the goods fresh. One side was for dry goods and the other for groceries. The place smelled of new clothes, leather, tobacco and spices. People were in and out all day long and she was never bored. Her quick mind and her neat penmanship were especially good for the bills and receipts that had to be handwritten and added up.

Tom would always come into the store when he came down off Sandy. The two would chat and make eyes at each other when Mrs. Plotsky wasn't looking. One evening, he waited for her to get off work and walked her home, up the track, holding her hand all the way. Jennie was scared that someone would see them, but Tom said what odds. So Jennie said, right, what odds, too.

Mam was looking through the window as he said goodbye to her at the gate and gently kissed her cheek.

Ralph never had much patience for schooling. He felt too confined in a classroom. The nuns gave him the heebie-jeebies. All those clothes: they wore long black dresses and black veils with white things on their foreheads. Looking at them made him sweat and long to be outside in the cool clean air. He was pretty sure that God never meant for humans to dress like that.

So he quit school. He and Vern and Tom Hillier just walked away from it halfway through the eleventh grade. Ralph, because he couldn't stand the nuns, Vern, because he thought he knew enough anyway, and Tom, because, at six foot six, he was too big to fit into the seats.

The young men wanted jobs in the lumberwoods. Grandfather had once told Ralph that it was called "lumberwoods" because of the lumber mill that was there at the turn of the century. Even though, since 1906, they had been cutting trees not for lumber, but for pulp and paper. However, the name lumberwoods had stuck. Grandfather had said that all the flat land in Badger, along by the Exploits River, once had big, tall pine trees, hundreds of them, forty, fifty feet tall. A white man and his crew had come, raped the tall pines from the land, sawed them up and shipped the lumber out. Without the trees to strengthen the riverbanks, the waters of the great Exploits overflowed onto a sad and barren land.

It sickened Ralph to see what the men put up with for a pittance of a wage to help their families survive in poor villages all over Newfoundland. The lumber camps were filthy and damp and in them the men lived like rats. All those bodies packed in a small space was too much for him. Ralph preferred to sleep outdoors. If the weather was bad, he built a bough whiffen and crawled in. But Vern and Tom slept in the crowded bunkhouse and put up with it.

In the summertime, swarms of flies ate the men. They crawled into their eyes, their ears and their mouths. It drove them crazy. They rubbed all kinds of concoctions on themselves, including bear grease, urine and kerosene oil. The flies never bothered Ralph. He hummed a song of the People that came on the wind that blew over the Great Mound and the flies and swarming mosquitoes stayed away.

Vern begged Ralph to tell him the secret. "Look, Ralph, a whole pack of baccy for you. All you have to do is tell me what kind of tune you're humming under your breath there. Sounds like Hank Snow to me."

Tom was there too. "Everything sounds like Hank Snow to you, Vern b'y. Don't pay any attention to him, Ralph. As for me, I likes the sound of it. Sort of calms me."

"Shut the fuck up, Tom." Vern hated Tom. Ralph knew it was because Jennie was casting him aside for Tom. As well, Ralph felt that Vern was also jealous of Tom's height while he stayed short.

Ralph laughed. "Tom, I guess if my humming could calm black-flies, it could calm anything or anyone," he said. "And Vern, my son, if I told you, it wouldn't make a peck of difference. You're not Indian. You wouldn't get it." Then, changing the subject: "So, which one of you fellas is taking out Jennie Sullivan these days?"

Tom turned as red as a beet. Mumbling that he had to file his saw, he shambled away. Vern, on the other hand, was furious. "Goddamn you, Ralph Drum. You fuckin' bastard, makin' me feel small in front of that big son of a bitch. Jennie haven't had nothin' to do with me in over a year, you knows that. I seen her makin' eyes at him, I did. I don't give a fuck, anyway. Lots of women down in Windsor that I could get if I wanted to."

Unlike Tom, who was destined to be a super-logger, Ralph produced an average amount, not because he couldn't do more, but because there was something inside him that hated to see the tall trees, some hundreds of years old, fall to the ground like dead soldiers. He never voiced that thought to the boys. They'd never understand. To them, a tree was a tree, not a soldier.

Company officials put pressure on the contractors to produce as much pulpwood as they could in a season. In turn, the contractors pressured their foremen, and the foremen pushed the loggers. It seemed to Ralph that there was always a race to see who could cut the most. Tom went at it like there was no tomorrow. Pretty soon he would be the best cutter in the Badger division. Vern hated it; hated the forest; hated the camps; hated Tom; hated Ralph because he wouldn't tell him how to keep the flies away. He was longing to get away, but there was no place to go.

After three months of cutting logs, Ralph got sick of it. He made his way over to the west coast of the island where he had many Mi'kmaq cousins. He stayed there until the summer of 1947. Then he came back home and decided to try for a job on the drive.

The three rivers converging at Badger were well-known to Ralph and to every boy growing up in the small town. They had fished and canoed on Badger Brook, swum in Little Red Indian River and sometimes even dared the mighty Exploits. As a teenager, Ralph would sneak out in the springtime when the drive was on and the River was full of pulpwood and try jumping from log to log. This was a dangerous game, but when you're young, you don't think about danger. A stick of pulpwood was five feet long, at least four inches thick, and as slippery as an eel. Sometimes he fell in and would swim under the logs and get to shore.

Tom hadn't gone around with Ralph and Vern much, due to religious issues with his parents, but when he did, he would try a log close to the shore. He used to say that balancing on the logs made him dizzy. Annie Drum, Ralph's Ma, said Tom probably had trouble with his ears. He had no balance. He'd slip off into the water every time. Vern had been too scared to jump logs, no matter how much Ralph called him chicken.

The River had always been Ralph's first love or, he thought, *my second love*. His first love – his love for the white woman Jennie – would always be a secret hidden deep inside him.

With pike pole and peavey, as the famous song said, he would join the other rivermen and work at moving the logs on their way to the Grand Falls mill. His drive boss would be Jennie's father, Ned Sullivan.

6

One day, in the summer of 1947, Jennie sat down at the base of the tall old pine tree on the bank of the River, pretending to be reading but actually hoping to see Tom come across on the cable boat. Ralph came by.

"Hello Jennie. Can I sit with you for a spell?"

"Yes, Ralph b'y, sit right here." Jennie made room for him under the pine. "Where have you been? I haven't seen much of you since you left school."

"I was over on the west coast for awhile, you know; had a job with Bowaters cutting wood on Glovers Island out in the middle of Grand Lake." He lit up a cigarette and blew the smoke into the air. "But I'm never content until I'm back home in Badger."

"Will you go up in the camps now? Vern says they're some state. He hates it, but Tom is happy enough; never complains."

"Yeah, I know. I guess I'll try to get on as a cutter for now. I have my name in with your father for next spring to get on the drive. I figure I can do that pretty well. I've been on that River all my life, sure." He laughed. "What about you, Jennie? Are you going to marry Vern or what?" Ralph had been away for quite a while and didn't know what was going on anymore. She saw him looking at her out of the corner of his eyes, as if he was anxious about it or something.

Jennie's quick anger flared. "No, Ralph, I am not going to marry Vern. I am not." She jumped up. "Sure you are worse than Mam and Pap! I am sick of them trying to make a couple out of me and Vern."

Ralph got up too. "I'm sorry. I only asked. I am actually glad you're not going to hitch yourself to Vern."

That stopped her. She had thought he and Vern were buddies, and that he was questioning her on Vern's behalf. "You are? Why are you glad, for God's sakes?"

Ralph turned away and gazed out over the surface of the River. "You deserves someone better, Jennie," he said softly.

Just then she caught sight of the cable boat. And there was Tom's red cap. Perhaps they'd walk up the road together. "Excuse me Ralph, I see Tom's getting off the boat."

Ralph didn't reply. He smiled at her and walked down to the cable boat to help the men ashore. As Jennie followed, she thought, *Sometimes I just can't understand Ralph.*

When Tom and Jennie made it known they were a steady couple, both sets of parents were dead set against it.

Mam was firm. "You'm not marrying no Protestant. No you're not! What about poor little Vern? Why can't you marry him?" And on and on she went. "What will the priest say? I'll never hold me head up at Mass again."

Tom told Jennie that his mother, Suze, wasn't about to let her only child marry no black Catholic. Jennie had heard others say that Suze was a crousty woman. They said that she had no good words to say about anyone, that she never laughed, and that she hated music and dancing. "Carryin' on with foolishness" was what she called it. Tom's father, Albert, was different; he seemed to be a more tolerant man.

Tom didn't tell Jennie everything that his mother said to him after she learned the news. All he would say was, "Mother is very upset, Jennie, maid. Her religion is important to her. She got up in church the other night and told the whole congregation about us during her testimony. She said that the Devil was leading her son down a wicked path to leave his true Christian religion and worship idols. Then the pastor had me up to the altar and prayed over me."

Good God Almighty, Jennie thought. *Suze is worse than Mam, and I thought that Mam was bad!*

After weeks of fighting with his parents, Tom hit upon a plan. He told Jennie about it one evening as he was walking her up the track. "Jennie, I got it all figured out. We'll get you pregnant. Then the families will have to let us marry."

Jennie stopped walking and looked up at him in open-mouthed astonishment.

Taking her hands in his, Tom said, "I know, I know Jennie that you wants to wait until we're married before you loses your cherry. But it's the easiest way. When everyone knows you're going to have a baby we will have to get married, and then they won't be so mad at us."

Looking up into Tom's strong handsome face, Jennie tried to think things through. Ever since she was a young girl Mam had always told her what a precious gift her virginity would be to her husband. But when Tom put his strong arms around her and kissed her eager lips it took every ounce of strength for her not to lie down and let him have his way with her. But she wanted Tom to respect her, for the townspeople to respect her, and most of all, she didn't want to disappoint her parents.

Turning away from him, she continued to walk up the track. "No Tom, that's not the way. We'll have to think of something else."

But Tom was insistent. "Come on. Let's plan for tomorrow night. Come on, Jennie. You knows I loves you and there'll never be anyone else for me. At least think it over."

So Jennie did think it over all the next day at Plotsky's. As she wrote out a bill of sale for a pair of logans and a washboard, she thought, *I won't give in to Tom unless we're married and that's that.* But as she wrote out another receipt for a pound of bologna and a plug of tobacco, her mind tipped the other way. *Tom's right. We love each other, so there's no need for us to wait.* By closing time, she still hadn't made up her mind.

Jennie met Tom down by Coleman's Restaurant and they walked over to the Highroad Bridge that spanned the Badger River. Farther down, as they meandered along, there were A.N.D. Company sheds. There was no one around when Tom pulled her in by the back of one of the sheds. It was pitch-dark, but Jennie didn't need any light to feel Tom's arms and his strong body. She arched her neck as he trailed kisses down toward her breasts. It was so good she felt faint.

"Oh Glory be to God." Tom's hot breath was down to her cleavage now. "I want you so bad. The smell of you is enough to send a man insane." One of his hands crept up her leg to the smooth inner flesh of her thigh.

"What do I smell of?" she asked, while the other part of her mind concentrated on Tom's hand on her thigh.

"Mmmm," he inhaled deeply, "some kind of flowers I think. I loves it." His fingers had undone her blouse and one of her soft breasts spilled out into his large callused hand. "Oh Jesus – God," Tom swore softly, forgetting his strict religious principles. "They're the most perfect things I ever saw. Can I kiss them?" He bent his head and his tongue touched the tip of her nipple.

A flash of fire ripped through Jennie such as she had never known. Tom had never gone that far before, and she was unprepared for the intensity of feeling that his tongue generated.

She tried to push him away. "Tom," she said shakily. "Tom! I never knew that it would be like this. No one told me." She laughed. "Sure I'm losing the strength out of my legs."

Tom slid his hands back up her body and buried his face in her hair. He pressed into her and she could feel his stiffness. He laughed low in his throat. "I knows somethin' that the strength is gonna take a long while to go out of, Jennie, and it sure ain't my legs."

Jennie thought she heard someone around the other side of the shed. She hushed Tom. As she buttoned up her blouse, she whispered, "All right, I promise you that we'll do it. We'll meet up on the hill." Jennie looked up into his earnest face and giggled nervously. "Think you can last until tomorrow night?"

As they walked up the track in the dark, Tom firmly attached his large hand to one cheek of Jennie's round backside, establishing his ownership.

All the next day Jennie went about as if she were in a fever. From the moment she got up in the morning, graphic pictures kept popping into her head – his brown hair bent over her breast, his hands cupping her face, his body pushing against her. Once, as she was putting cans of beans on the shelf at Plotsky's, she had to stop and sit down when fire seared right through her.

That evening she washed herself all over, paying particular attention to her armpits and between her legs. She dressed in her best underwear and her new lacy bra.

The moon was full when they met on the back of the hill. Tom was there first, sitting with his arms around his knees. Jennie stood for a moment looking at him. Oh how she loved this man. And now she was giving him what Mam called her most precious gift. But she was giving it willingly, was even in a hurry to give it. Some girls said that the first time hurt, but Jennie was so in love, so anxious to try it, to experience those new sensations, that she didn't care.

"Tom," she said softly.

He looked up. "Jennie. Come sit down."

The night was quiet and still. Side by side, they sat and looked down on the great Exploits River. "Jennie. Have you changed your mind? You can, you know. I won't be mad." He gently took her hand.

"Tom. Shut up talking and kiss me right now." She turned and, taking his shoulders, dragged him down on top of her.

They went down in the sweet grass together. The last words Jennie heard were, "I promise not to hurt you."

Later that night, lying alone in her bed at home, Jennie thought about what they'd done and how natural it had seemed. *I forgot to be scared. The other girls were wrong. There was no hurting. Then we did it a second time. It was wonderful. And we laughed together on the way up the track. Tom said "My jumpin's, Jennie, I dare say we put twins in you that time."*

It was wonderful to be in love. Summer turned to fall and when it got too cold up on the back of the hill they moved into the old A.N.D. Company barns, where the work horses were kept. Inside the barns they couldn't see the stars, but they made their own stars on those nights together.

One evening after supper Jennie told her Mam the news while they were washing dishes. "Mam, I think I'm in the family way." She couldn't look her mother in the face, but stared down at the soapy water in the dishpan.

Mam was drying a plate. It fell out of her hands and to the floor. For some reason it didn't break and Jennie thought maybe that was a good sign.

But Mam's eyes were filled with tears as she went over to the chair and sat down. "Oh Jennie, what have you gone and done?" Her tears ran unchecked down her cheeks as she gazed unseeingly at the plate on the floor. "Please don't tell me it is that Pentecostal boy in on Halls Bay Road. Tell me it's a fine, upstanding Catholic boy like Vern." Mam was looking for one last hope.

Mam must be crazy to think I would have anything to do with Vern, thought Jennie. "Sure Mam, you know it's Tom. We've been going out now for ages. And I loves him. We want to get married. You knows that." Jennie dried off her hands and went over and knelt in front of her mother.

"But what's the priest going to say? It's a mortal sin, you know, Jennie."

"There's no reason to be so upset. I'm still the same Jennie. Nothing's changed." But Jennie could see that Mam didn't believe her.

Bridey Sullivan was a strong woman, and when her daughter said she was expecting a baby, Bridey knew there had to be a marriage.

A child born out of wedlock had no chance in a world where people would call it a bastard.

In bed a couple of nights later, when Ned went to blow out the lamp for the night, Bridey stopped him. "We needs to talk, Ned."

"Can't it wait for morning? I'm fair beat out."

"No, this is the best time. All the children are asleep." She propped her pillow up against the headboard and took a deep breath. "Ned, you're going to have to speak to Albert Hillier and tell him that his son Tom has your daughter put in the family way. The Blessed Virgin only knows that I can't talk to Suze Hillier. She wouldn't give me the time of day."

"What? Jesus Christ, Bridey! That young son of a bitch of a Tom Hillier! How'd that happen?" Ned felt shocked and angry enough to seek out Tom and kill him on the spot.

Bridey calmed him down. "Listen b'y, this happens to many women; they gets caught before they're married. Just because Jennie is your daughter don't mean she's any different." She moved over in the bed to lay her head against his arm. "You knows that everyone does it on the sly. We did, or have you forgotten how hot you were to get inside my bloomers?" She laughed. "And you're still hot to get in there."

Ned looked at her and grinned, his anger waning. They both had great memories of their younger years together. "All right, Bridey, all right. I'll speak to his father tomorrow." He blew out the lamp. "Now go to sleep."

The next day, Ned went down to the station to see Albert.

Albert was a mild-mannered man who attended to his station master duties with rimless glasses perched on the top of his nose. "Good day to you, Ned. How've you been keeping?" he asked as he peered at Ned over his glasses.

"I'm doing all right, b'y," Ned replied. "If you can spare me a few minutes sometime today, I'd like to have a private chat with you about our two children."

"Ah, so it's come to that," Albert sighed. "I must say, Ned b'y, I'm not surprised. Tom and his mother have had a few words over him seeing your daughter, you know."

"Yes, Albert, the same thing has being going on at our house. I wish children would stick to their own kind. This marrying into other religions causes some fuss for the parents."

"Yep, it sure does," Albert answered, as he picked up his train schedule sheet. "Let me see now . . . I haven't got a train coming for another four hours. Why don't we take a little stroll together?"

Jennie was terrified. Mam had told her that Pap had spoken to Tom's father and that he had invited Albert, Suze and Tom to have a cup of tea together at the Sullivan's.

Mam was a bundle of nerves. She had the girls drove crazy as she made them clean and shine everything in sight. "Got to measure up to Suze Hillier's house," she muttered, even though she had never been inside it.

The Hillier family arrived. Jennie could see that Mam was quite in awe of Suze's fox fur stole that she wore around her neck and shoulders. The stole was complete with beady eyes, dangling paws and bushy tail. It was some kind of status symbol for Suze, who wore it on any occasion possible, summer or winter. For a moment, Jennie's stout heart quailed as she beheld Suze's countenance, black as thunder above the animal fur.

Jennie and Mam served tea. Suze never touched the tea, she never smiled nor spoke and her lips were pursed up as if she smelled a bad odour. Only Albert and Ned were at ease as they chatted away over their tea and sandwiches. Tom sat next to his mother and kept offering her a piece of cake, a sandwich, more hot tea to replace the cooling cup that she hadn't touched, all to no avail. Finally he cleared his throat, stood up, and put his hands on the table. Jennie went to stand beside him. "Me and Jennie wants to get married," he said before anyone could interrupt. "Jennie's in the family way." Their parents had already been told this, but Jennie and Tom felt it needed to be said again in front of everyone.

Jennie noticed how not one person sitting at the table would look them in the eye. They were all staring at their sandwiches and cooling tea. Mr. Albert was the first to look up and speak. He told them that they were welcome to come and live with them until they built a place of their own. Jennie glanced once again at Suze but still she didn't speak, or look up. Her lips seemed to be pursed even tighter and the fox's beady eyes gleamed.

Once Mr. Albert had spoken, Mam got up and started to bustle around clearing up the table. Pap sat back and filled his pipe with baccy and offered some to Albert, commenting on how adding a slice of apple to the pouch provided moisture and added a nice flavour to the smoke. Mr. Albert graciously declined, saying he and Suze had to be getting on and that they would be in touch.

And then the two families planned a wedding.

Jennie said she wanted her oldest sister to stand for her. Tom said that his mother wasn't fussy about having too many Catholics present. But Jennie was firm. No sister to stand up for her, no wedding. Tom was quick enough to change his tune then.

Mrs. Plotsky gave Jennie a lovely cream-coloured evening dress. It came to mid-calf and had an organza shawl. Her sister said they'd get blue forget-me-nots from the garden for her bouquet.

Tom was in a quandary who he'd ask to be his best man, seeing as he had no brothers.

"I don't care who you gets," his mother told him. "But get a Protestant. Don't you so much as offer to bring in that Sullivan fella, Phonse. I just knows they're dying for you to ask him." She went off down the hallway grumbling about too many idol-worshipping Catholics in her good Christian home.

Suze told Albert to ask the pastor to get one of the young men from the Youth Group to stand for Tom. She was pleased when he did. That meant there would be one less Catholic in her house. Tom didn't care. His mind was focused entirely on Jennie.

It was 1948. The pastor married them in Suze's living room.

Even though it was summer and they were indoors, Suze still draped the ugly fox stole over her shoulders as her son and his Catholic girl said their vows. There were only Jennie and Tom, Suze and Mr. Albert, Mam and Pap, and Jennie's sister Philomena. The boy from the Youth Group, who was only fifteen, was shy and uncomfortable. As soon as the ceremony was ended he mumbled goodbye and was out the door before anyone could stop him. Mam and Pap stood strong together, but their eyes were red and watery all the way through. *My God in Heaven,* Jennie thought afterward. *It wasn't that bad! You'd think I was marrying a criminal instead of nice quiet Tom.*

The women from Suze's church, at the request of the pastor, had produced tea and sandwiches and a small wedding cake. Bridey wanted to make Jennie's wedding cake herself, but Tom told Jennie that his mother wanted no wedding cake in her house that had been made with rum in it.

There was no gaiety. Suze's disapproving face and turned-down mouth put a stop to any attempt anyone might have made for a laugh or a joke. No one drank a drop because of the religion issue. No one danced, for the same reason. At one point during the long evening, Jennie thought of what fun it would be if Ralph were here with his fiddle. But there was no use thinking about that; Suze despised the Mi'kmaq people as much as she did the Catholics. Besides, the Mi'kmaq were both Indian and Catholic. According to Tom, his mother allowed that the Drum family was damned for all eternity.

✺

When Ralph heard that Jennie and Tom had gotten married, he got into his canoe and paddled for miles up the Little Red Indian River, to organize his thoughts. He wasn't sure if it made him happy because Tom was a good man, or if it made him sad because it wasn't him that Jennie Hillier loved. Ralph's own future remained uncertain to him. That night, Jennie's wedding night, he made camp on the bank of the Little Red Indian. As he lay back in his sleeping bag having a final smoke before going to sleep, Ralph saw a star shoot swiftly across the sky. He sent a silent wish after it, a wish that Jennie would be happy with Tom.

And then his thoughts turned to Vern Crawford, who had got himself a woman from Windsor after all, just as he said he would. Her name was Millie and Vern had married her that very same year. Whether he did it to show Jennie or not, Ralph didn't know. He and Vern weren't close buddies as they once were.

Ralph could never have guessed that two years later Vern would have a huge spot of luck, when Millie would inherit five thousand dollars from a rich uncle in the States. Before long, Vern was out of the woods and into a big Chrysler with a lit-up sign on top saying BADGER TAXI.

7

Millie Crawford was washing up the dishes and trying to ignore her excited husband as he paced about the kitchen.

"Millie," Vern said. "This is my big chance. I'm going to buy a taxi. No more lumberwoods for me, maid. Just thinking about the living conditions in those camps makes me shiver. Men housed in shelters not fit for henhouses, scroachin' all over with lice, forced to work long hours in all weathers for small pay – I can't take any more, Millie. I got a chance to get out of it, and I'm going to do it. Yessiree."

Millie wasn't too happy about her husband taking her money like that. She tried not to show it, but this evening she was banging the dishes about a little louder than usual. After all, it was willed to her from her bachelor uncle down in the States. She thought she should get to say how the money was spent.

"Vern, that's my money too, you know. Can't I have some for myself?"

Vern, oblivious to her feelings, said, "Sure what do you need it for? Don't I keep you fed and looked after?"

So she let him go ahead. A couple times he heard her muttering to herself about new clothes. Vern squashed that. "What do you need new clothes for? You never goes anywhere except to Mass and to bingo. No one's going to notice what you got on."

Vern's taxi became the love of his life, a '48 Chrysler 300, beige-coloured, with many miles to her credit, but a valiant and brave car

51

nevertheless. He'd bought her second-hand because he wasn't sure if the taxi business would pay off. She was scraped and scruffy-looking. The passenger's door handle was broken, so he had to lean across and open it when someone got in the front; inside, the brown vinyl was stained and torn. But for all her wear, Vern sometimes thought he loved her more than he did Millie.

Vern and his Chrysler worked long hours together. In winter, he attempted trips over Halls Bay Road, plowing his way through the snowdrifts when no one else would try it. He made daily runs to Grand Falls and Windsor and even a few long overnight trips to St. John's. Vern was a happy man. He was out of the woods camps, while fellows who had laughed at him, like Ralph and Tom, for instance, were still up there and working like slaves and being eaten by the flies. Well, not Ralph; flies left him alone. And Jennie's brother Phonse, who was on the drive, was stuck out in the wet and cold driving logs, while he, Vern, soaked up the warmth of his cozy taxi. Hah! That would teach them to laugh at Vern Crawford!

⌘

There was no baby for Jennie and Tom. There never had been. It had all been a lie.

Consumed with guilt about the great falsehood she had told, so she and Tom could get married and share a bed, Jennie's thoughts cast back to what had brought them to this.

No matter how much sex we had in the A.N.D. Company barns the winter before, I never became pregnant. Every twenty-eight days or so I'd see the dreaded stain on my bloomers and I'd have to tell poor Tom, "No baby, no marriage this month."

Spring had come and the barns were busy with the men and horses, so the good times in the hay were over. Getting desperate, Tom had said that they could lie. Jennie had not been too happy about lying. Mam's old saying had kept ringing through her mind, "Oh what a tangled web we weave, when first we practice to deceive."

"Tom, I can't. I can't lie to Mam," she had said. "There's no way I can tell Mam I'm having a baby if I'm not. That's a great sin that will surely haunt us for the rest of our lives."

"It will only be for a couple of months until we get married, and then we'll just tell them it was a false alarm," Tom had urged. "It'll be all right, you'll see if it won't."

Jennie was still reluctant, but wanting desperately to please Tom, she'd agreed.

And it did seem all right; right up to the time I told the lie to Mam and she dropped the plate and started to cry. It became worse when we had to stand in front of two sets of parents and lie again. And now is the worst of it all. I am stuck in a house with a mother-in-law who hates me.

Three months after they were safely married, Jennie and Tom told their parents that it was a mistake and she wasn't going to have a baby after all. Mam and Pap said nothing, but Jennie sensed their disappointment.

Suze nearly had a stroke. "Dirty crawling idol-worshipping Roman Catholic, you trapped my son into marriage," she spat at her when the two were alone. The two women spent many hours alone together while Tom was up on Sandy and Mr. Albert busy with his railway duties, but they took no joy in each other's company. Jennie was too scared to carry on a conversation. Used to her easygoing Sullivan family, Jennie had never before met anyone like Suze and she didn't know how to respond to her at first. Her mother-in-law had a way of undermining her self-confidence with sly remarks. Suze had a mean and dirty mouth when there was no one around to hear her but Jennie. *And to see her,* Jennie thought, *so pious and holy, testifying in church.*

Jennie didn't want to force a confrontation and hurt her beloved Tom. As her quick temper and saucy tongue were clamped down she became withdrawn and nervous. And she was too ashamed to tell Mam about the things her mother-in-law said about Catholics.

Back when they got married, Tom had encouraged Jennie to stay working at Plotsky's. The morning after their wedding night, which Tom had enthusiastically consummated in the bedroom where he had slept all of his life, Jennie had come downstairs. Tom had left at dawn to go back across the River to the woods camps. It was barely eight o'clock and Jennie had to be to work at nine.

"Good morning, Mrs. Hillier."

There was no answer from her mother-in-law, who looked like she'd been up for awhile, already dressed in her severe black dress and white apron. Jennie had reached for the kettle on the stove but Suze quickly brushed her aside without as much as an "excuse me," picked up the kettle and, walking to the back door, dumped the entire contents over the step.

"Oh, I was hoping for a cup of tea before I went to work, if that's all right," Jennie had stammered.

Suze had slammed the empty kettle down on the back of the stove. She'd gone to the cupboard and got out her stove blackening and her brush. "Well, if you wanted tea you should have gotten up at a sensible hour like a decent Christian instead of lolling about in bed until eight o'clock.

"I've been up since six," she'd continued. "Got my breakfast eat and am ready to work now. This is my day to blacken me stove. The fire is died down now and I'm not building it up for the likes of you." She'd waved the blackening in Jennie's face and motioned toward the door with the black brush. "So be off with you now!"

From then on, Jennie kept a pack of biscuits in her room to munch on in the mornings. She wasn't about to try and face Suze again in her kitchen.

At first, she'd tried going back to Suze's to make a sandwich for her lunch, but her mother-in-law quickly put an end to that. "If you thinks you can come traipsin' in here in the middle of the day, dirtying up my clean kitchen, wasting my firewood to boil the kettle, you can change your mind on that." Jennie ended up walking up the track to Mam's place where she was always welcome.

When Mr. Albert and Tom were at home, Suze Hillier was all goodness, cooking their dinner every day. Suze tolerated Jennie being there during those times; otherwise Tom would be asking questions.

The only happiness she had was when Tom came home and they were in their bedroom and in bed. They made the bedsprings creak, but they were so in love they didn't care.

In the morning Suze would say under her breath, "You two are like rabbits. Kept me awake all night with the noise, you dirty Mick. Certainly I wouldn't expect much more of you, the way you were reared. Eleven children! He must've been at her day and night."

But to Jennie and Tom's great disappointment, no matter how much loving they did, Jennie didn't become pregnant. She longed for a little baby to hold and cuddle and call her own, but every month, like clockwork, she would get the cramps in her belly and her flow would start. She came to believe that her monstrous lie, plus the fact that she had left the Catholic Church to marry a Protestant, was God's punishment on her.

Before long, to please her new husband and her new mother-in-law, Jennie threw herself into the Pentecostal Church. She went to all the services and became saved. They were glad to have her – another convert. The handsome new minister, Pastor Damian Genge, said to her, "You're a Christian now."

Jennie asked him, "What was I before?" He looked at her as if she had ten heads, opened his mouth to say something, closed it again and walked away.

Tom and his parents were all saved. It meant living a stern and strict life, which she knew Tom found hard. He said that he worked with men who cursed until the air turned blue. Tom occasionally used God's name where it wasn't appropriate, but he said he always asked forgiveness. He had tremendous sex drive, but he rationalized that by saying that it wasn't a sin as long as they were trying to make a baby. In Jennie's opinion the Pentecostals were no different from the Catholics: same beliefs, but presented in a different manner. But she wisely kept these thoughts to herself.

Jennie told her mother-in-law about her conversation with the pastor, and asked her what she thought she was before she joined the Pentecostals, if not a Christian.

"Was I Jewish, like the Plotskys?" Jennie asked her.

"Shut up, Catholic whore," the old woman hissed. "You've no business prying into religious subjects. You and your ignorant family, you're all whores. Whores!" She banged her big iron frying pan on the stovetop.

Suze was preparing to fry pork chops for her supper. It seemed to Jennie that the family lived on pork chops and bacon. She fried everything to a blackened crisp, calling it well done and saying that that was the only way to eat food. Tom and Mr. Albert ate her cooking because they were used to it, but Jennie had a hard time eating burnt meat, burnt fat pork and burnt onions. Jennie offered to cook a meal for the family once. Just once.

Suze had turned on her like a cat, hissing and spitting. "You get your filthy dirty Roman paws off my food, my lady. You're only here in this house because of my son. You can take no part in my kitchen, no part in my house whatsoever. And the day he gets tired of you and you walks out through that door will be a happy day for me."

Jennie had known then that there would never be any compromise with Suze. Three more years passed. Hard years: living with her mother-in-law, not having a baby. Tom seemed in no hurry to build them a house. He had lived with his parents all of his life and saw no reason to uproot himself and move out. Sometimes Jennie felt that all he wanted was for her to be in his bed, waiting, warm and willing when he came home. What happened to his wife outside that didn't hold much interest for him.

But then, sometime in those three years, Jennie's true personality began to reassert itself. She'd had enough. Suze had pushed her to the limit and her abuse began to roll off Jennie like water off a duck's back. She had no more tears left. Nowadays she often sauced her mother-in-law, giving as good as she got. The venom and hatred in the old lady's eyes became worse.

8

Ralph's great-grandfather Michael was half Beothuk, or so they said. They were nearly finished by the time the Mi'kmaq made their way inland. The white man had hounded them away from the ocean and into the interior and one winter the Drum family took in a Beothuk family: a man, two women and an infant. Whenever his grandfather, Peter, or his father, Louis, talked about all this, they became vague when they reached the part where the man was killed and the older woman died. Perhaps the family wasn't proud of whatever happened. The younger woman and her baby lived, they said, and Great-great-grandfather had fathered a child with her, a boy – half Mi'kmaq and half Beothuk. It was Michael who had been given the Drum family name.

Ralph felt all this must be true because he could feel the Beothuk blood in his veins when he stood on top of their sacred Mound overlooking the three rivers, and heard the spirits of the People speak on the wind. In the interior, he trod the paths that they trod.

There was a legend that said, hundreds of millions of years ago, the centre of the island of Newfoundland had risen from the bottom of the ocean. Perhaps the legend was right. Who could say? Ralph only knew that he had seen some unusual things deep in the interior, many of them unexplainable.

The Beothuk knew the places of powerful magic. Hodges Hill was one such place. The hill was sacred to the Beothuk and, later, to the Mi'kmaq as well. And that was Grandfather's territory. He'd told Ralph that right at the top there was a small cave. In it, in a hollowed-out rock, were two large freshwater pearls, beautiful to look at and magic to hold. His grandfather Peter claimed they'd been there since the beginning of time. He said *his* grandfather showed him, and that *he* had been shown by the Beothuk woman, his mother. *Never remove the pearls,* she had warned him. *They belong to the spirits of the high places.*

When Ralph was twenty, he decided he would go in and look at Grandfather's pearls for himself. He asked the old man to go with him, but he said no. His time to die was almost upon him, he said, and the young man had to find them for himself. "Hold the pearls in your hand, my son. Some say it will cause you to dream of the future."

Hodges Hill was about two thousand feet high, the highest point in Central Newfoundland. It lay northeast of Badger, near the Mary Ann Lake and Twin Lakes area, and was a visible landmark from the towns of Badger, Windsor and Grand Falls.

It took Ralph all day to trek in. He made camp overnight on the shore of Mary Ann Lake to the west of Hodges Hill. A deep, dark, cold lake, it had a boggy shoreline and the waters were a brown peaty colour. Like most lakes and brooks in the interior, it had lots of fish.

That evening, sitting alone by his small campfire, Ralph looked out over the smooth waters of Mary Ann. He thought of the time his father had shown him a funny little island in the upper end of the lake, about half a mile long and half a mile wide. It was actually a floating island, he said. Ralph was only thirteen then and had often gone with his father into the woods, to be taught the skills of trapping.

According to his father, Louis Drum, the making of the island had started with the body of some animal, perhaps a caribou onto which debris had gathered over the course of fifty years, a hundred years, or longer: old stumps and sticks, moss and clumps of peat into which grass, gowiddy, and alders seeds rooted, fertilized by the animal carcass.

Father had taken him out in canoe and said they'd climb onto the squashy mass. Ralph trusted his father. If he said it was safe that was good enough for him, but he hadn't looked forward to standing in the middle of a deep lake on a floating island.

Father had climbed out of the canoe at a certain spot, the only spot to attempt it, he said. Anywhere else around the perimeter, your foot would go on down through. He grabbed Ralph's arm and hauled him up, warning him to tread only where he did. One misstep and he'd be a goner.

The ground was spongy, as if the lake underneath was just waiting to take this piece of earth back. Ralph could feel a slight rocking motion as the island shifted and swayed. In the centre was a hole no more than two feet wide. Father had his fishing pole. The place for trout, he said. He cast in his line and in a flash had a fat mud trout. He gave Ralph the pole then, warning him again to watch his step. Ralph caught five fish in the next few minutes. They'd have three apiece for supper. *No need to take more than we need,* Father always said. Louis, like his ancestors before him, had great respect for the land and for nature.

In the morning, alone on the shore of Mary Ann, Ralph woke and looked up at the summit of Hodges Hill. It was covered in cloud, but it was a fine summer morning and he knew it would burn off before he reached the top.

The climbing was hard going. Much of the mountain's face was smooth granite with a crag here and there to get a foothold. Two thousand feet is no big deal when you think of the people who climbed Mount Everest, but this place spoke to something inside Ralph. He'd felt it before: his Beothuk blood. Their spirits were still there, hovering.

He gained the top around midday. The cloud had disappeared and the view from the top was spectacular. Over to the east, near Gander Lake, Mount Peyton reared up, a beautiful blue colour high above the forest. To the west rose the prominent Topsails. Far to the west, toward Grand Lake he could see Hinds Hill – even higher than Hodges Hill, they said. To the south he could just make out the yellow top of Mount Sylvester. To the northeast was the Bay of Exploits, and farther to the northeast he could see several of the outer islands of Notre Dame Bay. Ralph felt insignificant in the great scheme of Creation and wondered if his ancestors had felt that way too.

It was very cold at the top, even in midsummer. The bald rock was scraped smooth by the winds and harsh climate and no vegetation grew. The cave was to the side, under an overhang. A person had to be looking carefully to find it. Or maybe the spirits pointed him to it. Ralph scrabbled down carefully and crawled into a space so small that he couldn't stand up. He lit a match and looked around. It was clean and dry and he knew that Indians had slept there at some time in the past. Ralph decided that he would too, even if there were no pearls.

But there *were* pearls, just like Grandfather said, side by side in a cup-shaped granite hollow in the far corner – one pale, translucent pink, and the other purple, shot through with pink streaks. Ralph was there two hours before he mustered enough nerve to pick them up, one at a time. They felt warm in the middle of his palm. Magic to hold. Perhaps they weren't pearls at all, although they looked like pearls, but were as big as marbles. Whatever they were, Ralph knew they were put there for a reason. The reason may have been lost over time, but the pearls remained. He laid them back down in their nest of rock where they could continue guarding the cave, guarding the mountain, guarding the land.

He lit a small fire near the mouth of the cave, unrolled his sleeping bag, and prepared to spend the night. A feeling of peace and contentment came over him, more intense than ever.

As he slept, Ralph dreamed. He could see his own face, an older version of himself, and he knew it was the future. It was winter and hundreds of people milled around him. He clearly saw Jennie, older too. Suddenly, from out of nowhere, a large figure in a long black cape swooped into the scene and grabbed Jennie, wrestling her to the ground. He was choking her. Ralph could see her heels digging in the snow as she tried to get free.

He watched as his older self moved in slow motion, brought a stick up over his head, and savagely hit the black-draped figure. He felt his other self put all his pent-up love and frustration behind the blow and the black figure let Jennie go.

The little cave was on the eastern side of the mountain and the sun shining in his eyes woke him. Ralph lay still for a few moments, thinking of the dream, wondering what it could mean. He thought of the beautiful pearls in the little pocket of rock, a few feet away from where he had slept. Was Grandfather right? Had they caused him to dream of the future? How far into the future had he seen? Was Jennie in danger?

There was a noise outside the cave. He peered out. Looking straight at him from five feet away was a great bald eagle. Its golden eyes held Ralph's. It had finally happened. The Great Spirit had sent his spirit guide.

The eagle walked away from him toward the edge of the summit. Ralph squirmed out a little farther to watch as the great bird spread its great wings and flew toward the rising sun. At the top of its spiral the eagle banked and turned toward Ralph's home, the town of Badger, as if signalling him to go back where he belonged: to watch over Jennie and keep her from the threatening black danger.

9

Alf Elliott had what he called a "gammy leg." A childhood injury had left him crippled. He'd had a good education and, unable to do heavy physical work such as logging, had trained for Morse code. In 1945, he'd gone to work for the Newfoundland Posts and Telegraphs in the town of Badger. After Confederation with Canada, postal and telegraph offices were separated and then Alf became an employee of Canadian National Telecommunications.

When Alf and his wife, Mary, moved from Port Albert, a community in Notre Dame Bay, their oldest child, Amanda, was a small baby. His sons were born in Badger. The years passed swiftly. The children grew up in the Company town with good schools, electricity, a railway station and well-stocked shops, never knowing or thinking about the hardships of the logging industry. However, Alf, their father, knew. He conducted business with loggers every day and listened to their stories of the camps.

There were no telephones in Badger except in the telegraph office and in the A.N.D. Company manager's residence. Alf was often asked to go back to his office after hours for people who wanted to make private telephone calls. No money changed hands, and it was done out of courtesy, but now Alf would be owed a good turn: a meal of moose meat, a load of firewood, a ride to Grand Falls.

Over the years, mining companies and survey crews were back and forth to Badger as the mineral-rich interior was surveyed, mapped, and sampled. Alf, outgoing and friendly, got to know them all as they sent telegrams back and forth to their offices on the mainland.

There was a French fellow, Wilfred d'Entremont, doing mine surveys with a crew of men at Collishaw, up on the Gaff Topsails. He wired telegrams back and forth to his company in Quebec and made phone calls, after hours, to his wife.

Even though d'Entremont's English wasn't very good, and Alf spoke no French, they became friends. Alf did pick up some French swear words from the crew as they worked there that summer. Gradually, he learned that *merde* was shit and *mange la merde* was eat shit, *casse-toi* was piss off, *ferme la bouche* was shut your mouth, and *allez a l'enfer* was go to hell. Not exactly the kind of language that a father would use around his children, but Alf was interested enough to remember it.

He also learned that in Quebec the parts of a car all had English-sounding names: *le carburateur, le moteur, la batterie.* Alf thought that was the oddest thing and he wondered if it was because the car parts manufacturers were English companies and the French had had to adapt. The funniest one of all was the French word for seal – *phoque*, which they pronounced "fuck." It was a great laugh among both the English-speaking and the French-speaking men to say, "What a tasty piece of *phoque!*"

The crew had rented a house, and d'Entremont had a photography outfit that he'd brought with him to take pictures of the mine site, the minerals and the terrain. Alf would visit there occasionally, and somewhere during that time, he was bitten by the photography bug. It consumed his thoughts.

When d'Entremont and his crew were leaving to go back to Quebec, he gave Alf all the gear needed to develop and print snaps. Alf offered to pay the Frenchman something for it, but he said it would only be thrown away because it was too much trouble to lug it all back to Quebec.

In January of 1952, Jennie felt a slight shift in the air in the Hillier house. If anything, it felt heavier, like a storm brewing. Suze had a satisfied smirk on her thin lips and she would occasionally nod and smile to herself, as though she had come to a decision.

The storms were bad again that winter. The woods camp was closed down for a couple of weeks, which meant that Tom was at home. Suze picked a night when Mr. Albert was away, Jennie was working at the store until nine o'clock, and she had Tom to herself.

Not realizing how bad it was outside, Jennie had left Plotsky's to walk in on Halls Bay Road, but Abe Miller, who worked for the A.N.D. Company as a truck driver, happened along and offered her a lift. "Thanks for stopping, Mr. Miller."

"Well, Jennie my child, I wouldn't leave me dog out in this, let alone a person." Abe hauled his Company pickup down in gear and pushed through the snow that was accumulating on the road. "This storm blew up all of a sudden, didn't it?"

Abe dropped Jennie off at the Hillier house and continued on through the storm to his own place farther down the road.

When Jennie came into the kitchen there was no sign of Tom, just his mother standing by the stove with her arms folded across her chest.

"Where's Tom?" she asked. Tom always waited up for her.

"Gone to bed," Suze said. Her lips were pursed and her eyes gleamed with something. Was it the glow of satisfaction?

Jennie climbed the stairs to the bedroom. Tom wasn't in bed. He was sitting on it, fully clothed, and his face was white as a sheet.

"Jennie," he said, "are you going out with Vern behind my back?" She thought she would faint. Her throat closed off and she couldn't get a breath into her lungs. Spots danced in front of her eyes.

"Tom! How can you say something like that?"

"Mother told me that you and him rides around in his taxi together and that you're right chummy with him." Tom had his elbows on his knees and his head was bowed into his hands, the pose of a man crying. "She also said you and Ralph Drum are pretty thick, and that everyone says that last summer you and him went up on the back of the hill together."

In truth, Jennie hardly ever laid eyes on Vern or Ralph. She knew that Vern had gotten out of the woods camps and had somehow acquired a taxicab. She knew he'd married a girl from Windsor and that their little girl, Melanie, had been born in 1950. Missus Crawford went on and on about her grandchild to Mam, as if she were the only person ever to have one. As for Ralph, he came and went. No one ever knew where he was, although Phonse said he was likely in the deep country among the forests and lakes. Jennie hadn't seen him in quite a while.

"Tom, did your mother call me a whore? Do you really believe that I would sink that low?"

"My mother wouldn't tell me that if it was a lie, Jennie."

Well, my God, she thought, *how dumb are men? He actually does not know the stuff that old woman has been up to.* Something inside of Jennie snapped. Suze's lying and meanness had gone too far this time. Jennie was still wearing her coat; she whirled around and dashed down over the stairs and to the porch door. Suze was standing by the stove. "Goodbye, you Roman whore," she whispered, with a smirk on her face.

Jennie turned around and spotted Suze's precious fox stole lying on the chair, the stole that was lovingly combed every evening. The glass eyes of the dead fox looked at Jennie; its tiny teeth seemed to be laughing and echoing its mistress's words: *"Whore."*

Jennie grabbed the stole, lifted the cover off the stove, and stuffed it down in the fire headfirst. Suze screamed and hauled on her, but Jennie was bigger and stronger and very, very angry. The stole caught fire immediately, and the last thing Jennie remembered as she went through the door was the stink of scorched fur.

Tom came thumping down the stairs to see what the racket was about, but his wife had gone and his mother was hysterical.

Jennie slammed the door behind her and ran into the darkness of the snowy night. The wind swirled the snow around her nylon-stockinged legs. Too late she realized that she had forgotten her bandana. It was back on the bed where she had taken it off as Tom accused her of adultery. Anger surged up inside her again and gave her the strength to plow through snowdrifts that reached to her knees. All the way from the Hillier house in on Halls Bay Road and to her father's house up the track she went. It was more than a mile, perhaps two miles.

The storm was fierce, and as she turned west on the railway track the wind blew directly into her face, threatening to take her breath away. Her hair was matted with snow and had frozen onto her head like a cap. Jennie kept in the front of her mind the picture of her mother-in-law's face when she realized that her precious fox stole was burning. The satisfaction of that was fuel enough to keep her from falling into a snowbank and freezing to death.

Finally, she reached her parents' house and fell against the door. Pap opened it and Jennie collapsed into his arms. Mam and her sisters came rushing to her aid. They stripped off her frozen clothes, sat her by the stove so her hair could thaw out, and got her some hot tea. Her legs showed white spots of frostbite and her sister had to massage them to bring back the blood flow.

Tom was up the track to the Sullivan house at first light. "I would've been here before," he said to Mam, "but my mother had pains in her chest and I went to get the doctor for her." He was beside himself with shame from the realization that he had acted in a dishonourable way toward his wife. *And so he should be,* was Mam's opinion.

She gave him short shrift. "Jennie's too ill to be bothered right now, Tom. Go on back home and look after your mother. And think about this: a husband's first duty is to his wife, not his mother." And with that she slammed the door in Tom's face.

Jennie developed pneumonia and burned with fever for two days. In her delirium, Suze was chasing her, and right along at her heels ran the stole, a live fox again and not some dead thing with glass eyes. She cried out and kept running, but tripped over the fox and fell.

It was several days before Jennie could manage to keep her eyes open long enough to speak and to drink some broth. Mam nursed her tenderly, glad to have her daughter home again instead of in there on Halls Bay Road with the Protestant heathens.

Three weeks went by before Mam would let Tom in to see Jennie. He'd come every day, knocking on the door, cap in hand, inquiring about his wife, but Mam was firm. "She's still very sick, Tom. If there's any change for the worse, someone will come and let you know."

Eventually, Jennie was able to sit up in bed with the pillows propped behind her. Mam told her that Tom had been wanting to see her. "'Tis time to make a decision, Jennie. I knows you never want to live in with that old Suze again, but you and Tom have a marriage together. Tell me when you're well enough to speak to him."

Jennie fretted about her hair, lanky and sweaty from the fever. Her sister washed it for her, tied it back with a green ribbon, and produced a frilly bed jacket to cover her nightdress. Bed jackets were considered the proper bedwear for accepting visitors.

When Tom came again, Jennie told Mam to let him in.

His big form stood by the bed. No one offered him a chair as he shifted from foot to foot. "Ah . . . ahem," he cleared his throat. "Jennie, I don't know what to say. I am so sorry, so sorry I couldn't come after you that night. My mother had chest pains. You knows she has a bad heart. I had to walk to the doctor's house and get the doctor. I figured you'd be all right to get home, you being a big strong woman and all. I never thought you'd get so sick. I'm sorry."

Jennie listened to what he had to say. She could see that Tom had not changed in regard to his mother and waited for him to say that he didn't believe his mother's lies.

But he said nothing.

Jennie looked at him, the man she had married for better or for worse. Her eyes filled with tears.

"I still love you, Tom, and I guess I always will. Your mother treated me badly from the first day I went to live with her." He started to speak, but Jennie held up her hand. "Let me finish, please. I know you don't believe me, but hear this. I'll only come back to you on one condition: when you get a home for us away from your mother." She closed her eyes. "Please go now."

Whenever he came to see her after that, she would get Mam to say she was in bed, resting. At first he would knock on the door a couple of times a day. Then, in a week or so, it was only once every few days. Then he stopped coming altogether.

10

Father Kevin Murphy was parish priest of the Roman Catholic Church of Badger. His parishioners made up half the population of the town. The rest was made up of Protestant religions – United, Anglican and Pentecostal.

Father Murphy considered that he ran a pretty tight ship. The school was well-built and clean. The convent housed eight black-robed nuns who answered to him. He liked to think of his church as a jewel. It was small, not like the big one down in Grand Falls. The altar and the pews were of warm, hand-carved wood and seemed to glow from inside with their own light. When the sunlight came through the stained glass windows, it was as if God was saying, "This is a beautiful thing."

He remembered coming to Badger in 1952. It was his first posting in Newfoundland. He had arrived in St. John's from Ireland the year before and had applied for a parish with the archdiocese. Father Murphy never knew what chips fell into place for him to be sent to Badger, but he was a firm believer in the Hand of God guiding him wherever he was supposed to go.

His first task was to set up church, school and convent, all in one area. The Church had just purchased a block of land on Church Road, prime real estate for Badger. It included a lovely big house that had belonged to one of Badger's first merchants. It made a perfect convent for the Presentation Sisters.

The church, with the small school attached to it, had originally stood across the railway tracks on the other side of Badger. When the church officials decided to bring it across to the new property, they left the little school where it was, as they were building a larger one on the new site. The little school eventually became Alf Elliott's telegraph office.

Every able-bodied man in the town helped, and religion, always a hot subject, was put aside. The men put big logs under the church and poled them along. The church moved, inch by inch, foot by foot. When they came to the railway tracks, the Canadian National Railway helped by stopping train traffic and taking up a stretch of the rails in the path of the rolling church. Linesmen had to see to the overhead wires on the poles that ran along by the track. When the church passed over, the sectionmen worked frantically to replace the length of rails for train traffic to continue.

Once across the tracks, more logs had to be put across the railway's big drainage ditch. Then, to get the church to its new location, it had to come across Herb Day's garden to Church Road. Down came the back fence and the front fence. The church was eased through backward, so that when it arrived across the road at its final resting place, the entrance would be facing the road.

Father thanked all who helped. Some came back to the rectory with him for a dram or two of rum. They were all proud of themselves for a job well done. Friendships were formed that day that had nothing to do with religions. One of those was between Ned Sullivan and Albert Hillier. Although their children, Tom and Jennie, had separated, Ned saw no harm in asking Albert to come along. Albert pushed his Pentecostal religious principles aside, swallowed down the liquor, and hoped that Suze, his stern wife, would never hear about it. As the priest's rum slid down their throats and their tongues became looser, they laughed together and swapped stories. Albert, when he was away from Suze, was no different from any of the other men.

Father Murphy soon learned first-hand about living conditions in the woods camps. He'd been called up on Sandy one night to administer last rites to a man on whom a tree had fallen, crushing his chest.

The priest went with Abel Miller, the A.N.D. Company transportation man. The cable boat spun them across the deep, swiftly flowing Exploits and, once across the River, Father Murphy was bundled into an old Company truck and jounced along woods roads until they came to the camp.

When the priest entered the camp, he was astonished. There were at least forty men sleeping side by side on a platform with just boughs for mattresses. The only heat came from an oil drum that had a chimney running up through the roof. Hung all around the stove were the men's wet and dirty clothes, drying out for the next day.

Someone had moved the dying man out to the forepeak and onto the foreman's bunk. He was pretty far gone. They'd taken off his boots, but he was still lying in his wet clothes.

"Father," the man spoke softly, with an Irish lilt to his voice, "thanks for comin'. I'm from St. Mary's Bay. I got a wife and nine children." A fit of coughing overcame him and Father Murphy could hear the death rattle in his throat.

He quickly laid out his tools for Extreme Unction – holy water, oil, a candle, a crucifix – and donned his vestments. But the man wasn't finished. "Father, please write to the priest out there. Tell him to look out for my kids."

His eyes closed and his breathing slowed. Father Murphy anointed the man and said the prayers to send his soul onward. He wondered if he should bury the man in Badger cemetery. St. Mary's was a long ways away.

ॐ

Tom left Badger. Someone told Jennie he'd gone by train up to Buchans where he'd gotten a job in the mines. Working in the mines was dangerous work because of rock slides and cave-ins. It was good money, though, if a man could stay at it.

For Jennie, the winter dragged along. She didn't go to the Pentecostal church. A chance meeting with Suze was more than her weakened state could manage. Mam and Pap and her family trudged off faithfully to Mass every Sunday and Jennie stayed home and cooked dinner.

She kept as busy as she could. It wasn't hard to find something to do around the house with nine siblings to help look after. Mam was good to her, helping her gain back her strength by spooning Brick's Tasteless into her before every meal. In the evenings they sat by the wood stove and darned socks. Mam had bought some home-spun wool and, together, they'd knit wool stockings for Pap and Phonse for their logans.

Jennie knew Mam must have spoken privately to Pap and told him not to torment her. Being of Irish descent, he liked to take a drop now and then. With the drink in him, he could be a bit lippy about the Protestants. But Pap never said a word to her about Tom or his family.

Every evening at five-thirty Pap turned on the *Gerald S. Doyle News Bulletin*. No one was allowed to speak until he'd heard every bit of the news and weather. With all the girls and women in the house, this of course was impossible, so Mam had installed Pap in the little bedroom off the kitchen. With the door just ajar, he could lie on the bed, turn on his radio that operated on a huge battery, and listen to the news and weather in peace.

One evening, when Jennie and her Mam were sitting comfortably by the kitchen stove, Jennie got up nerve enough to talk to her mother about her own marriage. "Mam, I think that the reason I never had a baby is because I left the Catholic Church and went with the Pentecostals. Do you think that God is punishing me maybe?"

Mam finished knitting her round on the sock. "Perhaps you're like me, Jennie," she said. "I was married to your father for a good spell before I had you. Then, once I got started, there was no stopping the children from coming."

"Is there a secret, Mam? Is there something I can do? I mean, is there something I can do to have a baby if I get back together with Tom?"

"No, my dear. We're just slow to take, that's all. Don't you worry about it. You'll have a baby one of those days. First, though, you have to get your husband back and your lives straightened out."

Ralph Drum came to visit every now and then. He was cheerful and uncomplicated and just what she needed. Jennie would ask him to sit and play Auction Forty-Fives with her. Jennie always loved the game and she was good at it too, winning more than her fair share of hands. Ralph would play cards for as long as she wanted.

Auction Forty-Fives wasn't like Auction Hundred and Twenties. Two people could play Auction Forty-Fives and have fun. With Hundred and Twenties, you needed four or more people to get the trumps out on the table. Pap had the most unusual story about Forty-Fives. He said his grandmother, who had been born and grew up in Ireland, had told him that they played the game there too. However, she said it was called *Forte*-Fives and was based on a card game played in the 1500s by King James I. *Forte*, his grandmother allowed, also meant strong and, in the game, the five was the strong trump card. It all made sense to Jennie when she heard Pap tell the story.

Catholics loved playing cards, but the Pentecostals frowned upon it. Jennie had missed the card games while she lived with the Hilliers. If the day ever came when they had a home of their own, there'd be fun and good times and music. They'd all play cards too.

During these times, Ralph would tell her stories about his grandfather, about the Beothuk and the Mi'kmaq legends and his efforts to find himself a wife. One day he told her about a treasure up on Hodges Hill – two beautiful pearls, alone in a small cave. Jennie said she wished she could see them. She knew where Hodges Hill was. It was visible from anywhere in Badger and Grand Falls. People had an expression, "as old as Hodges Hill," meaning that it had been part of the landscape forever. Why was it, Jennie mused, that men were free to roam and women were not? Why couldn't she climb Hodges Hill if she wanted? Jennie told herself that one day she would try it.

Another time, Jennie asked Ralph about the blackflies story, back when he and Tom and Vern had first gone in the woods as young men in their teens. Tom had told her about Vern's obsession with getting Ralph to tell him the secret of why the flies didn't bother him and they had laughed about it. She missed the laughter. She missed everything about Tom.

"So, Ralph, the boys say you can make magic with yourself and the flies."

"Jennie, give it up! It comes to me on the wind, that's all I can tell you. But if I'd told the boys that, they'd have laughed and called me nuts! I dare say you think I'm nuts too. And perhaps I am, maid." He laughed.

But Jennie knew he wasn't nuts. She thought that Indians had a special relationship with the elements that white people had no clue about.

Up to that point, Ralph had never mentioned the split between her and Tom, no matter how often he visited. He thought Jennie would bring it up herself, but she didn't. He decided to ask her.

"Jennie, I knows 'tis none of my business, but what are you going to do about Tom? I heard the guys saying that when he left home he said he might never see Badger again."

Jennie folded the cards in her hand and held them against her heart. "I told you before, Ralph. Suze Hillier is a bad woman. I can't live in her house, you know. If Tom isn't man enough to get us a house, I'll stay here with Mam and Pap." Her eyes filled with tears and, to her embarrassment, she broke down and cried.

"Aw, come on, Jennie. Don't cry. I'm sorry I brought it up." Ralph seemed unsure how to deal with the situation. "Listen, how about I sing you a song? Would that cheer you up? Huh?"

Jennie sniffed and wiped her eyes. "Oh, shush, Ralph. You might be a fine musician, but you can't sing worth beans."

"I'll do Hank Snow for you! I will. Listen . . ."

That made Jennie giggle and she put aside her tears as Ralph tried singing through his nose.

"Oh, you foolish thing, stop it and let's finish our game."

She often thought of this in the years to come. Of Ralph's kindness and sweetness and what a good friend he had been to her.

11

At the back of Alf Elliott's garden was an old building called the "goat house." Years ago, people had kept goats for milk and meat, goats being easier to care for than large cows. The little building had been empty for a long time, but the strong odour of male goat still clung to its dirt floor. Low-ceilinged, snug and warm, once Alf had it cleaned up, he figured that it would make a great photography darkroom.

He asked Mary to get out her Jeyes Fluid, and together they scrubbed out the little building. It needed a floor, so Alf got a bit of lumber from someone who owed him a favour and Ralph Drum helped him nail it down. It made a fine little darkroom, but somehow the smell of male goat never quite left it. Mary wrinkled her nose every time she went in there, which wasn't often. Alf's photo lab was his private space.

He ran a couple of long extension cords from his house down to the goat house, joining them up with electric tape. For lighting, he only required a single red bulb. Along two of the walls he built countertops where he set up developing pans, the printer box and the dryer. He strung wires up like clotheslines, complete with clothespins, to hold the strips of film to dry. And Alf's photography darkroom was in business.

In the semi-darkness, he would unroll the long piece of black plastic film from the camera, attach clips to each end, and carefully slosh the strip back and forth in the negative developer acid. Then he would hang it dripping wet on the line, pinned with a clothespin. Any black streamer of drying negatives hanging from the line was a delicate thing, and one had to be careful not to brush against it.

Next evening, after supper, he'd go out to the goat house again and cut the dried strips into usable negatives, putting each set into a separately labelled envelope. Then came the printing of the pictures. He laid each negative on the glass inside the printing box, put a sheet of printer paper down on it, closed the cover, and flashed the light on it for a few seconds. This exposed the image to the photo paper.

Back to another acid tray – the fixer, this time with the printer paper and tongs. To see the image appear on a blank piece of paper was truly amazing. Alf would invite his friends in every now and then to watch. It was like magic to all who saw it. His own children, especially, were fascinated.

At first Alf snapped pictures of the family with a little box-Brownie that everyone used and cost about two dollars. But before long, he sent off to Eaton's catalogue for a Kodak Hawkeye camera with a flash, top-of-the-line photography equipment for the 1950s. This camera cost seventeen dollars, almost the price of a suit of clothes for a man. The Hawkeye also had a time delay which Alf tried one evening by taking his own picture. He was amazed that it really worked.

Alf let it be known that he was available for functions as Badger's photographer. Soon he was invited to weddings and anniversaries where he would snap shots of couples as they celebrated. The clergy often called on him too for their events. Some people asked for pictures at a wake and a funeral. Businessmen around the town would get him to take shots of their establishments. He also took pictures for the Badger section of the *Grand Falls Advertiser* and wrote the weekly social column as well.

As a result, Alf got into the habit of taking his Hawkeye with him almost everywhere he went. People were used to seeing him with its leather case slung over his shoulder. It was easy to use outdoors. All he had to do was aim and click. For pictures indoors he had to screw on the flash attachment and put in a flashbulb.

With his gammy leg, he limped all around town taking pictures of scenic spots. The rivers were beautiful in any season. The view from the large round hill was wonderful. He made up a set of post-cards and they sold well.

Out in the little goat house, he'd develop and print, cut, and frame his snapshots of history that he hoped would last for years to come. He could have made a full-time living out of it, but it remained a hobby.

By the spring of 1952, with Pap, Phonse and Ralph out on the drive, Jennie found herself missing Tom more and more. It gnawed at her insides: the not knowing, not seeing. Then, when Mam wasn't around, one of her sisters whispered to her that Tom had quit the Buchans mines, had come back down to Badger and was on the drive. That was weird, she thought. Tom had long had a balance problem, so he certainly wouldn't be out jumping from log to log. Neither could he swim, a carefully guarded secret that he'd only told his wife. So what on earth was he doing? And why had he come down from Buchans? Jennie longed to know.

She asked Phonse once, on the sly, if he saw Tom around any-where. "Jennie maid," Phonse said, "to tell you the truth, he asked me about you the other day, asked how you were feeling. You know he worked in Buchans mine all winter? He missed home, he said, so now he's wongin' on the drive."

Jennie was astonished. "Wongin'? Tom is wongin'?"

To people who didn't live near logging operations, *wonger* and *wongin'* were strange words, certainly not found in any dictionary. It all had to do with the drive, described very well in the song *The Badger Drive*. The logs were fed into various brooks and streams that flowed into the great Exploits River. Along the way there were hundreds of men who worked to coax the logs along and keep them from getting jammed up.

In anticipation of the logs reaching the River, a movable cook camp was established to feed the drivers and see to their sleeping arrangements. The logistics of moving and setting up again were carried out by the wongers. There was a wongin' boss too; he supervised the operation, including the five or six riverboats that carried the food and the men's belongings.

It was the wonger's job to pitch the sleeping tents and the cook tent on the riverbank, to be ready for the men coming ashore in the evenings to eat their supper – mostly bread, beans, lassy buns, and tea steeped in kettles called sluts – then they hunkered down to sleep. Next morning, each driver rolled up his clothes bag and set it on the riverbank for a wonger to collect. Then he was fed his breakfast – bread, tea, and beans – and went out for a day on the moving logs. The wonger-cook made up his bread dough and put it in a big warm iron pot to rise. Beans were put to soak in another pot to soften up for the supper meal. The wonger-helpers packed up everything, loaded it aboard the boats, and the convoy moved off down the River. The cook boat carried the iron pots with the bread rising and the beans soaking.

The drivers usually made only three or four miles in the run of a day. Sometimes they would stay in the same spot for a couple of days, until word came for them to move on downriver. It was slow work. The wongers, too, had to keep an eye out for the moving pulpwood. Whenever they reached a designated spot, everything was unpacked. The iron pots were buried in a firepit to bake the bread and cook the beans, and the sluts were filled to boil over another fire. After a number of years they got small stoves, but some wonger-cooks liked the firepits the best. More even heat, they said. In the evening, the men came ashore once more and the same routine started again.

The drive went on during the Newfoundland springtime, which was cold and wet in any year. The men were wet all day long from mishaps in the River and from the rain. At night they lay down in wet clothes, side by side in the tents. They slept in their canvas breeches and the seasoned men used to warn the new guys to keep their legs straight during the night, since the breeches would dry out and be stiff as a board the next morning. At night, you'd hear fellows saying to each other, "Now, b'ys, keep dem legs straight tonight. You don't want to look like a crippled old man in the morning." Pap and Phonse always complained that they were never dry or warm from the time the drive started until it finished.

Ralph was different from all of them. He didn't wear the canvas breeches. Cold didn't bother him, wet didn't bother him. Ralph was as one with the River.

This was off-season for cutters. Many of them were cross-trained to work on the drive as well, but Tom had never done it. He had a fear of the deep, fast-running River, perhaps stemming from his boyhood when he'd try to follow Ralph on the logs and usually end up getting wet.

When Phonse told Jennie that Tom was wonging, she knew it was for a reason. She hoped it was for the same reason that she'd thought he went to the Buchans mines: to earn extra money to build their house. Jennie prayed to God, Protestant and Catholic, *Please God, let the house be for me. Please God, if he ever loved me, let him come and get me.*

But the days went by and no word from Tom. No word from Suze or Mr. Albert either.

Mam said one day, "In a small town like this, you'd think that they would drop in to see how their daughter-in-law was doing. I always thought Mr. Albert liked us. But I guess old Suze has him firm under her thumb and has threatened him to stay away from us."

Jennie was too proud to go and seek out her husband. She felt that too much had happened in between to heal the breach. And, because she hadn't gone back to work at Plotsky's, she wasn't part of the hustle and bustle of loggers coming and going.

Jennie was given to crying spells. The doctor said that she had low iron, but Mam had a different opinion.

"Jennie," Mam said to her one evening as they washed up the supper dishes, "there's nothing wrong with you now except you're pining for that big Protestant galoot in on Halls Bay Road." She vigorously scrubbed the cooking pot with steel wool. "What you needs, my maid, is a change of scenery."

12

Rod Anderson's yearning for the sea lessened with time. Ruth's love helped heal the resentment inside him. He became tamer, less morose, but still, from long habit, he kept many things inside him.

Their daughter, Audrey, was born in 1936. If Eli had hoped for a boy to carry on in Rod's footsteps, he never said a word. And it didn't matter to Rod. He loved his little girl and was thankful she was strong and healthy. Soon the old man was holding her, letting her grasp his finger, and calling her Poppie's girl. One day he brought home a pram he had bought from one of the A.N.D. Company management for five dollars. It was the Cadillac of prams, woven with a combination of light and dark brown wicker and lined with flowery cotton. He said the man had told him it was made in England.

"Come see what I got for Poppie's girl," he cooed gently as he lifted his little six-month-old granddaughter and put her inside.

Even though Rod had married Ruth in the Catholic Church in Buchans, he didn't "turn" to her religion. Eli and Rod faithfully attended the United Church. Many years before, Eli had purchased a pew – a common practice among the more affluent Protestants. Every Sunday morning the two, father and son, so similar in appearance, marched up the aisle and claimed their own special place.

When Audrey came along, Eli spoke privately to Rod. They were walking home from church. "Me son, I wants with all me heart and soul to have that little maid raised up in the Protestant religion, as you were and as I was. Do you think you can talk to Ruth and come to an agreement without too much fuss?"

Rod understood his father's thoughts because he'd been having the same ones himself. "Yes, Pop, I agree with you. The Andersons have always been United Church. I don't have anything against the Catholic Church, but I think I'd like to see little Audrey raised as a Protestant." They had reached the gate of their home. "Let me deal with it, Pop. Say no more for now."

So it was that little Audrey was baptized, went to Sunday school and then to grade school, all in the Protestant religion. Eli never knew how Rod worked it out with Ruth and he didn't ask. There was a period, however, when the air in their house was tense and the cooking wasn't as good, so he knew that Ruth hadn't been entirely happy about it.

When Audrey was four years old, Eli Anderson decided to retire. "Now Rod, me son, you knows everything I can learn you. I'll be here if you wants advice, and don't be afraid to ask me, but I am never crossing the River again. I'm finished with the woods." Rod was twenty-five years old.

In 1942 the SS *Caribou* was sunk by a German torpedo with a great loss of lives. Rod thought of his dream and what Melv's spirit had told him so many years ago. On the day of the sinking, Rod walked over by the River in the quiet evening gloom. If it was true about the loon being his spirit guide, he felt that the loon's call would let him know that Melv was reinforcing his message of years ago. There was no call. *Maybe it's their migration time,* Rod reasoned, as the practical side of him took over.

ɶ

Eli lived to be seventy years old. One night, he died in his sleep, of natural causes, the doctor said. Rod was really on his own now. The old man was gone.

In 1953, Audrey finished her schooling at seventeen and went away to St. John's to work. Her mother's relatives helped Audrey get a summer job at Government House. In the fall she studied for a third-grade teaching certificate. At Christmas of that year, she came home to Badger to teach in the Protestant school. Over the winter, Audrey corresponded with a young St. John's man, whom she had met quite by accident, she said. When school let out for the summer, she went back to the city.

✺

Bridey Sullivan's cousin Margaret, one of the Aylwards from Stock Cove, was in-service in St. John's. Bridey wrote to her and asked if it was possible to get her daughter Jennie a job. Margaret wrote back and said for Jennie to come on in and she'd be waiting for her at the station.

Jennie didn't know what to do. She talked to Ralph. "B'y, I really don't want to go. All I wish is to be with Tom. No, don't say it. Don't!" she said, as Ralph started to interrupt. "You want to go and talk to Tom and tell him that I'm going away. I say no! Tom has to realize that if he comes in a package with his mother, I want no part of it."

Ralph laughed, threw his hands in the air, wished her well, and walked away.

On a mauzy May evening in 1952, Jennie walked down the track to the railway station to get the train. Pap carried her suitcase and her sisters trailed along behind. Halfway to the station they met Ralph coming up. "I came to see if you needed help with your suitcase," he said, taking it from Pap's hand.

At the station her father went inside to buy her ticket, leaving Jennie and Ralph on the platform. Her sisters milled about excitedly. No one in their family had ever gone on a train trip before and they weren't missing a moment of it.

Ralph cleared his throat. "Be careful in the big city, Jennie. 'Tis not much like Badger, you know."

Jennie nodded. "I dare say you're right, b'y. But Mam's relatives have prospered in there. They've all found work and adjusted themselves, so I suppose I will too."

Pap came back with the ticket. Because St. John's was an overnight trip, he'd scraped together seventeen dollars to buy Jennie a sleeper on the train. To have a sleeper was a luxury. Mam had asked him to do it because she was worried that the long trip would be too much for Jennie, who was still recovering from her illness. Most people travelled sitting up in the coaches, but it was a long, tiring ride.

It was a very new experience for a young woman who had never been any farther east than Grand Falls. If her heart hadn't been so sore and aching for Tom, Jennie knew she would've enjoyed it. The sleepers were like compartments. When night came, the conductor turned the seats, then hauled another one down and they became upper and lower bunks. You got into your bunk, pulled the curtains, and it became your own little world. Jennie was a bit nervous. She didn't know what to do about undressing. Suppose the conductor saw her in her nightie? But she didn't want to arrive in St. John's in a wrinkly dress. It was new, from Eaton's catalogue, mint-green with white polka dots, empire waistline and straight skirt. With her white shoes and purse, Jennie felt she was making the right fashion statement for the big city.

Finally she decided to take off the dress and shoes and sleep in her full slip. She intended to leave on her nylon stockings but the garters were cutting into her thighs. So off they came, and she poked them out into the toes of her shoes, which she kept beside her on the bunk. As she tried to drift off to the rhythm of the swaying cars, Jennie wished Tom were here to share the bunk with her, but it was no good thinking about that.

St. John's was big, dirty, sooty and noisy with people rush, rush, rushing here and there. Margaret met her at the train and they got the bus up to a big house on Kings Bridge Road, where she worked as an upstairs maid. It was a gorgeous place, set in among big trees, like a park. Jennie was awestruck. *The rich sure know how to live,* she thought.

"Now, my dear," Margaret said as they unpacked Jennie's clothes, "I've got you a job as kitchen girl. You have to wash all the dishes and the pots, bring in the scuttle full of coal, feed the fire in the big stove and peel vegetables."

Jennie pulled the uniform dress on over her head and tied the apron strings. "I dare say I can manage that, once I get the hang of it. Thanks Margaret, my dear, for getting me this place here with you."

Jennie was amazed how the rich people ate roasts of beef with blood still in them, surrounded by puffy little puddings. "Yorkshire puddings," cook said. Everything went on the platter: the beef, the Yorkshire pudding, the vegetables, the potatoes. It looked nice, but the meat was too rare for the Newfoundland servants to appreciate. The master and his lady always had dessert: sweet puddings with sauce and trifles with custard. Cook said they were English people and they ate in the English way.

"Sure, my dear, I s'pose they don't know what salt meat and pease pudding is all about," Margaret told Jennie.

"Well, for sure they never ever had a roast of moose or a piece of bear meat," Jennie added.

"I was thinking about going down to the waterfront and getting them some seal flippers," joked the cook, and they all had a grand laugh.

The mistress of the house was kind to them all. Jennie thought that she dressed some grand. Margaret showed Jennie the lady's closets, full of stylish dresses and hats. She had many fur coats, and a mink stole – more expensive than Suze's fox, but still as ugly. One of the lady's coats, a nice light brown wool, fawn-coloured, caught Jennie's eye because it was so soft and smooth. Margaret said the wool was cashmere that came from some kind of goat in foreign countries. Jennie never forgot the feel of it. To her it was better than mink and fox. Maybe because the goat didn't have to die as the fox did.

Jennie worked all spring and summer and it was as if Tom, her own husband, never existed. Mam never mentioned him in her letters and Jennie was too proud to ask. She made a few friends and went out to a couple of dances. A couple of fellows asked her to step outside with them, but her heart was with Tom and she couldn't begin to think of going out with other men.

❡

The Eastern Bible College in Ontario was an imposing place. Damian Genge from St. John's had been there for a year studying to become a preacher, a job for which he felt God had called him. On the last day each inductee was given an envelope with his assigned posting.

Damian was proud of himself. He figured that with his good looks, his eloquence, his ability to whip up religious enthusiasm in the congregation, and his impeccable knowledge of the Scriptures, he would surely get a posting in Grand Falls, or Corner Brook, or even in St. John's. Being from St. John's, he felt he was a cosmopolitan kind of guy with lots to offer the richer high-toned churches. So, when he opened his envelope and read BADGER, it was a shock. He had to get a Newfoundland road map to discover where it was located. A long look told him it was buried so deep in the interior that only a place like Buchans could be more remote.

As it turned out, it wasn't too bad at all. The church was a fair size, the parsonage was in good shape, many people came to the prayer meetings, and Grand Falls was only eighteen miles away. Still, he had a nagging feeling that someone somewhere didn't like him enough to give him a St. John's church. He was pretty sure that his friendship with Jonathan Frost, another student at the college, was viewed as just a close friendship and nothing more, but you never knew. There were eyes everywhere. Whatever it was, he was an ordained pastor and he was here in Badger to do his best.

It had been tough going at first and sometimes still was. His monthly letter from Jonathan was the only bright spot in his life. Jonathan was posted in Hearst, in Northern Ontario. It was a bigger town than Badger, but had a similar industry – forestry. It would likely be many years before they would meet again, if ever, but

Damian was determined not to dwell on sad things. Maybe God really did have a plan for him. However, no matter how many hours he spent on his knees praying, so far God had not seen fit to show him.

March 5, 1952

My Dear Jonathan:

Your letter was like a balm to my heart and soul. It took a month to reach me and I read and reread it eagerly.

Your town seems to be somewhat bigger than Badger. You say there are about five thousand people there and about one-fifth of them are your flock. Well, the whole town of Badger has only one thousand souls and about two hundred of them are mine – God's and mine.

I looked up Hearst in the atlas. It is about as far north as you can go in Ontario. You must miss the warmer climate of your native British Columbia.

As for me, even though Badger is inland and is not even remotely like St. John's, at least it is Newfoundland and we Newfoundlanders have a common bond that runs through us.

One thing that our postings have alike is the forest industry. You say you have a pulp mill there. There's one here too; not in Badger, but Grand Falls, eighteen miles away. The logs are cut here and sent to the mill via the Exploits River, which cuts its way through the landscape like a mighty scar.

It makes me wonder: did someone plan this for you and me? And I don't mean Divine Intervention.

I am doing fine, physically, as I hope you are too. However, I am very lonely. I have to say that I miss you more than I ever believed possible. When I think of the hours we spent together at the school, talking, arguing religious philosophy, laughing at each other, my heart aches. I will probably never see you again, but you will always be a part of my soul.

I promise, no matter what, to keep up our correspondence. May God be with you in all that you do.

Until next time, pray for me as I will for you.

Your friend forever,
Damian

Badger matured young Damian Genge. Church stewards wanted a pastor who understood about the hole in the church roof and how to get it fixed and how church funds should be spent wisely. Damian had to learn fast. And he did. His hair, his handsome face, his expensive suit were still his personal priorities, but not as much as they'd been in the beginning. Sometimes he even forgot to file his nails or shave his armpits. Slowly his life took on other priorities.

May 5, 1952

Greetings Damian:

Yes, indeed, it takes a month for a letter to go between us. I was overjoyed to hear from you. Since we parted last June, I have felt an incompleteness that I never knew was there, that I never even knew existed before you came into my life.

We are deep into the winter here. Some days it barely gets light at all. You're right, the intense cold does penetrate my thin west-coast blood and I am sure I'll never be warm again.

You'll laugh when I tell you how the ladies here are trying to matchmake. They are certain that I need a wife. I bet you are going through the same thing.

What will happen to us, my friend? Will we eventually

be forced to take wives onto ourselves? Do we have any
choice but to fit into this society?

I spend many hours on my knees praying to Jesus about
this. I read the Bible over and over. We were taught that
His Word is Law.

Yes, we will always keep in touch, my friend. We cannot
allow life to rip us asunder.

Yours, under God's protection,
Jonathan

Away in St. John's, on her own, Jennie didn't know if she was
Catholic or Pentecostal, so she took turns going to each church. The
Catholic churches were so big that no one noticed her, but the
Pentecostals welcomed her and the pastor shook her hand.

"Are you new in town, my dear?" he asked.

"Yes Pastor, thank you for asking," Jennie replied. "I'm in from
Badger."

He looked at her blankly for a moment.

"It's out by Grand Falls, you know," Jennie said. "Perhaps you
know Pastor Genge. Pastor Damian Genge."

Something flared in the man's eyes, then was quickly quenched, but
Jennie saw it. "Oh, indeed. Indeed. We were in Bible College together,"
he said and turned his attention to another of his congregation.

Something going on there, Jennie thought. *I always wondered*
how a handsome fella like Damian Genge, with his gifts as an orator
and evangelist, ended up in little Badger. This pastor isn't nearly as
good a preacher and for sure not as good-looking, but he has a
plummy St. John's church.

Another time, still torn over the lie she had told about having a
baby just to get married to Tom, Jennie went to confession. She
thought, *Big city church, no one will know me. Not like home, where*
the priest knows my voice. For sure I'll get absolution here.

"Bless me Father, for I have sinned," she said demurely. "Father, I burned my mother-in-law's fox-fur stole," Jennie blurted out, shocking even herself. She had planned to talk about the pregnancy lie.

"Is this a sin of coveting the stole, my child? Is that why you burned it?"

"No, Father. It is a sin of hatred. I hate her. She told lies and broke up my marriage."

"A wife's duty is to cleave onto her husband. You must go back and make peace with him and his good mother."

"Cleave?" Jennie was raging. "The only cleaving that is going to be done is by me, cleaving Suze's head open . . . or Tom's head, if he don't soon come to his senses. I'll give you cleave, Father!"

Because she wouldn't say she was sorry, the priest wouldn't give her absolution. Jennie stormed out of the Basilica. And that was that.

In October, she got a telegram from Mam that said the twins were sick. A boy and a girl, thirteen years old, Jennie's youngest siblings, were struck down with polio. The disease was raging throughout Newfoundland. Some years they would delay the opening of the schools, trying to keep the disease from spreading. A few years later, children were given the Salk vaccine, but by then it was too late for the twins. By the time Jennie got the train back to Badger, they were dead and buried. Doctor said that polio could progress to meningitis in some extreme cases, and that was what had happened with the twins.

Oh God, God in Heaven! Jennie's parents were beside themselves. She took over running the household and looking after everyone. Mam spent most of her time sitting in the rocking chair, looking through the window and crying. Poor Mam.

13

Although life as a Mi'kmaq was hard, Ralph was not entirely without friends among the white population of Badger. Some people welcomed him into their homes and their lives. Alf Elliott, the telegraph operator, often invited him to his house in the evenings. They'd play accordions together, with Ralph being the teacher. Another evening it was the harmonica. There was no instrument that Ralph couldn't play. He was a sought-after entertainer for weddings, dances and wakes. For dances in the town hall, the accordion was a must for stomp-'er-down music and the fiddle for step dances. The weddings wanted some of that, plus the guitar, but for wakes Ralph used only his fiddle.

Sometimes the groom paid him five dollars for his music; sometimes the people who organized the dance in the town hall paid him a little; sometimes a relative of the bereaved slipped him a couple dollars. Ralph considered this smoke money. Mostly, he played for free. He was never asked by the A.N.D. Company executives, the higher-ups, but that didn't bother him.

Rod Anderson's daughter Audrey had married a fellow from St. John's, a cop. They visited Badger a few times and, through Rod, Ralph came to know the young man's father. He was a police sergeant, and he could certainly play the fiddle. Ralph and he got together a few times and sawed out some sweet tunes.

Constable Richard Fagan had met Audrey Anderson at the Lieutenant-Governor's garden party. He was in his dress uniform and was standing at attention by the entrance to Government House. One of the constabulary always stood there as a formality during the garden parties, staring straight ahead and standing at attention as if he were guarding Buckingham Palace. Those chosen hated the job in the heat of the summer as they stewed in their wool uniforms.

The summer sun was blazing down on the young constable's white helmet, sweat was running over his brow, and his feet were hurting. And he was not in a good mood. The Lieutenant-Governor, Sir Leonard Outerbridge, and Lady Outerbridge were doing a walk-about. Ladies in fancy hats and men in pinstriped trousers and spats were bowing and scraping. The Church Lads Brigade Band was playing the *Ode to Newfoundland* in the background.

"Excuse me, sir," said a timid voice near his elbow. "Lady Outerbridge's cat has escaped and is over in the garden of the American Consul. Can you help me?"

Richard slowly looked around. "I cannot leave my post, miss." *Lady Outerbridge's cat?* he thought, trying to maintain a stern face. *Do I look like a cat catcher?*

"Oh please, please. I know she'll be upset if she loses the cat. I was supposed to be watching her, but I was helping the other maids cut the sandwiches for tea, and someone left the door open and – she was gone." Richard looked at her more closely and saw that her eyes were a deep blue and her glossy brown hair was pinned up under her white cap. She was dressed in uniform, black dress with a white apron cinching her narrow waist.

She certainly was a pretty girl, and Richard softened somewhat. "All right, let's hurry then. Just so you know, I can get in trouble too."

There was a gate to the back garden of the American Consul and they slipped inside. The darned cat was up in a tree. Preparing to climb, Richard took off his helmet and started to unbutton his blue uniform jacket, but the maid was up that tree before he had the first button undone. *Good God,* he thought, *look at her climb.*

Getting down, carrying a reluctant cat wasn't as easy. Audrey's foot slipped and she started to fall, but Richard caught her in his arms. He stood there for a moment, holding this maid and this vice-regal cat in his arms, unsure of what to do next.

Then he set Audrey on her feet. "Look here, miss," he said, "if you can climb that well, why did you need me?"

She laughed. "I knew I could climb up there, but I also knew I'd need help coming down holding the cat. I actually had a mind to toss the cat to you, but my foot slipped before I could get the chance."

Merciful God! She had planned to throw me the cat! Richard wasn't particularly fond of cats.

"Hmmph. Well, you're down now – you and the cat." Richard was grumpy, but intrigued by the girl with the nice laugh. "By the way, where did you learn to climb like that? You're as good as the cat."

Again she laughed that merry laugh. "Where I come from there are lots and lots of trees. Many of them are higher than that one."

"Where's that?"

"I'm from Badger. Bet you don't know where that is."

"No, I'm not sure. Somewhere out near Grand Falls, I think, or maybe Corner Brook."

The other policeman on duty called to him and Richard had to go. He held out his hand, suddenly reluctant to leave her. "I'm Richard Fagan. Nice to meet you."

She laughed and shook hands. "A funny way to meet, wouldn't you say? I am Audrey Anderson."

Richard hurried back across the lawn to his post. "Who you talking to, Dickie?" asked his partner, Bob Parsons.

"That was a nice young woman who wanted me to rescue the Lady's cat. And don't call me Dickie."

Bob paid him no heed. Some of his fellow officers who had known him since he was a boy called him Dickie. Richard hated the nickname. It brought back reminders of another life and another set of circumstances, long ago. So long ago that Richard could almost forget it.

Later that evening he got out a map of Newfoundland and looked for Badger in what was referred to as Central Newfoundland, but strictly speaking, it wasn't. The centre of the island was wilderness. Badger was actually centred midway on the railway line that went across the island. He could see it there, next to Grand Falls. Not many people of his acquaintance had been out as far as Grand Falls, except for a few guys who had gone there to play hockey at times, but none of them had reason to go to Badger.

Richard thought about Audrey off and on for the rest of the summer and fall, wondering how he'd get to meet her again. He could hardly march up to the door of Government House and ask for her.

Just before Christmas, Richard's mother said to him, "Would you come downtown with me today? I'd appreciate your help in buying Papa's Christmas present."

"Sure thing, Mama. And maybe while we're there I can pick up my gift for you. I saw some nice strings of pearls in Bowrings. Since you burst yours last year, I dare say you'd like a new strand."

They put on their coats and got aboard Papa's old Studebaker. "Now Mama, I'm all yours. You just tell me where you want to go."

"O'Brien's Music Store at 278 Water Street is supposed to be the best place, according to an ad in the *Daily News*. Let's try there."

Richard drove down New Cove Road, Kings Bridge Road and down over the Hill o' Chips to Water Street. "You haven't said what you're buying for Papa, but I suspect it's a fiddle. Am I right?"

His mother laughed. "Yes, that's it. The one he has doesn't have the right sound, he says. He picked near Christmastime to complain, hoping, I'm sure, that I'd get a new one to put under the tree."

Warm air flooded around them when they opened the door to O'Brien's. It felt good after the wind outside. There weren't many people in the small store, and Mama went looking at the fiddles while Richard waited for the clerk to finish ringing up a sale. Idly, he noticed the back of the woman at the counter. It was a nice, trim-looking back in a red coat. For no reason, Audrey flashed across his mind again, as she often did. Then the customer turned and it was her! For a minute they were face to face, speechless. Did she remember him?

"Audrey?"

"Why, its Richard, isn't it? Fancy meeting you after all this time." She was laughing. Richard could see that he hadn't imagined those eyes, that hair, that laugh. They were real.

The clerk hovered and Richard pointed to Mama. "See that lady over there by the fiddles? She's interested in buying one. Please tell her I'll be along in a moment."

When it was just the two of them, they both started to speak at the same time.

"I wondered about . . ."

"Are you still . . . ?"

"You first."

"Are you still at Government House? I've thought of you many times and . . . and wondered how Lady Outerbridge's cat is. I was tempted to call and inquire – about the cat, I mean."

"No, I'm not at Government House now. The cat is fine, I think." She laughed. "That was only a part-time job while I went to summer school. I've got my teaching certificate now, and I'm going back home to teach. I'm here to buy my dad a harmonica for Christmas." She held up her package.

Richard didn't know what to say. *Oh no, I just found her again and now she's leaving St. John's.*

Mama bustled over with the clerk in tow. "Dickie," she said. *Not Dickie.* Richard cringed inside. "I need a bit of help with the fiddle."

She looked quizzically at Audrey.

"Mama, this is Audrey Anderson." He didn't even know if he should call her a friend or what to call her.

Audrey held out her hand. "I'm pleased to meet you, Mrs. Fagan."

"It's Mrs. Abernathy, dear. Uh . . . Richard kept his family name when my husband and I took him in."

"Oh, I didn't know." Audrey looked confused.

"I'm buying a fiddle for my husband. The two of you should come over, as I would like your opinion."

ᛄ

The next morning, the look of surprise on Audrey's face when she saw him in the waiting room at the train station was worth his early rise. He liked to think she was pleased too. Or perhaps she wasn't. A man never knew where he stood with a woman.

As people were going out to board, he picked up her suitcase. "Audrey, I'd like for us to keep in touch. Do you think we might write to each other?"

"That'd be lovely, Richard. All you have to put on the envelope is Audrey Anderson, Badger."

"No street address?"

"Not necessary. Everyone knows me."

"How many people live there?"

"About a thousand, I think. Why?"

"I'm just trying to imagine a place where everyone knows your name."

The whistle blew. The conductor yelled. "All aboard for Port aux Basques and points between." Audrey quickly squeezed his hand and gave him one of her unforgettable smiles. As the train pulled out of the station, she went out of his life again.

During the winter of 1954, they wrote to each other quite often, and when summer came, Audrey came back to St. John's to stay with friends.

Richard was in a dither of excitement. Mama told him to ask her for supper, but before he brought her he said, "Now Mama, no calling me Dickie, please. I want to be called Richard. I hate that Dickie business."

They had a nice enough evening. Richard's foster parents liked Audrey, and he supposed she liked them. They didn't have much common ground, but they all tried. Audrey told them about her parents and about the little town in Central Newfoundland. Papa Abernathy was interested in the pulp and paper industry and the dense forests of the interior. He was that kind of person; wanted to know about everything.

Once, Audrey slipped and called Mama Mrs. Fagan. She apologized and asked her how old Richard was when he came to live with them.

Mama said proudly, "Dickie was seven years old, twenty years ago this winter."

Richard groaned to himself. *Stop with the Dickie!* He quickly changed the subject by jumping up and saying it was getting late and they needed to be going.

As they grew to know each other better, Richard asked Audrey how she felt about marriage. He hadn't declared himself to her as yet, but he wanted to sound her out.

Audrey said she was full of doubts.

"Richard, life is different in Badger. People are different. You have no idea. My family is very important to me. Perhaps you should make a trip out to Badger and meet them. After that, if you still want to, we'll discuss how I feel about marriage."

So the next step was for Richard to go to Badger.

∞

They planned their trip to Central Newfoundland. Papa's Studebaker would have to stay home. In 1954, the few roads there were in Newfoundland were unpaved, potholed and narrow, and when it rained there were many washouts. The best mode of transportation to the interior of the island was definitely by train.

From the old railway station in St. John's, it was a fifteen-hour trip to Badger. Richard had never been off the Avalon Peninsula before and being a city boy had no idea how big, empty and lonely the island could be.

After they crossed the isthmus of Avalon, the landscape changed dramatically: no more weird rock formations and desolate bogs.

Now there was heavy forest stretching unbroken for miles. Mountains and rivers and lakes wherever your eye looked. Richard was entranced. Audrey had seen it all dozens of times and pointed out things of interest.

And they had a fine day of it, laughing, talking and reading. Mama had packed a grand lunch basket: cold chicken, salad, ham sandwiches made with her own homemade bread, cookies and small cakes, bottles of ginger ale. They ate as they clickity-clacked along. Many others were doing the same thing, although some went to the dining car.

Audrey told him more about her family. Her father was a woods contractor, she said. She wasn't very knowledgeable about his work, saying that he operated a woods camp for the A.N.D. Company. She'd never been in a woods camp. Women weren't encouraged to do that. It was just the way things were.

The long summer evening came to a close and they rolled into Gander in darkness. When they got going once more, the conductor dimmed the lights and passengers settled down to doze as best they could.

Audrey slept on Richard's shoulder. He put his arm around her and drew her in close, resting his chin on the top of her head. He realized that, no matter what awaited him in Badger, or whether her parents liked him or not, Audrey was the person with whom he wanted to spend his life.

It was after midnight when the conductor walked through, calling, "Badger, next station." The train came to a halt. Conductors slammed open the doors. Richard followed Audrey onto the platform.

Mr. Anderson was there to meet them. The two men shook hands, sizing each other up as men do. The word that came to Richard's mind was staunch – a staunch man. Rod Anderson was of medium height, solid, compact, clean-shaven, dressed in a summer shirt and pants. He looked like anyone you'd meet on the streets of St. John's. Richard thought, *What was I was expecting, a Paul Bunyan – type person with a bushy beard, an axe over his shoulder, and a booming voice?* He felt somewhat ashamed to be thinking that way.

The house was nice, not as nice as his parents' home but nice just the same. It was late. Too late for cups of tea and talk. They all went upstairs to bed. Audrey's mother, Ruth, showed Richard the spare room, saying the bathroom was downstairs should he need it.

Next morning, Richard sat with Audrey and her parents for breakfast. He felt uncomfortable, as if he were under scrutiny. He supposed it was only natural, seeing as he was being viewed as a possible suitor for the Andersons' daughter.

He tried a little conversation. "Mr. Anderson, I am surprised to find that you have amenities like electricity, running water, indoor plumbing. In St. John's we always believed that the outports had nothing like that."

Mr. Anderson chewed his bacon slowly. "First thing you have to remember, son, is that Badger isn't an outport. We are sixty miles from the ocean. Second, this is a Company town. We're here because of the stands of timber across the Exploits River that supply the pulp and paper industry. This is the centre for the Anglo-Newfoundland Development Company's Badger woods division. Many Company personnel live here, from England and other foreign parts. It's necessary that they have good living conditions."

"I never knew any of that, sir."

"No reason why you should, son. Lots of stuff I don't know about St. John's, too. Before you go back, I'll take you across the Exploits – the River, we always calls it – and show you the woods operations."

Audrey was impatient to get out and about and show him the town. "Come on, Richard, finish your breakfast. It's a beautiful day. Let's take a walk around town before it gets too hot."

And it was hot. Audrey said that was the peculiar thing about living in Badger. Summers were very hot and winters were extremely cold. When she took him to the place where the three rivers met, Richard was amazed at the powerful waters. The only water he was used to was St. John's Harbour and Quidi Vidi Lake. The deep swift-flowing Exploits was a new experience.

Audrey's favourite spot, the great round hill, gave a panoramic view of the three rivers and the little town. The place had a magical, dream-like quality. "Beothuks used to be here," she said, as though that explained everything. She pointed out a mountain in the distance. "Hodges Hill," she said, "highest point of land for miles."

They walked around the town in half an hour. Everyone knew Audrey and she knew them. People shook Richard's hand. What a different way of life! Richard couldn't imagine how people lived from day to day, month to month, year to year with no pavement, no Water Street stores, no city buses, no Bowring Park. But then, what right did he have to look down upon the little town of Badger?

14

When Cecil Nippard was ten years old his mother died from stomach cancer. She was only forty-two years old. That was in 1952. His strongest memory of her was that at every mealtime, day in and day out, all she ate was bread and tea. She said anything else gave her stomach pain. When she died, it came to Cecil's mind that maybe she'd starved to death.

His father didn't know what to do with his two young children: Cecil, ten, and Emily, eight. Then he found a woman from somewhere over around Herring Neck, married her, and brought her to live with them in Rodgers Cove, Gander Bay. He used to go in the lumberwoods when he wasn't fishing. The woman from Herring Neck was fierce cruel. With their father gone so much, Cecil and Emily grew up to hard work, beatings, being barred in the attic, going to bed hungry.

When he was fourteen, Cecil went to work in the woods cutting pulpwood with his father. He was glad to get away from the mean woman his father had married and felt sorry for Emily who was left behind, but he had other more important concerns. Father said he had to learn how to survive in a man's world. That was 1956. If there was one thing Cecil was good at, it was dates. He could remember every date of any event, big or small.

Cecil didn't have much luck with the woods camps. Within a week, he sank the blade of an axe into his leg. The blade was dirty and the wound became infected. He was laid up in Badger, it being too far for him to go all the way home to Gander Bay.

That was when he met the Mi'kmaq lady, Missus Annie Drum. When they brought him down off Sandy with the leg all swelled up and red and throbbing like a son of a bitch, someone got him over to Missus Annie, who knew Indian cures, they said.

He lay on the daybed in her kitchen and watched the old woman set a match to a thick yellowish substance in a dish. It burned for a few seconds before she blew it out. While it was still hot she smeared the substance on a clean piece of cloth and bound it around his swollen leg.

Cecil was scared out of his mind. "What's that?" he asked.

She laid a kind hand on his fevered brow and spoke gently. "That, my son, is myrrh from the bladders on a fir tree. I cuts it off and squeezes out the sap."

He limped up the road from the loggers' staff house three times a day, and she would dress the wound until all the pus and infection was gone. He tried to give her some money before he went back to the camps. She wouldn't take it, so he left a two-dollar bill on the table, under the tin of Carnation Milk.

A couple of months after that, at another camp, while watching a little tom-tit eating crumbs of bread from his hand, Cecil was hit by a falling tree. It knocked him out a cold junk. He was dizzy and stomach sick afterward. The foreman told him to go on down off Sandy, ending his stint as a logger for awhile. He was told to come back when he was older.

In the same year, the family moved from Gander Bay to Windsor. Father wanted to be closer to the woods, and his sister lived in Windsor. The bitch stepmother came too. In the six years since he'd married her, she had produced five other children. Emily's life wasn't much more than that of nursemaid for them all.

Father told Cecil that he would have to try the woods again when things started up the next spring. By then he should be old enough not to keep getting hurt, he said. He was disappointed in his son because he didn't seem to be much good for any kind of work. The stepmother called him stupid, but his father always stopped short of saying that himself.

Pastor Damian thought long and deeply on what Jonathan had written him regarding conforming to society by taking a wife as was expected of him. He looked around Badger for someone who he thought would suit him. There were half a dozen young women who simpered over him, hoping to be noticed, but they all had flaws. One was too fat, another too skinny, another too beautiful – heaven forbid that his wife should outshine him in beauty. He didn't want a woman who was too smart or one that wasn't smart at all. After all, she had to be a pastor's wife and help with the congregation.

His housekeeper, Mrs. Adams, who did not live-in, but came to clean and cook three times a week, had a daughter, Virtue. Damian liked Virtue. She was the right age, a good Christian, and ordinary in her looks. He got to know her better when her mother broke her ankle and Virtue took over Damian's housekeeping.

Surprisingly, Virtue treated Damian differently than any other female ever had. His good looks didn't put her in awe as it did most women. She wasn't coy and wasn't what Damian considered foolish and romantic.

They took to walking along by the River on summer evenings.

"Pastor . . ." she said in her forthright way.

"Damian, my dear," he murmured. "Call me Damian, please."

She nodded. "Damian, many people are asking me if you and I are going to marry. I merely think of you as my friend. I am wondering how you think of me."

"I think of you in the same way, of course," he said. "It's too soon to tell if it would be more." *How will I ever force myself to take this step?* he wondered to himself.

Soon it was all over town that the pastor and Virtue were an item. Damian let the rumours continue, since it made him look good, although, so far, he had not so much as held her hand.

※

The year 1952 had been tumultuous for Jennie. She had nearly died from pneumonia, become estranged from her husband, went to St. John's to work, her twin siblings had become ill with polio and died, and now she was home in Badger caring for the family. It was a hard time for them all, but worse for Mam. She could not get herself past it. Her mother wouldn't eat, couldn't sleep, walked the floor or rocked in the rocking chair all night long. It became Jennie's turn to care for Mam as she had cared for Jennie. Pap was beside himself, grieving for his children so much that he didn't know how to go about comforting his wife.

Autumn set in. Days were shorter, and Mam seemed to fade as the light faded. She took to her bed early in November. The girls tried to tempt her to eat with bowls of custard and jelly. They would wash her face and braid her long hair, which had not been cut in her fifty-nine years in the world.

Nothing worked. When the sun dragged itself over the horizon on the first of December, Mam left the world behind.

※

The leather hinges on Mam's old brown trunk creaked as Jennie opened the cover. The sharp odour of mothballs stung her nostrils. This was where her mother kept what she called the "good" clothes for her family. There was the christening dress worn by Jennie, Phonse and their sisters, her father's good suit, the First Holy Communion dress and veil that all the girls had worn, and the white muslin dress in which her Mam had been married.

On top of the good clothes was her mother's prized and sacred possession, a personal burial shroud or "habit." Made from five yards of broadcloth, it was dark brown in colour, and long enough to cover the whole body, from neck to feet. Over the heart were the letters IHS embroidered by Mam's own hands.

Mam's people, from Stock Cove, Bonavista Bay, were of Irish descent, and good Catholics all. Carrying on an old tradition, the women of the community took great pride in making themselves habits to be worn only when they were dead and resting in their coffins.

Throughout the years, Bridey would occasionally show it to her daughters and she would quote a little rhyme:

> I'll sew five yards of cloth,
> To have and to keep,
> I'll need it where I'm going to lie,
> To warm me in my sleep.

The young girls, who thought that their Mam would go on living forever, didn't show much interest in either the shroud or the rhyme. But now the time had come for poor Mam to wear it and suddenly the rhyme and the habit took on a different meaning.

Her coffin was made by hand. Phonse was friends with the man who worked in the A.N.D. Company carpenter shop. He told Phonse to get the pine together and, yes, they would make her a coffin. Phonse told Jennie later that the carpenter did the oddest thing: he saved all the shavings that came off when they planed the sides and the cover. When the box was finished, he put them in the bottom. He told Phonse that was from the old ways, when people believed that if any stray shavings from a coffin were accidentally carried into anyone's home on their boots, someone else was bound to die soon after.

Jennie bought some nice white satin to line the box. Her sister sewed a lace pillow for Mam's head to rest on. The Catholic women of Badger washed her and dressed her in a long, snow-white night-dress. Pap himself lifted her in his arms and gently laid her in the pine box. Then the women put the habit on her, from front to back, tucking the open part in behind her body, and tied the hood under her chin. One of her daughters threaded her prayer beads through her folded hands.

Pap's house had the usual front room or parlour, which wasn't used much. One thing that parlours were used for was to lay out the dead and that was where they put Mam's coffin.

So Jennie and her sisters readied the room for the wake. Phonse borrowed three benches on which to rest the coffin and got the kneeling pad from the priest. They put two candles at the head of the coffin and two at the foot. These would burn until poor Mam was taken to the church the next day. By the door of the parlour, where people could dip their fingers in it, Jennie put Mam's holy water font. It had belonged to her grandmother and had been brought all the way over from Ireland. Mam always kept holy water in the house and Jennie poured it into the font.

Straight-backed chairs were placed around the room for people to sit. Phonse scrounged up some rum and some moonshine, but people would bring their own flasks too. The sisters cooked a pot of moose soup and made tea buns. Friends and neighbours would also bring food. All was ready.

That night, the Catholic population of Badger and many Protestant friends came by to pay their final respects to Mam and to mourn with the Sullivan family. A couple of Pap's cousins came down from Buchans. They were put up for the night at Rod Anderson's house, as they were also relatives of his wife, Ruth.

Jennie was pleased to see Pastor Genge come by. With him was Albert Hillier, but without his wife, Suze. Mr. Albert shook hands with Pap and sat on a chair beside him. Watching them, Jennie thought once again of how Mam used to say that the two men, across the vast gulf of religious differences, had a kind of friendship.

Pastor Genge didn't stay long. Perhaps the smoking and drinking bothered him, Jennie thought as he said good night to her. Pap and Phonse, in the Irish tradition, loved to sit with friends and relatives and have a drink and a smoke.

After the pastor left, Jennie, busy with seeing people were

looked after, noticed that Mr. Albert had stayed. She saw him accept a glass of rum from Phonse. Jennie was glad he was there beside her father. It seemed right, somehow. She thought about the telegram that had arrived, among many others, during the day. It was from Tom. He had addressed it to Pap.

BUCHANS DECEMBER 2, 1952
MR. NED SULLIVAN BADGER, N.F.L.D

SORRY FOR YOUR LOSS STOP

THOMAS HILLIER

She had only given the telegram one glance and passed it back to Pap. Her tears were close to the surface and she hadn't wanted her father to see. *He never even mentioned me – his own wife. I'm sure now that he doesn't love me anymore.*

Jennie pulled herself back to the present and to the task of caring for her Mam's mourners. She felt bad for thinking about her own marital problems when her poor father was trying to deal with his wife's death.

The Catholic visitors flicked a drop of holy water on their fingers and blessed themselves. Everyone, Catholic or Protestant, knelt by the coffin, looked at Mam's face, and said a prayer. Most everyone left a Mass card, a black-edged card stating that the Holy Sacrifice of the Mass would be offered for the soul of Bridey Sullivan. But they didn't write Bridey. They wrote Bridget. Mam's name was Bridget Sullivan.

There was lots of food in the kitchen. It seemed that everyone had brought a covered dish of something. *People can be some good, you know,* Jennie thought. The men would sit and smoke and drink with Pap and Phonse, then drift out to the kitchen and have a bite to eat and a cup of tea. Then they would go back in the parlour to sit again. It was a long night, made bearable by the presence of friends.

Pap held up well during Mam's wake, seemingly relieved to see his poor wife resting so peacefully at last. He had shown Jennie the death certificate, signed by the doctor. It said "heart failure." It should have read "broken heart" because Mam never got over the death of her twins. Jennie wondered if her spirit was joined with them now. Were the twins on hand to welcome Mam to the other side? *My Scared Heart of Jesus*, she thought, *it's all some big mystery*.

By two in the morning, most people had gone home except for family and close friends. Ralph was there, as was his mother and a sister. His other brothers and cousins had been in earlier, but had left as well.

Ralph could play wonderful music on the fiddle. All night he kept low-key background music going as people sat around the room, talking, drinking a drop of rum and smoking. Some of the tunes he played would break the heart of a grindstone. Many a tear was shed as he played *Nearer My God to Thee*. People associated that with the *Titanic* disaster, which was still fresh in people's minds after forty years. It was somehow appropriate for a wake as well.

The candles guttered low at the head and foot of the coffin. Conversation had pretty much run out. In the quiet of the night, Ralph pulled his chair close to Mam's coffin and, slowly and sweetly, played *A Mother's Love is a Blessing*. He played it for Jennie, Phonse and the girls, but he looked straight at Jennie as he played, the dim candlelight reflected in his dark brown eyes. The notes fell and lingered on the air in the shadowy smoky room where Jennie and her sisters, even Pap and Phonse, wept softly.

Mam was buried next to the twins. Her favourite flowers were lupins, with their tall purple spikes. Within two years, there were lupins growing on Mam's grave where none had ever been planted, the only grave in the cemetery that had them. *Things like that,* Jennie thought, *makes you believe in life after death*.

15

Mr. Anderson insisted Richard use his first name and call him Rod. On the second morning of their visit, Rod said he had some work to do up at the camp and asked Richard if he would like to come along. Interested to see first-hand what life was like for men who cut trees to make paper, Richard readily agreed.

Soon after breakfast they bid farewell to the women, set off and walked down to the River. The large flat-bottomed scow was tied up, attached to a cable. On the same cable was a small boat with an outboard motor. Rod explained that the scow, often loaded with horses, tractors, equipment and supplies, was slow and ponderous. The little boat was there to give a hand to nudge the scow out into the eight-knot current. The small boat could also go across on its own, for quick trips across the River to Sandy. They both climbed aboard and Richard noted that Rod was very adept at using it, a skill most Badger men learned from boyhood.

Rod angled the boat slightly upriver and the power of the current whipped them across to the other side. The two men got out of the boat and climbed onto a small wharf and sent the boat back along the cable for the next person to come along. When Richard asked how they would get back again, Rod pointed to a large bell attached to a pole on the side of the dock. Richard thought the cable boat and scow setup was ingenious and commented so to the older man. Rod told him that some engineer had invented it back in 1910.

A dusty red pickup truck was parked on the other side and they climbed aboard. Rod's camp was about twenty miles in on a narrow woods road. As the truck bounced along in the ruts, Richard looked out the window, his city eyes taking in the dense forest that stretched for miles and miles.

Finally, they pulled up to the Anderson camp in a clearing. Getting out of the truck, Richard looked at the low log building in front of him. He could see no one about and figured all the men were out working in the woods nearby. He followed Rod into the building and entered what appeared to be the office, known to the loggers as the forepeak. A table built into the wall served as a desk. It was littered with papers and tools, tin cans used as storage containers, and old enamel mugs with blackened bottoms. Rod walked over to the desk and started rifling through some of the papers. Richard looked around the room to see a small cot on the opposite wall where he supposed Rod slept when he came up to work.

Without looking up, Rod said to him, "I got a bit of work to do, my son. Feel free to look around on your own."

Richard wandered out the small hallway into the loggers' sleeping quarters, a long, narrow room with a small window on the farthest end. Along both sides, pushed up against the rough-hewn walls, were old war-surplus army cots. Quickly counting, Richard could see there were ten sets of bunk beds per side, making room for forty men to sleep. Clothes were strewn about everywhere, beds were unmade, cardboard suitcases and clothes bags littered the floor. In the centre of the room was an oil drum on its side. A door was cut in the end of it and a stovepipe led out of the top and disappeared into the roof. Beside it were tossed a few junks of firewood.

Walking over to one of the walls, Richard peered to the outside through one of the small spaces between the logs. Most of the holes had been stuffed with moss and old newsprint, but there were still many gaps. Even with the ventilation from the holes, the air still smelled of dirty socks. Richard wrinkled up his nose.

"Can I help you, young fella? Are you from a newspaper or something?"

Richard turned to see an older man standing behind him. He was trimming the wick on a kerosene lamp.

"Oh no, no sir. I'm just a visitor," Richard replied, straightening up and moving away from the wall.

"Never seen a woods camp before, I bet." The man laid down the kerosene lamp on the makeshift table and chuckled.

"No, sir. I haven't."

"Well, my son, this is a good camp. 'Tis rough work, make no mistake about that," the man said. "Oh, I'm the cookee, by the way. Bert is me name." He held out his hand to shake.

Richard shook it. "Richard Fagan. Pleased to meet you, Bert." The hand that shook his was gnarled and dirty.

"Yes, my son, we've had some improvements lately since the war." He hawked and spit on the dirt floor. Richard couldn't help but step back slightly. Bert continued. "For years and years the men slept on wooden platforms with only spruce boughs for their mattresses. But after we joined Canada in '49 we got these cots from the army. They're a lot better than them spruce boughs, I can tell you that. That is if you don't mind a few lice and bedbugs. We tries to get rid of them, but they always seems to come back. But what do you expect with a bunch of men living together, eh?" The older man coughed and hawked again, but instead of spitting, he eyed Richard and, at the last moment, decided to swallow it.

"What do you do out in St. John's, me son?"

Richard turned to look about the room again. "I am with the city police."

"Are ya now! Well, a policeman! First one we ever had up here. Not that we ever needs one. There's nothing up here to steal and most times the men solves their own disputes. Hey, would you like me to show you around? Maybe you might like a job if you gets tired of being a policeman."

Richard looked into his guileless eyes and wondered if Bert was a bit simple-minded. Knowing he meant no harm, he smiled and said that, yes, he would like to have a tour.

"Well this is the bunkhouse, as you can see. That there is the oil drum we uses to heat the place. Gets pretty cold in here if that thing goes out. Sure, one time last October it went out during the night and I woke up with the frostbite on me ears." He laughed, showing broken, tobacco-stained teeth.

They walked back out in the hallway and Bert showed Richard three enamel pans that were sunk into a table against the wall near the entranceway. "That's the door where the men come in through, and the first thing they do is to wash up."

Richard saw a barrel filled with cold water and a dipper. It would seem that this was not only the men's washing water, but their drinking water as well.

Pointing out through the door and toward the trees, Bert said, "If you needs to go, that's the outhouse up through that way. I've worked in all the camps up here. They're all Company property, but some are worse than others. This one got the cots and the roof don't leak as bad as some of them. Rod tries to run a good camp and he's fair with the men." He sniffed and wiped his nose with the back of his hand.

"Well, the day's a-wastin' and I got to get me bread on to bake. 'Tis nice to meet ya."

Richard shook Bert's hand again and watched the older man amble into the kitchen area.

He wandered back out to find Rod. *I could never live a life like this*, he thought.

When he walked into the forepeak, Rod was busy with the time sheets for the men. "I'm just finishing up here, Richard. Usually my foreman does this, but he's off with the flu. I have to bring these sheets back with me so the men can get paid."

When Rod was finished, the two of them climbed aboard the truck. On the drive back down the narrow woods road they didn't say much. Rod was thinking about the time sheets and Richard was trying to absorb what he saw.

He wondered how the loggers felt about things. Bert, the

cookee, seemed satisfied enough, but Richard wondered how men could live like that. Then he remembered another place, a house with a dirt floor.

$\wp$

A few days later it came time for him and Audrey to leave. In Richard's mind, the visit hadn't been a great success and he blamed himself. He had felt awkward and out of place. The Andersons were kind and friendly, but he knew he was a city fellow and always would be.

Standing on the platform at the Badger station, he thanked the Andersons for their hospitality and invited them to St. John's for a visit. Audrey hugged both her parents and, with Ruth dabbing at her tears, the young couple boarded the train. Richard had paid for two sleepers this time. Although Audrey was sad to be leaving her parents, she was excited at the thought of getting a sleeper.

For supper, Richard took Audrey to the dining car with its snow-white tablecloths and silver cutlery. They enjoyed a meal of pan-fried cod. When they finished their meal and the steward had served coffee, Audrey sat back and looked out at the landscape as it rushed past the windows. It was a beautiful evening and the couple lingered, watching the fading evening light. They hadn't talked much; neither of them knew what to say.

Finally, Audrey put her cup back in the saucer. "Richard, what did you think of my parents and my home?"

"Oh, great. Great. Your folks are great, Audrey." He looked out the window. *I have to tell her,* he thought. *She thinks I am a glorified city fella, always used to the best. But I'm not. And she deserves to know.*

"Richard, what is it? Was Badger that bad?"

"No, no, Audrey. I just felt I didn't fit in there, but that's to be expected, I suppose. I have never cut down a tree or shot a moose."

"We both knew, at least I knew, that the lifestyle back there is different." She leaned across the table. "People who live outside St. John's hardly know it exists. The city is like another world to the many small towns on this island."

"Audrey, I love you and I would like for us to marry. If you'll have me, that is." Richard stopped and looked down into his coffee cup. He wanted to say more but couldn't.

Audrey's brow furrowed. "What is it, my dear? You must tell me what's troubling you."

Richard looked into her earnest young eyes. He took a deep breath and squared his shoulders. "Not now, my dear. Trust me on this. It's not the time or place. But there's something I need to show you and tell you, when we get back to St. John's." He finished his coffee and set his cup on the table. "Come on. Let's go back to the sleeper car."

Trustingly, Audrey tucked her hand into his arm as they left the dining car together.

The conductors had everything made up for the night. Audrey's bunk was on the top, Richard's on the bottom. After they were settled in, with the curtains pulled and the lights off, Richard crawled out and sneaked up into the sleeper with Audrey. He expected her to kick him out, but instead she opened her arms to kiss and cuddle him. Richard thought he was the luckiest man alive.

After a few kisses he lay back on the pillow and pulled her close to his heart. He felt he didn't deserve this fine young woman, because he knew he hadn't been open and honest with her. After awhile he could feel her deep breathing and knew she was asleep. He slipped quietly from her arms and went back to his own bunk, where he lay awake for a long time, listening to the steady rhythm of the train's wheels on the track.

16

As Christmas of 1952 approached, it was a miserable, quiet time for the Sullivan family. All were wrapped up in their grief, thinking of Mam and the twins up in the cemetery buried in the frozen ground.

On Christmas Eve, Jennie prepared a supper of boiled salt fish and homemade molasses raisin bread as Mam had done for years. They sat around the table, pushing more food around on their plates than actually went into their mouths.

Jennie looked around the table at her father and sisters. "Just look at us! Mam would be disgusted with us sitting here, moping about." At the mention of Mam, Pap's head came up and he looked across the table at her.

Jennie continued. "Mam always said dying is for the dying and living is for the living. We all know that life must go on. So let's get ready and go to Midnight Mass, as Mam would want us to."

Pap nodded his head in agreement. "I know you're right, maid. Yes, we *will* go to Mass. We'll need to get there early so we can sit up front just like your Mam used to do. Girls, help Jennie clean up from supper now. I'm going to get a shave."

As the girls were washing dishes and Jennie swept the floor, a rap came to the door. Jennie left her sisters and went to open it. Standing on the step was Tom Hillier with his cap in his hands. It was snowing softly and, as he stood there, the flakes settled on his shoulders and in his hair. Jennie thought she would die. Her chest felt like she would never again get any air into it.

Jennie looked into Tom's eyes for several long seconds. One of her sisters yelled from behind her. "Will ya close the door? You're letting in a draft!"

Suddenly able to find her breath, Jennie said, "Tom, won't you please come in." She was surprised and proud of how calm she sounded, though she could hardly hear her own voice over her pounding heart.

"No, no, Jennie. I'll drop by tomorrow. I just want to give you this tonight." He took her hand and pressed into it a thin wrapped package. "I was real sorry to hear about your Mam." With another searching look at her he turned and started to walk back down the path.

"Tom, wait . . ."

He turned and looked at her. "You looks good, Jennie." Pulling his cap on over his head, he went on out in the snow to the railway tracks.

Shutting the outside door, Jennie went into the parlour and sat down on the settee. She was shaking so badly she could hardly open the package. It was clumsily wrapped in Christmas paper and Jennie could tell Tom had done it himself. Pap and the girls came in to watch her.

From the paper she pulled out a folded piece of blue cardboard tied with a ribbon. Jennie pulled open the ribbon and unfolded a legal document onto her lap.

She started to cry. "Oh God, oh Sacred Heart of Jesus!"

Her father, with one side of his face still lathered from shaving, came over to her and looked over her shoulder at the deed to a house – the house – made out in her name, Assumpta Jennifer Hillier, in a fancy script. She thought her head and heart would burst. Tom still loved her. Tom still loved her.

Later that evening, as she sat in the pew next to her father and sisters, Jennie held her handbag in her lap. Inside was the precious document to her house. She prayed to the Blessed Virgin that her marriage was about to begin again.

∞

Jennie got up early on Christmas morning with one thought in her mind: perhaps today Tom would be back as he said he would. She looked out her bedroom window. Everything was blanketed in a coating of white, and the morning sky was a pale, frosty blue. It was going to be a good day; she could feel it in her bones. Her handbag was on the chair where she had laid it last night after Mass. Inside was the house deed. Jennie smiled. She felt that her mother was watching over her and helping her.

"Thank you Mam," she whispered.

Phonse and his wife came over with their daughter Madeline and little five-year-old Bernie for Christmas dinner. In the parlour, they had set up the Christmas tree and Jennie smiled at Pap down on the floor playing with a train set he had gotten for the boy. It helped to have children in the house. The sisters cooked dinner, and although it wasn't the happy, boisterous meal of years past, they all made the best of it.

Tom came by again in the afternoon and sat with them. He played with little Bernie, who by this time was strutting around wearing a pair of six-shooters, complete with red embossed holsters and real shooting caps. Tom and Bernie played Cowboys and Indians and Jennie couldn't help but laugh at their antics. She thought that Tom was like a big kid himself. Bernie, crouched behind the table, yelled, "Bang, bang, you're dead, fall down!" Tom obligingly rolled on the kitchen floor, clutching his chest and shouting, "I'm shot! I'm shot!" Jennie realized anew the preciousness of this man. And she remembered Mam saying that they'd have a child of their own. *Please Mam,* she prayed silently. *Please ask God to make it happen.*

When Tom went out to the porch to pull on his boots, Jennie went with him. They stood close, so close she could feel his breath on her forehead. She looked up at him and whispered, "Thanks for coming over today, Tom. And thanks for the Christmas present. I'm sorry that I have nothing to give you in return."

"That's all right. It was kind of a gift for both of us anyway. How about if I come and get you tomorrow and show you the house?" Tom chuckled and wiggled his eyebrows. "We might even be able to discuss my gift then as well." Jennie pushed him teasingly out the door, laughing for the first time since she couldn't remember when.

✜

On St. Stephen's Day, or Boxing Day, Tom came shortly after breakfast and got Jennie. She bundled herself up and held his arm as they went to see their house together. She had not even seen the outside of the house that Tom had been building, never mind the inside. Jennie was that stubborn, no matter how curious she'd been. She hadn't allowed herself to walk in on Halls Bay Road for a sly look. *I will not look at it*, she used to think. *I will not. Supposing he is building it for someone else.*

As they rounded the corner, he made her close her eyes and led her through the snow until she was standing directly in front of it. When she opened her eyes, she gasped in wonder.

They were standing on a piece of land Tom's father had given him years ago. Facing her was a bungalow painted yellow, with a peaked roof. It was built up high because of the floods, and they climbed the steps and went inside. Jennie breathed deeply at the smell of new lumber and paint and rushed from room to room. There were two bedrooms, a darling little kitchen with nice cupboards, a lovely front room and – Oh, wonders! – a bathroom with a big claw-footed bathtub. It was beautiful.

Tom said, "Now Jennie, we'll go down to Cohen's in Windsor and you can pick out all the furniture yourself. I don't care as long as you get me a nice comfy chair that I can sit in and listen to the news after supper."

Jennie ran into his arms and kissed him all over his face. "Oh Tom, I love you, I love you!"

Tom moved her gently from him and she could see that a deep red colour had spread up his face; even the tops of his ears were pink. Clearing his throat self-consciously, he said, "Do you think we might discuss my Christmas gift now?"

Without waiting for her to respond, he walked over to a cupboard and opened it to reveal a big quilt neatly folded on the shelves. He took it down and with Jennie by the hand led her into the bedroom.

They were starved for each other, after a year. Tom spread the quilt on the floor and they made up for lost time. "We're christening the house, Jennie," Tom said. And then their stars came down . . . and nothing else mattered.

Later, as they lay on the quilt, Tom said, "Well, Jennie girl, that's the best Christmas present I ever had," and he pulled her close. "Never again will I let anything come between us."

Jennie laughed and nestled into his chest. "Give me a chance to get me breath back and I'll gladly discuss your Easter present too."

They didn't move in until spring, but before that the house was christened many times. And finally they talked about what had driven them apart. Tom said that his mother had admitted to Mr. Albert that it wasn't true what she'd said about Vern and Jennie or about Ralph and Jennie. Actually, she said she hadn't lied, just that she'd made a mistake.

Jennie left it at that. Mam used to say *let sleeping dogs lie.* But she was wary and mistrustful of her mother-in-law forever after, even though, for the sake of Tom and his father, they eventually became reconciled enough to sit down for an occasional family meal.

Tom and Jennie settled down to their lives in the spring of 1953. By this time they both figured there would never be any children. Jennie never went to a doctor and neither did Tom. They were the kind of couple that the old women talked about over their knitting:

"My dear, she never had any children, you know. Dey sez she got inward trouble."

Or: "My dear, dey sez that he had the mumps when he was young and dey went down on him."

None of that was true, but they didn't care what people said anyway. Tom and Jennie had each other. "What odds," Tom said.

"Right, what odds," Jennie agreed.

That fall, a stray cat followed Tom home one evening and decided to stay. Tom always had a soft spot for the felines and called her Bucksaw. The cat followed him everywhere. That Christmas Tom brought home a little white crackie with brown spots. Jennie called the dog Freckles. The little family was healthy and happy in the house Tom had built.

Part II

THE LOGGERS' STRIKE

17

In 1958, union organizers started coming into Rod Anderson's camp to talk to the loggers, to tell them what their working life *should* be like.

The first time was on a fine Sunday in late summer. The men were hove back for the day having a rest. A rest just meant that there was no cutting on Sunday. They used the time to file their saws and sharpen their axes. Some of them washed both their clothes and themselves in a nearby brook or lake. The cooks were working flat out. Besides having to feed the men their Sunday dinner, bigger than other days, they had to catch up as well with the usual making of bread, molasses buns and, perhaps, some pies.

Into this scene walked two strangers. They introduced themselves as organizers from the International Woodworkers of America, the IWA.

"We're here, boys, to tell you about logging camps in British Columbia. Now, you might think that is pretty far away and has nothing to do with you fellas, but you're wrong. It is far away, but Newfoundland is part of Canada now and has been for the past nine years. It's time for Newfoundland loggers to be treated like other Canadian loggers. Do you know that camps on the mainland have showers, indoor toilets and central heating?"

This got the men's attention. Most of them didn't even have those kinds of things in their homes. They were from small isolated outports still struggling to become part of the twentieth century.

"Now, gentlemen, we propose to change all that. We propose to give you a new union that will improve your working life and give you a better wage to pass on to your families. We're asking you right now to sign up with us. Membership dues are one dollar. If you haven't got the fee right now, you can pay us later."

Rod listened to what the union organizers told the men. Perhaps they had a point. So he said they could have supper with the men and stay overnight. It being Sunday, the meal was boiled dinner: salt meat, pease pudding, doughboys, potatoes and turnip. Then the organizers bedded down in a spare bunk with the loggers.

The recruiters' hair and clothing became lousy that night, and in the morning their arms and legs were covered with red welts that the men told them were bites from bedbugs. This was part of the life of a logger. Rod had slept on the same bunks and eaten the same food when he worked for his father and he had accepted it.

He mentioned, in passing, to other contractors that maybe they should see about building better bunkhouses, but they had laughed him into the ground. "My son," they said, "if we was to improve anything, our profits are gone. The Company won't give an inch on any upgrading, you know that. Besides, what do we care? It's not our property; it belongs to the Company."

＄

Sometime later, on a trip across the River to Badger, Rod was called into the A.N.D. Company manager's office. Mr. Cole was long gone and had been replaced several times by managers brought in from England, St. John's and mainland Canada.

"Well, Rod. I hear you're allowing union men to take over your camp."

For a moment Rod was too astonished to answer. *Take over his camp? What was this all about?* "Well, sir, I wouldn't say they are taking over anyone's camp," he said. "They're trying to organize a union. What's wrong with that?"

"The Company doesn't want the IWA, that's what's wrong with

that. We've been getting along fine here for fifty years. So, my advice to you is: no more being friendly with the union organizers. There are lots of contractors willing to take your place and you know it."

Rod passed along word to Bill, his foreman. "If the union fellas come back wanting to stay overnight or have a meal, just say you're sorry, but we have no room. And say the Company has said they can't be fed."

Other contractors did the same, some with more forcefulness than Rod. But it was too late. The IWA had made serious inroads into the camps. Every logger had signed up on the spot. They were all focused on the new union's promise of better camp conditions, a shorter work week and a wage increase.

The IWA began broadcasting a radio program called *Green Gold,* aimed at informing the loggers of the current happenings. In the camps at night, after supper, the men gathered around battery radios to listen to news of the union's progress. Rod turned a blind eye to the activities of his men. If they signed up, he didn't want to know about it. All he wanted from life was to do his job, look after his family, and live in peace.

ॐ

On the first of January, 1959, the loggers went on strike and Badger changed overnight. Most of the town, aside from Company employees and contractors, seemed to be pro-union. The IWA set up picket lines at every exit and entrance to the community. Other places were similarly affected: Millertown, Peterview, Terra Nova, Glenwood and Gambo; wherever the A.N.D. Company had a woods operation, IWA organizers were there.

Rod Anderson's camp emptied out. Bill Hatcher said he'd help him get his tractors down off Sandy for friendship's sake, but then he was going to go. His cook and cookee left the camp as well and joined the picket lines.

The Company manager called a meeting for all the contractors.

Twenty-two of them from the Badger Woods Division gathered at the A.N.D. Company office.

"Now, boys, we can't have those camps lying idle. We have men who are willing to work and they aren't signed up with the IWA. We're going to fill up them camps, you know, by hook or by crook."

Some of the contractors protested, saying that it was a waste of time and money to have untrained loggers up on Sandy; they'd be a hazard to themselves and to others.

But the Company manager wasn't interested in hearing any of this. "My orders are from higher up, gentlemen. The camps will be filled. It will show the public that the IWA has no support. The public will see that there are lots of Newfoundland men willing to work for us without a union. The Company will send recruiters into the outports and snap up anyone willing to come into the woods."

Rod came out of the meeting knowing there was trouble ahead. As he walked up Church Road toward his home he met clusters of men on the street. They were loggers who had joined the union when the organizers had come through. When the strike began, they came out of the camps, went home to their communities to see their families, and then returned to stand on picket lines wherever the A.N.D. Company had a woods operation. Badger, a central location and the closest town to the paper mill, had four picket lines leading in and out of town. The IWA rented three deserted houses for the out-of-town strikers. The most popular one, owned by Mrs. Noel, was on Church Road, across from the Roman Catholic Church. Here strikers tended to congregate.

The main picket line was at the River crossing, where the Company tried to take scabs across in broad daylight. The strikers stood firm, shoulder to shoulder. The only way to go through them would have been to mow them down with the Company Bombardier, but the A.N.D. Company, as anxious as it was to fill the camps, wouldn't go that far.

Undeterred, the Company went farther downriver, just off the Grand Falls Highway where the Exploits was shallow. Under the cover of night, scab labour was transported across and trucked into the camps. Within two weeks, Rod's camp had forty men again. But loggers they weren't; many had no idea how to cut and limb the timber, how to pile it, nothing. Some of them were sick and coughed all night long. Rod wondered about TB.

$\wp$

Vern Crawford was a daredevil and had been all his life. He was willing to try anything. He seemed to have no conscience, no remorse. But for all that, there was one thing about Vern that made people who knew him think that he was a half-decent fellow who was just a little crazy. It was his little daughter, Melanie, born in 1950. She idolized her daddy. Vern doted on her. Whenever Vern came to the door, Melanie would run to him with her arms held out to be lifted up. When she'd learned to speak, she'd cry, "Daddy, Daddy." Vern always had something to surprise and delight her. Some days he would bring her chocolate or candy, other days he might have a small toy or even a larger gift tucked away in the trunk of his car. It warmed Millie's heart to see them together because, by the time Melanie was born, she knew that she had married a "devil-may-care" man.

In the autumn of 1958, Vern heard about a union that was up in the camps trying to sign up loggers. The A.N.D. Company refused to recognize the IWA, even though their certification with the Newfoundland Department of Labour had given them legal right to bargain and to strike. It was no surprise to Vern or anyone else when the union *did* call a strike on New Year's Eve.

When he heard talk that the A.N.D. Company was bringing in non-unionized workers to put into the woods camps, Vern hoofed it on over to the manager's house and knocked on his back door.

"Good evening, sir," he said when the manager answered the door.

"Good evening, uh, Vern, isn't it?" The manager stepped out onto the veranda and looked at the much shorter man standing before him. What he saw was a slight person with thinning, sandy hair, and small sharp eyes that darted around nervously as he worried his cap in his hands.

"Yes sir. Vern. I drives taxi, sir."

"Yes. Yes, you do. What can I do for you?" He didn't ask Vern to come indoors. *Not a very friendly guy,* Vern thought. He seemed full of himself, puffed-up, like, but that could be in part to the big round belly that protruded over his belt. The manager had a cigarette fitted into an ivory holder and took long draws from it. *Jesus, what an uppity fucker,* Vern thought.

"I was thinking that you might need help transporting men into the camps," Vern said. He didn't dare use the word scab. In the A.N.D. Company manager's mind the men were legitimate workers.

"Yes, we do, as a matter of fact." The manager reached back and closed the door. He only had on his white shirt and the sleeves were rolled up. Vern was shivering with the cold, but the manager didn't seem to mind the dark January evening. As they spoke, their breaths made white puffs in the air. The manager sucked another long draw through his ivory holder.

The A.N.D. Company manager was so tall and large that Vern had to look up at him. "How much will you be paying, sir?"

"We'll give you five dollars a man. More than you get arsin' around in Windsor with groceries."

Vern knew they were desperate to get the scabs up in the camps. "It's dangerous work, sir. Very dangerous. I'll be going through picket lines wherever I go. Fifteen dollars per man."

The manager drew in the smoke again, all the while watching Vern with wary eyes.

"Ten dollars," he said.

"Done, sir!"

Vern held out his hand to shake with him, but the manager ignored him and went back into the house. *Ignorant son-of-a-bitch,* Vern thought. Perhaps he was cold, but what odds if his balls froze and dropped off on the steps. Vern was going to get ten dollars a head. Five men in the car was fifty dollars.

He jumped aboard his taxi and spun the wheels as he raced up the street.

It wasn't that Vern was against the loggers. He understood their plight. Sure he did. *Guaranteed,* he thought. Hadn't he worked as a logger from the time he left school? Hadn't he suffered the hardships the same as any other logger?

But, Vern reasoned, he had a right to make a living too. He had to keep his family fed and clothed, put gas in his taxi, and he needed money for upkeep as well. But there was more to it than that. Vern looked forward to the challenge and the excitement of what might be ahead.

Alf Elliott and his Brownie Hawkeye were busy during the strike. He took pictures of strikers on winter mornings at the main picket line down on the bank of the Exploits River. They were bundled up against the cold, dressed almost identically in laced-up logans and wool socks, brigs, heavy coats and sweaters and stocking caps. Grim and unshaven, smoking hand-rolled cigarettes. Behind them was the frozen Exploits, the deep swift River that governed the life of the town.

One night, Landon Ladd, the IWA president, held a packed meeting in the town hall. Ladd was a popular and powerful speaker. Alf, with the help of a couple of men, hitched his gammy leg up on a table at the back of the hall and shot a picture over everyone's head. The photograph captured the backs of the heads of the audience, and on stage, an animated Landon Ladd delivering another inspiring speech.

During February, the violence against the scab workers escalated when a car carrying non-unionized workers was overturned in the centre of town. Alf walked over on his dinner break and took a few shots. Taken against the snowy backdrop, the pictures captured a sorry sight: the car with its windows smashed, its four wheels facing the sky.

In January 1959, Ralph turned thirty years old, as would Jennie, Tom and Vern, later in the year. As he sat with his family having a drink of rum that evening he thought about all the things that had happened in the last decade.

Last year, Grandfather had finally given himself up to the Great Spirit. The family estimated that he was one hundred years old, although he had no birth certificate. He'd outlived his son, Ralph's father Louis, who was found the winter before, dead and frozen up on his trap lines. Missus Annie said she knew it was coming. For weeks she'd heard him complaining of chest pains. The morning he had left to go check his traps she had told him to stay home, but he wouldn't listen. Although Ralph knew she grieved quietly and deeply, she never shed a tear. His death was the way her husband would have wanted to go.

All Ralph's brothers and sisters got married and his ma had grandchildren everywhere. In the past few years he had had a few girlfriends, but could never get himself interested enough in a woman to ask her to marry. Sometimes Ralph felt ashamed to be carrying a secret torch for Jennie all these years, since she was devoted to Tom and would be shocked if she knew. It would destroy their friendship and Ralph wanted to hold onto that.

Two years ago Jennie told Ralph she was going to run for community council and became the first woman ever to sit as a council member. Ralph admired his Beothuk Wonder Woman. He chuckled to himself as he went to refill his glass. He still liked to think of her as that.

Back in 1958, rumblings had started about a union wanting to organize the loggers. The men were all for it, and when the ballot boxes went around, Ralph was among them as they cast their votes.

Ralph had seen Jennie down at the postal office and was delighted when she remembered it was his birthday. They got to talking about the union. Jennie told Ralph how disgusted she was with the way negotiations were being handled.

"What's wrong with men? And how foolish is that A.N.D. Company, dilly-dallying back and forth over whether to bargain with the IWA or not? My jumpin's, I would've cut right through all that, and said, 'Listen here: we are loggers; we are the ones getting the pulpwood for that mill; we want better conditions, more pay and a shorter work week. If we don't get it, we don't cut any more wood.'"

Jennie had the kind of voice that could carry far. When she spoke, heads turned, and seeing it was Jennie Hillier, the woman with opinions on everything, they simply nodded and smiled. Ralph could see that they agreed with what she was saying.

Ralph was in a musing frame of mind that evening and, as he sat there, he had a thought that their lives, all of them, were just like the logs on the River, sometimes hitching up and getting jammed, but with a bit of help, or sometimes on their own, they usually managed to get straightened out again.

He drained his glass and sat back to watch his sisters and nieces bring in his birthday cake with thirty candles. He missed Grandfather and wished he were still there, sitting in the old rocker by the stove.

That night Grandfather came to him in his dreams. He was in the old rocking chair, smoking his pipe. "My son, hard times are coming. Remember what I told you about being unable to stop what is happening. You will be caught up in the river of time that flows on and on. Don't let anything drag you under. Care for the young white woman."

18

Vern was having a hard time of it. He'd made a couple of trips out around White Bay, Green Bay and Notre Dame Bay, rounding up anyone who was willing to work as a scab. The A.N.D. Company recruiter went with him at first, but he got busy with something else, and Vern was left to scrounge around on his own. The lure of ten dollars for every man that he could coax into the taxi and up in the woods kept him at it.

Even Vern would later admit that he'd done some weird things. One time he picked up some fellows to go through Badger and up the Buchans Road to Millertown. Vern knew the pickets would give him a hard time, so, after he passed through Grand Falls he pulled into Rushy Pond, a small village between Windsor and Badger. Out behind a railway shed, in the darkness, Vern stopped the car.

"Okay fellas, get out. I need a little help here."

The five passengers scrambled out, not knowing what to expect.

"Now then, see those railways tracks? Well, me sons, we're going to put my car on those tracks and I'm going to drive you to Millertown Junction on the railway."

The men started to protest. "Christ, ole man, that's too dangerous."

"Go on b'y, no one can drive on railways tracks, you're nuts."

"How are the tires going to fit on them there rails? Sure, they're too big."

"Aha, that's where you are wrong," Vern told them. "This is a

Chrysler 300 and her chassis is wider than the span of the tracks. My tires will fit on either side." Vern was pleased with himself to have thought of it. "Come on now. Give me a hand here. We'll be there in a couple of hours."

Vern put the car in neutral and got out. He kept the driver's side door open and, giving the steering wheel an occasional twist to get her straight, he and the men pushed until she was over the rails with the tires straddling each side.

There was enough snow on the railbed to smooth the way a little – kind of bumpy in spots, but not too bad. The small trestle over Kitty's Brook, one mile east of Badger, presented no problems, but Vern knew that the big trestle crossing Badger River was bare of snow. He was worried that he might have to turn back. With the Chrysler in second gear, he eased her along, bump, bump, bump. It took awhile, but he made it. Then, in the darkness, they sailed on through Badger on the snow-covered railway ties. It was a clear, frosty night. If it had been stormy, perhaps Vern would've thought twice about taking such a risk. He certainly was a daredevil, but he wasn't crazy enough for that. Or was he?

Before the taxi got to Millertown Junction, they heard a train coming down the grade from the Gaff Topsails. The engineer had seen them and the mighty blast of his diesel's horn sliced through the frosty night.

Vern jammed on the brakes.

"Come on men," he yelled. "We have to drag the car off the rails. Quick! Quick! That train's bearing down on us fast, and buddy can't stop her on the grade."

The scabs and Vern grabbed the car by the front end and, huffing and cursing, hauled the big Chrysler off the track. She came clear just in time as the huge diesel roared by, pulling twenty ore cars from the Buchans mines. The men fell back into the snow, exhausted and terrified.

And so the legend of Vern Crawford was born. The tale of driving on the railway tracks was told, and retold, and embellished along the way.

Another time the A.N.D. Company recruiter told him to go to Millertown and pick up some scabs they had up there on the dam and bring them back to the Badger camp. It was a pitch-black night. Vern was driving along, doing about fifty on the icy, hard-packed snow of the Buchans highway. The radio was playing Hank Snow, and every once in awhile he was taking a swig from a flask of rum. He had only recently taken up drinking a drop every now and then to relieve the stress. The scab-running business was more wearing than he had anticipated.

Suddenly a dark shape appeared out of nowhere. It was a moose. Vern couldn't stop in time, so he ducked down sideways on the seat, still holding the wheel steady as the moose came up over the bonnet, crashed through the windshield, and landed in the back seat.

The car slewed sideways into the snowbank on the side of the road and stalled out. Vern sat up and brushed off the glass shards that were all over him. There wasn't a sound. Just him and the moose. He looked over the seat at the animal, wondering where he'd come from. Moose were common, but with the high snowbanks on the Buchans highway, Vern wondered how the animal had ever gotten out over and onto the road. Not very big, as moose go, he looked like he might be last year's calf. Poor young devil wasn't moving. *Perhaps he's broken his bloody neck. Otherwise he'll kick the devil outta me car,* Vern thought. *Jesus, what a smell! Fresh moose shit. So much for that, got to get to Millertown.*

He put the car in reverse. The Chrysler 300 had plenty of power, so she came out of the snowbank easily. Vern tipped the rum bottle up to his lips and took a good long swallow, floored the gas and off he went again, moose and all, toward Millertown, with Hank Snow singing *The Wabash Cannonball* and the cold wind blowing in his face, freezing the blood from the small glass cuts.

When he reached the Millertown dam there were six men waiting. Great. Sixty dollars. He got out of the car, three parts drunk and not giving a damn for anyone at that point.

"Boys, I got a passenger in the back seat. He needs some help to get out before you fellas gets in."

Vern watched their faces as one of the men opened the door. They got some fright when they beheld the moose slumped in the back.

The six of them hauled the young animal out. They got some water, threw it in on the seat and cleaned up the shit. Someone had a piece of tarpaulin and laid it on the wet seat. Vern was no help. He was too drunk; he just sat on the snow and laughed and laughed.

He heard someone saying, "Sure, b'y, that's fuckin' Vern Crawford. Dey sez he's crazy. He's capable of anything. Didn't you hear how he drives on the railway tracks?" And that made him laugh even more.

They got to Badger late in the night. Vern put the men on the A.N.D. Company steps, where Abe Miller met them and bunked them down for the night. Vern had his money. Millertown had a moose. The A.N.D. Company had their scabs. Hank Snow was singing *I'm Movin' On*, and all was right with the world.

The next morning, when Vern went outside and looked at his taxi, last night's happenings didn't seem so funny anymore. He looked at his poor, worn darling. Her windshield was gone and the back seat was wet and smelly. The first order of business was to get her cleaned up, so up to Barrett's Garage he went to nurse her back to health. Repairs were going to eat into his profits.

∅

When the IWA called the loggers' strike, the justice of it appealed to Ralph and his family and they supported the union. Most people of Badger and other logging communities thought the same way. They saw it as the wealthy pulp and paper tyrants versus the down-trodden loggers.

All the people of Badger took the dispute to heart, in one way or another. It became bitter and families turned against each other. Fathers, sons, uncles and cousins found themselves on opposite sides. It was the same story in other towns affected by the strike.

People were much the same no matter where you went. And they all had their own reasons for doing what they did.

Ralph saw Vern every now and then spinning the wheels of his Chrysler around town, acting the bigshot. The two men didn't get together anymore as they had done when they were boys. But when one of Ralph's brothers told him that Vern was sneaking loads of scab workers through the lines, Ralph went looking for him.

Vern was in his driveway polishing the headlights of his taxi when Ralph called out, "Hey Vern, how ya doin'?"

Vern raised his head and looked at him. Ralph knew he was probably one of the last people Vern wanted to see. "Oh, hello Ralph b'y. Cold weather, what?"

Ralph came right to the point. "Vern, I hear you're running scabs."

"Who, me? Naw b'y. I wouldn't do that, sure." He stopped his polishing and stood with the rag in his hand, as if he wasn't sure whether to run or stay.

Ralph could see that Vern was scared and he suddenly remembered about the white man believing Indians would kill them. Vern and he used to joke about it when they were young. Perhaps he was remembering the old stories too.

Ralph put his face right up close to Vern's and made himself look as fierce as he could. "By the Jesus, Vern, if you had never been a logger, if you never slept in them camps, I'd excuse you and say you were just some dumb fucker who didn't know the difference. But you know the difference, Vern. Our men are fighting for their livelihood, and you're aiding the A.N.D. Company by running scabs to the camps. This is about money, isn't it? Fuckin' money. You lousy son of a bitch." Ralph was so angry with him that he wanted to shake Vern like the rat he was.

Vern turned and ran toward his house. Ralph yelled after him, "If I ever catches you, buddy, you can start saying your prayers."

Rod Anderson was never to forget the evening of February seventh. It was after dark when Bill Hatcher came to his back door. Rod and Bill had known each others since they were youngsters. They went to school together, fished and hunted together, learned to smoke, chased after the girls. The fun had gone out of Rod after his illness and his brother Melv's death. Rod withdrew into himself. But that didn't daunt Bill. He kept niggling his friend to go places and was with him up to Buchans on the night he met Ruth, and was best man at his wedding.

As they grew up and Rod assumed responsibility of his father's camp, Rod told Bill that he would think it a great favour if he came to work with him. Bill Hatcher was a good logger and knew the woods life well. However, Rod wanted him as his second hand. This meant that when he wasn't in camp, Bill would be in charge. He'd keep track of the time sheets, the purchases from the van and the scaler's reports, and deal with problems as they arose between the men, the cooks and cookees.

Bill was overwhelmed at first and told Rod that he wasn't sure he was able to do it. But Rod eased him in slowly and, in no time at all, Bill became his trusted foreman. However, Bill's loyalty was only to Rod, and not to the A.N.D. Company. When the IWA signed up the men for the union, Bill gave them his dollar too. When the strike was called, Bill went out on the picket line.

He had told Rod straight out, "Rod b'y, nothing against you and all the years we've been together, but I spends enough time with our men to know that they needs more than they're getting. The Company don't treat them fair. They don't treat you fellas fair either. But I knows you can't go out on a picket line, being a contractor."

Rod had told Bill that he understood his position and wished him well.

In light of the fact that Bill now did picket line duty, Rod was surprised when he opened his back door and saw Bill on the step. "Bill, what are you knocking for? Come on in, b'y. What is it? What's wrong?"

Bill was acting skittish and nervous and not his usual self at all. "Close the kitchen door," he said. "Don't turn on the light."

They stood in the dark porch, the only light being the snowshine through the window.

"Badger is in some uproar out there, my son. Christ, the men are some fired up tonight." He glanced nervously through the porch window. "Rod" – his voice was low and hurried – "there's something going to happen tonight up on Sandy. The strikers are going up to drive the scabs out of the camps."

"What? Why are you telling me this, Bill? Sure, you're supposed to be a loyal union member, b'y. The others would kill you if they knew you were here."

"I know. I know. But I owes you a lot, b'y. I'm just tipping you off, that's all." Bill hesitated. "Besides, Rod b'y, 'tis too late now. Not much you can do. I gotta go."

Bill slipped out through the door leaving Rod standing in the dark porch trying to digest what he had just heard. He knew his camp would be the first the strikers would reach. *My God,* he thought, *those poor, poor, foolish men. They shouldn't be up there in the first place.*

Ruth was waiting in the kitchen when Rod came in from the porch. "What is it, Rod? What did Bill want?"

"Nothing, Ruth. Nothing . . . well, yes, something. I think there might be trouble up on Sandy. Turn off the lights and crack open the front door."

The Badger night was alive with sounds: groups of men running up and down the road, carrying torches, and shouting. In the distance, someone fired off a gun. The shot echoed on the frosty winter air. The glow of fire barrels could be seen here and there.

Later that night, after Ruth had gone upstairs to bed, there was another knock. This time it was Abe Miller, the A.N.D. Company transportation man.

"Rod, me son, they sez your camp got trashed." He snarked snot into the back of his throat and spat into the snow. "They sez the strikers drove them poor buggers out in the snow."

There's no point of going up there in the middle of a cold, dark,

February night, Rod thought. *What's done is done.* "We'll wait for daylight," he told Abe.

"Very good, I'll meet you by the River around seven."

⌀

The next day dawned cold and windy, with a wind out of the north-west eddying the snow into drifts. As Abe and Rod approached the picket line down by the River, Rod could see several women standing around the fire barrel.

Ralph Drum nodded to them as they walked by. A couple of others said good morning. Rod and Abe got aboard the A.N.D. Company Bombardier snowmobile and went off across the frozen River and up the woods road. About halfway up, with the old Bombardier putt-putting along, they saw a line of strikers and Mounties straggling down. *The wind is right in their faces and the poor things look froze to death. Some of them have to have frostbite. The Mounties too,* Rod thought. *Well, old Jack Frost doesn't care if you're the law or the lawless when he wants to bite.*

Abe would probably have offered them a ride if they'd been going the same way. He wasn't a bad fellow. Neither was Rod. They felt sorry the loggers who, after more than a month, had made no progress with their strike against the Company. But they had to look after their own jobs – Abe as the A.N.D. Company transportation man and Rod as an A.N.D. Company contractor.

The strikers had trashed the camp, all right. It was a miserable sight in the cold light of morning. Every window was broken out. The stovepipe was torn down from the roof. The door was yanked off its hinges and thrown down in the snow where it was quickly drifting over. Rod picked it up and stuck it by the side of the wall. He went inside and, even though he never spoke of his feelings on it to anyone afterward, he was terribly frightened by the destruction in front of him. The brutality and violence of the angry strikers was everywhere to be seen.

Abe was scared too. He stayed in the doorway with one eye on his snowmobile, as if he thought someone was going to grab it. But there was no one about. The place was long deserted.

The doorway opened into the forepeak, which was in shambles. The foreman's time book was ripped to shreds. All the bottles of Gerald S. Doyle medicines – Witch Hazel, Friar's Balsam, Cough Syrup, Cod Liver Oil, Worm Powder – had been smashed. Someone had poured the cough syrup over the foreman's bunk.

Rod was reluctant to visit the cookhouse, but it was unavoidable. Every bit of food was dumped out – flour, sugar, beans, tea, yeast, molasses. *Name of God . . . we'll never get this cleaned up. 'Tis better to put a match to it and burn the whole camp down.*

The bunkhouse was worse, if that was possible. The scabs had banked down the stove for the night and it was still hot. When the rampaging strikers arrived, they'd hauled the stovepipe off the old oil drum and stuffed the scabs' clothes down in it to burn. The stench of charred wool was heavy on the cold air of the bunkhouse.

Rod was sick to his heart with it all. What was going to become of them all? "Come on, Abe b'y, my eyes can't take no more."

ℬ

Cecil Nippard wasn't a member of the IWA, seeing as he wasn't working as a logger at the time. But his father was a logger and a union member. He was assigned the picket line down by Peterview, near Botwood.

One evening, while Cecil was hanging around the pool hall in Windsor wishing someone would give him some change to play pool, a station wagon pulled up and a guy asked him if he had worked in the woods at some time. "Would you like to have an easy job now that the loggers are on strike?"

"At what?" asked Cecil.

"Oh, the A.N.D. Company wants some men to go up in their camps to man them, sort of. Not much to it."

The old bitch stepmother was acting up pretty badly these days with Father on the picket line and not much money coming in, so Cecil agreed, just to get away from her.

He was driven to Badger where he and others were trucked up on Sandy and into a deserted woods camp. The men came from all parts of Newfoundland. None knew much about the work since none of them were loggers. They were just fellows who weren't much good at any trade. One guy said, "They must've scraped the bottom of the barrel to get us." Everyone thought that was a fine joke.

They made a half-hearted attempt to cut some wood. Cecil knew a bit about it, having been in the woods before, but some of the men were straight out of the fishing boats. The whole camp of forty men didn't cut a full cord for the whole week. The Company wanted to start the haul-off, getting the wood out to the riverbanks for the drive, but they weren't much good at that either. They'd stack the wood on the sleds wrong and it usually fell off before it got to the riverbank.

One night they were talking around the old oil drum stove. One of them said, "I s'pose you guys knows dey calls us scabs, what?"

Someone else piped up, "What's a scab? Is that like when your cut is gettin' better?"

A guy over in the corner said, "Geez boy, you're some stunned. We're the ones who didn't join the IWA."

The men were quiet for a bit, thinking, working through it, wondering what being a scab might mean. They didn't think it meant anything good.

After three weeks up in the camp, they were raided by the real loggers, the union men. To the scabs they were like savages, not human beings at all. They were asleep when avenging strikers burst into the bunkhouse, screaming and yelling. They threw the scabs out of the bunks, refused them time to get their clothes, and pushed them out in the snow. It was cold enough to freeze the balls off a brass monkey. All Cecil had on were his long johns and socks. He ran through the snowdrifts as fast as he could go, his legs and his heart pumping together with the terror. He didn't even feel the cold until afterward. There were a couple of strikers running behind him at first, but they gave up the chase after awhile.

At last, through the drifts of snow Cecil spied a trapper's tilt. He crawled in, buried himself in the old garbage and dead leaves, and fell asleep. Next thing he heard voices outside. It was the A.N.D. Company man with the Company's snowmobile picking up scabs here and there, and he had spied Cecil's tracks. He helped him outside, but Cecil was so cold and scared he could only shake and jibber at him. The Company man gave him an old blanket to cover his shoulders and got him aboard the snowmobile.

Back at Badger, the scabs were hidden in a back room of the A.N.D. Company offices. Clothing and footwear were scrounged up for them and they were offered another chance to go back to the camps or take their wages and go home. All of them, traumatized by what had happened, took their wages and left town.

Cecil went back to Windsor to his father's house. His clothes and his logans were gone and never seen again. Bitch-stepmother didn't know and didn't care where he'd gone. Emily wouldn't talk to him because she was too scared of the older woman. Father came home for a few days, but Cecil was afraid to tell him what he had been up to. After all, father was IWA. He'd be mad if he knew that his son was a scab, taking loggers' jobs.

It wasn't long after that, perhaps a month, when he met the taxi driver, Vern Crawford, who was recruiting scabs just as the first guy did, only this time it was to go up on the Millertown Dam. Cecil agreed to go along again.

19

Jennie had been at the River picket line all night, standing around the fire barrel with other women waiting for the men. At the beginning of the strike, when he made his speech in the town hall, Landon Ladd had decreed that the strike was a family affair and women could do picket duty too. The women had stood along-side the men ever since.

The strikers had gone across the River last night, headed for Rod Anderson's camp. The A.N.D. Company had been bringing in scabs to fill the camps to prove they could always get men to go to work. The strikers claimed that Rod's camp was full.

There was a gathering around the fire barrel. Someone threw more wood in; flankers flew up and disappeared into the dark cold sky. There were a dozen women and several men worrying and waiting. Ralph was there too, standing beside Jennie. She asked him, "How come you're not gone up there too, Ralph?"

He walked a short distance from the group around the barrel, nodding for her to follow.

"I was all set to go," he said, "but Landon Ladd asked me if I would mind staying here. My brothers and cousins are gone, and I was raring to go too, but he said that if there were arrests he would rather I wasn't among them."

During the past month, Jennie had often noticed how Landon Ladd depended on Ralph to help organize the men and the picket lines. Now, fear gripped her heart as she immediately thought of Tom being in danger. "Are they going to be arrested, Ralph?"

"Jennie, keep what I am going to tell you quiet. There are spies everywhere, you know that. I received word awhile ago that the Mounties have gone up there too. And you know what that means. Someone's told them where our boys were headed."

"Oh no . . ."

"Not a word, Jennie. Don't frighten the other women. It might not be right, after all."

As the grey winter dawn came in the sky, Jennie walked over to the bank of the River. Across the frozen surface she could see the black outline of the trees and the clearing at the landing on the other side. The outline of the three A.N.D. Company fuel storage tanks stood black against the white snow. Jennie expected that this was where Tom and the others would emerge from the forest.

Behind her, the sound of motors broke the morning stillness. Jennie turned and saw two yellow buses pull up. Ralph went over. Several Mounties got out and talked to him. They pointed toward the landing across the River and she saw Ralph shake his head. He turned and walked toward her. He peered across in the early morning gloom as if he expected to see someone emerging from the forest. The sky was getting lighter by the minute. Jennie touched his sleeve. "Ralph, what is going on?"

"The information was true. The Mounties are waiting to arrest the men, Jennie. They're expecting them any minute." Jennie turned away from him, seething inwardly. *It can't happen. I won't let it happen. My Tom can't go to jail. He can't.*

Then she saw them – at first as a thin black line straggling out through the trees; then they stepped onto the ice and the long line became more visible. *Oh God.* With no thought for the consequences, Jennie ran toward them. That one – the tallest one – had to be Tom. Behind her, someone yelled "Stop!" Not Ralph's voice. It had to be one of the Mounties by the bus.

Up close, the strikers looked terrible: cold, exhausted, defeated. The Mounties that had been sent into the woods were a sorry sight too. She could see icicles clinging to one guy's moustache. They were almost back to the Badger side of the bank. And there was Tom!

Jennie ran out on the ice and grabbed his arm. "Tom," she said hurriedly, "the Mounties are waiting with buses to arrest all of you. Let's be fast. We can race down the riverbank and around the point. Pass the word. Some of you can get away."

He nodded and spoke to another striker behind him.

They were across; the Mounties by the buses rushed forward to round up the men. Jennie started to run down the bank of the Exploits toward Pope's Point, waving for others to follow. A Mountie grabbed at Tom but he pushed him away and ran behind Jennie. A dozen or more scurried after them. They circled around Badger, past the trestle and Badger River, dodging through backyards. Some residents, the early risers, saw them. Some were startled. Others waved them onward.

Safely home, Tom and Jennie took off their snow-covered clothes and hung them up behind the stove. Jennie put on the kettle. She sliced off some homemade bread and put the butter and molasses on the table in front of him. Tom was starved.

"I'm dying to hear what happened up on Sandy," she said as she sat down at the table beside him.

"Jennie, maid, we put the boots to them scabs, I can tell you." Tom slurped his tea and slathered butter and molasses on two thick slices of the bread. He continued. "They were all asleep when we got there. Not a light anywhere. We beat on the door, yelling for them to open up. The guys started to throw rocks at the windows until they had them all broken out. Someone crawled in through and opened the door for us. It might have been the Drum boys." Tom chewed his bread. "You had to be small to get in through a window. It wouldn't be me," he laughed, all two hundred and eighty pounds of him.

"We piled in through the door. By this time, the scabs were all awake and scared out of their minds. We were screaming and cursing at them. They tried to grab their boots and trousers, but we weren't having any of that. It was into the snow with them, bare feet, bare arse, we didn't care. They were taking our jobs and we were fighting for our rights." Tom, her once-gentle Tom, pounded the table as he said this.

"We never hit no one, mind you," he went on. "After all, they're Newfoundlanders like us. We weren't out to hurt, just scare. And by God, did we ever! We were making so much noise that you'd think a bunch of devils was descending on them. B'y, did we ever give them scabs a fright!" He slapped his big hand down on the tabletop once more. Cups and spoons jumped. The cat, Bucksaw, leaped down from his lap and skittered away.

"We hauled down the stovepipe. Their clothes was hangin' to dry all around it and we took the clothes and rammed it down in the oil drum. That douted the coals but the clothes smouldered and burned enough that they wouldn't get to them and put them on. Then we beat up the forepeak. Ripped up whatever the foreman had on his table. In the cookhouse, we dumped out the flour and beans, poured the molasses all over the floor, made as much mess as we could. By the Lord dyin', we left some mess for the A.N.D. Company to clean up. As for the scabs they were out in the snow with the flaps of their long johns hanging down. Some of the men chased them for miles. Serves 'em right. Lousy goddamn scabs."

He stood to his full height, stretched, and yawned. "C'mon, Jennie girl, let's get in bed."

Tom and Jennie cuddled down together; they still did a good bit of cuddling, even after eleven years of marriage. They were toasty warm and almost asleep when a rap came on the door. Tom got out and hauled on his trousers. Jennie was wearing her long flannel nightdress.

Two Mounties stood at the door. "Tom Hillier? You're under arrest for being part of the group that destroyed Anderson's camp."

Jennie pushed her way in front of Tom. "No. You're wrong. Tom and me have been home all night."

Tom took her arm. "Jennie, leave it alone. I have to be with the men. I won't lie to them about it." He put on his logans and reached for his coat and cap. "Don't worry, I'll be okay." He gave her a kiss and a hug. When his lips were near her ear he said, "Get Ralph. You women have to fill the gaps on the picket lines while we men are in jail. Tell him to pass it along to Landon Ladd." Then he went out the door with the Mounties, leaving his wife to deal with it as best she could.

The fiasco up on Sandy landed the men in the Grand Falls jail. Ralph, who had spent all night out by the River waiting for the rampaging strikers to return, was now at home with his Ma. He was just finishing breakfast when Jennie came to the door.

His mother opened it. "Good morning, Jennie. Is something the matter?" She often expected to go out on sick calls if the doctor wasn't in town.

"Good morning Missus Annie, morning Ralph. No, everyone's well, thank you."

Jennie was standing in the morning light, rosy-cheeked and sparkly-eyed from the frosty air. The sunlight through the window shone coppery on her hair. Ralph's hidden heart turned over in his chest at the sight of her.

She turned to him. "Ralph, Tom is gone off to jail with the rest of them. He said to tell you the time has come for the women to come forward and fill in for them on the picket lines. He said you need to get Landon Ladd to speak to them."

Missus Annie loved for people to drop in, even if it was only eight in the morning. She got a cup and saucer for Jennie and hauled out a chair. "Sit down my child, and have a drop of tea with us."

"That's a good idea, Missus Annie. Thanks. I'm nearly frozen. Some frosty this morning."

My God, Ralph thought, *I never thought the day would come when my Beothuk Wonder Woman would be in my home having tea.*

He cleared his throat to find his voice. "Landon Ladd will be here later on, Jennie. If you can get the women together, we'll have a meeting over on the picket line by the River. We're going to need everyone you can gather up. There will be a lot of gaps in the lines with the men gone."

Ma made Jennie a slice of toast to go with the tea and inquired after Jennie's father and her sisters and Phonse.

"The family is all well, Missus Annie. Thanks for the tea and toast. It hit the spot. I must get going now and round up the girls."

Ralph grabbed his coat and cap. "Wait, I'll come along with you." He wouldn't look at Ma's eyes. Ma was pretty sharp. She'd know how he felt about this white woman if she got a look at his eyes.

They tramped all over Badger that morning. The two of them visited every logger's house in town. And everywhere the women said they were ready for whatever the police and the A.N.D. Company threw at them.

But Ralph's greatest secret accomplishment was being next to Jennie all day, laughing and talking in their old easy way. The Badger loggers were fighting for their livelihood and he was mooning after a married woman. But he could no more help it than he could help breathing.

When Landon Ladd came to meet with the women, he told them that their men were lodged in the Grand Falls Armoury because the Grand Falls jail couldn't hold a hundred strikers. He recommended that some of the ladies might make themselves available to carry food, paid for by the union, to the prisoners.

He's such a handsome man, Jennie thought as she watched him. *It isn't sexual attraction. No way. Tom is the only man I'll ever want to go to bed with. It is just that, when he speaks, people – men, women, and children – just stop and listen. He has that way about him.*

"Ladies of the IWA loggers strike," said Landon Ladd. "We spoke about this a couple of months ago. We said the time would come when you would be needed. And now you are needed more than ever before. I will never forget you, brave staunch women that you are. I know you will stand in good stead for your men. Don't worry; we'll have them back to you before long."

Mr. Ladd went among the women, shaking hands, patting a shoulder here, a shoulder there, his head bent, listening to them intently. He had the common touch, people said. *That man could go places,* Jennie thought. She sneaked out her hand and touched his overcoat. It was a light fawn colour, so smooth and soft. Cashmere, like the rich lady's in St. John's. *And his dark hair is perfect, with a lock falling on his brow, just so. They say that Joey Smallwood is afraid of him; of his charisma and his ability to hold a crowd spellbound when he gives a speech. I know one thing: the women would vote Landon Ladd in for Premier in a minute!*

He told the women to guard the Buchans Highway. Word had filtered through, he said, that the Company was taking advantage and had a busload of scabs coming in to go to the camps in the Millertown Division.

The women assured him. "No one will get past us. No cops. No buses. No scabs. No one." Landon Ladd said he knew how good they were, how dedicated to the cause.

$\wp$

A week went by. It was hard for the women, without their husbands. Jennie had a commanding presence; people liked her and listened to her. Her husband, Big Tom Hillier, had, according to reports, led the assault on the woods camp full of scabs. The women expected her to lead them. And she did. Ralph was a great support, by her side all the time. If it was anyone else but Ralph, Jennie, with her own husband down in jail, would have worried that people might have talked about her being with another man. But, she reassured herself, it was only Ralph, who had been her good friend forever.

She asked Pastor Genge if he'd get his parishioners to bring down some Thermoses of tea and a few sandwiches. They did, God love them. Even Suze helped; for Tom's sake, Jennie supposed. For that they were thankful, seeing as they couldn't get a chance to go home and cook something for themselves. But you could see the women who brought the food were nervous and disapproving, especially the older women. Jennie could almost hear their thoughts: *Women shouldn't be out on picket lines with men. It don't look right.*

Father Murphy would come down to the River picket line sometimes. He'd stay for awhile, talking to everyone. Jennie heard him telling Ralph and the boys that he was originally from Northern Ireland, and had come to Newfoundland twenty years ago. He told them about the unrest over there. Jennie thought: *We thought we had troubles; sure, ours were nothing compared to what the Irish had to put up with from the English. And, speaking of trouble, we have to watch out for that sneaky Vern Crawford. You never know what he's about. With just women on some of the picket lines, if he thought that he could sneak a scab through, he would.* Jennie would've liked to give him a clout over the head. And to think, if she'd listened to Mam and Pap, she would've been married to him. Christ! That didn't even bear thinking about.

After a week, the unionized strikers were released. Jennie and the other women were glad to see them home. But four of them didn't come back. There were low rumblings that they had been sent to the Salmonier prison farm. No one was sure why. They were advised to keep quiet.

As the days went by, Badger became a tense, ugly place. Loggers patrolled the roads or stood on street corners. Police patrolled too. The people of the town were now beginning to see police in Newfoundland Constabulary uniforms along with those of the RCMP. A rumour went around that some of them were really mill workers dressed in police clothes, and not real officers at all. They were grim and silent, and, maybe, nervous. The strikers were grim too, but definitely not silent.

The women continued to back up their men for the rest of February. The weather was rough. There was a lot of snow and the cold was bone deep. The strikers were boiling with frustration and anger, disgusted with the way the provincial government and the

Company were treating this whole affair. Jennie had a feeling in the pit of her stomach. *There's going to be a showdown.*

✆

On an afternoon in mid-February, Alf Elliott faced four angry men over the counter of his telegraph office.

The night before, Joey Smallwood had finally broken his silence regarding the loggers' strike. Every radio in Newfoundland was tuned to his speech. His venom and fury toward the IWA and the strikers was something no one was prepared for. Joey, the man who had given them Confederation, had been their idol, their god. It was unthinkable that he would attack the loggers and their union. After all, he'd formerly been a union man himself.

But attack them he did. "The IWA strike is a failure," he stated, "and they have failed the loggers of Newfoundland. It is not a strike they have started, but a civil war. How dare these outsiders come into this decent Christian province and try to seize control of our main industry by spreading their black poison of class hatred and prejudice?"

Smallwood then announced that he would be forming a union of his own. He even had a name for it already: the Newfoundland Brotherhood of Wood Workers. He also announced that his new union would be headed up by Max Lane, a Liberal MHA.

Overwrought and angry at what they considered the Premier's betrayal, Joey's speech was the last straw for the strikers. This was an insult. The loggers already had a union; they didn't need another one. A group of furious strikers decided to telegraph Joey Smallwood to let him know their feelings.

"Boys, I'm sorry," Alf told them. "I can't send this kind of message. Canadian National Telegraph forbids the sending of telegrams with foul language." Alf was a slightly built man, and he knew he'd be no match for these men if they resorted to violence. But they weren't bad men, just tormented, disappointed ones. He was anxious to help them out, if he could.

"Look, reword it," he told them. "Take out the goddamns and the fucks. State your feelings to him, and then I'll send it. Sure I'll even help you word it, if you want."

A taller, rough, unshaven guy elbowed the others out of the way and grabbed Alf by the collar, knocking off his glasses. "Buddy, I'm tellin' you, if you don't send that goddamn telegram, we'll beat up every last thing in this office. We'll break out the windows, haul out the telephone wires, throw the typewriter out in the snow and kick your cowardly arse through the door."

Whether he would've made good on his threat or not would never be known. The door opened. It was Ralph Drum and his brothers.

"Well, Frank Jones, whattya at, me son?" Ralph clapped his hand on the shoulder of the big guy who was holding Alf captive by his collar. "You're not givin' the telegraph operator here a hard time, are you? Aren't you the feller who was preachin' to everyone else the other night about keeping a cool head and no violence?"

Jones released Alf's collar and straightened up. "We just want our damn message sent, right?" He looked at Alf. "I s'pose I shouldn't have grabbed you like that." He bent over and picked up Alf's glasses and passed them to him.

"We'll deal with the telegram another time," Ralph told him. "My brothers want you fellas to go with them now, Frank b'y. The main picket line has gaps and we have to keep it up to strength, you know."

The irate strikers left their flaming message to Joey on the counter and obediently followed the Drum brothers out the door. Jones must have felt somewhat sheepish because, just before the door closed behind him, he looked back at Alf. "Sorry for what I said, sir."

Ralph stayed behind.

"My son, I'm some glad you were passing by," Alf said. "I think the boys there would've put the boots to this office in another minute."

"Someone told us what they were up to, Alf b'y. They've been drinking all afternoon; some of them do that, you know. 'Tis a hard time on the men; they're far from home, they're cold and tired. A drop of rum comes in handy."

"Yes b'y, I know everyone is having a hard time of it." Alf looked at his watch. "Even though it's only three o'clock, I think I'm going to close up early. I don't want to have to deal with more of this today."

"Yes b'y. Proper thing. I'll see you later," Ralph said as he went out the door.

His little office had become a busy place. As the strike escalated, news reporters came into town. They filed their stories back to their newspapers in St. John's and on the mainland with long wordy telegrams sent off collect, to be paid for at the receiving end.

As the strike wore on, more and more men were pouring into Badger and telegrams were flying back and forth on both sides of the dispute: IWA officials were contacting their executive offices; A.N.D. Company personnel wiring for potential strikebreakers; unionized loggers from out of town sending telegrams to their families out in the bays; and their families sending messages back to them. Money was being wired back and forth.

Alf gathered up the cash box and receipts and locked the door. As he walked up the road he thought about the delicate job he had treating the Company and the strikers, all the same. He couldn't publicly be pro-union or pro-Company. If the Company wanted to send telegrams, he sent them; same thing for the union. He was under oath never to divulge the contents of his work. People trusted him. But no matter how neutral he tried to be, his heart was with the loggers who were out there on the picket lines, day after day, in bitter winter weather.

20

The church was crowded on the Sunday morning after Joey Smallwood's speech decertifying the IWA. Father Murphy pondered his sermon. Church leaders had been pro-union, but not so much now. Should he speak out against Smallwood's decision?

His heart told him yes. What he saw in those camps was horrible. How could the A.N.D. Company condone living conditions like that? He stepped forward to his pulpit. Many eyes focused on him, waiting patiently for him to speak. The pews were full and some parishioners were standing along the walls. There were strangers there as well, loggers from other communities in town to support the cause. Father Murphy knew the clergy of the other two churches were facing the same dilemma.

"My friends, I wish to speak about the current labour troubles in this town and this province. I want to advise against rash actions.

"Outside, the streets are littered with overturned cars, and loggers patrol the picket lines armed with birch sticks. Police officers – RCMP and Constabulary – patrol our streets armed with their own weapons. Never in the history of this town has anything been known to equal this. The people of Badger have faced forest fires that have come so close that some have been forced to flee their homes. Every year the rivers flood the town, some years worse than others. Through it all we have survived. And together, we will survive this.

"We have to remember that innocent people live here too. Do

not let your rash judgments allow any of our citizens to be harmed. Remember our children. Shield our children above all else.

"Let us pray to God to bless and protect us all."

⚥

Nineteen fifty-nine was a great year for twelve-year-old boys in Badger.

On Saturdays, with no school and no homework to be done, the boys were given plenty of freedom. The hill behind the school was a great place to slide. Most youngsters didn't have slides, but used a piece of canvas or cardboard. It didn't matter. Anything was fun when you were young.

They spent much of their time digging snow forts, with long, intricate tunnels. It was a wonder that no one was buried and smothered. They played not Cowboys and Indians, as they used to, but Strikers and Police. To the Badger boys, strikers were the good guys and police were the bad guys.

The bell that announced school's opening on Monday morning was rung by hand. Several generations of teachers had held this solid brass bell on which was engraved the words BADGER AMALGAMATED SCHOOL, PRESENTED BY THE A.N.D. COMPANY, 1921. The school was very proud of its bell. It alone had survived the fire that had burned the first school to the ground in 1941, and only because the principal, as he did occasionally, had taken it home that night to clean and polish it.

The same bell rang on Monday, February 15, to announce recess time. David Elliott and Harold Hatcher scrambled through the class-room door with the rest of the class. Rough-and-tumble boys, both twelve years old and in grade seven, they saw the whole town as their playground.

"Harold," yelled David, as they rushed up over the stairs from their basement classroom, "I got fifty cents. Let's run down to Plotsky's. I can race you. Bet I can."

"Fifty cents?" Harold's freckled face and bright eyes were all interest. "Where did you get all that money? Steal it?"

They burst out through the door into the winter air. David grabbed Harold in a hammerlock and pummelled him. "Shut up, you shithead. I don't steal stuff. I earned it, cleaving splits for my grandfather." David was proud of a dirty word like shithead. He knew there were even worse words that he could use, but shithead was pretty good.

"Okay, okay," cried Harold. "Ow! Let me go!" David released his grip. They could see the Catholic boys, who were out for recess too, coming down the road. Their friend, Bernie Sullivan, stood out among them with his bright red hair, a mark of all the Sullivan family.

"Hey Bernie." Harold ran forward. "We're going to Plotsky's. David got fifty cents."

"Yeah, sure, we might see some friggin' strikers while we're down there," said Bernie. Friggin' was his latest safe-around-school swear word. Everything was friggin': friggin' school, friggin' recess, friggin' books, friggin' strike, friggin' winter.

All together, from both schools, there were about fifteen kids on the road that Monday morning. Three or four were girls, although most girls didn't go out for recess in the wintertime unless they planned to go sliding on the hill out back. Then they came prepared with snowpants under their skirts.

The Badger children were in a continual state of excitement over the IWA strike that had taken over their town. They all imagined themselves to be strikers too. The sons of loggers and their friends spent as much time as they could mooching around the fringes of the picket lines, listening to the men, watching them.

Harold's father was employed with Mr. Anderson in the logging camps and Bernie's worked on the drive. David's dad was the telegraph operator.

"Come on guys, let's go," said David. "We haven't got much time." The three lads streamed down the road toward Plotsky's. Their only objective was to get fifty cents worth of jawbreakers. They never made it.

School Road joined with Church Road, the main street. Just

before they reached the town hall the children came upon a group of strikers and two cars.

Harold, out in front, skidded to a stop. "Geez, there's me father."

His father, Bill Hatcher, was to the front of the strikers involved in a scuffle with scabs. The children crowded around, all thoughts of Plotsky's and jawbreakers evaporated.

Two cars were upside down on the road, tires sticking up like the legs of a turtle on its back. Around the car was a bunch of angry men, cursing and yelling. If ever the boys wanted to add to their list of swear words, this was the place to be.

David remembered his dad telling him to stay away from anything associated with the strike. Other kids had had the same warning, but, like the jawbreakers, it too was forgotten. This was a big happening, exciting and scary at the same time.

"That's scabs," Bernie informed them. "I heard my father say that the A.N.D. Company was sneaking them through to Millertown."

No one had to ask Bernie to explain scabs. They all knew that it had nothing to do with a cut on your finger. Every man, woman and child in Badger now knew the meaning of the word scab as well as they knew the meaning of strike, picket line, union, trashing, jailed, decertified. A year ago, even six months ago, none of those words meant anything to them.

"Look. Look." David's voice cracked. That happened lately, especially when he was excited. He pointed toward the cars, his hand shaking slightly. "They're crawling out through the windows."

No one could predict what might happen. Perhaps it would turn to violence with Newfoundlander fighting Newfoundlander. Maybe not. Around the corner came a police car.

"Watch out, the police are coming," someone yelled.

Five Mounties piled out. "Stand back! Stand back," they shouted, moving forward to separate the loggers from the men who were crawling out of the cars.

"Goddammit," muttered Bernie. "My father is missing this. Hold on till I tells him."

David and Harold looked at him in admiration. Bernie had dared to use a Big Swear Word.

Far up the road, the school bell could be heard faintly, announcing the end of recess. Like a flock of sparrows, the children turned as one and flew up the road toward the school.

Loggers, scabs, and police were left to deal with life's adult problems.

ℬ

Sacred Heart! Would that Sister Mary Agnes ever shut up? She'd been wailing for the past half-hour. Not even Mother Superior could get a word in edgeways. At times, the nuns were a big responsibility for the priest. Mother Superior oversaw them and she deferred to him in matters of household expenses. Things normally ran along smoothly, but from time to time there were bumps in the road that were hard to know just how to deal with.

The six teaching nuns taught religion, history, music, literature, algebra, geometry, arithmetic, geography and social studies. They had all been at it a good many years. All except Sister Mary Agnes. She was new. Their old history teacher, Sister Mary Augustus, had recently passed away.

From the first day they brought in the new nun, Father Murphy had an uneasy feeling about her. Call it the Irish in him, but he could sense something unstable about the woman. She was the Bishop's niece, sent there by the Bishop himself, so he couldn't put up any objections.

The school had children from grades one to eleven, with twelve to fifteen students in a class. Sister Mary Agnes took over the grade sevens. There were several big boys in her class, rowdy rambunctious young fellows whose last thought was to learn anything.

Since the strike had consumed Badger, the Catholic boys, like the boys from the Protestant school, played hooky more often than not. No matter how much Father Murphy preached to them all, it didn't matter. As far as they were concerned, they were loggers too, and had to be in the thick of what was going on. They couldn't understand the danger of being youngsters among angry, desperate men. They had never known fear and they refused to recognize it now.

Sister Mary Agnes, being from Grand Falls, the headquarters of the A.N.D. Company, had no sympathy for the loggers, and was no match for the boys whose fathers were strikers. They refused to do their homework, didn't listen to what she said, and left her in tears every day.

One morning, totally frazzled, she dared to speak out. Father Murphy wasn't present when it happened. He sat in on the nuns' classes occasionally, but he had other responsibilities as well. He heard all about it afterward from several sources, however, including from Sister herself.

She'd told Phonse Sullivan's boy, Bernie, that he looked like a ragamuffin, just like the fellows on the picket line. Bernie, all twelve years of him, said that was because he belonged on the picket line with his father. Sister Mary Agnes told him those men ought to be ashamed of themselves, leaving their good jobs because they were too lazy to work, and standing around all day doing nothing.

That did it. The boys went crazy. Threw their books at her. Terrified, she crouched down behind her desk so she wouldn't be struck. Then the whole class just got up and left, with Sister running behind, ordering them to come back.

When Mother Superior had finally taken Sister Mary Agnes away, Father Murphy was faced with the task of pacifying a mob of angry parents.

"Excuse me, Father, my daughter came home from school today because everyone walked out of class. She says they had to follow the strikers' sons or else."

"I'm sure it's a mistake, Father. The nun was within her rights, I'm sure."

"Listen here, Father, my boy is a good learner. He's not mixed up with that crowd that chases around after the strikers."

"By the Sacred Heart of Jesus, Father, those men on the picket line are not lazy! No sir! They're fightin' for their rights. How dare she – that relative of the Bishop's – speak to the youngsters like that? What's the world comin' to?"

Phonse Sullivan also had his say. "Now listen here, Father, what kind of stuff is that to teach our children, huh? Here I am out there all winter, freezin' me arse off with the police breathin' down our necks. And now a teacher, and a nun to boot, goes and says things like that to our youngsters. 'Tis enough to turn you, Father. Enough to turn you."

It went on and on and got louder and louder. The priest told them that Sister Mary Agnes would be leaving. That quieted them down somewhat. What he didn't tell them was that all the nuns were leaving and the school would immediately close down until the unrest was over. The orders had come from the Bishop himself.

What would be the end of this? Only God knew. Father Murphy went to his church to pray for the people of Badger and for the loggers.

21

Alf Elliott's daughter, Amanda, was fourteen and in grade nine during the autumn of 1958. She heard her parents talking about a union being organized to help the loggers get better pay and better living conditions in the woods camps and it didn't interest her at first. But some of her friends' fathers were loggers, and the young girls talked among themselves. Those in the know said the men were going on strike, but others weren't quite sure what it meant to be on strike.

There were many things happening in Amanda's own world. She was becoming a woman and her childhood was being left behind. Her mother talked to her about strange new things, like sanitary napkins and what they were used for. She even sent away to Eaton's catalogue for a brassiere for Amanda.

Elvis Presley, the American rock and roll idol, was all the rage. Amanda and her friends were no different than other teenagers all across North America as they oohed and aahed over him and his music. Television had recently come to Newfoundland and was broadening young people's view of the world.

And then, suddenly, in January of 1959, things changed. Many strangers were seen on Badger's streets. Loggers from the outports poured into the town to support the union. The words "strike" and "IWA" were on everybody's tongue. Reality hit, and even young people were jarred out of their safe little lives.

School life wasn't the same either. The principal, Mr. Summers, who was also the teacher for grades nine, ten and eleven, didn't seem to notice if someone was shooting wads of paper with their slingshots or using their huge World History book to hit a person in front of them over the head. He often absented himself from the classroom, something he had never done before the strike occurred. The boys would go wild then, jumping over the seats, tormenting the girls, seeing who could swear the best – or worst – and everyone talked in a classroom where, at one time, it was so quiet that you could hear a pin drop. Everyone shared news of the strike. The kids considered themselves experts on what was happening.

February came, and the strike was becoming violent. The young girls saw overturned cars in the streets and angry men standing around fire barrels. However, no one ever bothered or threatened them, and they were allowed to walk freely about the town. Susan Foote and Madeline Sullivan had fathers who were on the picket lines. Susan hadn't seen her father since the trashing of the woods camps on the seventh of February. He'd been carted off to jail with many others, but hadn't come back home when the rest were released. Her mom said that he was sent off to a prison farm out in Salmonier, but Susan didn't know why. No one ever explained things to kids.

Amanda's younger friend Madeline was part of the big Sullivan family. Her father, Phonse, and her Uncle Tom, even her Aunt Jennie were strikers too. Madeline was pretty sure the strikers would win their fight.

❦

As the town became more unruly, Rod had a mind to send Ruth in to St. John's to stay with their daughter, Audrey. Since the episode in the camps almost a month ago, tension had become so bad that some Company personnel were afraid to let their kids go to school.

Every Company employee and contractor who stayed in town had a police car parked outside their door. Ruth went out every now and then and offered them tea and buns. She was like that, kind-hearted. Sure, all Badger was like that, or was like that at one time, before the strike. Now everyone was afraid of everyone else. Rod could understand the loggers' position, but the town itself was paying a high price.

They were having supper. It was the beginning of March and the evenings were starting to get longer, but you still needed the light on to eat supper. Rod's father used to say that by the middle of March you could have your evening meal in the daylight. He would plan his winter around that event, every day getting a bit longer, a sign that winter was loosening its grip.

Looking across the table at his wife, Rod said, "Ruth, why don't you pack up and go in St. John's for awhile? See Audrey and the girls. I'll wire a message to have Richard meet the train."

Ruth got the teapot from the back of the stove. She'd cooked pea soup with dumplings for supper; it was one of her husband's favourite meals, even though he always complained afterward that it made him gassy. They were finishing off with a bit of fruitcake and tea. "What about you, Rod? Will you be all right here in the house?"

"My dear, don't worry. I've lived here all my life. What can happen to hurt me in little old Badger?"

Next day, Rod went off to the Canadian National Telegraph office and sent a telegram to Audrey.

"Good many people leaving town, Rod," said Alf Elliott, as he carefully counted the words of the telegram.

"Yes b'y. Badger has become a rough place these days. When this strike is over, I wonder if it will go back to the quiet way it was."

"I wonders the same thing. That's fifty-two cents, Rod my son. I'll send one of my kids over with the reply, when it comes through."

"Thanks Alf, I'd appreciate it. I'm hoping to get Ruth out on the train tomorrow evening, if I can."

The telegram came back:

ST. JOHN'S MARCH 5, 1959
MR. ROD ANDERSON, BADGER, N.F.L.D.

RUTH IS ALWAYS WELCOME STOP PLEASE ADVISE WHEN ARRIVING STOP

RICHARD FAGAN

Ruth was excited to be off to St. John's by herself, even if she was worried about leaving her husband behind.

22

The old St. John's railway station was a bleak place. Lining the walls, wooden seats offered hard invitations to the backside. Constable Richard Fagan chose to walk around as he waited for his mother-in-law to come in on the morning train.

Others waiting to board the train or to meet someone eyed him warily. People were always on guard when they saw a police uniform, thinking that the officer might be there to pick up a prisoner or arrest someone.

Richard had been on the night shift: eight hours of drunks, family squabbles, one robbery and one accident. He had told Audrey that he would go to the train station on his way home and pick up her mother. His wife and their two little daughters were at home waiting to see her.

People began to stir and drift toward the back door of the waiting room. Through the window he could see the train easing its way into St. John's station. Most railway stations had the tracks running by the main door, but in St. John's the front looked like an imposing Victorian mansion, which Richard thought was the idea when they built it back in the 1890s. You came in through the front door and the train sneaked along the back where a door opened out on the platform.

As he stepped outside he thought about faraway Port aux Basques where this train started, and all the little places in between, like Badger, where his in-laws lived which was his wife's hometown. Richard never ceased to be amazed about the largeness of the island of Newfoundland.

He saw Ruth being helped off the train by the conductor, and moved forward.

"Good morning, Momma Ruth. Did you have a good trip?"

Ruth reached out and hugged him. "Richard, how nice to see you. And you in your nice uniform too! Yes, the trip was fine. My first ever alone, you know. I had a sleeper and slept all the way from Gander to Whitbourne."

Richard installed Ruth in the front seat of his car and stowed her baggage in the trunk. "So this is the new car, Richard," Ruth said, patting the dash in her affectionate way. "Audrey wrote about it." She looked out the window at the miserable March weather – dirty snow on the ground and drizzly rain looking like it was about to turn to freezing. "When the summer comes, you all will be able to go for nice drives outside the city."

Richard drove on up Water Street and up over the Hill o' Chips onto Duckworth, then past the Newfoundland Hotel and onto Kings Bridge Road.

"How is Rod doing, Momma Ruth? I've been reading the papers about the loggers' strike. Sounds like they're having a rough time of it." He turned left onto New Cove Road. Richard's house was only a few doors down from his father's. "Audrey reads me your letters. You said that the strikers beat up Rod's woods camp. Will the company stand to the expense of cleaning it up and rebuilding?"

"I suppose so, Richard. Everything is so uncertain with the A.N.D. Company these days. Rod sent me in here because it's too dangerous in Badger right now. Hundreds of strangers roaming about the streets, Mounties everywhere, cars and buses overturned in the middle of town. Company personnel who are staying – and many have left – have police cars parked outside their doors. Rod says he'll be all right, but I'm not sure if he will be."

At the house, Ruth got out and quickly went on up the walkway while her son-in-law got her suitcase. She had been here twice before. Richard and Audrey and their children had visited them in Badger too, but the distance was so great – four hundred miles – that the families didn't see each other often enough.

Richard heard the excited squeals from the children before he got up the step. Ruth was on her knees and the children were hugging her. Everyone was laughing.

Richard went on through to the bedroom to take off his uniform. He was dead tired and felt like he could sleep for a week. Audrey peeked in.

"Breakfast, Richard?"

"No, sweetheart, I'll just go on to bed. We had a busy night last night."

"Mom and I are going to take the children up to your mother's as soon as they're fed and dressed. You'll have a quiet house then. Later on, your mother is cooking supper for all of us."

Richard climbed into bed as Audrey closed the door. He thought about what she'd just said: "Your mother's house." Strictly speaking, Mama was his foster mother. Richard seldom thought about the life he'd lived before being adopted by the Abernathys, except when he had been preparing to marry Audrey and felt compelled to tell her about his unsettled past.

When Richard awoke hours later it was mid-afternoon. The house was empty and quiet. He made himself some tea and sat staring out the window as he sipped it. The city was still grey and cold, but it hadn't gotten the freezing rain that had been forecast. As he sat there in the silent house, gazing out the window, Richard's mind started to drift back over the years that had brought him to this point in his life.

He was jarred back to the present when the porch door opened. The tea had gone cold in the cup and the March evening had closed in outside the window.

It was Papa. "Dickie, the family sent me over to wake you up, my son. You must have slept some sound; they were ringing the telephone and there was no answer."

"Sorry, Papa. I'll come right away." He grabbed his coat and hat from the rack and hurried out the door after his father.

🍃

That evening, sitting in the Abernathy living room while the women cleaned the dishes, Levi told Richard about the Constabulary's involvement in the strike. "Government has ordered fifty members out to Grand Falls to supplement the RCMP," he said, keeping his voice low so the women in the kitchen wouldn't hear him. "You know what we read in the *Evening Telegram* and the *Daily News*. The papers say that the A.N.D. Company is standing firm in its resolve not to acknowledge the IWA. And the Premier has condemned the union and decertified it outright. Here in St. John's people are having a hard time understanding that because Joey Smallwood was once a union man himself. One time he walked across Newfoundland on the railway tracks to organize a railway union."

"So, what do you think?" Richard asked him. "Will our boys be much help to the RCMP?"

"I suppose so, Dickie my son. Most likely it's just for patrols to show a presence. Let's keep quiet about it for now. Poor Ruth is worried enough about Rod as it is."

The embers snapped in the fireplace as the women's voices drifted in from the kitchen. The two children were kneeling on the floor by the coffee table, colouring in the books Ruth had brought for them. In the middle of such domesticity, it was hard to think of desperate loggers standing outside in cold and snow fighting for what they believed to be their rights.

The women joined the men then, and the little girls rushed to them with their coloured pages.

Richard had to work another overnight shift. They bundled everyone up and walked off down the street to home. The children had their bath and went off to bed, and Ruth declared that she was tired too, so she went to bed as well.

Audrey sat on the arm of Richard's chair. "Richard, you've been quiet and moody all evening. What's wrong? You don't mind my mom being here, do you?"

"No, no. Nothing like that, my dear. I just have a heavy feeling and I don't know why. I got up from my sleep this afternoon and started thinking of us – you, me and the girls, Mama and Papa, Rod and Ruth. Then I got to remembering how we first met, and how fate played a heavy hand in us meeting again."

Audrey kissed him on top of the head. "Wasn't that something, though? I always say if it wasn't for a cat, a harmonica and a fiddle, we'd never be together."

Richard got up from the chair and turned to the darkness outside the window. "When the weather clears a bit, I think I'll go down and visit my mother's grave."

What brought on that thought? Audrey wondered, as she helped her husband with his jacket and watched him go out into the night.

When Richard finished his shift the next morning, he headed down to the Anglican Church Cemetery on Forest Road. It was still overcast but not raining, with an easterly wind whipping down Quidi Vidi Lake. The paths were clear and the headstones and monuments were bare. Most of the plots were still covered with old winter snow dirty with soot from the numerous chimneys. Richard walked quickly along the path bordered by giant beech trees that looked forlorn and naked without their leaves.

Richard read again the plain stone that marked the resting place of his mother's poor crippled body: MARY ANN FAGAN, 1908-1944. Thirty-six years old. She had died when he was only sixteen. Then his unsettled mind went flying back over the years again to the 1930s when his mother had been discharged from St. Clare's Hospital. The Welfare Department had installed her in a boarding house on Brazil Square. The Abernathys had never kept any details of his life from him. They believed that things should be done the right way. That was why he still had the Fagan name.

Mama had told him it would be the proper thing to visit her. She coached him carefully. "Now Dickie," she said gently, "I want you to go and see her. She is your real mother. I am your adopted mother. I love you as if you were always mine, but I want you to know your birth mother."

"Will I have to go and live with her? And leave you and Papa?" The young boy was terrified. He had only been with them a year. The tragic happenings that had brought him here were still fresh in his young mind.

"No, my darling boy, no. You are with us forever." Mama smoothed his hair back and kissed the top of his head.

After that first meeting, and as he grew into his teens, with some prodding from Mama, Richard would go visit Mary Ann alone. But there seemed to be no feeling between mother and son. His mother, who had given birth to him, was a stranger and he was a stranger to her. Thinking about it, he supposed that, given the circumstances of his birth, it was not surprising that they had never formed a bond.

As Richard stood in his uniform, fur cap and greatcoat, he hardly knew what he was doing, standing at the grave of the long-dead woman who had given him life. Why was he now filled with so much sadness and foreboding? He had a good life and a fine wife and family. He shrugged off the feeling as best he could and retraced his steps out of the cemetery. He looked forward to getting home after a long night.

∅

Mary and Alf Elliott were alone in the kitchen. Alf was preparing his pipe for his after-supper smoke as Mary did the dishes.

"Mary maid, there's something strange going on with the people of this town. I need to discuss this with someone and you're the only one I can trust." He opened his tobacco pouch and pinched out a portion of tobacco.

Mary, standing by the cupboard wiping a plate, said, "You know I won't say anything, Alf. It's your job we have to think about, b'y. I wouldn't want you to get into trouble."

"Many Badger people believe the propaganda that Joey's been spouting over the radio for the past month. His rantings have turned the tide of opinion all across this province, you know. The churches have even come out in support of him now." Alf applied a match to his pipe and sucked in to make it draw.

"Since he made his first speech on radio last month, dozens of people have been sending telegrams to the Premier's office, congratulating Mr. Smallwood, telling him he's right and offering their support. Over a hundred messages in less than a month." Alf drew deeply on his pipe and the smell of Amphora Pipe Tobacco wafted through the kitchen. "Since word came through today that the House of Assembly has decertified the IWA, I was even busier. This afternoon I sent off forty messages to him."

Mary was still occupied with the dishes. "I s'pose it's just the A.N.D. Company crowd and the business people, is it?"

"Well yes, for the most part. But there were also messages from people who had no direct connection to any of it, who must just feel the need to put in their two cents worth." Alf got up from his chair and walked across the kitchen to look out. It was snowing again this evening. It had been a hard winter for snow.

"What surprises me is some people who have relatives in the union, and some union members too, are sending telegrams to Mr. Smallwood saying they know him to be right. That's betrayal, Mary, and there's not a damn thing that I can do about it."

Mary sat down on a kitchen chair with her dishtowel in her hands. "Alf, be careful. I know it seems wrong, but you can only take them telegrams over your counter and say nothing. Don't forget you're supposed to be neutral." She twisted her dishtowel as she looked at her husband anxiously.

Alf turned his back on the snowy scene outside the window. "And you know what else bothers me, Mary? Outside of my office, going about town, I meet the same people staunchly affirming their support for the IWA when, only the day before that, they'd sent Joey a telegram telling him that he was right in calling the IWA an unscrupulous foreign union."

He went over to the stove, removed the cover with the lifter, and knocked the half-smoked contents of his pipe into the flame. "My God, they know that I know. They do! Yet they look at me as if daring me to say something. I'm disgusted with it all, Mary. Disgusted."

"If you did decide to talk, who would you tell? Landon Ladd? Ralph? Who?" Mary stood up and faced him. "You can't do it, Alf. There would be a backlash at us, your family, and you'd lose your job."

"Yes, I know you're right. I know you are, but it burns me up inside to see such a two-faced crowd. I agreed with Landon Ladd, and I knew he was on the right track with what he was doing. But now it's all over. The loggers won't get to keep their union, thanks to Joey Smallwood."

"I understand what you're saying, Alf. And I trust you to know what is right. I'm just asking you to keep your family in mind."

Alf turned from the stove and limped back across the kitchen. "I think about them poor buggers out on the picket lines with no legal union to back them up. 'Tis terrible times, Mary. Terrible times."

Their second son, Thomas, thumped down over the stairs. "Dad, let's have a game of checkers."

"Yes, all right, my son, you go in the dining room and lay out the board."

As he turned to follow Thomas, Alf said to Mary in a low voice, "Bloody Joey controls Newfoundland like an emperor and I think he sees that control slipping away like his rubber boot and his chocolate factory slipped away." He shook his finger at Mary. "Mark my words. This is the beginning of Joey Smallwood's downfall."

23

Richard was scheduled for a day off when he got the call to go down to the drill hall. He called his partner, Bob Parsons. Yes, he said, he had to go too. Richard said he'd pick him up.

There were about twenty of them. The assistant chief was there and Sergeant Abernathy was with him. Richard and his father always maintained a strictly professional relationship at work. To Richard he was Sergeant Levi Abernathy. To Levi, his foster son was Constable Richard Fagan.

That evening, in the drafty old drill hall, Papa's craggy face looked drawn and worried. He looked at Richard and shook his head slightly. The assistant chief announced that he would wait awhile for a few more men.

Bob, always restless, said, "I'm going to get a Coke and have a smoke. You want to come along?"

Richard shook his head. He was feeling worse by the minute. He had a sinking feeling in the pit of his stomach, fearful that they would be following the larger contingent out to Central Newfoundland.

In all, there were twenty-four men. The assistant chief told them they were going on a secret mission and no one was to know where they would be. No civilian clothes; just uniforms. They would be immediately taken to a train coach that was waiting off on a siding at the station.

Someone spoke up. "Where are we headed, sir?"

"You'll know when you get there, Constable."

At the last moment, Bill Moss and another officer rushed into the drill hall, apologizing for being late. Their arrival brought the unit up to twenty-six men.

Sergeant Abernathy helped the officers to get ready, making sure that they all had their badges, nightsticks – which the constables called batons – and their winter gear. He spoke to Richard. "You're going to Central Newfoundland. Orders have come down from the Justice Department. It's just to help the RCMP keep the peace during the loggers' strike. Badger hasn't been mentioned, just Grand Falls. But I think it might well be Badger, based on what Ruth has told us. It would be a good idea to stay away from Rod and anyone else you know."

Richard agreed, not surprised by the news. "Look after Audrey and the girls," he told him. "I don't know what you're going to tell her and her mother."

"I can't tell them anything, my son," his father answered. "There won't be much to it. Don't worry. Likely they won't even need you men and you'll all be sent home again in a couple of days."

The officers boarded the private train coach in the darkness. It was soon coupled to a diesel locomotive that set off across the Avalon, off the isthmus, non-stop. No conductor punching tickets or yelling, "Whitbourne next station!" Just twenty-six men sent into the unknown, uncertain where they would end up.

A few of the members got together in one end of the coach to play poker. Richard was too depressed and anxious to do anything but sit hunched in his seat, eyes closed, pretending to sleep. He was remembering again. His mind going back to when he had married Audrey.

Richard had never thought it would ever happen, but it had. After Audrey and he were engaged, Rod and Ruth came in from Badger for a visit. The woodsman and his wife from around the bay and the St. John's police sergeant and his townie missus became friends, starting with Richard and Audrey as their common ground.

They had been married in March of 1955 in Corpus Christi

Church on Waterford Bridge Road. Richard was in his dress uniform, the same blue that he wore when they met at the Garden Party. Many of his fellow officers were there. Audrey was beautiful in the traditional white. They had a reception in the parish hall.

Audrey had become pregnant soon after their marriage, and by 1957 they had two little girls. Richard's adopted parents became doting grandparents. The young Fagan family made a few trips out to Badger, sometimes with the Abernathys in tow. In a short time Levi learned more about the woods operations than Richard ever would. He met other contractors and company officials; that was Levi's' way. He could talk to anyone. Back in St. John's, that was what made him a good policeman.

People of the town came to know Richard and the Abernathys on sight. Richard hadn't formed any friendships, but Alf Elliott, the telegraph operator, and several other people would say, "How ya getting' on, Richard?" when they met. Sometimes Richard would go over to the field to play ball with Rod's neighbour and friend, Bill Hatcher, and his two rowdy boys, Walt and Harold, and big, tall Tom Hillier. Through them Richard met Ralph Drum.

During one of the Badger visits, Ralph said that his old grandfather wanted to talk to Richard. Richard said that he was sure that his father, Levi, would like to meet Ralph's grandfather too. But Ralph said no, Grandfather just wanted to see him alone.

"It's you he'd like to see, Richard. I'm sorry. Just you," Ralph said.

"How strange," Richard answered. "I didn't know he even knew who I was."

"He said that he saw you over by the River one time, getting aboard the scow." They walked over to the Drum house. "My grandfather is getting ready to die, Richard. Our people always know when their time has come upon them. We think he is over one hundred years old, although there's no birth certificate to prove it."

How strange, Richard thought. *How does a person get ready to die and how do the Mi'kmaq people know when their time is coming?*

Ralph paused and looked intently at Richard as if searching his face for something. "Richard, I never question my grandfather, but

I have to warn you that he has some unusual thoughts. When he asked me to get you, he said that you have "the Blood." That's Grandfather's words, not mine. Do you have any idea how that may be so?"

Richard looked at him dumbly. "What blood?"

"Beothuk blood, Richard. Grandfather can recognize it. And he values it highly."

They came to the house. The wizened old man was sitting propped up in a chair with pillows and quilts near the kitchen stove. The skin on his bald head and his gnarled old hands were the colour of strong-steeped tea, but his eyes were as sharp, black and alert as his grandson Ralph's.

"Sit, my son," he croaked. "Allow me to tell you some history."

Ralph pushed a stool forward and Richard sat.

As Richard and Ralph listened, the old man spoke of a time when there was no paper mill and no railway; when the land along the River was thick with sixty-foot pine trees. He told them about Hodges Hill and the pearls that guarded the interior and about the Mi'kmaq people and the Beothuk. Ralph was used to his grandfather's stories, but to Richard, another world was coming to life.

Richard couldn't hold in his curiosity any longer. "Excuse me Mr. Drum, but if you don't mind, I would like to know why you asked to speak with me. Ralph said that you think I have what he called the Blood. If that's so, how did I get it?"

The old man cackled. "Surprised, are you? Many Newfoundland people carry the Blood. It came to you through your mother, my son. She, who is long dead, left you a legacy."

At the thought of his poor mother, emotion welled up inside Richard. Good God! How did this old man know about his biological mother?

"Her people came from the bottom of Trinity Bay. Yes?"

"Uh . . . yes sir, I think they were from somewhere around Blaketown."

"Just so, my son. Beothuk land until the white man took it from them."

Then old man Drum said, "Ralph, my boy, I never told you this before, so now I'll tell you and this young man together so both of you can carry it into the future. White men think the Beothuk race was wiped out. They weren't. They removed themselves to another time."

Ralph frowned. What was Grandfather trying to say?

"After they put the railway through, fellas told stories of trains appearing and disappearing, their lights cutting through the night. After it happened many times, they came to be called ghost trains." The old man lay back against the pillows and closed his eyes.

Ralph said, "Yes, Grandfather, I have heard stories about the ghost trains, on the Gaff Topsails especially."

Richard was spellbound. *What a story,* he thought. He was sorry that his father was not there to hear it.

Grandfather opened his eyes again. "Gaff Topsails is a huge plateau where time is different – where the world thins out. Nothing that happens in time is ever lost. It still exists. The trains that men see are leaking through the thinness. When the Beothuk realized that they could no longer live in this place the white man wanted so badly, they gathered themselves together and went to the high plateau of the Gaff."

He looked at them with his bright black eyes. "Do you believe what I am telling you?"

Amazed, Richard and Ralph nodded in unison. Neither spoke.

"Up on the Gaff, they waited for the right moment, and then, the few that were left walked through the thinness into another time – perhaps back to a time when they were happy and prosperous on this island."

"My God, Grandfather," Ralph exclaimed. "How'd you know that?"

"So my father, Michael, said, and so his mother, the Beothuk woman, told him. She wanted to go too but he wouldn't let her." He closed his eyes again. "I am tired now. Let me shake your hand, young policeman from St. John's."

Richard held out his hand and Grandfather grasped it. "Time is like a river, my son. Long ago, the Beothuk couldn't stop it and you won't be able to either. Keep that in mind when your time arrives."

Richard was overwhelmed by his visit with the old Indian man. He truly didn't know what to make of it.

Ralph told Richard that the next time he was out for a visit he'd take him in to Hodges Hill or even up to the Gaff. Richard thanked him and said he'd look forward to that. He knew nothing about hiking or trekking in through rough country. He'd never been any farther west than Badger, so he'd never experienced the high plateau that they called the Topsails. Ralph said, "Don't worry, b'y, we'll make a woodsman out of you in no time." Richard wasn't sure if he should be apprehensive or not.

Ralph played the fiddle, as did Levi, so they sometimes got together at the Andersons', where Rod would join in with his harmonica. Alf Elliott would come by too with his accordion if he wasn't busy with his photography. It made for a pleasant way to pass the evening and, slowly, Levi and Richard became part of the fabric that wove the town of Badger together.

Richard liked to go into the American Bargain Store owned by the Plotskys, who knew the Wilanskys in St. John's and their famous store on Water Street. Richard asked Mr. Plotsky why he chose to run a business here in Badger, when he could be in St. John's. Leonard Plotsky replied that he'd been born in Badger; it was his home.

$\wp$

"Hey Dickie! Wake up." Bob Parsons plunked himself down in the seat beside him, laughing maniacally. He was waving a fistful of money. "Get a look at this, boy. Forty dollars! I whipped their asses. No one plays poker better than I do."

Richard peered down to the end of the coach. Several of the members were shaking their fists at Bob and yelling obscenities.

"Uh . . . what time is it?" It was still pitch-black outside the windows.

"'Tis about four in the morning. I don't know where we are. I think I'll have a nap too, now that I've got all their money." He tipped his cap down over his eyes.

Richard stared through the train window in the blackness of the night. After awhile his eyes got used to it and he could see a house here and there with the light on over the door. The train swept past a small station. He could barely make out the white painted sign. NORRIS ARM. Not long now, he thought. There was a thin light in the sky. Somewhere he'd read that it was called the false dawn. False. The word made him remember the most painful memory of all.

His mind went back to the day before his wedding. He had felt strongly that he should tell Audrey about his early life. It was always in the back of his mind, like a festering sore, never quite healing. She deserved to know the shame he felt, shame that no amount of love from the Abernathys could erase.

Audrey was a good woman. She had never pressed him for details of his adoption; she always called him Richard, even when Mama slipped. Yes, she deserved to know just who and what he was.

First he had taken her to Mundy Pond. The old house was still there. There were some miserable-looking kids scrabbling around the door. It could have been Richard and his brothers of twenty years ago. As he'd looked through the car window at the desolate scene, memories flooded through his mind. His throat was constricted with emotion and for a moment he couldn't speak. He coughed to clear the choking sensation from his throat.

"That house was my home until I was seven years old, Audrey. Perhaps when you hear what I'm going to tell you, you won't want to marry me. Well, here goes. Father wasn't much of a provider at the best of times. He worked at a meat shop downtown and drank most of his earnings. Our house in Mundy Pond was as poor as could be. Five of us kids slept in one bed by the stove with one scrawny blanket to cover us. The floor was just packed earth – no floorboards. My father never repaired the broken windows. They were stuffed with cardboard or rags to keep out the wind and rain.

We had an old stove that gave no heat, even if you were two feet away from it. There was no running water and no toilet."

Audrey sat there, staring at the house, saying nothing.

Richard continued doggedly. "I was born into this world with tuberculosis. Did you ever hear tell of that? Well, it's true. Congenital tuberculosis. My mother had it while she carried me and I got it through her blood. They say there were only three hundred cases worldwide and ten of them were in Newfoundland."

Audrey pulled her gaze from the house and looked at him with widened eyes. "You had TB?"

He nodded miserably. "I was told, years later, that immediately after my birth, Mother and I were taken to the Sanatorium. They separated us then. Infants had their own isolation unit. Mother wasn't allowed to see me or hold me or feed me for a year. I wonder about that now and then. Is that why my mother and I had no mother-son bond between us?"

Richard paused and looked out at the decrepit old house. "After I went with the Abernathys, I had to have a patch test every three months to check and see if the TB had come back. Then it was every six months. By the time I was fifteen, it was once a year. It never returned. I think that was due in part to my upbringing by the Abernathys. Good nourishing food, restful surroundings and a lot of love and care. I have been TB-free ever since I was released from the San at just a year old. I suppose those old cures really worked, or at least they did for the baby that I was."

He waited for Audrey to say something, but she was silent.

"My mother's stint in the San with me as an infant threw the rest of the family into disarray. My brothers were left with no mother and a father who couldn't look after them. The Children's Aid packed them off to Mount Cashel. When I was one year old, they discharged Mother and me as cured. We came home to Mundy Pond and my brothers were sent home from the orphanage. Mother still wasn't very strong. Certainly not strong enough to care for all of us. Father was never there for her. When he wasn't working, he was off some-where drunk. I don't know how my poor mother coped at that time."

Richard stopped talking and put his head down on the steering wheel of the car. He hadn't wanted Audrey to see his tears.

She gently touched his arm. "Richard, that's enough. Let's go."

He put the car in gear. "I want to take you somewhere else. I have to finish this story."

They'd driven across town to the Anglican Cemetery and walked to his mother's grave.

Standing in the graveyard, Richard continued his story. "One evening, when I was seven, Father didn't come home after work. That happened quite often. We had no coal for the stove. We were cold and had no fire to cook supper. Mother said she would go out to buy a bag of coal. I was bundled up in scarves and sweaters to go with her. She left the other boys at home huddled on the bed, trying to keep warm from their body heat.

"It seemed to me, with my seven-year-old legs, that we walked a long time before we came to the place where they sold the coal. I tried to take it from her and carry it, but I was only a slight little fella and I couldn't lift it. Mother hoisted it on her shoulder and, taking my hand, began to walk back home. It took us even longer this time because of the heavy sack. Mother had to stop every now and then and put it down on the sidewalk. I tried to get the attention of some passersby, but they only brushed me aside and ignored Mother.

"It was a cold and windy night and there were patches of ice around. My boots weren't very good and I kept slipping. We had to cross Campbell Avenue to get to Mundy Pond. I slipped and fell down right in the middle of the street. It was a busy street with cars coming down over the hill from Pennywell Road. Mother tried to haul me to the side of the road and carry her coal at the same time.

"This big black car came speeding down the hill like a monster from a nightmare. I screamed. Mother screamed. But there was no time. I watched my mother being tossed over the bonnet of the car as though she were a rag doll. It swerved, narrowly missing me. I crouched, frozen with terror, on the coal sack.

"Traffic came to a halt. There were sirens and whistles, police cars and an ambulance. I watched them load my mother on a stretcher and put her in the ambulance as I screamed for her not to leave me. A policeman hauled me up and asked me to show him where I lived. I was confused but managed to say Mundy Pond. I knew that. He took me over there and I pointed out the house.

"We went in. Father still wasn't there. My brothers were curled up together on the cold bed. I jumped up and curled with them, trembling and crying, seeking comfort from them. The policeman told them that their mother was in an accident. I remember how scared we were, huddled together, trying to be brave.

"The police sent in the welfare officers and they took us off to foster homes. I suppose they found Father in some beer parlour and told him, but I never knew. I never saw him again. They took Mother to St. Clare's Hospital. Her spine was broken, they said.

"My brothers were scattered here and there. No Mount Cashel for them this time. A couple of them were adopted on the mainland and I never saw them again. I was put with a real fine couple – the Abernathys – who gave me good warm clothes, a nice clean bed and lots of good, wholesome food. It was like heaven to me.

"I never went back to Mundy Pond again. I saw my mother a few years later. Father was dead by that time. Poor Mother. She was crippled and pitiful. Such a hard life. They put her in a boarding home on Brazil Square, and there she lived out her last few years."

When Richard had finished his tale, he'd felt empty and light, light enough to float up over the cemetery and out over Quidi Vidi. All his worry and anguish was laid before Audrey to accept or not accept.

Sensible, wonderful Audrey had taken his arm. "Come on, Richard. We have a wedding to plan."

⌀

The police special stopped at daylight. The contingent of Constabulary officers disembarked into the cold sulphur-tainted air of Grand Falls, so different from that of St. John's with its fog and drizzle. The RCMP were there to usher them to buses before news of their arrival would spread.

The Grand Falls Armoury was cold, echoing, and devoid of comfort. Richard was physically sick with dread. He frequently had to visit the armoury washroom. Sometime during that day the thought came to him that the old Mi'kmaq man really might have been able to foretell the future and this is what he'd meant by not being able to stop time. Maybe he'd foreseen that Richard would soon be caught up in something over which he had no control. From the moment the Constabulary group had been called together in St. John's, Richard had felt that he was rolling along on a river of time and going so fast that there was no stopping it.

The constables stayed most of the day at the armoury, eventually being billeted out. Patrols were organized, and the Newfoundland Constabulary officers were dispatched to Badger where Constable Richard Fagan's wife had grown up, where his in-laws lived, where he had made a few friends, and where none of them knew that he was there. He was afraid that he'd meet Rod or Ralph, Alf or the Hatchers. What would they say to each other? Pulling his cap firmly down to his eyebrows and turning up his collar, he prayed no one would recognize him.

$$\wp$$

When Joey Smallwood decertified the loggers' union in early March, the strikers felt that the tide of opinion had truly turned against them. During the last two weeks of February, Joey had been on the radio almost every day. People began to believe him when he accused the IWA of being communists and white slave traders. Only the loggers, the strikers, knew the truth.

On instructions from Landon Ladd and his executive, the call went out to men from the west coast and to every bay in Newfoundland, to come to Badger to support the cause. This kept Ralph pretty busy. Somehow, he had become the accommodations man. The union rented another vacant house for the men to stay in, but it still wasn't enough. Many of the Badger loggers let the out-of-towners sleep on their floors, wrapped in quilts.

Jennie and Tom were always together as they worked for the union's cause. Jennie was a superb organizer. Just the sight of her lugging a ten-gallon pot of steaming hot soup out to the picket line, followed by other women with ladles, bowls, buns and tea, was for Ralph a wonderful sight.

He sometimes went all day without thinking of her. Then, they'd meet somewhere. On the picket line or in someone's house. He'd look furtively at her rosy cheeks, her bright hair, her robust frame, and his heart would jump in his chest as it had done for twenty years.

Two days after Smallwood decertified the IWA, Ralph went over to meet the train. Fifty men were coming in from Trinity Bay. It took him until daylight to get them all bedded down. This brought the union supporters up to three hundred. The streets of Badger were crawling with men, who stood in clusters around the fire barrels, smoking, talking and watching for scabs. Landon Ladd had ordered no violence. They obeyed him, but it was hard. They were all discouraged and disheartened.

Once again, late in the night, Bill Hatcher snuck over to Rod Anderson's house after the police had gone back to their barracks in Grand Falls. Perhaps they'd been afraid to spend a night in Badger. Bill was a bundle of nerves and there was sweat on his forehead. Rod could see that this strike was getting to be too much for his friend, as it was for many others as well. His hand was shaking as he drank the drop of rum that Rod poured for him.

"Rod b'y, I think tomorrow is going to be the big day."

"How do you mean?"

"Can't say too much, you know." Bill held out his glass for another tot.

"There's a lot of talk going on. We're coming out in force, that's all I can tell you. And that goddamn Joey Smallwood will be sorry for the day he sent in the Constabulary. We'll show them that the loggers ain't afraid. Men are saying that perhaps we'll spill a drop of blood while we're at it. That'll drive the sonsabitches back to St. John's."

"Christ, Bill, them's hard words, b'y. You should watch what you're saying. Don't go gettin' yourself in trouble." Rod thought of Bill's wife and family. He thought about other strikers who had families depending on them. What was happening to everyone?

"Rod, Rod. Listen." Bill gulped his tot of rum. "'Tis not only me that's saying it, b'y. Others are saying it too. The men have been gathering all day. Most of them are at the end of their rope. We got nothin' left to lose now. A few of them have had a drop to drink and there's bragging going on about killing a fuckin' policeman."

"Bill, 'tis late. Go on home. Don't go back down with those guys tonight. Whatever comes tomorrow . . . well, whatever comes, comes. Just don't get yourself hurt."

After Bill left, Rod locked his door and lay down on the daybed, where he tossed and turned all night. It was most likely only bragging from the guys who were drinking. How in the name of God could a bunch of loggers, with no weapons, hope to kill a policeman? Foolishness, he decided. But still he couldn't sleep.

24

On the tenth of March, the principal of the amalgamated school, Mr. Summers, told the students that there would be no classes in the afternoon. He said that all of the children should be at home where they would be safe. There was a lot of violence in the air and children shouldn't be exposed to it.

The Protestant girls walked across the back road and through the fence by the Catholic School, which had already been closed the week before. Everyone was on their way home with their school books, but few had any intention of staying home. There was too much going on for that. Along the way, the girls met other youngsters, including Amanda Elliott's brother, David, his friend Harold, and Madeline's brother, Bernie. The boys were excited. They'd heard a rumour that there would be a load of scabs going through to Millertown and the strikers were going to block the road. Bernie said that he'd heard the police were going to break it up, and a bunch of the boys were heading up the road to watch.

When Amanda walked into the house, her mother was feeding her baby brother, Alvin.

"Hi Mom."

"Amanda, you're home early. Where are your brothers?" her mother asked anxiously.

"Mr. Summers closed the school and told us to go home and stay home. He told us that it's dangerous out on the streets right now, but we all think he's being a fuddy-duddy. David and Thomas are gone up the road with some other boys. You know what they're like; if there's anything going on with the picket lines, they want to be there."

"Oh dear." Her mother spooned more food into the baby's mouth and deftly swiped the spoon across his chin to pick up the excess. "Your father was home for his dinner and he said to make sure that the boys stayed in the house when they came home after school. All morning there's been policemen walking up and down the street. Perhaps you should go and find them and tell them they have to come home."

Amanda told her mom not to worry. Nothing was going to happen in little old Badger. Hadn't they lived there all their lives? Amanda, a sensitive child, felt that their bodies and souls were in tune with the rhythms of the rivers, the deep vastness of the forests. Nothing could ever happen to change them. Her mom, busy with running a household, caring for a young baby, didn't have time to think about rivers and forests. All she wanted was for her children to be safe.

Amanda grabbed an apple from the bowl on the table and went outside. Madeline Sullivan was just coming out of her gate. "Come on, Amanda," she called. "Let's go. Everyone is heading up by the Pentecostal Church. There's supposed to be something happening up there."

Together the two girls went across to Church Road. There they saw dozens of people, young and old – loggers, women, children – heading toward the junction of Church Road and the Buchans Highway. There were police wagons parked off to the side and many police standing around. They didn't attempt to stop the curious residents as they streamed past and up toward the intersection.

Amanda and Madeline joined with the crowd and climbed up on the snowbanks to get a good view. Danger was the last thing on their minds. It would be many years before they would understand things like greedy foreign pulp and paper companies, corrupt governments, international trade unions, and mob violence that could quickly spiral out of control.

Nine-year-old Melanie Crawford knew that all was not as it should be in Badger. There was something going on with the adults, but she wasn't sure what. Her mom and dad, usually happy with each other, now raised their voices and argued.

Melanie was in grade four at the Catholic School, where her father, Vern Crawford, had gone before her. Her life centred around herself and her friends – whether or not to wear her hair in braids, like her mom wanted, or wear it down straight; how many dolls she owned and would she get more; but most of all the little dog that she'd received for her birthday.

For as long as she could remember, her dad had driven the town taxi. Sometimes he'd take his wife and little daughter to Windsor and Grand Falls to go shopping. They always went to the Cozy Chat Café and had a lunch. Chips and a hamburger with a Coke was a big treat.

Mostly, though, her dad was away. He spent long hours in his taxi. Melanie's mom said he was making money for them to have a nice house and good food. When he came home, the house was full of fun and laughter. He always brought her something, a special surprise, like the time he made a trip into St. John's. He was gone almost three days, and when he came back he brought Melanie a real doll's carriage with a baby doll in it, complete with her own nursing bottle. Dad also brought her mom a new red sweater.

Her little brown dog, Cocoa, had been a present from her dad for her ninth birthday. He said he got it from a man in Baie Verte. Melanie wasn't sure where that was – not for certain. In grade four, the Sister was getting them to draw a map of Newfoundland and put places on it. So far, they had marked Badger, Grand Falls, Corner Brook and St. John's – little red circles that they drew with their coloured pencils. The Exploits River they drew in blue from almost the middle of the map to the sea, which was coloured blue as well.

Melanie's school was closed, but the amalgamated school let out at lunchtime on March 10 and Melanie was there waiting for her friend Jean, who had a blue wooden slide. Melanie loved it. She still had to make do with her old coaster that she'd had for three years, though she was sure that her dad would eventually come home with a new one, when he got time. The small hill behind the school, snow-covered and smoothed by countless coasters, slides, toboggans and pieces of canvas, beckoned to the two little girls.

Melanie forgot all about lunch, forgot all about her mom in her eagerness to go sliding.

The afternoon passed quickly. Bump, bump, bump down the little hill, along by the side of the school, and then across the road to the fences. Some of the older children went up on the big hill, coasted down onto the little hill, over it, and down across the road. But you had to be good to do that, and in at least grade seven or eight.

Gradually, the rest of the children drifted off home, Melanie's friend Jean going with them. Melanie's new pink wristwatch – Dad had got it over in Corner Brook – said four o'clock. In another hour it would be getting dark. The little girl realized it was time for her to go home too.

Born and raised in the small Newfoundland town, allowed to roam freely since she was five, Melanie had no qualms about walking down School Road, across Church Road, over the railway tracks and onward to her house near the high road bridge. She'd walked home from school almost every day since grade one. All of the children walked. There was no bus and few cars. Walking was a way of life.

Melanie took her time. She was thirsty, so as she meandered along she patiently chewed off the little snowballs that were stuck to her green woollen mitts. So absorbed was she in this exercise that she didn't hear the loud shouts up ahead of her.

At the intersection of School Road and Church Road she saw many people hurrying along. She wondered briefly what they were doing, but grown-up things didn't really interest her. She kept to the side of the road and continued until she reached the town hall.

The crowd was thicker there, and she saw many policemen. No one was paying any attention to her. Men were shouting. They even had sticks. The police had sticks too. Melanie stopped near the town hall, uncertain where to go. For the first time, a small curl of fear started to form in the bottom of her belly.

It was then that she saw Dad's taxi. "Dad!" she shouted. "Dad, wait for me!"

But her dad didn't hear her. He was driving up the street and he was surrounded by the men with sticks. The police were pushing them back so her dad could get through.

Melanie ran after him. She had to catch Dad. Among the crowd there were women and other children, but Melanie was blind to them. She had to get to her dad. When he knew she was there, he'd take her in his car. She'd be safe then. Perhaps he'd have a chocolate bar. She sure was hungry.

On she went, as fast as her little legs could go, dodging between the legs of the grown-ups, looking neither left or right, focusing on Dad's tail lights. The lights disappeared, blotted out by the bodies of the crowd around her. Still she pressed on until she came to the place where many policemen stood, wearing long black coats. Melanie saw some boys – that nice boy, David Elliott, among them – skirt around the police and climb the snowbank on the side of the road. She followed them.

Small and nimble, she made good progress along the top of the bank. The view was better too; there were no adults blocking her. She saw Dad's taxi – finally. He was stopped and many men were gathered around his car.

Melanie didn't stop to consider if something might be wrong. She was just nine years old. She merely wanted to get to Dad's taxi, get in with him, and check the glove compartment to see if he had a chocolate bar.

ɶ

For a scab-runner like Vern Crawford, getting around Badger during the strike wasn't an easy matter. The centre of town, near the railway station, the area around Plotsky's Store, Coleman's, and the post office looked like a war zone: overturned cars, a bus on its side, and fire barrels with loggers clustered around them for warmth. Media people were everywhere, searching for the big story that their instinct told them was to be found here: the *Evening Telegram*, the *Daily News*; even, someone said, a reporter down from the mainland; the *Toronto Star*. Picketers patrolled the streets, some of them armed with birch sticks. Police patrolled too, always in twos, never alone.

On this day Vern had more scabs to deliver to Millertown. Scabs were getting scarce by this time. Because they weren't regular loggers, they didn't last long up in the camps. After two or three weeks, they'd quit and scravel off home. The recruiter from the Company told Vern to scout down around Windsor and see if he could pick up a few guys who were doing nothing. Well, that trip got one, the guy in the front seat. The two men in back were hitchhikers that Vern picked up as he was coming back from Windsor. They stuck out their thumbs and Vern had them. Trying to get home to Springdale, they said. *To hell with that,* thought Vern. *They're coming with me. Three men – thirty dollars.*

He was confident that he'd have no problems getting to Millertown. Then he crossed the main railway crossing in the centre of Badger and noticed more strikers and police. *What's on the go?* he wondered to himself, not wanting to say it out loud and upset his skittish scabs. *It'll take me some spell to drive from the tracks up Church Road and onto Buchans Road. I knew I should've waited until later. Perhaps I might have attempted the railway tracks again. Too eager. Too eager. Millie says that I'm always letting the almighty dollar rule me.*

The local loggers recognized Vern. They knew what he was doing. Swearing and shoving, they tried to block the taxi, but the Mounties formed a cordon and stopped them. The crowd closed in behind the car as it inched along. At this point there was no turning back.

Cursing, Vern gritted his teeth and lit up another Camel. *Goddamn smoking is going to kill me,* he thought. *And I have the piles too. They say it's a taxi driver's complaint, from sitting too much. I think I got them from sitting in the snow up in Millertown, loaded drunk and laughing my fool head off at the boys and the moose. My sore arse feels like I'm sittin' on a bunch of hot grapes. All Millie had in the house to smear on them was Vaseline. I used it; put a big dollop on me tender rectum, but all that done was leave a big round grease spot on the seat of my pants. Well, to hell with it. You can't have all sunshine and roses. But right now – right now – I'm in enough misery with my sore arse to take on the whole fuckin' IWA. Let the Mounties look after the fellas trying to kill me. By the Christ, they can't stop Vern Crawford. I'm going to get to Millertown.*

He released the clutch and continued on up Church Road past the United Church, past the Roman Catholic Church, past McDonald's Uptown Store, past houses of people he had known all of his life.

The inside of the taxi was smoky and stank of sweat, the kind that men sweat when they're scared. Vern had smelled it before. It smelled acidic and metallic at the same time. Sharp to the nose.

I'm afraid to slacken the window, he thought as he inched along. *Someone might try to poke me eye out with a stick or something.* Just up ahead, he could see a cluster of loggers. *Jesus. The goddamn picket line must be two hundred strong! They knowed I was comin'. Someone ratted on me. My God, there are spies everywhere these days.*

He stopped the taxi at the junction of Church Road and the Buchans Highway. On his right was the Full Gospel Tabernacle Church; on the left, homes and gardens. The snowbanks were high, crowded with women and children. He couldn't go ahead and he couldn't go back. What to do?

He spied Jennie Hillier out in front of them all. There she stood, legs apart, hands on her hips, big bosom thrust forward. *Holy fuck. That woman!* he thought. *What an armful! She must be nearly six foot. I dare say I'd have married her if she hadn't walloped me so hard that time when I told her to go on a diet. What man wants a woman who can beat him up?*

"Get the hell off the road, Vern!" He heard Jennie screech so loud that he could hear her over the roar of the crowd, even with the car windows rolled up.

The angry loggers surrounded the Chrysler with its cargo of scabs. Ralph Drum was out in front of the picket line blocking Vern's way. He rapped on the window. Vern screwed it down an inch or two. "Well you son of a bitch. What did I tell you about running scabs? I told you that you'd be the sorriest bastard that ever walked." Ralph's face had that fierce look that he had used on him before. *Frightens the shit out of me every time I see it,* Vern thought.

At a nod from Ralph, the loggers began pounding on the bonnet of the taxi with their sticks. *The sonsabitches have cracked the bloody windshield! That's the second windshield this month.* One of the guys in the back seat moaned that he wanted to throw up. Another prayed to God to get him safely back to his wife and kids. He promised God that he'd never leave them again. Buddy in the front seat was holding his crotch and whined that he shouldn't have drank them beers 'cause now he was sure he was gonna piss hisself.

Vern had almost decided to go for broke – put her in gear and crash through the picketers – when twenty big, furious men, Tom Hillier among them, physically grabbed the car. They all reached down and took hold of the undercarriage. Vern's mind and his car were caught in slow motion. *They got her off the ground! Bloody bastards! They'll ruin my car! Oh Christ Almighty!*

Up, up, and around. For a few seconds the car was airborne. Then it dropped on its four wheels. Something cracked. *Goddamn it!* Vern's mind screamed. *That probably broke the shock plates!* Muffler and exhaust pipe clunked against the road. Shocks and springs complained loudly. The undercarriage squeaked and trembled. A tire went flat, inner tube and all, with a loud bang.

Vern clutched the steering wheel so hard that he felt his knuckles crack. Buddy banged his head on the dash and the smell of his hot urine mixed with the already pungent air of stress and sweat inside the car. The guy in the back puked. The sour smell of his vomit added to the other odours. The third man was silent. Perhaps he had fainted.

Vern's abused, darling Chrysler was now facing away from the Buchans Highway and the route to Millertown. As he looked back down Church Road he could see black-coated Constabulary officers marching up toward him and the loggers.

Ralph Drum rapped on the window again. They used to be friends before this strike. They'd go rabbit catching and canoeing together. *Perhaps we will again, if this is ever over,* thought Vern. But right now he couldn't imagine setting another rabbit snare with Ralph, or with anyone else, for that matter.

"Had enough, Vern? If you haven't, we can demolish the god-damn car." Ralph's fierce eyes glared over the top of the window. The picketers crowded around the car, their sticks raised to wallop it again.

Vern was frantic. If he lost his taxi, he might well end up back in the lumberwoods, his worst nightmare. He had to escape.

"Christ Almighty, Ralph, I think buddy in the back there is having a heart attack or something. Listen to him moaning. Goddammit, Ralph, I promise never to run another scab if you let me go."

Ralph looked at the frightened men in the car. "All right, you cowardly weasel, go on. Take the side road; there's no one over there to stop you. I'm saving your scrawny neck, but you don't deserve it."

Ralph's attention turned and focused on the marching police column that was almost upon them. Vern saw the men lining up across the road, sticks at the ready. He seized the opportunity and put the gas to the floor. The Chrysler, his faithful, crippled darling, skidded on three wheels onto the side road heading toward the Exploits River and the big hill. It would take him down to the A.N.D. Company property. Like a stream of urine, his taxi left behind a trail of gasoline leaking from a hole in her gas tank.

The scabs were in shock. The guy who was saying his prayers muttered that no job was worth this. Buddy who was full of stinky piss said he wished he'd stayed home with his stepmudder, bad as she was. The poor devil in the back who threw up was moaning. Perhaps he really was having a heart attack.

As for Vern, he didn't care. He just wanted them out of his car.

It would take a month to get rid of the stink of piss and vomit. Perhaps she was done for; perhaps there was too much damage to the undercarriage.

He met no one on his way down to the A.N.D. Company office. The big action was going on up by the church. Vern hustled the men out.

The vomit fellow whined, "You can't leave us here like this. The strikers will kill us before daylight."

Vern answered, "I don't care what happens to you. Just fuck off." He left them on the step shaking in their boots, hanging onto each other for support, wondering where to hide.

The Chrysler limped home. Vern's house was empty. He figured Millie was up there on the snowbanks with the rest of Badger. Where was Melanie? Was she up there too? He knew things were getting pretty ugly up there. Who would know better than he would? Hadn't he just left it?

The thought of his little nine-year-old daughter in the midst of a riot galvanized Vern into action. He had to go back up there. *I'll walk up the back way,* he thought. *I'll make it look like I am just another bystander.*

His abused Chrysler was in the driveway. As Vern passed her on his way to find his precious daughter and his wife, the car seemed to moan at him. Vern felt like moaning too. It had been one bitch of a day.

25

On this day Pastor Damian Genge's mind wasn't on his usual preoccupation – a rich congregation posting in his home city – as he peeked from the corner of his church window that overlooked the intersection of Church Road and the Buchans Highway.

He smoothed back his glossy black hair with shaky fingers. He was terrified. Nothing in his life had prepared him for this. Even though he felt that he had a calling, he also thought that he had certain other characteristics that helped him preach the Good Word. He often practiced in front of the mirror, flashing his even white teeth and using his intense brown eyes to appear to be looking deeply into a person's soul. He knew he was good at making the glorious prayer words undulate off his tongue like sonorous drum rolls. Sometimes he knew how an actor must feel, as he watched people respond to what he considered his magnetism.

Badger was his trial-by-fire posting, but he'd never expected there to be this much fire in his life.

Below the window of his church were more than two hundred men – loggers, in brigs and logans, rough woollen sweaters and stocking caps – all caught up in the violently escalating hysteria that had gripped them and the townspeople alike.

Many of them were his parishioners. His eyes picked them out as he scanned the scene below. There was Jennie Hillier on the snowbank, screaming and shaking her fist. Bright red hair, tall, handsome and outspoken, the woman was foremost in everything.

At prayer meetings, she was the first to stand up and proclaim her faith in God. She had put herself in charge of the Women's Mission, collecting and rolling pennies from the other ladies and directing the proceeds overseas to missionaries in Africa. She was also the only woman on the community council. Pastor Damian hadn't been a bit surprised when he heard she was running the women's side of the picket lines. In his mind, Jennie was capable of whatever she took on. There was something about her that intrigued him. But then, he'd always felt a bond with strong women – the slight masculinity in them, he supposed, made them safe to be with because they didn't expect anything from him, things he wasn't able to give.

Only about one third of the men gathered at the crossroads that evening were actual Badger residents. The town was overflowing with strangers from places like Bonne Bay, Lewisporte, Seal Cove, Springdale and Roberts Arm, places Damian had heard of but never visited. But evangelical arms reached long into outport Newfoundland and he had seen some of the strangers at his Sunday services. These men brought their beliefs with them as they rallied to support the loggers' union.

Standing at the front of the men was Jennie's husband, Big Tom Hillier, stick in hand. The Mi'kmaq man, Ralph Drum, and his brothers and cousins stood beside him. Several other Badger men clustered around them.

Damian thought about how the men had asked him if they could stow their birch billets in the church porch. Confronted in the middle of the night by determined brawny loggers, he never even considered saying no. The slim birch sticks, all of them exactly eighteen inches long, were specially cut by the strikers to defend themselves should the need arise. And now it seemed the need to use them *had* arisen.

Something was astir. A beige taxi came slowly up the road and was stopped by the picketers. Damian could see Vern Crawford at the wheel. The pastor wasn't well-acquainted with Vern, a Catholic, but he'd heard rumours that Vern moved scabs around in his scruffy-looking car.

The strikers were attacking the vehicle! Damian cried out, his eyes fixed on the scene below. *Blessed Jesus, have mercy.* He began to pray. The men lifted the car and turned it around! He could see the scared white faces of the men inside. On the outside were the determined, set faces of the loggers as they battered the windshield of the car with their sticks and fists.

Oh my Lord, no, no . . . how has this come to pass?

Ralph Drum, near the front of the group, seemed to have his attention diverted from the taxi by something that was happening back down Church Road. Damian watched as Vern seized his chance and slithered away on the side road toward the River.

The strikers formed a solid line across the road, their billets at the ready. Pressing his face against the glass and looking to the left, Pastor Genge could see down Church Road. Black-coated police were marching toward the picket line.

As he gazed down at the scene below, Damian wondered if God was looking through his eyes. Had God created mankind to hate each other in this way? Whose side was God taking in a time when everyone was taking sides? Or did God allow man leeway to chose? Was there a lesson here for him to learn? He prayed fervently for guidance, for his own safety and for the safety of his flock.

⚲

Cecil Nippard huddled deep into the collar of his jacket as he stood on the steps of the A.N.D. Company office. He was shivering, partly with fright and partly because of the stain down the front of his brigs. He was glad that the sun had gone down. In the darkness no one would see that he had wet his pants.

All he could think about was how sorry he was to have gotten involved with that bastard of a taxi driver, Vern Crawford. A few hours ago he'd been standing outside the pool hall in Windsor. He had just played and won two games of pool. No one could beat Cecil at pool. The prize was two bottles of homebrew. Cecil, not used to drinking, had downed them too fast. Now he felt somewhat dizzy.

His father had been on the IWA picket line in Peterview for the past two weeks, him and his sister Emily left with their stepmother and her brood of five kids that she'd had for his father. Their stepmother was particularly bad when Father was away, and beat him and Emily with the broom as often as she could.

As he had rounded the corner of the Brown Derby Café, a taxi had cruised by and stopped by the curb. A guy rolled down the window and asked Cecil if he was interested in going up to work on the Millertown Dam. Because he was cold and broke and didn't want to face the old stepmother, he opened the front door to the cab and hopped in.

The man sitting in the driver's seat was talking fast, and Cecil, who wasn't real good at words and speech, had to struggle to keep up with him. The man didn't seem to notice, or even care. His name was Vern. He fired questions at Cecil. "You ever work in the woods?"

"Yes, sir." Cecil watched furtively as the taxi driver lit up a cigarette. He wanted to ask him could he have one too.

"When was that?"

"Last year."

"How old are you?"

"Seventeen."

"That's old enough I s'pose."

"I worked as a scab too." Cecil thought he should tell Vern that he had work experience in that field as well.

"What? Jesus Christ!" Vern's taxi swerved as he swivelled his head to look at Cecil. "How did a young fella like you get to be a scab?"

"Uh . . . uh . . . I dunno. Just happened. We went to Badger and went up in a camp. We wudn't there no more than a couple weeks and real loggers came and drove us out in the snow."

"Go on, b'y! So you must've been part of that crowd that was in Anderson's camp when they beat it up. Did you get a good fright? Where'd you run? Who picked you up?"

Cecil hadn't been able to keep track of the questions that had come out of Vern's mouth like machine-gun fire. He was sorry he'd mentioned it. He shrunk his head down into the collar of his jacket again as if by doing so he would become invisible to the world.

As they'd approached the Oasis Tavern, halfway between Windsor and Badger, they saw two fellows standing on the side of the road with their thumbs out. Vern muttered, "Poor bastards out in the cold, they looks like they needs a job too."

He put on the brakes and rolled down the window. "Need a ride, boys?"

"We're hitchhiking to Springdale and we don't have any money," one of them said, as he eyed the taxi sign on the roof of Vern's car.

"That's all right, boys, jump aboard. 'Tis too cold to be out on the side of the road, and you mightn't see anyone else for hours."

That was all the men needed to hear; they scravelled into the back seat.

As the beige Chrysler hurled up over the road to Badger, Vern had kept up a constant stream of chatter. Approaching an intersection, he slowed down and turned left into the town. One of the men in the back piped up, "Excuse me, buddy, we're going to Springdale, so if you could take us up onto the Halls Bay Road, we'll see if we can't pick up a ride there."

"Now boys, listen here. I got a proposition for ya. How would you like to go back to Springdale, or wherever it is you comes from, with a few dollars in your pocket? Wouldn't it be grand to go home and show your women a bit of cash for a change? Well I knows a way you can do it and it don't take nothing at all."

By this time the car had moved over the railway tracks and into the centre of Badger, where the evidence of the now-famous loggers' strike was in plain view. The men in the back nervously eyed a number of overturned cars with the windows beaten out of them.

"Now listen here, old man," one of them said, "we don't know what you have in mind, but we knows what is going on up here in Badger and we wants no part of it. Sure look out the windows. It looks like a war happened here, b'y. Stop the car and let us out."

Cecil also looked out through the window of the taxi. The beer he'd drunk an hour earlier had filled his bladder and was making him squirm in his seat. Seeing the overturned cars and the fire barrels had started him feeling scared again, remembering his last trip to Badger.

"Go on with ya. There's nothing to this. You just sit back now and watch me. I'll have you up in Millertown in no time." Vern manoeuvred around the corner onto Church Road.

Even Cecil had seen there was no way the taxi was getting up to Millertown. The street was lined with police and loggers. Some of them had recognized Vern's taxi and were yelling and cursing at him, as Cecil and the two men in the back tried to hide their faces.

It had taken a while, but with the help of the police, Vern had made it up the street to where the road turned toward Buchans and Millertown. Then things had deteriorated pretty fast. Their way was barred by about two hundred men.

Cecil thought he'd never seen so much anger, not even in his stepmother when she beat him. When he got older and bigger, she'd had to pass that job over to his father and his thick leather belt. The men pounded on the bonnet and the windshield of Vern's taxi with their sticks. Then a ring had formed around the car, and bodies had pressed in close to the windows. Before Cecil could figure out what they were doing, they lifted the car off the road.

It had been too much for the young man. His full bladder let go – piss or urine, call it what you want. When the car banged down on the road, he couldn't take any more. He felt the dreadful wet warmth as it spread out from his crotch and down one of his legs. Through the curtain of his misery, terror and shame, Cecil could smell vomit. It wasn't his, thank God, so that meant that one of the guys in back had thrown up. *Vomit's worse than piss, isn't it?* He felt a bit better to know someone was suffering worse than him.

Vern had been screaming at them all. "You dirty bastards! Not fit to get in a car. Friggin' animals are cleaner than you fellas."

Cecil, overwhelmed with the noise and confusion, never knew

how it happened, but somehow Vern had managed to escape. The men in the back seat said afterward that the taxi driver was as lucky as a shithouse rat.

But Cecil and the two men hadn't been so lucky. Vern put them out on the A.N.D. Company office steps. They'd cried that he couldn't leave them, certain they'd be killed before daylight. Vern had said that he didn't give a fuck what happened to them – just get the hell out of the car. All three had tumbled out and the taxi roared off on three wheels into the night.

Cecil was shaking, too scared to know what to do. One man tried the A.N.D. Company office door. "Son of a bitch is locked up tighter than a virgin's hole," he said. "We're leavin', buddy. What you gonna do?" Cecil couldn't answer; his thoughts jumbled around inside his head and his speech deserted him.

The Springdale men disappeared over among the A.N.D. Company warehouses and sheds. Cecil was left all alone.

He thought of the bad luck that had dogged him from the day that his mother had died. He thought that if life was no better than this, it was best to die or be killed and have it over with. He wanted to cry, but his stepmother always told him that only sissies cried.

He was jarred out of his jumbled thoughts by the presence of a woman. It was dark, about six or seven o'clock.

"Cecil? Is that you, my son? Where'd you come from?"

"Missus Annie," he sobbed, and he couldn't say any more. He wondered if God had sent her.

She took him by the arm and led him over the road to her house. His pissy brigs were stiff with the cold. They chafed his private parts as he stumbled along behind her.

Her kitchen was like a warm womb, and smelled of baking bread. Poor Cecil was shivering with cold and delayed shock. He clung to the woman's arm like a small child. Missus Annie knew what needed to be done. She'd dealt with this young man before and she knew he couldn't handle a lot of words at once. She handed him a pair of knitted underdrawers and a pair of worsted brigs and motioned to the back room. Cecil shambled inside.

He changed as fast as his shaking hands would allow. Forgetting his heap of soiled clothes on the floor, he went back out to the kitchen. That was another of Cecil's problems: he often forgot things in the moment, but could recite dates and happenings from years and years ago.

Missus Annie had a lunch on the table for him: tea, fresh bread and butter, some cold meat. Bear meat, she said, as she sat opposite him and watched him eat ravenously.

"Are you a logger with the union, Cecil?"

"No, missus."

"So you're one of the other crowd then, what they calls scabs."

Cecil concentrated on his steaming teacup, unable to look at Missus Annie's eyes. He felt even more ashamed of himself than when he'd been pissing in his pants. Since his mother died, no woman had cared for him as this Mi'kmaq woman had. Cecil wished she was his mother, wished that he belonged to the close-knit Mi'kmaq community.

The door burst open. "Ma, ma, you'll never believe what's happened!" It was one of the Drum men. He saw Cecil and stopped. "Who the fuck are you?"

His mother shook her head and pulled her son into the other room, leaving Cecil alone to chew on his bear meat. Not that he had much appetite. He figured her son was a striker. *Just wait until she tells him about me. I'm dead now, for sure.*

The time when he was with Missus Annie for the infection in his leg, someone had told Cecil that she had twenty-two children. They said she had ten sons, but Cecil never learned their names and he didn't know this one. After a few minutes, this son and Missus Annie came back to the kitchen. She laid her hand on Cecil's shoulder. "My son thinks it would be best if he took you over to the railway station now," she said. "You might hitch a ride on a freight train. You can hide under the station stand until one comes along."

Cecil thanked Missus Annie. He wanted to hug her, but couldn't get up the nerve to do so. In his mind she was the mother he'd lost, and he loved her. As he walked out to the road with her son, he could see her standing in the door, the lamplight silhouetting her short, round, motherly frame.

It was late, nine o'clock. By this time Badger was swarming with Mounties and Constabulary officers as they searched out fugitive strikers. Cecil barely had the strength to walk over the road with Missus Annie's son. He was quaking with fear.

When they reached the railway station, Missus Drum's son held out his hand for Cecil to shake. Cecil was grateful for the handshake. No one had ever held out their hand to him before. When their hands parted there was a two-dollar bill left in his. It came to Cecil's mind that it might be the same two-dollar bill that he'd given Missus Annie back when she healed his leg. Before he could say anything, the Mi'kmaq turned and walked away. Cecil put the money down in the bottom of his boot. It was good money, enough to play pool for weeks.

The station platform was deserted. The nor'west wind was whipping down the tracks. It had been mild earlier, but the wind was up now. There was no freight train in sight. Cecil saw the dark hole under the station stand. He thought about it for a bit. He'd never liked dark places. They reminded him of his stepmother and the attic. But it was cold, and he was afraid that a cop or a logger might come by.

And it *was* dark. Cecil could hear breathing and snores and curses as he crawled in. Someone kicked him in the ribs – hard – when he almost knelt on him. After awhile, another body crawled in. Cecil kicked him as hard as he could, just because someone had kicked him.

He dozed off. Stepmother always said, "That stupid Cecil! He'd fall asleep in a snowbank." If she only knew how true that was, but Cecil wasn't about to let her or Father know about all this goings-on. All he wanted was to get through this night and see daylight.

Part III

THE RIOT

26

It's been four days since Ruth left to go in to St. John's. This hasn't been too bad, I think. Ruth has been looking after my comforts for almost twenty-five years. I miss her, but after all, I am a grown, independent man. I can do this.

There's nothing to keeping house; just wash a few dishes, maybe sweep up the floor. I can wash my own clothes when I get them dirty. The clothes that I have on I've only been wearing for five days, and there's hardly a peck on 'em. I think women washes clothes too much anyway. Something for them to do, I guess.

There's no point in me going upstairs to sleep in our bed. That would only dirty up the sheets unnecessarily. And yes, I have to admit, it would be too lonely in that bed without Ruth. I'll get that quilt again, and a pillow, and make up a bunk on the daybed by the kitchen stove. Ruth will never know. I'd have it all put away on the day she comes home.

I'll keep myself busy all day long. "A man's work is never done, though he toils from sun to sun." That was my father's favourite quote. There's some firewood to be sawed up, cleaved into junks and stacked in the woodshed. The felt on my roof has come loose on the corner. Won't be any good if Ruth comes home to a leaky roof! First thing she'll ask is what I've been doing all the while she was gone.

I get my ladder and climb up on the roof, nail the loose piece down with felt nails and smear some tar over it to keep the wet out. It's a mild day, the first mild day of the year. The sun has the power now, as my father used to say, and when it's shining down on the roof felt it is warm enough to spread a bit of tar. No good trying to spread tar in cold weather.

I wake up next morning to a cold kitchen. The damn oil stove is not lit anymore and the house is cold. It must have gone out several hours ago. The tank is full of oil, so there must be something in the line. This happens every now and then. I tinker with it, taking apart the oil line, spilling oil on the linoleum. I'll have to clean that up later. All of this, before I have my breakfast, only serves to make me cranky. I say a few choice swear words, guiltily enjoying the sound of them in my empty house. Sure enough, in the copper tubing I find a little piece of bark. "Blood of a bitch," I mutter to myself.

So I put the damn oil line back onto the damn stove, relight it and boil the kettle. Our icebox has eggs and bacon, but that's too much trouble. The frying pan is still in the sink anyway, dirty from yesterday. So I forage around in the cupboard and get a half dozen Purity Jam Jams and that, with tea, is breakfast. My hands stink of stove oil, but I am halfway through the tea and Jam Jams before I notice it. I glance at the calendar. It's Tuesday, March the tenth.

As I sit there in the quiet, sipping my tea, I miss Ruth even more. If she were here now she would be bustling about the kitchen, fussing over me, making sure I had enough to eat. But most of all I miss her next to me at night. I heave a big sigh, take my cup over to the sink and add it to the pile of dirty dishes. I'll get around to washing them sometime before she comes home.

As I go out the door, I remember that I never wiped up the stove oil that dripped out of the line. There's a puddle on the floor behind the stove. Well, I'm not going back now. Bad luck to do that; everyone knows that it's bad luck to go back in the house right after you leave.

I go down to the A.N.D. Company garage. It's a mild March morning. The sun is glinting off the snowbanks as I stroll down Church Road. It's a relatively short street compared to High Street in Grand Falls or Water Street in St. John's. It might be a mile long and is arrow-straight. Residents say it's built on an old Beothuk trail.

People who come here always comment on the big twenty- or thirty-foot trees that line it. These stately trees probably looked down on the Beothuk as they look down on the goings-on today. Along the sides of the road the houses are well-built; most have white picket fences. Also on the street are three fine solid churches, which give the road its name. The United Church is at the southeast end, the Roman Catholic in the middle, and the Pentecostal toward the northwest end.

As I walk down the road, over on the left-hand side I see a crowd of men over by Mrs. Noel's house. They seem to be just milling about, having a smoke. The IWA rented the house a few months ago for loggers to stay during the strike. They're all strangers to me, so I just keep on my way. A couple of police cars pass by slowly and, although I don't know them either, I put my hand up to them hoping I look friendly. They seem to be keeping an eye on the Noel house and ignore me as they go by.

First, I head over to the forge shed. I need to get the blacksmith to make runner chains for my tractor and extras to take up in the woods with us. I while away an hour or more chatting to Jack Travers, the blacksmith, and to a couple of other men that come by. When Jack goes for his lunch I bid him goodbye, telling him I need to head up to the garage to check on the tractors. Old Jack says, "Rod b'y, you are one busy man. No one can say that you won't be ready for the haul-off when it comes – if it comes."

I head out the door feeling pretty good about myself as I trot on over to the A.N.D. Company property. The boys are working away in the garage. They have the big garage door pulled up this morning to let in the fresh air and sunshine, and a couple of them are working on my tractor. Abe Miller, who manages transport for the Company, is there too, fixing the track on his Bombardier.

"Hey boys, how's it going?" I ask as I saunter up to them.

Abe turns his face away from his labours and looks up at me. "Hey there Rod, my son. Is there much on the go up your way this morning?" Abe lives in on Halls Bay Road.

"Yeah, I saw a lot of men up by the Noel house as I was walking down the road. Nice few police around too. Looks like more than yesterday. Maybe they sent out more from St. John's."

One of the mechanics speaks up. "That should never be happening. Dem police got no business out here in Badger. This little town is in some friggin' mess with all the goings-on here."

The men talk together for awhile. I've used this downtime to get some general maintenance done on the tractor, and the mechanics are doing a good job with it. A few days ago I gave the head mechanic a bottle of rum on the sly and asked him if he could put me up first. And that's what he did. They replaced the fuel pump and the engine sleeves. There were repairs as well, to the final drive. They even replaced the track pads. The old tractor will be ready to go whenever this strike is over.

I spend the better part of the afternoon there helping Abe and chatting with the boys.

Around three o'clock, a Mountie car pulls up and from out of the back swaggers the Company manager. He's flanked by two Mounties. He never goes anywhere these days without police protection.

"Time to finish up, men. We need you all to secure this place," says the manager. "We're securing all Company property. The situation in this town is a bit dangerous right now." I look at the faces of the two tall Mounties with him and they look pretty serious.

Without a word, the mechanics put away their tools, pull down the garage door, and the manager locks up. The mechanics walk on over to the A.N.D. Company staff house where they're staying. The Mounties and the manager climb back in the police car. Abe asks them if he can get a ride home to Halls Bay Road. They offer me a ride too, but I tell them I'll be fine. Don't worry, I like to walk. I put my hand up to them, then continue to head back up Church Road alone.

As I walk, I can see that there seems to be quite a lot more activity going on than there was this morning. There are dozens of people streaming past me – loggers, women and children. A man I don't know runs by me yelling, "Come on b'y, get a move on. We're going to block the road to Millertown."

I guess he thinks I'm one of the loggers.

I suppose I don't actually look much different from a logger or, I suppose, a striker now. I wear the same kind of clothes: rough pants, wool socks, logans. My sweater might be a bit better quality and my coat might be warmer, but not outstandingly so. I am a contractor, but you don't see me in a suit, white shirt and tie. No sir, not Rod Anderson. I've always been a part of the men who work for me.

$$\wp$$

It has been a restless day for me. As the priest of a busy parish, it's strange for me not to have administrative duties anymore. The school is closed, the nuns are gone.

In the morning, I walk around Badger, now a cheerless place, strangers everywhere, the mood dangerous and ugly. This usually quiet, snow-blanketed little town looks ill-used and invaded.

There's a big police presence, more than previously. It looks like their numbers have swelled overnight. Some of them nod to me or tip their cap. There is no attempt at conversation. The officers look uncomfortable and out of place. Government has plunked them down in a place that doesn't have any setup to house and feed them. They've had to bunk in Grand Falls, eighteen miles away over a slippery, snow-covered gravel road.

Joey Smallwood has decertified the IWA, calling them foreigners and white slave traders. The Bishop has advised me to keep quiet on all issues. All right for him to say; he doesn't live here. He said not to show support to the loggers. Clergy all over the island have swung toward Joey in recent days. The battle is indeed lost.

After lunch I decide to go out and open up the church. Someone might need to pray or talk and I feel I should be available. Some ladies come in, bless themselves with holy water, genuflect to the altar, light candles and kneel to pray. I go down by the door so I can speak with them on their way out.

"Good afternoon, ladies. How are you doing today?"

"We're on our way up to the Buchans Road picket line, Father. We have to be there to support our men, you know."

"And you came to pray?" I know they are loggers' wives; the famous ladies of the picket lines.

"Yes, Father, we needs all the prayers we can get. May God protect our men this evening."

After they go, I pray awhile, read the scripture, straighten the altar a bit, but mostly I have one ear cocked to the shouts and screams out on the street. I want to lock up and go check it out, but something tells me that I should have the church open for anyone who might have need of a sanctuary. If ever a place of peace and calm was needed, it is now.

❧

My house, the Anderson house, which has been in our family for three generations, is about three-quarters of the way up Church Road. As I approach, I can see a police bus parked by my front gate. Across the street, where the little side road crosses the track, there's another bus and two police cars. Everywhere, black coats of the Constabulary are moving around.

The scene puts me on edge, maybe because my son-in-law belongs to this same police force. They stand around, straight as arrows, with their fur hats on their heads. They're not attempting to stop anyone going up the road and I guess they're just there waiting for orders.

I walk over to my gate and stand there with my back to my house, looking around. People run past me. I see Alf Elliott's young girl, Amanda, and some of her friends skirt around the black coats and head up the road. I remember my daughter Audrey used to babysit her years ago. Children sure grow up fast. The Hatcher boys clamber over the back of their father's fence, taking a shortcut through the snowy gardens. They're on their way to join the crowd of people up by the church. It's close to four o'clock, with an hour or so of daylight left in the sky.

I think I hear someone say "Dickie." I whip around, scanning the faces of the black coats. Richard can't be here, can he? I'd heard Becky Abernathy, Richard's adopted mother, call him Dickie once.

Audrey told me later that it was a sore point with Richard. He hated it, but some of his fellow police officers who had grown up with him still called him Dickie.

With those black fur caps, the policemen all look alike. I don't see anyone I recognize. There isn't a chance that Richard would be picked to come out here. If he were, wouldn't he have come by to see me? Or wouldn't Ruth or Audrey have let me know? However, Richard must know these men. He works with them; likely he's even friends with them. But I am not comfortable with approaching the uninviting group and asking.

My stomach growls and I remember that I haven't had anything since the Jam Jams this morning. But hunger or no hunger, I'm too curious to see what's going on. Besides, there is no point in going into the empty house. There's no wife waiting for me, no fire going, no supper cooked.

I too head up the road until I see the intersection with the Buchans Highway. There's a mass of loggers assembled, surrounding a taxi. They seem to be giving it a hard time, banging on the window and shaking the car. I look up on the snowbanks that are now lined with the people who have just passed by me. There's the young Elliott girl with her friends, and over on the other side I spy the young boys scampering around the legs of the adults.

I'm standing well back, almost into the alders, on the right-hand side of the road leading to the intersection. Suddenly, the police fall into formation. I never heard anyone give the order, but right away they start their march up the road. They are quite the sight as they go past, their bodies rigid in their march, with their nightsticks on their right shoulders, all swinging their left arms in unison.

The unit goes past the Pentecostal Church and out of sight. They must have turned about, probably up by the sawdust dump, because next I see them marching back down. I don't see what happens next, but suddenly the police are among the loggers and the loggers are among the police. Sticks are swinging on both sides. I hear screams from the women on the banks and children crying out.

Oh my Christ! Police marching the streets of Badger! If someone had told me two months ago that the loggers' strike would come down to this, I would've said they were nuts. I start forward to head toward the violent scene, but then realize I have no business there. I'm a Company man. I tell myself that this is not my concern. But it is. This is my town, and my town has been invaded. The Badger loggers are my friends. Some of them work for me. I stand there, frozen, torn. I don't know what to do.

Ⅻ

"Ralph," Bill Hatcher says to me as we walk up Church Road with our fellow strikers. "The men think that the A.N.D. Company is more determined than ever to carry on. We're nothing to them, you know. Nothing. We've been on strike and suffering the cold picket lines all winter and they don't give a damn. Do they?"

We've left Mrs. Noel's house and are heading up to the road that goes to Millertown. Tom Hillier is up front in the lead, while I'm farther back, walking along with Bill.

I have only one response for Bill and it's cold comfort for him. "No, Bill, they don't give a damn. And they never did." I have a foreboding on me that this evening will be our last stand. Since Smallwood decertified us, do we have a chance of winning anything at all?

Earlier this afternoon, about a dozen of us went down to the centre of town by the railway tracks and turned back a busload of scabs. The bus driver didn't even attempt to push through. I figured he cared too much for his bus. Not that I blame him. Bus and taxi drivers always retreat. No one is foolhardy enough to try to get through a picket line. They don't want to see their vehicles ruined and their livelihood gone.

When the bus was gone on back to Grand Falls, we went to Mrs. Noel's house. The men were restless and keyed up. They were talking about getting back at Smallwood because he went and did them dirty. They felt the need to take out their frustrations on someone, something. I tried my best to calm them down, but Bill

Hatcher and Tom Hillier arrived with word that more scabs would be attempting to get through to the Millertown camps.

The town is maggoty with police. Badger is a powder keg about to blow. The men are heading to the intersection of the road to Millertown, opposite the Pentecostal Church. Last night, Tom told me that he and a group of men went and cut some birch sticks and stowed them in the Church porch. "We're going to need some protection against the police and their nightsticks," he said. "I hope to God it doesn't come to that, Ralph, but a man has to be prepared to do what he has to do." This strike has changed mild-mannered, law-abiding Tom Hillier so that he seems to be another person entirely.

By the time we arrive, townspeople have gathered and the high snowbanks are already starting to crowd with women and children. I don't know how word gets around so fast. The wives of the Badger loggers – the women of the picket lines – are there as well. I look for Jennie and spy her standing high on a snowbank. Her red hair, poking out of her bandana, is bright against the snow. I catch her eye for a moment and she gives me a brave smile. Our men amass in the open area where the street turns onto the highway to Millertown. By sheer numbers we effectively bar the road.

I look for Tom among the men. I push my way through to him. "Come on, Tom," I say. "Fellas like you and me need to be up front."

It's close to four o'clock. We wait for the scabs we know are coming.

Not much happens for half an hour or so. We see police gathering farther down the road, but no one heeds them. They've been around for days, not interfering, merely watching. I think how people have become immune to the police presence in so short a time.

The townspeople drift up and down the street: women, many walking arm in arm, identical-looking with bandanas on their heads; townsmen, serious and intent as they avoid the eyes of police and logger friends alike. Young boys run through the gardens. Young girls squeal when someone pushes them off the snowbanks. The only ones standing tense are the loggers.

Around half past four I spy a vehicle making its way up through the crowd. The police, farther down the street, are clearing a path for it. I can see a taxi sign on top of the car. Are the police nuts? Where do they expect a taxi to go at this hour of the evening? To Millertown? Do they expect us to step aside?

Next to me, Tom sucks in his breath, and for the first time in my life, I hear him swear. "Well, I'll be goddamned! It's that fucking Vern Crawford's taxi and he got a load of scabs aboard too." Tom raises his stick over his head and shouts, "Get ready boys, he's coming through!"

I can't believe my eyes! Sure enough, there is Vern's beige Chrysler heading right for us. Vern is either the bravest son of a bitch alive or else the biggest fool on two legs, coming up here to face this crowd this evening. From the men behind me I feel anger rise to match my own. I grip the birch billet and get ready.

⌀

I'm standing on a snowbank with other strikers' wives. I look down and see my husband, Tom, and Ralph standing side by side out in front of the rest of the men. It's the first I've seen of Tom since early this morning.

He left our house around eight o'clock. I'd cleaned up the dishes and then mixed up my bread dough. Standing in the kitchen, I punched the dough extra hard. I'd been expecting my period this morning, but there's still no show. Dare I hope, after all these years, that I'm pregnant? I cursed myself a fool. I felt like a bloated whale as I pounded the dough. Foolish, foolish, foolish. I tried instead to think about Tom, who loves homemade bread. He likes it with a cup of tea, and I pictured him slathering up a slice with butter and molasses later this afternoon when he got home.

While waiting for the bread to rise, I made up the bed and swept the floors. It was a nice mild day outside and I would've loved to open a few windows and air the place out, but then I thought of Mam always protecting her bread from drafts. No, it would just have to stay a bit stuffy in the house today, and I added another couple of junks of wood to the stove.

Around one o'clock the bread was out of the oven and the buttered loaves were cooling on the table. I got ready to go up the road to see what was going on, when a knock came to the door. It was Bill Hatcher's wife, Flora. I invited her in.

"No thanks, no time, Jennie. Come on, all the women are going up to the road. There's a lot going on today. Where have ya been all day?"

"I wasn't feeling too well; that time of the month, you know. Besides, I had to make some bread and clean up around the house. Strike or no strike, we still got women's work to do," I grumbled at her.

"Well come on, get on your coat, we needs you, Jennie."

"Just let me cover up my bread and grab my bandana."

As we trudged out Halls Bay Road, Flora told me about how the men had turned back a bus in the centre of town earlier. "Bill thinks there's something gonna blow. He said that the strikers have had enough of this shittin' around. They're expecting more scabs through, and all the men are going up by the Pentecostal Church. We figure we'll turn out in force and show the A.N.D. Company once and for all that we are not putting up with this."

So here I stand a little while later. Looks like almost all the town is here this evening. The snowbanks are high and there are women and children everywhere. I think that little children shouldn't be here. Supposing something happens. Little children . . . I wonder about whether I'll start my period.

I hear Tom shout, "Get ready, boys!" and look down the road. Oh oh, too late now, here comes a taxi, full of scabs for sure. It's Vern Crawford's taxi! I can't believe it. The man must be off his head! Everyone starts shouting all at once.

"Get the hell off the road, Vern," I shout. He has the windows rolled up, but I can see by the look on his face that he's seen and heard me. I can see him hunched over the steering wheel of the car and, by golly, he looks scared. There are three men in with him and they look like they're about to die. But does that stop Vern? No siree! He keeps inching along, bit by bit, still hoping to break through. What a nerve!

Tom and some of his bigger buddies grab the taxi by the under-carriage, pick it up, turn it around, and let it thunk back down on the frozen road.

Well, what a bang! Vern's pinched little face is as white as a sheet. And Ralph looks some angry with him. The men are hitting the bonnet with their sticks. Someone cracks the windshield. Oh God, Vern's face is priceless to behold! Serves him right.

Someone shouts, "The police are coming!" I turn around and there they are, a long line of black-coated Constabulary marching up the road.

27

"Help me up, Madeline." I grab her coat sleeve. It's brown, with brown fur on the collar. The air is damp and her coat feels damp.

"Amanda," she says, as she assists me up the high snowbank. "What were you thinking not to put on your slacks?"

When I'd gone home after school let out, I was in such a hurry to get back outside that I had forgotten to change from my skirt into my snow pants. As I stand there with Madeline and students from my school, I can feel the cold on my legs. My fur-tops are filled with snow and I dig it out as best I can.

I look around at the scene, trying to spot my brothers. There are so many youngsters racing around that it's hard to pick out who is who. The loggers are gathered at the intersection, maybe a couple of hundred of them. Almost all the people of the town are here, up on the snowbanks with me. When Madeline and I were coming up the road, we passed a group of policemen. They've been around for days. They've pretty much ignored us and this evening was no different.

The men have stretched out their line now, and the road going up to Buchans and Millertown is blocked. The strikers are waving hockey sticks, baseball bats and regular sticks. They're shouting and swearing. Madeline's Aunt Jennie and the other women who have helped out on the picket lines this winter are there too, yelling to the men to stand firm.

Now I see a taxi that has somehow driven up the road among

the people. The strikers are banging on it with their sticks. Oh the noise! There's Madeline's Dad; he's right there too, banging on the windshield. Oh my God! The men have grabbed the taxi and lifted it in the air! How could they lift a car? They have turned it around! Madeline and I hold onto each other. The shock of what we are seeing goes through us and I can feel her trembling. The younger kids are crying. I can see my brothers now, farther up the snow-bank. Like the other boys, they've been pretending they're strikers too.

߾

As I stand there with the other women, my eye catches sight of a little child falling off the bank of snow. She lands under the feet of a running striker. The man is so intent on joining the crowd of men who are blocking the road that he doesn't even see her.

I hear her cry of terror. I spring forward and grab the little girl. It's Vern's daughter, I realize now. What cruel irony, I think. She must be trying to catch her daddy. The poor little thing is crying.

"Jennie," yells one of the women. "Come back up this way. Get ready. The police are coming."

I pick up the little girl's green mitten and give it to her, wishing I had something to give her to wipe away her tears, but I have nothing. I turn to hail Vern, but I see his car has slipped off down the back road and away from the scene. I can see my niece, Madeline, up on the bank. With her is Amanda Elliott. I hoist little Melanie Crawford up to them. "Keep her with you! Don't let her go!" I shout to them.

I sprint back to the women. The police are almost abreast of us. I look at the strikers; my eyes search for Tom. He's ready, him and Ralph. They've formed a line across the road. Most of them are armed with sticks of various kinds. "Stand firm, men," shouts a logger.

The bystanders – children and all – are silent. We are silent too. This is it; this is what's been in the pit of my stomach for a month.

It is as if the air holds its breath. Onward the police march, hup, hup, hup.

✆

I wipe the moisture of my breath from the inside of the church windowpane. My hand is shaking. Oh Lord God, they're right below the window. Maybe I should run back to my house behind the church and bar the door. But I can't move.

Jennie Hillier looks up and sees me peering out. She holds up her hand to me. I can see her lips moving. "It's the pastor," she is saying. Others have seen me too. I want to draw back but I cannot. I feel riveted to the glass.

The perfect line of black fur caps marches past the church and goes farther up the road. The strikers are standing in their own line, watching the police pass by not five feet away. No one moves. Not the men. Not the people on the snowbank.

As I watch, the police unit turns around and comes back down. It's abreast of the loggers now. Everything is dead quiet. An officer shouts: "Right wheel!" The constables turn right and face the strikers. Even from my God's-eye view, high above the crowd in the church window, I can feel how tense they are – tightly coiled like a spring.

Someone, deep in the crowd, throws something. I can't see what it is, but I see it glance off the shoulder of a policeman, who whips around. His nightstick connects with the arm of a striker, who hits back.

And that is all it takes to start a riot.

The police wade into the crowd, raining down blows left and right. I am horrified. Merciful Lord, those men are no match for trained police. They'll beat the daylights out of them. I am so terrified that I forget to pray. My hands grip fistfuls of my hair in anguish – hair which never has a strand out of place. I rub my face and realize I am crying, crying for the cruel, brutal injustice being meted out below.

Jennie, no! Stop! Of course she can't hear me as she jumps from the snowbank and onto the back of a policeman who's grappling with her husband. All three go down together, swallowed up in the legs and bodies around them.

In slow motion it seems, below – slightly to the right and a little apart from the main body of the fighting – I see a striker and a cop struggling against each other. A stick is raised; the policeman ducks, but the vicious blow connects with the left side of his skull.

Even through the window, I can hear the crack. Lord, oh Lord, in my whole lifetime I never expected to hear a human skull break open. The crowd has heard the peculiar broken-flowerpot kind of sound too. Everything stops and the crowd parts. There, in the snow, lies a police officer. Blood pools around his head and seeps into the snow, making a pillow of red.

God's voice, inside my head, galvanizes me into action. It's as if my whole life has been building for this moment. I am a man of God, and God is telling me to run. I race up through the church, out through the side door, and into the parsonage. I grab some towels and, with God's voice still upon me and the wings of angels on my feet, I tear around the end of the church and onto the road.

$$\wp$$

"Look, Madeline, the Mounties are coming. No, not Mounties. The Constabulary!"

"Should we go, Amanda? No, we can't go." Madeline's voice is high-pitched as though she's almost crying. "We can't go down on the road. The police are coming up it. If we go down the other side of the snowbank and get inside that fence, we'll get soaked. There's water under the snow." We both know, from living in Badger all our lives, that the River has a way of creeping slowly in under the snow at this time of the year.

"Wow, look at those police, Madeline. Those heavy long, coats! Must be hard to march in them." I'm still clutching her damp coat sleeve.

The policemen are staring straight ahead as they march, three abreast, up the road. Every one of them has a nightstick on his shoulder. Black fur caps. They are some grim. This is serious. Something is going to happen. The crowd is silent. The air crackles with tension.

The taxi has gone down a side road toward the River. The men seem to have forgotten it as they turn to cope with a bigger problem. They're watching the threatening line of police coming toward them, three abreast. The strikers stand aside and the formation marches on up the road, past the church, toward Mrs. Sharpe's house on the left. As they pass, the men mutter among themselves, not sure which way to turn. I think they're relying on the ringleaders out in front to show them what to do.

Oh, here they come back down. The loggers surge forward. Now the police are viciously attacking the men! Oh my God, the loggers are no match for this! Those men are trained to use their nightsticks. Crack! Crack!

We're all crying now. Our minds can't take it all in, such incredible violence. No one has seen anything to compare with this.

I try to keep track of my brothers, but the crowd is too thick. The strikers are putting up a strong fight. Crack! Oh my God. Oh! A policeman is down. His fur cap is knocked aside. There's blood on the snow. Everything stops. I forget to breathe.

❧

"Jennie." One of the women grabs my arm. "Jennie, I'm scared."

I nod. "I'm scared too," I tell her.

The police march up the road. My God, the sight of them is enough to scare anyone, and I fear for Tom. They're so menacing, so black, so tall and straight. Such perfect marching order. It's like the war pictures of the German soldiers that they used to show in the town hall before the main feature of Roy Rogers and Dale Evans or Gene Autry. The sight of the Germans marching in such perfect order used to scare me. I remember thinking, back then, how lucky I was not to be living in Germany. And now, fourteen years after the war, I'm watching something so similar that I shiver with terror.

The loggers watch silently as the police file past the church. A movement in the window catches my eye. It's Pastor Genge. He sure has a bird's-eye view, looking down like that on everyone, the same kind of view that God must have. Has God put the pastor up there as His representative? What a thought!

The police have turned around up by the sawdust dump and are coming back. What are they trying to prove? I suppose by marching in formation they think they can intimidate us into letting the scabs through. But there are no scabs here now. Vern and his scabs have escaped. Surely they can see that.

The men stir restlessly, as men do when in a crowd. They mumble among themselves. I catch Ralph's eye. He nods ever so slightly. He is thinking that all hell is going to break loose. He and Tom stand side by side at the forefront of the men.

After its turnabout, the menacing black line comes back and stops in front of the strikers, wheeling to face them. Someone, deep within the strikers' group, throws a snowball, or something like it. It's possibly just a saucy gesture. The thrower could never have foreseen the consequences of his act. Whatever has been thrown glances off the shoulder of one of the officers.

The anger-charged atmosphere is affecting the police as well as it affects us. They're tensed and waiting to strike out. Clunk! A nightstick connects with the shoulder of a striker. A striker's birch billet connects with the shoulder of a policeman. Ralph, quick, wily Ralph, ducks under a nightstick held high. He grabs the arm and twists. The policeman drops his weapon. Ralph kicks it in under the milling feet of the men. Ralph releases the man and scoots away. The officer immediately looks around for someone to grab.

I see the cop making for Tom, who is tussling with another one. The cop leaps onto Tom's back. I can't take any more. I leap off the snowbank and onto Tom's attacker. We all go down, Tom, the policeman and me. Tom shakes free in an instant and is whirled off into the crowd of police and loggers. But I'm not. The policeman has me in a hammerlock, his strong arm around my throat. I can't breathe. Stars dance in front of my eyes. My heels drum uselessly on the frozen ground. *Tom, help me.*

Suddenly I am free. I roll over onto my knees and raise my head. The cop is on the ground and Ralph is standing over him with his stick. Tom is lost somewhere in the crowd.

"Ralph! Thanks. Geez, I think he would've choked the life outta me." I'm shaking like a leaf. I look at the policeman lying on the snow. Not a gig in him.

All around us the place is gone mad. Ralph stares at me as if he's in a trance. "Jennie. My God, Jennie, I dreamt this event ten years ago."

I don't understand what Ralph is saying and I pay him no heed. I crawl over to the downed officer.

"He's not moving, Jennie. What have I done? Have I killed him?"

"I don't know. Let me look after this. Go, Ralph. Get away before someone sees you. Go. We've lost our chance and we can't win this anyway. Go on, I say."

"Go? What about you? I can't leave you."

"Don't worry about me, b'y. Tom will see to me. You get yourself away from here as fast as you can. We don't want to see you end up in jail. Go. Go now." I lean over the policeman and roll him over. When I look up, Ralph is nowhere in sight.

Tom finally gets clear and rushes to me. "Jennie. What happened? Are you hurt? What's wrong with that feller? Is he dead or knocked out?"

"He's knocked out, Tom. See, he's coming around now." Sure enough, he's conscious, with a cut on his forehead. He sits up, groaning.

Another officer comes over. "Here, what happened to you?" He helps his fellow policeman to his feet. "Who hit you?" He turns to me angrily. "You?" I look at him. "Christ! You're a woman."

Then we all hear it: a sharp, clear crack like someone broke a flowerpot. Time stops. The policeman turns from me toward the sound. Tom raises his head like a fox on the scent. Utter stillness falls over the scene. The people on the snow aren't yelling, the men aren't cursing and yelling. Nobody is scuffling with anyone else. We're all just a bunch of human beings standing still in the silence.

Time starts up again, and the sea of strikers and police parts to reveal someone down on the snow. There's blood . . . oh my God! This one is hit seriously. I start to sob, great heaving sobs. Part of it is delayed reaction to being nearly choked; part of it is from what I am witnessing. It feels like my heart is crushing inside my chest and I can't get the air into my lungs.

Tom grabs my arm and turns me about. "Run, Jennie," he whispers hoarsely. "Run. I don't want you to get arrested. This is more serious now."

I don't need any urging. I am out of there. I can't control myself. I can't stop crying. I don't really know what has happened except I saw a policeman on the snow and a lot of blood. I just know that, for the second time in my life, I am out of control. As I run down the road, something deep inside me is welling over with terror, with grief, with regret. For certain, the loggers have lost.

Around three o'clock, my wife, Mary, sends word to the office that our children have gone up to view the gathering near the Buchans Bridge. I know that most of Badger is up there too. Some think of it as a bit of excitement to liven up the dreary winter.

Once again I close the telegraph office earlier than usual. Flurries of people have been blowing in and out of my office all day saying the strikers are planning something for the afternoon. Rumours are that the picket line will be up near the intersection of the Buchans Highway and Church Road to stop scab workers from getting through to Millertown. Mounties and the Constabulary patrol Badger's tiny streets; loggers stand in groups on their picket lines; residents scurry back and forth, going about their private concerns with heads bent, trying to be as inconspicuous as possible.

As I turn the key in the lock of the telegraph office, I'm thinking that if the loggers and police are going to clash, children shouldn't be present. Who knows what might happen? I decide to go and look for Amanda and the boys.

I cross the small side road that goes over the track. It's then that I see Vern Crawford hurrying down the railway track toward me.

"Hey, Alf. Wait! What's happening up the road?"

Vern is out of breath, his eyes darting around everywhere. He looks scared. As he comes close to me, I can faintly smell vomit. What's he been up to? Vern has gained a bad reputation during this strike. He's known to have taken scabs through the picket lines. I've heard some pretty weird stories about him. I'm surprised to see him without his old taxi.

"Don't know for sure, Vern b'y," I answer. "But I think the strikers must have tangled with the police. We knew that had to come, sure. I wonder what brought it to a head."

"'Tis hard to say, b'y. It could've been anything," Vern replies. "I just got back from Springdale meself. I stinks of vomit. Someone threw up in me taxi."

The side road takes us across to Church Road. As we get closer we can hear screams and shouts. Men are running, jumping over ditches and fences. Hot on their heels I can see police chasing after them. There are two police wagons and three or four police cars parked nearby.

"Where's your taxi now, Vern? How come you're on foot? I never see you walking anywhere."

"Oh . . . well . . . er . . . she stinks too much from the little girl throwing up. I have to clean her out after I finds Melanie and her mother."

I look at him. His face is pale and his eyes are wild. He's been up to something more than just driving back from Springdale.

As we reach Church Road, we both see Jennie Hillier running toward us, wild-eyed, sobbing, her arms flailing. She cries, "'Tis all over! 'Tis all over! Someone is dead!" In passing, she spies Vern. She grabs him by the shoulders, shaking him and screaming, "This will all be on your conscience, Vern!" She lets him go and keeps running.

Vern seems to have had such a fright that he turns tail and runs back toward the railway tracks.

I sidle up the right-hand side of the road, keeping close to the alders. I almost bump into someone standing off to the side keeping out of the way. It's Rod Anderson. I remember that he sent a telegram in to his son-in-law a few days ago, asking if Ruth could go and visit. Come to think of it, wasn't the son-in-law, Richard, a city cop? Newfoundland Constabulary? The same ones as the police involved here?

Four large Mounties block my path. "Sorry, sir. No farther."

Over the Mounties' shoulders, I can see pandemonium. There are police everywhere, yelling to people to get off the snowbanks and go home. They move off slowly, as though the violence-infected atmosphere is affecting their bodies. The police are grabbing strikers, knocking them down into the snow, hitting them with nightsticks. Angry shouts and curses fill the air. Children and women are crying. I can see many children, of all ages, dodging among running strikers and police. Somewhere in this commotion are my own children. But where?

❧

I sense someone near my elbow. It's Alf.

"Hello, Rod," he says. "What's goin' on up there, b'y?"

"I dunno, Alf, but it wouldn't surprise me if someone gets hurt out of this."

"I have to find my kids. You didn't see them, did you?"

I remember glimpsing them earlier. "Yes, I did see them about an hour ago. They were up there with the rest of the school kids. And it sure isn't a place for children to be this evening."

"No, Rod b'y, 'tis no place for children or grown-ups," Alf answers. He tries to move past the Mounties, but they block his way.

Something has happened up there in the midst of the melee. The fighting has died back and men are running everywhere – through the gardens, over the field toward the River, through the alders behind me that lead out to the railway tracks. The police are giving chase. I watch as two of them run down a fleeing striker and club him to the ground right in front of me. They pull him to his feet and lug him toward one of the buses.

I decide that it's time to get out of here. I turn to go back down the road toward my house and see several RCMP officers. They seem to have joined forces with the Constabulary and are trying to break up the crowd.

From behind me a big hand grabs my shoulder. "Hey you, where do you think you're off to? Trying to get away, are you?"

I'm caught totally unawares. "No, no, officer, I am not a striker. I'm an A.N.D. Company contractor."

"Right. And I'm the Premier! Come on, buddy, into the van. You're under arrest."

He starts to push me toward the van. I try to pull away. "Let me go! I'm not one of them!"

He tightens his hold. "I don't care who the hell you are. Into the van!" He raises his free arm and brandishes his nightstick at me. I grab him by the wrist so he can't swing it. He is strong, but I'm stronger.

Realizing he needs some help, he yells out, "Hey, Dickie! Give me a hand with this troublemaker, will you?"

Dickie?

Suddenly, I am clouted from behind. A heavy nightstick cracks down between my shoulder blades and I buckle to the ground, crying out in pain. Rough hands haul me to my feet. A bright flash almost blinds me, the flash of Alf's camera as he snaps our picture. In that split second I look up into the eyes of my son-in-law, Richard Fagan. We are face to face in the midst of the Badger Riot.

✄

Unable to get up through the Mounties to find my children, I move back into the alders on the side of the road. I slip my Hawkeye out of the case. It's already rigged with a flashbulb.

Rod has moved out of the bushes and is heading off down the road. A policeman grabs him. They wrestle a bit. Another cop moves in to help him. My God, they think Rod is a striker! The two of them beat him into the snow with their clubs. No one notices me. Click. I have the picture. I back away again so they won't see who took it.

A Mountie shouts, "Make way! Make way!"

Four policemen come through the crowd. They are carrying a stretcher. On it is another black-coated officer. Around his head is a towel soaked with blood. His eyes are closed. His face is as white as the snow around him.

And here it is, I think to myself: the result of government inter-vention. Someone has struck down an officer of the law. A policeman whose unit should never have been sent out from St. John's in the first place.

My feelings about Joey Smallwood have come true. He's stopped this strike by foul means. The loggers and the IWA can never get past this.

I notice Rod staggering past me holding his shoulder. The last I saw of Rod he was being strong-armed toward the police van. Why did they let him go? Did he convince them that he wasn't a striker?

"Rod. The cops let you go. What happened? Need some help there?"

"That fucking cop walloped me, Alf. Son of a bitch walloped me."

Rod is sobbing, crying as though his heart is breaking. Men don't cry like this unless they have a tragedy in their family. There's some-thing going on here that I don't understand. I can't just leave him staggering about hurt and crying.

"I'll help you to your house, Rod. Come on." I take his good arm and steady him along; he seems to be in a lot of pain.

When we get into his kitchen, Rod sits down by the table, groaning and crying.

"You need a doctor, Rod, my son."

"No, not now, Alf. Go on out and get your children."

I hesitate, but Rod is right. "Why don't you lie down for a spell?"

"Nope, not lyin' down. Get me the rum bottle in the bottom of that cupboard, will you? Some goddamn family I got, I must say."

I get the rum bottle but I don't understand Rod's remark about family. I don't know what to say to him.

"Go, Alf. Get your youngsters before some fucking townie cop hauls them off to jail too."

I hurry out. Just as I'm about to close the kitchen door, Rod whispers hoarsely, "Alf."

I stop and look back.

"You'll never believe who hit me with his fucking nightstick . . . my own son-in-law." He starts to sob again.

His son-in-law? Richard Fagan? There is nothing I can say except, "I'm sorry, Rod."

I have to get back out there and find my children.

⌀

The riot has broken. Loggers are fleeing in every direction with the police on their heels. The snowbank spectators are in shock. The crying of young children is particularly distressing.

The Constabulary officer lies on the snow. I hurry forward. I am here, Lord. I am doing as You bid me to do. A policeman grabs the towels and wraps the officer's bleeding head.

Gladys Sharpe, who lives across from the church, rushes out with a blanket.

"I seen who did it! I seen who did it!" she screams hysterically. She sees me and points her finger. "There's Pastor Genge. He was looking through the window of the church. He saw it too."

An officer leads her aside quickly, talking to her.

The RCMP are shooing people off the snowbanks, telling them to go home.

A way is cleared and officers lift the unconscious constable aboard a van. The doors close and they make their way back down Church Road.

I stand there, amid the ruins of loggers' dreams and

Constabulary pride, and stare down at the pool of blood at my feet. I think about Jesus, my personal Saviour, and about the free will of mankind. I think about the evil that stalks among people, an evil ready to be let loose wherever man allows it.

Someone touches my arm. It's the policeman who took Mrs. Sharpe aside to talk with her.

"Excuse me, Pastor. Mrs. Sharpe says she saw you at the church window. We'll need a statement."

❦

"Come on, Amanda, let's go." Madeline jumps down off the snowbank.

She gives me her hand to help me climb down, but I am too upset to care anymore about being proper in my darn straight skirt. I sit on the snow and slide down on my backside, feeling my nylons tear and the snow cut the backs of my bare legs. Then I see them.

"Oh, look, Madeline, the Mounties are on the way up now. We can't get back down the road. Let's cross the road and go in behind the church and get out on the railway track." I grab my two brothers by the hoods of their parkas and Madeline keeps a tight hold on Melanie.

We scurry across the road.

A policeman sees us, but he only says, "Get on home now, kids. Go on with you, now."

We're behind the church, heading for the railway tracks when an adult figure looms out of the darkness behind a shed. We scream, but it's only Melanie's father, Mr. Crawford. She launches herself into his arms, crying to break her little heart. Perhaps I am mistaken, but it sure sounds to me like Mr. Crawford is crying too.

He says over and over, "Melanie, Melanie, are you okay? Are you okay?" Then he realizes who we are. "Your father is looking for you," he says to me. "Go on down the track and you'll meet him on the side road, I'm sure. Go on now."

We hurry down the track. There's Dad! My brothers race to meet him screaming, "Dad, Dad! We saw someone hit a policeman."

28

He was choking her. The cop had her neck in the crook of his arm and he looked like he was squeezing the life out of my Jennie. Jesus, what am I saying? She's not mine. To her I am just good old Ralph, her friend from childhood. The feelings and the frustration that I had kept carefully locked up inside of me all those years suddenly burst. A red mist came in front of my eyes.

I struck that policeman to make him let go of Jennie, but I think I struck to kill too. And when I did, my ten-year-old dream washed over me. There he was, the black-cloaked figure of death – or, in this case, a black-coated cop – and the danger to Jennie was very real.

Jennie was still alive, so that part of the dream was right. I did protect her, but perhaps I killed the policeman. Were they right? Was it natural for an Indian to kill a white man?

But I should have stayed. I deserted my friends.

I was soon over by the big hill, out of breath from running. Then I heard shouts behind me and turned around. Dozens of our men were racing over the same road, some toward the hill, and some toward the River. What was going on? Why were they all leaving? Had the police triumphed? What had happened?

I scooted across the grounds of the convent and came out by Church Road. It was full-dark now, the night air filled with strange sounds. I stood in under the tall old trees to catch my breath. I thought of the running strikers and I knew that, somehow, the picket line had been broken. Should I go back up the road? Or should I follow the men that I'd seen streaming toward the River?

Then I spied Tom, hurrying along, all by himself, with his long, loose strides. My nerves were raw, and my voice seemed unnatural, like a hiss. "Hey, Tom."

In his haste, he wasn't paying any attention.

"Tom," I repeated, and this time he stopped.

"Where'd you pop from, Ralph? You're like a ghost, always creepin' me out, b'y."

I grabbed hold of his arm. "Why are you running away, Tom? What's going on? Where's Jennie? What's happened up the road?"

"A policeman is down, Ralph. You must've seen it. You were there too, though, come to think of it, I lost sight of you after the police waded in. Anyway, he was hit on the head; blood all over the snow. The men got such a fright when they saw it that they scattered. I made Jennie run away too. The police are like devils up there now, chasing our boys down, clubbing them, putting them in the wagon." Tom shook his big head. "I'm never going back to jail, Ralph, no matter what. Come on, let's get off the road."

We went back across the Catholic property and over the hill to the River. There were people and police everywhere. Others were running along with us. We seemed to gravitate to the River for some reason, as if it was at the centre of all our troubles.

There were about forty of us. A couple of the organizers were there. "Boys, it would be much appreciated if any of you know places where we can hide some of our men for tonight." From Badger there was Tom and me, Bill Hatcher and a few others. The rest were strangers from out of town. We all agreed, anxious to help our union brothers.

I stepped forward. "We'll take ten for now. I know some places to hide them. We might be back for more later. Everyone lay low and out of sight."

Tom and I started off down the riverbank with the men following us. Tom was using the same route that was taken by the strikers back in February, when they came down off Sandy after trashing the camp. It kept us close to the rivers and in the trees until we put some distance between the police and us.

Sometime during that dark cold night under the railway station platform, I awoke to shouts and lights.

It was the Mounties. "This is the police! Up and outta there! Up and out now!" They shone their big flashlights in, scaring me half to death. I raised my head a little and I could see the other bundled-up bodies all around me, packed in like rats.

The Mounties yelled at us to crawl out, and to do it fast. I was one of the first to be hauled up by the scruff of me collar.

"What's your name?" a Mountie barked at me.

"Cec . . . Cecil Nippard, sir."

Oh my, I was some scared. I was shivering and shaking with the cold and fright. There were thirty-six of us. I had them counted as they came out, one by one. I always like to count things, even people. It helps to make me calm. Earlier in the evening, when we were up there by the church in the taxi and the strikers were all around us, I counted two hundred and thirty-six men. Then I pissed in me pants and lost count. I hated to lose count.

Many of the guys under the station stand were tramps or hobos or something, living on the rails. There was this one man, especially. They said he had no legs. He was in the war, what my father called World War Two, a veteran whose legs had been shot off and who was shell-shocked. He walked around with stilts under his pants legs, making him about seven feet tall. I had seen him around many times. He used to be at the Windsor station too. His height, and the creaking sound from his stilts, hidden under his long pants legs, scared me so much that I couldn't look at him full-on, only from the corners of my eyes.

They hauled him out too, poor feller. Two cops sat him up on the platform. He looked some pitiful without his stilts. Watching him, I realized that he didn't scare me anymore. He wasn't some strange giant at all, just a man with no legs. And he certainly wasn't a logger. Everyone knew that, even the police. They even seemed to treat him with some respect. More than they did any of us, that's for sure.

At the pool hall, the men used to discuss World War Two and I would listen. Someone said that it had ended in Europe on May 8, 1945. They called it VE Day and I knew, right away, that was five thousand and fifty-seven days, almost fourteen years ago. I didn't have to pause and think about leap years, because somehow I always counted them in, even though I didn't know I had until someone told me. Stuff like that has always stayed in my mind. Dates are important things. And they'd talk about the war veterans that had become hobos. They lived on the rails, from boxcar to boxcar, place to place. Many of them suffered war trauma, were shell-shocked and were lost in their minds, where the battles of the war went on forever. I never forgot what they said, maybe because, sometimes, I felt that I was lost in my mind too.

Some of the men tried to make a run for it, but the police weren't having that. They gave chase, knocked the men down in the snow, clubbed them with their big ugly sticks. I was shit-baked; afraid to even blink, let alone move. The Mountie who had hauled me out from under the station came back to me again. "Well, buddy, what are you at tonight? Hiding from the law, are you? Are you a striker or what?"

"No . . . no, sir." I could hardly get the words out of me mouth, I was so cold and scared. "I works for the A.N.D. Company."

"Yeah?" he sneered. "A likely story. Who you think is going to believe that?"

Another Mountie came over. "I know him. He's that foolish young fellow from Windsor. One of them skeets that hangs around the pool hall. He'd sell his mother for money to play a game of pool. They say he's real good at it too. No one can beat him."

"Whatever he is, champion or not, get him into the truck." The Mounties all laughed.

Oh my, oh my. I wanted to speak up, to say that I had no mother, and, if I did, I certainly wouldn't sell her for any amount of money. I wanted to say I'd love her and stay with her and be her good boy forever. But I couldn't form the words; I couldn't get them past my lips. I wanted to cry so bad, but only sissies cried.

The ones that the Mounties knew by sight as hobos were left to go back to sleep in under the station. They even helped the legless man off the platform so that he could scrabble in under, pulling his stilts in after him.

But twenty of us were herded aboard an open stake-bodied truck and off down over the road to Grand Falls. The dark night was freezing cold. In the open truck, even though we were strangers to each other, we huddled together for warmth. And no one tried to kick or punch me or call me stupid Cecil.

The guy huddled down next to me really was a striker. "What a fuckin' night this turned out to be. We're guilty of nothing, nothing, I tell you, except standing on a picket line for our rights, and now they're hauling us off to jail." Two or three others mumbled in agreement.

I didn't know much about that part of the goings-on, not being a member of the IWA union and having never stood on a picket line.

When we arrived in Grand Falls the strikers were sent off to jail. The rest of us were let go and some were ordered to leave town. Coming on toward daylight one of the Mounties dropped me off at me father's house.

I was never to know what would have happened if I had gone out into the fray that evening, because at that moment the church door opened. It was a police officer in his greatcoat and fur cap. And I knew him. Oh my God, did You keep me here for him?

He took off his cap. "Father Murphy, I have to talk to you." His dark hair was plastered to his forehead with sweat and his skin was pale. His eyes were frightened and glassy. "Can we go in back where I can't be seen?"

I sized him up. What had happened? "All right, then. Let's go this way," I said, as I led the way in behind the altar.

He was Richard Fagan, married to Rod Anderson's daughter. He'd been coming back and forth to Badger for two or three years now. Even though Rod was a Protestant, his son-in-law was a Catholic. We'd chatted together a couple of times. I had even seen him at Mass once.

In the sacristy, his legs seemed to give out under him and he sat down abruptly. "Father, you know me, right? You know that Rod Anderson is my father-in-law, right?"

"Yes."

He drew in a deep shaking breath. "Father, I think I have ruined my life. I hit my father-in-law with my nightstick, and I think he might be injured."

I didn't know what to say. I looked at him and he looked at me.

"My son, start at the beginning. What has happened up the road? How did this come about? Did you and Mr. Anderson have a disagreement?"

"No, no, Father. He didn't even know I was here. I . . ." He hung his head and started to sob.

I pulled up a chair and sat down next to him. Laying my hand upon his shoulder I told him, "Take a deep breath now. Start from the beginning."

Tom had said, "Run, Jennie," and I ran. My feet had a mind of their own, and I was heading for Pap's house – up the track.

You might wonder why I didn't go on to my place and wait for my Tom, but we live in on Halls Bay Road, a long walk in a community gone insane with violence. Pap's house was no more than five minutes from the scene of the clash between loggers and police.

Then I met that friggin' Vern again. He'd scooted over the back road, got rid of his scabs somewhere and ditched his taxi too, all in the past half-hour. Now, here he was, standing innocently on the side of the road alongside of Alf Elliott, the telegraph operator.

The anger erupted out of me. I grabbed him, shook him and screamed in his face. I don't know what I was saying, but the shock on Alf's face was enough to sober me a bit. I let him go and, instead of turning toward the track and Pap's house, I continued running down Church Road.

I don't know where I would have ended up. Perhaps I would have kept running until I reached Halls Bay Road. I just don't know. It was dark. There were people everywhere crying out in fear and shock.

Then I saw the Catholic Church, lit up like a beacon in the cruel night. I thought of its warm, smooth pews, the smell of incense, the statue of the Blessed Mother. Perhaps I'll drop in and rest a minute, I thought.

I cautiously opened the door. I hadn't been inside in years. Nothing had changed. As I crept to a seat and knelt down, I could still see myself up at the altar as a little girl making my first Holy Communion, so innocent in my white dress and veil.

And now here I was looking up at the same altar almost twenty-five years later, a thirty-year-old woman whose coat had the buttons gone where a cop had hauled me around. My blouse was undone too. There was blood on my bosom. Whose blood? Then I remembered it was the cop that Ralph had struck to keep me from being choked. As he was regaining consciousness I had held his head in my arms.

My hair was across my eyes and I had snot and tears on my face. I scrabbled in my pocket for a tissue. A hand held out a handkerchief. I looked up into Father Murphy's eyes, then back at the hanky. It was lovely and white and so nicely embroidered. I suppose the nuns did that; funny how irrelevant little things skitter across your mind at the strangest times.

"Father Murphy, I'm sorry. I should go on out. Were you locking up?"

"No, no Jennie. Stay, my child. Compose yourself. Pause a moment. Talk to God about whatever has happened to you."

He knelt in the seat across from me and closed his eyes to pray. I prayed too. I asked God to look after my Tom, still out there somewhere; to protect Ralph, wherever he might be; to help the loggers whose government had declared them criminals and sent the blackcoats to break their spirits by breaking their heads. I prayed to God that the policeman wouldn't die. If he did die, whose fault was it? Was it ours? Or was it the A.N.D. Company's and the Government's? Oh the poor man, to die out here in an unknown place. Somewhere he had a mother who was keeping vigil this night, waiting for word of her son.

I blessed myself and looked at Father. "If you wouldn't mind, Father, I'd like to make a confession and tell you what happened."

※

"Dad, Dad!" The high-pitched voice of my son David was music to my ears. Thank God, the three of them were safe. Amanda looked at me with round frightened eyes. She didn't speak as she grabbed hold of my arm. The boys were talking a mile a minute. One more camera snap of the scared shocked townspeople and we were away and down the road to home.

My children were traumatized by what they had witnessed. I realized that they should never have been there, but who knew that they'd be in the midst of a riot and see bloodshed? Badger had been a small, safe town where children could run freely. Had this changed forever?

We were eating our supper and trying to behave like it was a normal evening. Amanda's face was white and strained as she picked at her food. The boys were naming names: So-and-so said he saw who did it, Dad. He said he saw this fellow hit the cop with a birch stick.

This was going to lead to trouble. Poor little youngsters. They didn't know the difference. I was stern and forceful with them. "Say nothing. Understand? Say nothing. You'll only bring trouble upon us by repeating rumours. Keep quiet, no matter what someone asks you. Let the loggers and the police settle this."

A knock sounded on the door. I opened it warily, half expecting it to be the Mounties. It was the reporter from the *Toronto Star*. He needed to file his story. Would I go with him to the telegraph office so he could telephone with some privacy?

He had a car and we drove down. The riot had happened two hours ago, but people were still on the move – Badger residents making their way home, and police prowling around, looking for loggers. No one in this town had ever experienced such a time. It was a wild night.

The reporter needed light to read his report into the phone. I didn't want to turn on the light, the tumult outside was such that police or strikers were sure to investigate. We used my big flashlight which I shone on his notebook as he read. His voice was urgent as he communicated to colleagues in Toronto the horror of what had taken place in faraway Central Newfoundland.

෫

The police sergeant wanted to come inside the church. "It would be better if I could take your statement inside, Pastor Genge," he said. "Perhaps you could show me where you were standing at the time of the altercation."

I moved away from the blood splotch on the snow and slowly climbed the steps to the church. I felt the weight of grief upon me; grief for a lost cause, perhaps a lost life. I opened the door. It was dark inside and I reached to turn on the lights.

"No lights, Pastor, if you don't mind. First I want us to look out through the window."

In the gloom I led the way over to the window overlooking the road. He stood beside me and we gazed out at the scene, visible because of the white snow. Most people had moved farther on down the road, encouraged to do so by the RCMP. The strikers, those who had escaped, were long gone. The blood patch was visible even up here through the window. But now it looked black in the night. As we watched, an officer came by with a shovel, scooped it up and went off down the road carrying the stained snow. It was a hard thing to look at. The sergeant was affected, I could see. He turned away.

"Turn on the lights now, Pastor," he said. He nodded to the other policeman who had accompanied him. "The constable here will write down your statement. So tell me what you saw."

We sat in the back pew. I told no lies. I didn't paint the strikers as victims. I didn't paint the police as aggressors. They knew what had happened as well as I did.

He listened and the constable wrote in his black notebook.

"So, Pastor Genge, tell me. Did you see Constable Moss struck down?"

"Yes sir, I did. I saw him when he fell. That was when I ran into my house to get the towels. I felt that God had been preparing me for that moment all my life."

"Hmm. Are you getting all of this, Constable?"

"Yes sir. I have it all down, sir."

"Good. Now then, Pastor, I need you to tell me the name of the person who struck the blow, if you know it."

The door of the church opened. The sergeant swung around. It was another policeman. "I thought I told you not to disturb me," he barked.

The young constable looked scared. "Sorry sergeant, but a call just came through on the RCMP radio from Grand Falls. Our headquarters in St. John's wants you to call them right away."

The sergeant looked at me. I could see the indecision in his eyes. Should he keep grilling me or should he obey the summons from headquarters? Headquarters won out. He turned to me. "Where's the nearest telephone?"

"Alf Elliott has one in the telegraph office. He'll go down and open up for you." I told him how to get to Alf's house.

"Okay we'll go then," he said to the constable. "I'll be back,

Pastor. Don't go anywhere. You can close up the church and I'll find you in your house."

✄

As I locked up the office after the reporter was finished his call to Toronto, a police car stopped. A Mountie screwed down the window. "Which one of you is the telegraph operator?"

"That's me," I said, "and this gentleman is from the *Toronto Star*."

"We need to use your phone. The sergeant has to make a long-distance call." The door opened on the passenger side and the officer got out.

The sergeant motioned for the reporter to stay outside while he and I went into the office.

"Mr. Elliott, is it?"

"Yes. Can I help you?"

"We went to your house and your wife told us where to find you." He held out a piece of paper. "Here is a phone number in St. John's. Can you put the call through for me? Make it collect."

All long-distance calls are routed through the main switchboard in Gander. It was an efficient system and the call went through quickly.

The sergeant took the phone, saying, "Please wait outside, Mr. Elliott. This is a private call."

The reporter was still there, no doubt looking to get another story for his paper.

The Mountie was sitting behind the wheel of the car with the window down. "Will you give me a ride home after he's finished?" I asked him. "What about this reporter? He can go on, can't he?"

"Yes sir," he answered. "He can leave. You get in the car with me to keep yourself warm."

The Mountie was with the Grand Falls detachment and we knew each other slightly. The sergeant was on the phone for quite awhile, so we talked a bit. We talked of inconsequential things like the weather, the ice in the River, the ruts in the road to Grand Falls, but not once did we discuss what had happened up by the Pentecostal Church on the road to Millertown. Neither of us spoke of the horror of a human being lying near death because of it.

When I got home the boys were in bed asleep. Amanda was sitting up with her mother.

"Go on to bed, Amanda," I told her. "You have school tomorrow."

She headed for the stairs, then stopped. "Dad, we all saw something this evening that we weren't supposed to see. Am I right?"

She was fourteen years old. How could I explain it to her? "Yes, you did, my child. I wish you hadn't, but it's too late to talk about that now. I hope you have enough sense to keep quiet. No matter who asks you – even if the police question you – always say you saw nothing."

"Okay. Goodnight, Dad. Goodnight, Mom."

Mary and I were ready to go to bed. There was another knock at the door. I opened it. Oh my Christ! It was Ralph Drum. Beside him was Tom Hillier. They slipped inside quickly.

Ralph whispered, "Alf, we got four fellas outside, two from somewhere out near Lewisporte and two more from somewhere down in White Bay. The police are hunting them down. We got more than a dozen hidden at various places around town."

I looked at them both. Ralph had a black eye and Tom's lip was bleeding. The two of them looked as wild as hawks.

"What do you want me to do? Hide them? I have young children and no spare room."

"You got the goat house, Alf," said Tom. Big Tom Hillier was a quiet, gentle kind of man, mostly. People said he had a temper, though, and that he had practically beaten up a woods camp all by himself.

"Yes, Alf, you got the goat house. Just give me the key," Ralph said, "and I promise not to let them touch your photo equipment." Ralph knew how much I valued my stuff.

"No b'y. I'll go down with you. There are a dozen strips of film hung up to dry on the line. I need to take them down so the guys won't get their heads tangled up in them." I didn't say so, but most of the negatives were shots of the strike.

We went down the path in pitch-darkness to the goat house. I didn't need a light as I knew the little path well, and I dare say Ralph could see in the dark anyway. Tom had never been there before, and he stumbled along behind us. I knew his big frame would never get in the door of the little low building. He'd have to stand guard outside.

I cleared away the negative strips and put away the acids. Ralph went out and brought in the four strikers.

When he had the door closed, I screwed in the red bulb.

Well, whattya know? The fugitives that Ralph wanted me to help were the same boys who were going to beat up my telegraph office and kick my arse out the door!

The red light washed over their scared faces. They recognized me too, and Ralph knew that it was an awkward moment. I could see it in his face.

"Alf . . . I know you know them. But the boys are sorry they gave you a hard time about sending the message to Joey. Aren't you, boys?"

They coughed, cleared their throats and shuffled their feet. "Oh yes. Yes sir! We are. Guaranteed."

"Jesus, Ralph, I've put a lot of money and effort into this photo setup. I don't want it wrecked, b'y."

"No sir. We won't wreck it. We're sorry about before. We had a few drinks, ya know."

Ralph corrected them. "Actually, you guys were loaded drunk that time."

"Well, we're not drunk now, b'y. We just needs a place to hide from them Mounties, what?"

I had no choice. I couldn't allow the poor unlucky devils to be tossed in jail, when they were guilty of nothing more than being on strike. "Okay guys. But you dare touch any of my equipment and it will be your arses kicked out the door this time, right into the Mounties' arms. And don't piss in here. If you want to piss, go out and do it now because, once you're inside, I'm locking the door behind me."

They went outside again. I stood in the door alongside Big Tom. Our eyes were used to the dark now and I could make out the steam rising from four arcs of urine as they hit the snow.

We put the strikers back in the goat house and left them there. I snapped the padlock closed. If someone decided to investigate, it would look like what it was, an old, locked-up goat house.

Ralph and Tom went on their way, to round up others, I presumed, but I didn't ask. It was a time when the less you knew, the better off you were.

∅

After the sergeant left, I walked up the aisle to the altar. I knelt at the railing where so many sinners had come to accept Jesus into their hearts.

I did what I could do best: I prayed. I was unsure of myself. Perhaps I was mistaken. The events had unfolded so fast, so swift and horrible. I stayed there for a long while. Then I got up, turned out the lights, locked the door and went into the parsonage.

An hour later, there was a knock at the back door. I walked over and looked out through the little window, wondering why the sergeant was knocking at the back door. But it wasn't the police. It was Tom Hillier standing on the step. I could barely make out his face in the darkness, but his size was enough for me to recognize him. Behind him were three dark figures. Well, no worries about them if Tom was with them. He was one of my flock, as were his parents. I opened the door.

Followed by the strangers, Tom hurried in and closed the door. I stood there in the little hallway, not sure what to expect. "Pastor, how you gettin' on? Sorry to disturb you." I had the distinct feeling of being part of a play. Nothing was real. Here was Tom, playing a part, being polite – how was I getting on? Sorry to disturb me? Good Lord. And the three men, what parts were they playing? I knew without being told that they were fugitive strikers.

"We can't risk being seen, Pastor." Tom reached over my shoulder and switched off the lights. "I'm wondering if you can put these gentlemen up for the night."

"Are they being hunted down by the police?"

"Well, uh . . . yeah. We are all being hunted down, Pastor. Hunted down and dragged off to jail. I know my way around Badger and I won't get caught, but the boys here are strangers, from Notre Dame Bay, and they haven't got a clue where to go."

Tom's big frame took up most of the space in the hallway. I moved into the kitchen with them. He continued. "So I thought you might help. They are Pentecostal, if that makes a difference."

"That doesn't make a difference, my son. I cannot refuse you or them. This is a hard thing, Tom. A hard thing. Are you staying too?"

"No, Pastor, I'm going off again. I'm worried about Jennie." He turned to the men. "Now boys, the Pastor will look after you. You might have to go up in the attic if the police come by."

Tom went out the door, ducking his head automatically. The men and I looked at each other. "Boys, the police are coming here tonight. There's a sergeant who's been questioning me, but he didn't get to finish because he had to make a telephone call. He said he'd be back."

"Do you have an attic, Pastor?" asked one of them.

There *was* an attic. I remembered seeing the hatch in the old back pantry when I first came to live here. I'd never gone up there, though. Cobwebs, dust and spiders are things I try to avoid. "Yes, there is an attic here. I should get you some food before you go up."

We went into the back pantry. The tallest of them got up on a chair and lifted the hatch. He said they'd be able to swing up there when the time came. We left the hatch open and the chair ready in case they had to move fast. I knew that the sergeant might be back at any time.

So I got them a lunch – bologna sandwiches and cups of tea. I kept the light out in the kitchen, but there was enough light from the front room for us to see. It turned out that they were strangers to each other. The conversation around the table as they gulped down their hurried meal was mostly "where's you from?" and "who's your father?" and "do you know such-and-such?" I couldn't join in. Being from St. John's, I didn't know anyone from White Bay or Notre Dame Bay.

I proposed a word of prayer before they disappeared into the dark upper reaches of my house. I was good at praying. Jonathan always said that the words slid off my tongue like warm molasses. *Oh, Jonathan, I wish you were here beside me now in my time of tribulation.*

I gave the men a flashlight and some blankets. They climbed up into the attic. When he was hoisted up, the first man shone the flashlight around. "Ever been up here, Pastor? Buddy, there's some stuff here. You should see it."

"Uh . . . yes, some other time." No one would ever get me up there. Ugh! All that dust.

The boys replaced the hatch and I took away the chair. It was almost ten o'clock and still no sergeant. I sat down in the front room and took up my Bible. I needed a couple of good quotations for my Sunday sermon, quotations pertaining to violence and bloodshed.

Midnight. Still no police. He hadn't forgotten me. I'd see him in the morning. I was sure of that. I turned out the light and went to bed.

29

It didn't take long for Dad, my brothers and me to hurry away from the remains of the riot, across the road and home. Mom was relieved to see us. She held the door open for us as we came through the front gate.

"Are you all right? What happened? I was frantic with worry."

"Oh Mom," I cried. "My two feet are soaked from the snow that got into my fur-tops when I climbed up on the bank. And I ripped my nylons to pieces when I slid down over the bank."

Mom tut-tutted. "Amanda, how many pairs of nylons do you tear up, at all? Get the wet stuff off right away before you catch cold."

The kitchen was warm. I hauled off the ruined nylons and put on a pair of vamps. Then I turned down the tops of my boots and put them behind the stove to dry out for the morning.

Mom had baked rabbit for our supper. Around here folks ate a lot of wild meat – rabbit, moose, caribou, bear, even beaver. Dad always told us that it was the best thing for us, always available, and fresh too. The only fish we got, being so far inland, was trout and salmon, in season. Sometimes someone brought us something from places like Roberts Arm or King's Point – cod, or seal or herring. We picked and ate many kinds of berries too. Mom was forever boiling up pots of them and at every meal there would be a bottle of partridgeberry or blueberry jam on the table. We also had bakeapples, which I never liked very much, probably because they were so hard to pick. Or maybe it was the orange colour – a colour I never liked.

Supper was a strange affair that evening. None of us were really paying much attention to what we ate. My brothers, animated with excitement, were saying that they knew who did it, that everyone said they knew. Mom and Dad cautioned them to keep quiet. Dad said you cannot be heard accusing anyone without proof. You'd only get yourself in trouble.

A knock came on the door and Dad answered. When he came back to the table, he told Mom he had to go to the office for a reporter to use the phone.

No homework for us tonight. I turned on the television. Rex Loring was giving the CBC news. Ooh, he's so handsome. I did well in Current Affairs at school because he's so cute to watch.

Fidel Castro and the revolution in Cuba absorbed me. Castro and his guerilla army had taken over that country and ousted the dictator. The general opinion seemed to be that he wouldn't last long. Rebellions like that seldom did, people said. The teacher told us to write about it for our Current Affairs essay. I would've liked to write that I admired Fidel Castro for his rebellion, but that wasn't the accepted view and, if I wanted a good mark, I had to stay within the guidelines of the subject.

The Soviets had put a spacecraft on the moon. Then there was a piece about the IWA in Newfoundland. Diefenbaker had refused to send in more RCMP. Dad said that the riot would certainly be on the news tomorrow, when the country heard about what happened here in Badger.

&

So here I was, eleven o'clock in the night, making my way up the street to Rod Anderson's house. I was stopped three times by cruising RCMP cars. I identified myself and two patrols let me pass. The third one stopped. The Mountie rolled down his window. "Good night, Father. May I ask where you are going? Even a priest needs to be careful tonight."

I would not tell lies. "I am on my way to Mr. Anderson's home.

He isn't feeling well." The Mountie didn't know that Rod wasn't part of my flock and that I normally wouldn't be going to see him, especially late in the night, so it wasn't a lie. To myself, I called that a sin of omission.

"Okay, Father. Keep a sharp lookout. There's a lot going on." He rolled up his window and continued on down Church Road.

Richard was back at my residence. Jennie was too.

I had left Richard in the sacristy to go back to the front door of the church and lock up, when I spied a woman kneeling in one of the pews. It was Jennie Hillier. Her parents were Catholics. She had been too, until she married the Pentecostal boy, Tom. I found her in terrible anguish and it took me half an hour to calm her and listen to her story. To tell the truth, because Jennie had such a terrible tale to tell, I almost forgot Richard.

"Jennie, God has sent you here this night. I have a task for you. Come with me."

I led her into the sacristy. The poor woman jumped with fright when she saw a police officer. He jumped with fright when he saw her. And, of course, they knew each other, however slightly. After all, Badger was a small town.

I got the two of them out of the church through the back door and into my residence. Richard wanted to leave and go back to his job, but I was firm. There were enough lawmen out there that night. He was to stay put at my house until I found out about his father-in-law.

"I'll be suspended if I am missing at roll call."

"What is more important?" I ask. "Your family? Or your job?"

He put his head down in his hands. Poor young man. What a dilemma.

And with that I was out the door, leaving the two of them gawking at me.

The cold night wind whipped around the tail of my soutane as I stood on the veranda of Rod Anderson's house, knocking on the frosted glass panel of his front door. Nothing. I looked out at the street. The people had left the road now; everyone had gone back to their homes; the strikers were God only knew where. I wondered what dramas were being played out this night in other parts of town.

Perhaps I should go around back, I thought. As I walked around the side of the house, I could see a light in the back window. The back door was not even latched. I pushed it open and called out, "Rod. Rod! It's Father Murphy. Are you here?"

He was sitting at the kitchen table. There was a bottle of Lamb's rum and a glass in front of him. He raised his head and looked at me with bleary eyes.

I had never been in his home before, but I hauled out a chair and sat down without invitation. This was no time to think about manners. I waited for him to speak.

"Sorry, Father Murphy, sir." His voice was slurred. "This has been a bad night, not only for me but for Badger as well." He moved a little and winced in pain. "Get yourself a glass in the cupboard. I'm not too good at moving right now."

I knew all about his shoulder, of course, from Richard's account. "Your shoulder is hurt, Rod."

"Yes sir. My shoulder, my heart, perhaps my life." He swallowed a good measure of rum and rambled on. "You know, Father, I loves my two little grandchildren."

I got the glass and poured some rum. Not much – it was going to be a long night. "Is your shoulder broken, do you think?"

He flexed it a little. "Might not be. Some damn sore, though. 'Tis paining too."

"Perhaps the doctor needs to look at it."

"Doctor's gone, sir. He's hightailed it off to Grand Falls with the rest of them." He focused on me unsteadily. "What are you still doing in Badger? The bishop got everything belonged to you closed up."

I sighed. "This is the place that I think God wants me to be right now, Rod."

"How did you know about my shoulder? And what are you doing here in my house so late at night? I'm not even a Catholic."

Then he added, "Not that you're not welcome. Of course you are." He tipped his glass up to his lips again. "Yes you are. Yes."

I had to be careful. In his inebriated state, he might do anything when I told him. "Rod, Richard Fagan is at my residence."

"Jesus Christ!" Rod exploded. "That goddamned townie corner boy attacked me with his fuckin' stick. I knew I shouldn't have let Audrey marry him! He's a goddamned coward, running to his priest instead of coming to me like a man. I could be dead, sure, and he wouldn't even care."

"He was so scared, Rod, that he didn't know what else to do."

"Little townie fucker. All them little townie fuckers. They should never have been out here. And what was his father thinking about, sending Richard out here and not wiring me a telegram to say he was coming? I just can't understand it, sir."

Suddenly, he lurched out of his chair and toward the door. "Excuse me, sir, I'm gonna be sick. Ow! My God, me shoulder!" He was gone out into the snow.

I followed him and held him as he emptied the contents of his stomach into the snow. He stopped retching after a bit. He wiped his mouth on the sleeve of his coat.

"Oh Christ, I'm sorry, sir. I'm so sorry. I never had any supper; nothing to eat since the Jam Jams for my breakfast, and the rum must have hit my stomach like a brick. Ah my Jesus, I got some bad shoulder."

We went back into the house where I boiled the kettle, found some instant coffee in the cupboard and measured out two heaping teaspoons to make it strong. I cut and buttered some bread. There was a tin of bully beef sitting on the counter, so I made him a sandwich of sorts. If someone had told me twenty-four hours ago that I would be in Rod Anderson's house making him a meal, I would've said they were crazy. But here I was.

Rod sat in a daze all the while. But when I put the food in front of him he had sense enough to eat.

I sat and watched him as he finished the sandwich and drank the strong coffee. Then I asked him, "Do you think that the food helped your stomach, my son?"

"It feels much better, sir. Thank you very much for helping me like this." And indeed, the vomiting and the food had sobered him somewhat. At least he wasn't cursing anymore.

"How about we go to my place, Rod?" I coaxed gently. "You and I and Richard can talk. I'll help you sort it out. This terrible mistake has to be resolved."

"I can't, Father. I can't face him, sir. I don't trust myself. I'm likely to kill that townie bastard."

"Rod, think of the alternative. Richard explained to me about your wife being in St. John's with your daughter, Audrey. They have no idea Richard is out here. He was sent out on a secret mission. His father had no control over it. Just a routine patrol to keep the peace, he was told. Richard hoped to be gone and never see you. This is a cruel twist of fate. We have to work it out. Many lives stand in the balance – your own, Ruth's, your daughter Audrey's, the two little girls and Richard's. And two more – Richard's parents."

30

I don't know who got the biggest fright, the young policemen or me. Before we could gather our wits about us, the priest hustled us out through the back door of the church and into his residence. Then he left the two of us there and made off for Rod Anderson's.

As he went out the door, he said to me, "Now Jennie, I am depending on you. Stay with Richard until I get back. Get tea and some food for yourselves. I am hoping to bring Mr. Anderson back, but he might be injured. I'll need you then too. Stand by, both of you."

I started to get us a cup of tea. It took me a bit of searching to find cups and spoons, a sugar basin and some milk, which turned out to be what we called "fresh" milk and not the tinned Carnation kind that most of us used. The priest's kitchen was spotless. I was half afraid to touch anything. Oh Mam, if you could see me now. Father Murphy had a housekeeper, but she wasn't here. Perhaps she was sent away with the nuns.

Richard was restless. For sure he figured he should be out there with his unit, chasing down loggers. Privately I thought that every cop that the loggers didn't have to worry about, the better. Of course I never said that to Richard, and he never said anything to me about chasing down loggers. We each respected the other.

I actually didn't know what to say to him, and that wasn't like me. I was never stuck for words. We'd only met a couple of times. I always thought him rather nice, but reserved. Tom played ball with him over on the field sometimes. He said Richard was hard to get to know. He wasn't much like his father, Mr. Abernathy, who talked to everyone, right from the A.N.D. Company manager down to me. Most people in Badger called him by his first name, Levi. Everyone said, "What a nice man; never know he's a police sergeant."

I got our tea. I found a cake tin with a rich, dark fruitcake in it. Trust the priest's housekeeper to make fruitcake when it wasn't even Christmas. I cut off three or four pieces, put them on a plate – lovely Royal Albert china – and laid the plate in front of Richard.

"How are Audrey and the little ones doing?" I asked. "I heard that Ruth went in to St. John's to be with them for awhile." That was putting it delicately. Rod had hustled Ruth off because contractors in Badger had been threatened and Rod was afraid for his wife being alone in the house if he was across the River.

"They're all well." He spooned some more sugar into his tea. I was counting, and that was six teaspoons. I was pretty sure that he didn't even know he was doing it. "None of them has a clue I'm out here, you know."

Well! What kind of tangle was that? "And where's your father? Is he out here too?" I had this vivid image of Levi Abernathy – Police Sergeant Abernathy – galumphin' through the snow, striking loggers down with his nightstick.

"No, my father's not here. Thank God for that. He loves this town and its people. He'd never go along with what has happened here tonight. He'll never believe it when he hears. I can hardly believe it myself." He sighed and put his head down in his hands. "And now, this thing with Rod . . . I don't know. I don't know."

I patted his arm in sympathy. I was always a good arm patter. Mam was too. She always said human contact, an arm pat or a shoulder pat, was important when someone was in trouble. "Tell me about you and Rod while we wait for Father Murphy to come back."

And he did. Poor Richard. What a miserable stroke of luck, and no fault of his own. If Joey Smallwood or the A.N.D. Company officials were to ever hear the story of how lives were ruined this night, how many people would never be the same, how children's minds were scarred forever, would they care? I thought not.

Back came Father Murphy, towing a half-drunk Rod who had a sore shoulder and a lot of anger.

I knew it wasn't going to work when they walked in. I could see it in Rod's eyes. The friggin' rum, you know. It makes men say stuff that they later regret.

So Father Murphy tried to patch it up between them. Richard was sorry; scared and sorry. Father encouraged him to say what he was feeling. "I don't know what came over me to hit someone. I never have before, in my whole career. It was as if I was caught up in the violence, in the power that we were exerting by defeating the strikers and breaking them up. I know it was wrong. I can see it now. I'm sorry."

But Rod didn't want to listen. He lurched out of his chair. "Father, can I use your bathroom? I think I'm going to be sick again. And you, you goddamn townie bastard, get back to St. John's. Send my wife back to me, and tell Audrey what you did to her father. See how she feels about it." With that he was gone down the hall with the priest, groaning aloud about his shoulder.

Richard looked at me. "I'm leaving."

"No, Richard. Stay. Please."

"Sorry, Jennie, there's nothing else I can do. He's only going to get madder." He was dressing as he spoke, putting on his heavy black greatcoat, fur hat and gloves. His ill-fated nightstick was on the table. He picked it up. "I'm gone now. Thanks for your help. I hope we meet again under happier circumstances."

"Wait . . . wait . . ." But he was gone out into the cold dark night. I wanted to tell him to watch out for Tom and Ralph and others that he knew. Surely he would. Surely he wouldn't get caught up in the savagery any more. But I worried about it all.

ℬ

I left the priest's house on a run. My father-in-law's anger and pain was too much for me to watch.

Ducking under the big trees, my gaiters sinking through the snow, I reached the road. There was no one in sight. It must be nearly one o'clock in the morning. Had my entire contingent gone?

A lone patrol car coasted past. I waved frantically. The driver must have seen me in his rear-view mirror. His brake lights came on and I ran forward. It was the RCMP. "What are you doing out here alone, b'y? Most of the members have gone on down to Grand Falls."

"I had a bit of trouble," I answered. "Got knocked down."

"Climb in back there. We're going to cruise around for another bit and then we're going to head on down too." I climbed in the back of the police car.

"You okay back there?" one of them asked.

"Yeah, sure. I'm good. Thanks." They weren't Constabulary; they were Mounties, strangers to me. There was always a certain rivalry between us. If you were accepted into the RCMP you were considered to be a notch above the Constabulary. However, despite the rivalry there was a brotherhood. We were all police officers. We would always watch each other's back.

We cruised the streets for awhile. Streets that I had walked with Audrey. Streets that now had witnessed extreme violence. There was no one about. The boys decided to call it a night and head back to Grand Falls. When we arrived, they dropped me off at my billet on Cromer Avenue.

Rod and Father came back. The priest looked around. "Where's Richard?"

"He thought it better if he left."

"Well, so much for that. Let's hope he doesn't get into more trouble out there tonight." Father Murphy sighed. "Jennie, I'm keeping Rod here with me tonight. He needs that shoulder looked at. Maybe I'll send someone for Mrs. Drum. She'll know if it is broken, at least. You can stay too, my child, if you wish."

"No, Father, thank you. I have to get home to my house. Tom

will be worried about me, as I am worried about him. I don't know where they all went."

Rod looked at me. I think he was relieved to see Richard gone. He was a sorry sight, as pale as death, his eyes pain-filled, angry, yet defeated at the same time. "I bet you never thought you'd see the day when a good Protestant like me would sleep in a priest's house, did you, Jennie?" A small smile touched his mouth at the irony of it all.

Father Murphy was getting more tea. I cleared away the cups that Richard and I had used. Rod picked up a piece of the untouched fruitcake and started to eat it. I hoped he wouldn't get sick again.

"I wish there was someone to walk you home, Jennie," the priest said as he poured the boiling water into the teapot.

"Don't worry about me, Father. I can look after myself. I know all the shortcuts in Badger, all the hiding places. This is my home. I'll be all right." I pulled on my coat. There were no buttons left to do up. The cop had torn them off earlier.

So I left them. Out I went, into the darkness under the big trees, following much the same path as Richard must have done. It was one o'clock in the morning, and the whole length of Church Road was dark and silent.

No one stopped me as I walked down the road, turned left toward the railway tracks, passed through the town's centre and on in toward Halls Bay Road. I looked neither left nor right. I focused on getting to my little house, my haven. As I walked, I prayed that Tom would be there waiting for me.

ℬ

The morning of March 11 dawned cold and frosty. The mild spurt of weather was over.

As I walked down the road to my telegraph office, I could see that poor old Badger looked used and bruised. Every inch of snow was trampled in a town where stretches of land never saw a foot-print all winter. There were a couple of overturned fire barrels, their charred wood and ashes smeared across the whiteness. The Mountie cars were still around too. I wondered about the policeman who was struck down last night.

I had not gone back down to the goat house to check on the fugitives before I left. I figured Ralph would look after that when the coast was clear. I was worried about my film and about them pissing on my floor or in my acids, but nothing could be done about it now.

Not long after I opened the office, Ralph came in. He looked worn out. "Ralph, my son, you look like you could use a nap."

"Yes, Alf b'y, we had a hard night. We got everyone away, though. Only nine fellas were arrested. Half of Badger got people hiding."

"Here, Ralph, take the key to the goat house. Will you have them fellas gone before I get home?"

"Yes, Alf, they'll be gone. Don't worry." He pocketed the key. "Did you hear about Landon Ladd?"

"No. What about him?" I had forgotten about the IWA president. There were so many things on the go that I never gave a thought where he would be.

"He had a head-on collision with a meat truck last night. Demolished his car, but he never got hurt." Ralph rubbed his hands over his tired face. He looked like he was on his last legs.

"Where did that happen? On the road to Grand Falls?" I had assumed Ladd had been staying down there.

"No. Out on the Halls Bay Road. Someone said that he was staying at a cabin on the Halls Bay Line."

"Hmm. First I ever heard about that. Perhaps he's not wanted in Grand Falls these days. The mood is ugly down there too – in a different way than it is here." I tidied away the office as we talked, sweeping the floor, wiping off the counter, setting out a fresh message pad with the carbon paper in it.

"Yeah, I dare say you got that right."

"So, Ralph, what do you think of what happened?"

Ralph shook his head. "That was terrible, Alf. I was up there, b'y. Me and Tom were right up front. We were having a great laugh at Vern trying to sneak the scabs through." He leaned on the counter and scrubbed his hands over his face, as if he were trying to wipe away his fatigue. "Then we saw the police marching up and we didn't know what to expect. We thought it was their way of showing force. But they must have been ordered to destroy us, because when they came back down the road, the head cop shouted 'Right wheel,' and there they were, right in our faces. Then the police waded in among us with their nightsticks swinging."

"Did you see who struck down the policeman?"

"Naw. Too much going on for that. Maybe it was one of the police themselves who struck him."

Ralph turned away from me and looked out the window. Hmm, maybe the less that was said about last night, the better it would be for us all.

"Well, poor Landon Ladd," I said. "I guess he lost his fight after all. What do you think the loggers will do now, Ralph?"

"I dunno, b'y. The IWA is decertified. All of Newfoundland is on Joey's side. That friggin' Joey is like a dictator. No one will speak out against him. I'm thinking the loggers will be forced into joining Joey's union if they want to keep their jobs."

My phone rang. It was the Grand Falls office, ready to transmit incoming telegrams. Ralph nodded, jingled the goat house key at me, and went on out the door. As I took the messages, my mind was only half occupied with my work. The other half was thinking about what Ralph had said – and what he hadn't said.

Later in the day, Arnold Brown dropped in. Arnold works on the trains as a conductor. He was on his days off. "Jesus, Alf, I don't know what to do. I got four strikers hid up in me attic. I knows someone else who got some hid down in his basement."

"Arnold b'y," I said, "that's dangerous stuff, wouldn't you say?"

"Goddamn right, buddy. Anyone caught at that will be in some trouble."

Christ! I hope Ralph got them fellas outta my goat house.

31

I was nearly dead on my feet. What a night! Alf gave me the keys of the goat house and I trudged over to let the boys out, keeping my eye out for any stray Mounties that might still be around.

The men were cold, hungry and needed to use the outhouse. At least they never pissed on Alf's stuff. They all knew their asses had been saved last night, and now, by whatever transportation could be found, they would make their way back home. The loggers, all of them, were broken, defeated men. Their high hopes of January had been destroyed forever.

The buzzword around town was that the cop who had been struck down was in a coma at the hospital in Grand Falls. Doctors didn't expect him to live. Bad news always travelled fast. Was it the same cop that I had knocked away from Jennie? Or was it another one, struck by someone else? *I shouldn't have run.* This thought kept racing through my tired brain as I tried to clue up my tasks.

After we had stowed the men in the goat house, Tom and I had split up. I went back down to the River and he took three more fellows to the pastor's house to hide out. Tom was worried about Jennie. Jesus, I was worried about her too, but I couldn't let on to Tom. So I told Tom to go on home when he finished at the pastor's. I said I was going to hide some men up in the woods in a couple of old tilts in among the trees.

I couldn't ask Tom directly about striking the policeman. He hadn't seen me do it. Probably didn't even know I was near Jennie at the time. When the cop grabbed Tom, Jennie jumped from the snowbank onto the back of the cop, who turned and grappled with her. Tom was swung away from them in the furious ebb and flow of loggers and police. When I sprinted over to help her, he wasn't even close.

Tom said he never knew what happened for that cop to be hit so hard in the head. He kept repeating that it could just as easily have been a logger who was down in Grand Falls Hospital right now, there were that many of us clubbed to the ground.

As for me, I never let on to Tom that I had run from the scene because Jennie and I thought I had killed someone. I was purposely vague about what part of the riot I was involved in. We didn't have a lot of time for chit-chat that night. We were pretty busy hiding men in attics, basements, sheds, outhouses, garbage barrels, wherever we could find.

I had to talk to Jennie, but it would have to wait. I needed sleep and headed for home.

Ma was just getting home too. I figured she'd been making a house call, maybe delivering a baby. She was often called upon when the doctor was away, and I'm sure he'd been whisked away by the Company while this was going on.

We went into the house together and took off our boots and coats. "Hard old night, Ma," I said. "I'm going for a nap. Wake me if anyone comes for me." I had a feeling that, before the day was over, I'd have my hands full with helping the strikers that had to get out of Badger and away from the roaming police units.

"Yes, my son, I know it must've been a hard night for you." She put a junk of wood in the stove and moved the kettle over on the part that would get the hottest. "I just came from the priest's residence. He had Rod Anderson there. He got injured in the riot."

Huh? How could that be? An A.N.D. Company contractor injured? What was he doing at the priest's house? And Rod was a Protestant. How could that be? But my mind was numb with fatigue. I just shook my head and went on to bed.

Deep into sleep, I had a dream. It was born, I suppose, out of exhaustion and trauma. I was walking along by the banks of the

Exploits River. It was summer. The waters flowed swiftly, reflecting the blue sky on its surface but hinting at the darkness beneath. I heard a shout. When I turned I saw cops chasing me. They were shouting, "Get him! He killed one of ours!" In the dream, the riverbank was endless and I ran and ran. I could feel a pain in my side as I gasped for breath. Then I tripped and fell. I could distinctly feel the grass under my cheek and I could see the toes of a pair of old rubber boots close to my face. My eyes followed up the legs and there was Grandfather.

"Oh no," I yelled. "They're coming, Grandfather! Run, or they'll get you too!" Grandfather and I looked back together but there was no one there.

Suddenly, a great calmness came over me. I sat up, and Grandfather sat beside me on the green grass by the mighty Exploits. I told him about the riot, how we lost our bid for the union of our choice, how many men were hurt and, lastly, I told him about believing I had struck down a policeman. I kept inside my heart why I struck him and about Jennie. But I might have known Grandfather could see inside me.

"Go and talk to the young woman with the bright hair, my son. She has the answer for you. Then, when you are done, make a journey to our cave and speak with the eagle spirit. Keep in mind the river of time that I told you about."

In my dream, I looked out over the Exploits, toward Sandy, the centre of Badger's woods operations, thinking, Yes, that is exactly what I want to do. When I looked back, his familiar old face was gone and, in my dream, a hawk rose up in the sky, wheeling away.

"Ralph, Ralph, wake up." The voice was Ma's. I opened my eyes. The feeling of emptiness that one always gets when dreaming of a lost loved one was strong upon me.

"Ralph, some fellas from the union came by. They said to tell you there's a meeting at the Noels' old house up by the church." I looked at my watch. Nearly noon. I'd been asleep for five hours.

I awoke to Mom's voice calling me. "Amanda, it's time to get up for school."
I opened my eyes and last night's events came flooding back to me.

"You'd think they'd cancel school for today," I grumbled sleepily. "The Catholics are the lucky ones – they have no school." We envied the Catholics. Their school was closed when they took the nuns away.

My father had already left for the telegraph office. Mom got us our breakfast and, with her admonishments to my brothers to behave themselves, we were out the door.

On the school grounds, the kids clustered in little knots talking in low voices, looking scared. There was no running around, no horseplay. The shock of what had happened still seemed to grip us.

Mr. Summers spoke to us. "Don't go repeating rumours," he said. "No matter what you heard or what you might think you saw, say nothing. You're not grown-ups. You are children."

∅

It seemed like no time when I awoke to someone shaking my shoulder. One of the strikers was bending over my bed. "Pastor. Pastor. Wake up. There's a police car outside."

"What? What time is it?" I was groggy with sleep. Late nights don't become me.

"It's eight o'clock. We've been up for awhile. Too nervous to sleep. Got ourselves a drop of tea too. Hope you don't mind."

"No, it's all right. Oh my Lord, I overslept." I was hauling on my pants while he stood in the door.

Then I heard the knocking on the front door.

"That's the police. My two buddies are up in the attic again. I'm gone to join them." He disappeared in the direction of the back pantry. He was a pretty cool customer, that guy.

I scravelled to open the door. Sure enough, it was the old sergeant.

"Good morning, Pastor. Looks like I woke you up."

"Uh . . . yeah . . . I'm sorry." I hadn't had time to comb my hair. Never in my life have I appeared in public with uncombed hair.

"Come in, sergeant. Come in." I had to keep him to the front room in case there was a sound from the attic.

"I won't keep you, Pastor." He stood there, just inside the front door, dressed exactly as he was yesterday, in his long black coat and fur hat. I wanted to ask him if he'd been up all night. But something in his hard keen eyes as he looked around my front room, missing nothing, stopped me.

"I never got back to you last night. There was a lot going on and I had to go back to Grand Falls."

"That's all right, sir. How is the injured officer doing?" It was just as well to get this conversation to the point and get it over.

"He's not expected to make it, Pastor. I would like to find out who struck him."

"I'm sorry, Sergeant, but I have no name for you. There were many strangers down there. Everyone looked pretty much alike." The answer rolled smoothly off my tongue, surprising even me. I had gone to bed with indecision in my heart, but God had decided for me as I slept. "If you want me to testify, I will. I'll testify to the event, but I have no name."

He seemed to weigh my words. "Because you viewed the incident through a window, your testimony isn't admissible, but I would've personally appreciated a name from you."

I wished he would leave. My shirttail was hanging out and I was in my bare feet. Never had I felt so embarrassed.

"I am sorry, sir. There's no name." Help me here, Lord. "I will pray for your injured man. If it is God's will, he'll come through."

"Hmmph. Well, goodbye, Pastor." He turned and left me standing there in the front room, wondering what the new day would bring forth.

※

In the morning I was present at roll call in the armoury at six o'clock. I thought I was free and clear, that no one had noticed my absence in last night's turmoil, but I was wrong.

The sergeant beckoned to me. "Fagan. Come here a minute."

I went over, my heart racing. "Yes sir."

He was about the same age as my father. The two of them knew each other, having come up through the ranks together.

He looked at me, his sharp eyes missing nothing. "You weren't around last night, so I hear. I was told that our unit came back from Badger without you. What happened?"

I hesitated. Perhaps I should tell him. After all, I had done no real wrong. Maybe I did more right than wrong because I was too occupied with my own concerns during the riot to be out there clouting the loggers. And I was honest with myself: there's something takes hold of men in times like that. Anger – the Vikings called it *berserker* – that makes you want to strike out, to crush, to even kill. It affected me too. I know, because, God forgive me, I wanted to hit that guy and hit him hard, for no reason except that I *could*. Then I found out that he was my father-in-law. By then it was too late.

The sergeant interrupted my thoughts. "Isn't that girl you married from somewhere out this way? Buchans, is it?"

"No, sergeant. Badger. My mother-in-law is from Buchans, but Audrey is from Badger."

His bushy eyebrows went up in astonishment. "Really? You probably know a few Badger people, then. Hmm. I know it was a rush job to get you guys aboard the train and out here, but you shouldn't have been sent out here to a place where you have close family ties. But then, no one thought it would come to this. We were merely a supplement to the RCMP, you know. A show of force. Keep the peace."

I nodded.

"So you were a part of last night's confrontation."

"Yes sir."

"And?"

"As I said, my wife's parents live in Badger. Her father is an A.N.D. Company contractor. He was a bystander at the riot and became mistaken for a striker. There was a lot of confusion there for awhile."

He sighed. "Yes, a lot of confusion." I didn't envy the sergeant his job today. There were many things for him to sort out, and he had one of our members in hospital in serious condition.

"Well. Sir, I . . . I . . . hit him with my nightstick."

"What? Good God, man! Your own father-in-law? How badly did you hurt him?"

Just then another member came by and told the sergeant that the RCMP inspector needed to speak to him as soon as possible.

I said quickly, "I struck him hard, sir, I'm sorry to say. I don't know if there's a bone broken or not. We came eye to eye, and we recognized each other."

"Stay there a minute. I have to go and speak to the inspector, but I'll be right back to you. Don't move." And he hurried away.

I cooled my heels for almost an hour before he returned.

"All right, Fagan, here's what is happening. They think there will be more violence in the wake of last night's. The Department of Justice is sending out fifty more of our members. When that train arrives we are going to send her back to St. John's, and you are going to be on board." He looked at me keenly. "Are you going to be okay until then?"

I nodded miserably. All I could think of was Rod and the pain I had caused him. My thoughts kept tumbling to Papa, Mama, Audrey, Ruth, my daughters. What would become of our small family circle?

Once again I was on the train as it made its sinuous way toward St. John's. I was lucky enough to have a sleeper berth, but I didn't sleep. I lay in the bunk, listening to the squeaks and rattles of the train, and I worried. I had to tell Ruth that I had struck her husband.

I had to tell Audrey that I had struck her dad. I had to tell Papa that I had acted in a way that was the opposite of all that he had taught me. And then another thought raised its ugly head. Was my true lineage coming to the fore? Was I really a chip off the old block after all? My real father, the hardcase Joe Fagan, had done nothing but drink and fight his way through a short, brutal life. Did blood really run true?

I hailed a taxi from the train station and went to my parents' house first. Mama and Papa were having breakfast. They were surprised when I opened the door and walked in.

"Richard!" Papa jumped up so fast he upset his chair. "Richard, what are you doing back already?"

"Oh my God, my poor boy! You look worn out. Levi, let him sit down." Mama bustled to get a cup of coffee.

I sat down. "I was sent back early," I said. "Papa, what a mess out there in Badger."

Papa's face was sombre. "Yes, I was at the station when the news came through. One of our members was down; the report told of violence and bloodshed. We didn't think this would happen."

Mama gave me the coffee. It felt good to sit there in the kitchen where I had grown up. The hot coffee warmed my insides.

"Papa, I have myself in a terrible pickle."

He leaned forward. "A pickle? What do you mean?"

"I came to speak to you first, before I went home to Audrey and her mother." I drank some more coffee. It went down too fast and scalded my tongue. "Papa, I was with the unit that went up to Badger on patrol. We marched up through a large group of strikers. Something happened – I'm not sure what – and we became engaged with the men. They were armed with billets and we had our nightsticks."

Mama's mouth was a round "O" as she listened. I looked away from her frightened eyes.

"The ferocity of the clash was incredible. It was almost dark, and police and strikers grappled viciously with each other. I was as bad as anyone."

It was very hard for me to tell them what had happened. I couldn't look into their faces as I spoke. "Papa, I struck Rod. On his shoulder, with my nightstick. Maybe I broke it." I started to cry. "Oh God, oh God."

Both of them jumped to their feet. "What?" Mama came rushing over to put her arms around me.

Without sparing myself, I told my parents all of it, even the part about the *berserker* feeling. My shame was heavy on my heart. "I have to go and tell Audrey and Ruth now."

Papa went over and grabbed his coat. "I'll come with you."

Mama pushed back the dishes. "I'll come too. The little girls will need me."

So my parents and I walked up the street to my house where Audrey, Ruth and the girls were happily getting ready to start their day, unaware of how I was about to spoil it.

32

Tom came back in the afternoon. "Pastor Genge," he said, "thank you for putting yourself out for the boys last night. You saved them from going to jail. The union is shipping guys out of town as fast as they can.

"There's a freight train down at the station going east. We have about thirty men in one of the boxcars. My father knows but, like the rest of us, he wants to get this town cleared out as soon as we can. As station master, he'll turn a blind eye."

The men thanked me for my hospitality. Hospitality? Hah! Jonathan would've laughed at that one. Then they filed out the door.

Somehow, with the resilience that all human beings have, and with the help of God, the people of Badger, the former strikers and I, got through the day after the riot. A pall hung over the town as everyone held their breath, awaiting news of the stricken constable. If he died, it would be an entirely different tale than if he lived. I heard nothing further from the police.

ℬ

Well, Father beat the shit out of me. Unknown to me, Father was up in Badger on the very picket line that the taxi tried to crash through. He was among the picketers who were brought in to swell the numbers.

How was I supposed to know that? No one tells me nuttin'. When I walked into the house, after the Mountie let me off, there

271

was Father. I don't think he had gone to bed at all. "Well, Cecil, you snot-nosed little good-for-nothing, I seen you. Yes I did. You was in the taxi. Is that what you've been up to these past couple of months? There's me on a picket line, fighting for my rights, and you behind my back, working as a scab."

There was Stepmother over by the table smirking at me. I didn't know how to answer Father. I couldn't. Just stood there and looked at him. Father was taller and bigger than I was. I don't know why I didn't grow much, but I was always the smallest in the family. Jesus, I was more scared of Father than I was of the Mounties, the crazy picketers and the legless man all put together.

He had his big old leather belt in his hand. I was no stranger to that belt. My sister wasn't either. Neither were the children that Stepmother and Father owned together. Father used that belt all the time. Perhaps Stepmother was beaten too, but I never had no pity for her.

He let me have it – right across the side of the cheek. I dropped down on my knees, covering my face and head. My arms got it then. There was no escaping the angry swish of that belt. He went on and on, all the while yelling at me. "Your stepmother is right, you *are* a useless, stupid, good for nothing."

There! Stupid. I was stupid. Father believed what she had told him all along. My last hope was gone. If Father thought it, well, it had to be true. I was stupid and no good.

His arm must have gotten tired of swinging the strap and he stopped, but not before I was bleeding in what seemed like a million places. Every inch of me was burning. I crawled away, sobbing like a ten-year-old. Come to think of it, I wasn't very far from ten, being only seventeen, but I felt like I'd been around forever. Last words I heard before I passed out was that friggin' stepmother: "What a big baby, crying over a lickin'."

When I awoke, it was night again. I'd been asleep or unconscious for all day. I heard Emily's voice. "Cecil, wake up. Everyone is gone to bed except me. Wake up."

I rolled over. When me sore, raw back touched the mattress I almost died. Emily was bending over me. "Get up, Cecil, and I'll tend to your back. Shh, be quiet. Don't wake anyone."

There were three bedrooms in the house. One was for Father and Stepmother, one was for Emily and the two baby boys while the third was for the three older boys. I slept on a daybed in under the stairs off the kitchen.

We crept out to the kitchen table. The house was dark. Even though there was electricity, Emily wouldn't turn on the light for fear that it would wake Stepmother. She lit a small candle.

"Take off your shirt now," she whispered.

I hauled off my shirt and singlet. The singlet was stuck to my skin with the dried blood. When the singlet came off, the welts started bleeding again and I could feel the warm blood running down over my back. The pain was almost enough to make me faint.

The water in the kettle was still warm from Father's nighttime lunch. Emily poured it into an enamel pan. From somewhere she got an old cloth – not one of Stepmother's good face cloths – and sponged my back. I was used to being belted, but this one was the worst yet. It smert – it smert real bad. I wanted to cry, but I was brave.

Stepmother kept Mecca Ointment up in her cupboard. Emily reached up and got it.

"No, Emily. Stepmother will beat you if you uses that."

"To hell with her," my sister answered as she gently applied the soothing ointment to my skin.

I was so astonished to hear my meek young sister say a word like *hell* that I almost forgot about me back.

"You swore on her," I whispered. "You did! She'll wash your mouth out with Sunlight Soap for that."

"Shh. Be quiet, Cecil, and stay still." Emily finished me back and put the ointment back in the cupboard. She sat down at the table across from me.

"Cecil, I have something to tell you. I'm leaving here. I can't stand it any longer. I have a job as housekeeper to old Mr. Soames."

"Wha . . . ? Stepmother is going to let you go? Who'll look after the kids and do the housework for her?" Suddenly I was frightened all over again.

"I don't care about that. I'm going, Cecil, and that's that."

"Emily . . ." I didn't know how to say it. "Uh . . . you know . . . fellas at the pool hall sez that Mr. Soames is a dirty old man."

Suddenly Father's yell could be heard upstairs. "What's that light? Is someone up down there?"

Quickly, Emily blew out the candle. "Hurry, get into your bunk. I'm gone to mine." And she disappeared like a shadow. I crawled in under the stairs and onto the daybed.

33

In the evening of March eleventh, rested, and with Ma's good supper in me, I walked up the road to the meeting at the IWA house. But more pressing than any meeting was my anxiety over a question.

Was I responsible for that cop being in the hospital or not? My dream hung over me like a mantle. So strong was it that I only paid half an ear to what was being said at the meeting – me, formerly so passionate for our cause.

The union boys were there. There was no further news on the fallen policeman, they said. Then they told us that the IWA was accepting defeat. Landon Ladd would make it official later on, but for now we were to consider there was no other option but to go back to work and hope that our sacrifices had not been in vain. It was a hard decision, but we all knew it had to be. We had made our last stand at the picket line, and we well might have won, had it not been for a policeman struck down in the snow and, for all we knew, dead by now. It had taken the heart out of us.

When we disbanded, I came outside. Out of the corner of my eye I saw Jennie going into the Catholic Church across the road. Should I follow her? This might be my chance to get her alone and ask her what had happened after I ran away.

The church was empty. It was almost dark outside, but the lights weren't turned on. In the niche of the Sacred Heart, a red light glimmered and some small candles flickered, lit for the souls of the dead.

At first I didn't see her, but I knew she was there. I always knew when Jennie was nearby. Over to the far right, up near the front, I saw her faint outline. I walked up.

She jumped. "Ralph," she whispered. "I never heard you come in. How are you? I've been worried about you."

I sat down beside her. "This is a hard time Jennie, a hard thing for us all to accept. You can pray all you like, but it won't change the fact that we are finished as a union. We're wiped out. The men are in a terrible state."

"I know, Ralph. I have been with the women. There's a lot of tears have been shed the past twenty-four hours."

The Sacred Heart's red glow illuminated her face a little. I could smell her more than see her, her special scent that had been with me since I was twelve years old. I couldn't touch her. I couldn't even hold her hand. But we could talk as we always had.

She leaned forward and looked into my eyes. "You were just in my mind, Ralph. I was thinking of what you said when you hit the cop to get him off me. You said you had dreamt it at one time. Did I misunderstand that? Or did you really say it?"

"I dreamt that scene, Jennie. In it was an older me, an older you and a black figure choking you. Remember the time that I went up Hodges Hill and found the pearls? I spent the night in the little cave where they rest. I think I told you that part, didn't I?"

"Yes, you did, Ralph."

"Well, that was when I had the dream. Grandfather warned me that handling the pearls could make a person dream the future. Perhaps that's how Grandfather himself knew so many things."

Jennie was paying close attention. We were so close that I could see the lashes on her eyelids, her moist lips, feel her breath on my face. I forced myself not to tremble.

"My God, Ralph, all those years and you never told me."

"No, maid. To tell the truth, I thought the black-caped figure was Death coming to get you." I laughed, a little embarrassed. "It was a police officer's greatcoat instead."

Being so close to Jennie was unsettling my head. I slipped to my knees on the kneeler. My back was to her and she couldn't see my face. "Jennie, how did you get on after I ran away from you? I'm some ashamed of that, you know. I should've stayed. To hell with the consequences."

I felt her hand on my shoulder. "Ralph. That was my fault. I was so scared for you. I didn't want you to go to jail."

"We're not cowards, you know. My family are not cowards." I couldn't look at her.

She patted my back. "Come on, Ralph. Sit back. Let's get past this and go on. I don't think you're a coward. And I am sure no one else thinks so. I shouldn't have been up there, I suppose. I should've been at home like any good housewife, like Missus Suze kept saying all along. She told Tom I was too bold, mixing in men's affairs."

I sat back in the seat. "There's one thing I haven't asked you, and you have to tell me straight. Is the cop that's in the hospital the one I hit or not?"

I startled her. Her eyes and mouth formed "O's" together. She sucked in her breath. She reached out . . . she reached out and put her arms around me. I was as still as a little sparrow in the hands of a giant. Except I was no sparrow, I was an eagle, even if I was a beaten one. And Jennie, she was no giant. She was my Amazon Beothuk Woman, bigger than me, yes she was, and the feel of her was some good. And she held me.

"Ralph. Oh my son, I am some sorry. I never realized . . . oh my God. No b'y, you didn't. You are not responsible for that. Oh God, I should not have told you to run. Oh Ralph, I am so sorry." I could tell that she was crying. "Afterwards, it never came to my mind that you weren't there when the other cop was struck down. How'd you ever get that in your head? Didn't Tom tell you about it?"

What could I say? She still had her arms around me, but I had to move sometime. We couldn't stay like this forever and ever, frozen in time, dust gathering on us, perhaps becoming statues, like St. Theresa and St. Joseph and the Virgin Mary. People would light candles to us in a hundred years' time, thinking we were holy saints or something. Jesus, what a weird thought! Being in Jennie's arms had really unhinged my mind.

It took every bit of my willpower to do it, but I had to move away from her. "Tom didn't know that I hit the guy to get him off you," I said. "He was whirled away with the crowd and into the crush. You were on the outskirts, by the snowbank. He never saw us."

My heart was pounding in my chest. I got up, walked outside the pew and stood by the Sacred Heart niche. Jesus, in His red robe, His head bowed, His hand pointing to His bleeding heart, was no more sorrowful than I was at that moment. If I stayed in the seat, I was going to put my arms around her, I knew it. By God, when this was over, I was going deep in the country, perhaps to Hodges Hill, and live like a hermit.

Jennie wiped the tears from her eyes. "I knelt down by the policeman to see how bad he was. He was groaning a bit, so I knew he wasn't dead. I kind of cradled him in my arms – I even had a bit of blood on my blouse afterward – and then, another policeman came along yelling at me, until he saw I was a woman. Then Tom got clear and came over too. It was all a big tangle. But the important thing is that he got up and walked away on his own. Actually, he swung back into the fracas, as strong as ever."

Jennie sighed and stood up too.

"Well, thank God," I said. "You've taken some load off my mind, Jennie. None of us ever set out to kill anyone. Or I don't s'pose we did. I never did, anyway." Now I needed a smoke after all that. "Let's go."

"No, you go on. I have to stay for a bit. I think I am going to return to my own church, you know. Tom won't mind. Missus Suze will be furious and go on and on, but I don't care. Perhaps the pastor and the priest will let me alternate. Anyway, I need to sit and think for awhile."

I started down the aisle, toward the door.

"Ralph."

"What?"

"I hope we'll always be friends. I hope this doesn't change anything."

"Never, Jennie. Always friends."

Then I was outside in the cold evening air, hauling the cigarettes out of my jacket pocket as I walked.

∞

My sister, Emily, was gone before the week was out. She just disappeared one night while everyone was asleep. She didn't own much clothes or even a suitcase to put them in. I supposed that she used a paper bag.

One morning, when I rolled out of the bunk under the stairs, Stepmother was in the kitchen with the five little boys and she was going crazy. The boys were whining for breakfast. The smell of shitty diapers was strong, and she was cursing and screaming at them.

"Hey, Cecil. Idiot!" she yelled at me. "Where's your stupid lazy sister gone? She's supposed to be here to feed them youngsters. That's her job, what pays for her room and board in this house. No good to check the bedroom," she said, as I headed toward her room. "Her clothes is gone too."

That night, when I crawled into my bunk in the little cubbyhole under the stairs, I felt a lump under my pillow. It was a bit of brown paper tied with string. I opened it. Emily had left me our mother's blue handkerchief. It was the only thing that we had left from her. When I was ten and Emily eight and our mother died, Father had passed it to us, saying, "Here's something to remember her by." It had smelled so nice then. Emily said it was lavender. But the smell had left it over the years. I remembered that Emily and I would take turns holding onto it when Stepmother barred us up in the dark attic. Now, my sister had left it for me.

If Father cared about Emily's leaving, he didn't show it. He told Stepmother to get off her lazy arse and wash the diapers herself, and if she didn't stop complaining he'd give her the back of his hand. I secretly enjoyed the scared look on her face when he said that.

Turning to me, he shook his finger in my face. "Now, me laddie-o, since they had the fuss up there in Badger, the strike is over. I'm signing on with Joey's new union. I'm signing you up too. When the summer cutting starts, you're going back in the woods and I'll learn you to be a logger if 'tis the last thing I ever does."

With Emily out of the way, Stepmother stepped up her cruelty. She wouldn't allow me any food. I lived on scraps from the garbage cans of the Cozy Chat and the Brown Derby restaurants. Then she locked me out of the house.

It was the last straw. My sister was gone, my father wanted me to go in the woods again, there was no one who cared if I lived or died. I couldn't take anymore. I walked back down toward the pool hall, wondering vaguely where to spend the night. A westbound freight train was pulling into the railway station across the street. I remembered the hobos that I'd seen in Badger who lived their life on the rails. Without thinking much about what I was doing, I sprinted across the street and hoisted myself up into an empty boxcar. Next stop: Port aux Basques.

34

The riot happened on a Tuesday. I heard nothing from Ruth and Audrey. I didn't know what had happened to Richard and his police unit. Ruth never wired or phoned, but arrived late on Thursday night and walked up the road with her suitcase.

It wasn't a long walk, but it was winter and it was nighttime. Also, being such a small town, with everyone living in everyone else's back-yard, so to speak, by now they all knew that my son-in-law had clunked me, and they all knew that Ruth was in St. John's. Therefore, if anyone saw her plodding up Church Road all by herself with her suitcase in the night, they were sure to say, "Ah, Rod Anderson never met his wife at the train. What's going on with them since his son-in-law nearly killed him?"

I was asleep. I hadn't used the bedroom at all since Ruth left. Too much trouble to undress. I'd been crashing on the daybed by the stove. The house was messy, especially the kitchen, where I'd been living practically full-time. Jesus, I had a sore shoulder, sure. You couldn't expect me to do housework.

I woke to her standing over me.

"Rod. Wake up. Wake up."

I was a bit stunned and, I suppose, a bit drunk too. I'd taken to having a few shots of rum to ease the pain. The glass and the bottle were still on the table, plus the supper dishes. Over in the sink was a week's worth of dirty dishes.

"Ruth. How'd you get here? You never sent a message. I would have met you."

"There was no time to let you know. Besides, I'm capable of looking after myself, Rod." She surveyed her filthy kitchen that she took so much pride in. "That's more than I can say for you."

Because of my shoulder, I couldn't hoist myself up off the daybed as I normally would. Daybeds are not very high, and all I could do was roll over onto the floor and get to my knees, and from there, with the aid of a chair, I would get to a standing position.

Ruth watched me do this. I was still somewhat drunk and perhaps I overdid the groaning just to get a bit of pity from her. If I did, no one will ever know that but me. When I was up and facing her I said, unnecessarily I suppose, "Maid, my shoulder is some bad."

She didn't answer, but turned away and busied herself at the dishes. She planked the rum bottle down in the bottom cupboard and slammed the door.

"Have you been sleeping in your clothes on that daybed since I left?"

"Uh, yeah."

"And you saw the doctor about your shoulder?"

"Well, no. The doctor left town when things got too rough, they say. It's a long story, but Father Murphy got Missus Annie Drum to look at it."

She was wiping off the table. She stopped in mid-wipe, cloth in hand. "Who? Father Murphy? Why Father Murphy? What's been going on?"

"Never mind. I'll tell you tomorrow. 'Tis one o'clock in the morning."

She came close to me. I thought we would hug and have a kiss, seeing she'd been away for more than a week. But no. She sidestepped me and sniffed at my underarms.

"Phew. You smells some bad, my son. Booze, dirt, sweat. First thing is get the bathwater running and then off comes those dirty clothes. Come on." She bustled off toward the bathroom just off the kitchen. It used to be a pantry in Father's day.

"Ruth, no one has a bath at one o'clock in the morning."

"You got two choices, Rod. Have a bath and get in our bed with me, or have no bath and sleep in your dirty nest on the daybed."

Name of God! She stripped me off and got me into the water. By that time my manhood and my pride were a lost cause.

I wouldn't give in and say it to her, but the warm water felt some good on my shoulder. I should've thought of it before and had my own bath. All I had thought of was a drop of rum to dull the pain, and I'm not even much of a drinker at the best of times.

Afterwards, Ruth rubbed my shoulder with liniment and we got into bed. B'y, 'twas some good to have a wife, even if she was an angry one. The atmosphere was so chilly between us that there was no chance of me turning to her in the bed for a hug. There was a barbwire fence running up and down through the middle of the mattress, and I dared not cross it.

I slept later than usual and woke to the smell of bacon cooking. My God, I don't think I'll ever let Ruth go away again. Bachelor life isn't for me. I got up, dressed and went downstairs.

"Good morning, my duckie." The kitchen was back to the spotless condition that it'd enjoyed before Ruth went to St. John's. "You must've been up early."

"I was." She firmly placed the bacon and eggs in front of me. I wouldn't say she banged it down, but not far from it. Uh, oh, still mad.

Well, whether she was mad or not, I enjoyed my breakfast. I think I'd lost ten pounds the past week. I even had to take my belt in a notch.

When I finished, and was having a smoke with my cup of tea, she sat down at the table so we were eye to eye. "All right now, Rod, let us talk. You're clean, rested and have a good breakfast into you. I know your shoulder is hurting, but it's not broken. I couldn't believe the mess you were in last night. How can a man let himself go like that?"

What could I say back to her? Nothing. Guilty as charged. So I stayed silent and hid my eyes behind the cigarette smoke.

Ruth is a sensible woman. I should have remembered that. She didn't rant on about poor Audrey, poor Richard, poor little girls and bad old Rod. No sir. She said, looking at me with her steadfast blue eyes, "First, let me tell you this. Coming through on the train last night, when we stopped in Gander someone got on board and told everyone the news. The young constable that was struck down, struck down right here in Badger not a hundred yards up the road from this house, has died, Rod. How could something like that happen in a small town like this?"

The news jolted me. I'd been so immersed in my own affairs that I had given no thought to the policeman who had been hit. "Well, I am sorry to hear that, Ruth. I'm really sorry. What a terrible thing to lose his life over. Poor young lad should never have been out here in the first place."

"You're right, of course. I listened to people talk on the train. They all seem to be blaming Joey Smallwood and his government. But, still and all, the name of Badger was mentioned in every conversation. I think that it's going to end up being a black mark on us all." She pulled her chair closer to the table and leaned forward. "Now then, Rod, if you don't mind, I'd like to hear what on earth happened between you and our son-in-law. Richard was beside himself with remorse because he claimed that he'd accidentally hit you. Is that true?"

Well, yes. Blood of a bitch of a townie. But I never said it out loud. Instead I told her what happened after I had put her on the train.

I told her how the A.N.D. Company locked up their premises and the personnel left. How I was walking home and saw all the action on the road leading up to the intersection by the Pentecostal Church. I stood on the sidelines, I said, like everyone else, and watched the police force form a line, and I told her how Richard flashed through my mind. I told her of the women crowded on the snowbanks, and of young children, some of them no more than six or seven years old, running about over fences, along by the police, and mixing with loggers amassed at the intersection. As I recounted it to her, I realized that it was a hard scene to imagine if one hadn't been there.

Ruth said nothing as I went on to describe the formidable police unit marching up the road. When I reached the part of police among strikers, and strikers among police, she held up her hand to stop me.

"What caused that to happen? Didn't you say it looked non-threatening enough for kids to be playing around?"

"Yes, my dear, it seemed that way at first. I don't know what actually caused the clash. I was too far down the road to see and there was a big crowd of onlookers."

I hesitated then, unsure how to describe my meeting with Richard. "I look like a logger, Ruth, you know I do. I wear much the same clothes. This policeman mistook me for a striker and wouldn't listen when I tried to explain. We roughed each other up a bit and he called his friend to help him get me aboard the van." Christ, this was hard to tell. It brought the sweat out on me. "The other cop was Richard."

Well, I wasn't getting any pity from Ruth. I could see that. She's just sitting there, watching me sweat. It never occurred to me until much later that maybe she was too shocked to speak. Once again, I was too immersed in my own self.

"Goddammit, Ruth. No one told me he was out here. Someone could've got word to me somehow. Richard himself should have got in contact with me. What am I, fuckin' no one? Not worth being apprised of family happenings?"

I jumped up from the table. Now I was angry again. I thought I had it under control, but it was there, rising above the surface.

"Rod. Sit down. Tell me about the rest of it. Where'd Richard go from there? Did he bring you home?"

"No, shag it, Ruth. I've said enough. You haven't told me one word of what that snot-nosed townie coward told you. Come on. Out with it."

"There's no 'out with it' to tell, Rod. Audrey and I never even knew where Richard had gone. His father wasn't allowed to say. It never entered our minds that he was gone to Badger."

She stood up and grabbed my plate and cup. "Richard came home on Thursday morning," she continued. "He told us of how you were mistaken for a logger. Yes, he admitted he hit you, by accident.

But he didn't share any details with me except to say that he was sorrier than words could ever say and would I ask you to try to forgive him. Whether he told his father more I cannot say. I had no further discussion with him. We were, all of us, confused and upset. It was too much for me, so I went into my room and closed the door. The train was going west at two o'clock that same afternoon and, after saying goodbye to Audrey and the children, I took a taxi to the railway station and boarded it. I had no further conversation with Richard."

Well! He never told her about leaving me, about going to the priest. Nothing. Hmmph.

God only knows where she and I would've gone with our conversation after that. Perhaps God intervened, because the back door opened. It was Bill Hatcher. He'd come over every day to check on me.

"Rod, how are you today, b'y?" He spied the wife standing by the table with the dishes in her hands. "Ruth! I didn't know you were back. You must've come in last night. Rod, you never said." He looked from me to Ruth. "Have I butted in the middle of something?"

"No, no, Bill. That's okay," I said. To tell the truth, I was kind of glad he had butted in.

"There are a lot of our men down to the A.N.D. Company office, Rod. They want to go back to work. You knows that Joey said they have to join his union first?"

"Yeah, I heard that. Perhaps you and me should go down and see what's goin' on with them." Yes, I thought, anything to get away from Ruth right now.

So we mucked off down the road to the office. Let Ruth stew all afternoon. I was too crooked to care.

There were twenty-five of my crew waiting to see me. They all said they were joining Joey's union. But none of them had any smiles on their faces as they said it. They would sign anything, do anything to have their old jobs back. I pitied them, I did. All they had fought for . . . gone down the drain. So I signed them all up and then I went over to Alf's telegraph office and wired for the rest.

The A.N.D. Company had sent men up to my camp last month, to clean up. Most everything had to be hauled out and burned. Before then, the Company manager had called me into his office after the men trashed the camp and after Joey had made his surprise speech on the radio, condemning the IWA. This manager wasn't as gimlet-eyed as old Hughie Cole was, but he was no pussycat either. I suppose the managers had to be tough. They had bosses too, higher up.

"Well, Rod, there's a fine mess up in your camp. A few of us went up and looked at it the other day. Do you have plans to go back there?"

"I'll go back there, sir, if you guys will clean it up."

"Why us, pray tell me?" He had very high thoughts of himself as he stood there by the window in his gleaming oxblood leather boots, one foot cocked on the radiator, smoking his cigarette in a holder. I bet the foolish arsehole practiced that pose in front of his mirror at home.

And I was no pussycat either. No siree. So I kept my face carefully bland as I answered. "If I may say so, sir, this was your strike; it was your scab labour. You can find no fault of mine in any of this."

He drew deep on his cigarette holder, sucking the smoke into his lungs. "Yes, I suppose we agree with you on that. Anyway, I'll tell you what we're going to do. We're going to make an example of your camp. To show that we keep our camps in good condition, we'll do it up a bit. When she's ready to go, we'll get someone from the *Grand Falls Advertiser* to come up and take some pictures. That's the idea that the Company has. What do you think?"

"Yes b'y, if it's no expense to me. When are you going to start?"

"Right away. The IWA might call them scabs, but we have a hundred men up in the woods right now with not much to do. They'll start cleaning it out tomorrow."

So the Company had the camp cleaned out, made a mountain of the stuff and set fire to it. Then they put Tentest over the log walls, with some insulation stuffed between. We got an oil stove in the bunkhouse, new mattresses and cots. The cookhouse got a new stove as well. They installed a generator that gave us electricity and a hot water boiler so the men could wash in warm water. It wasn't much, but it was a long way from the old camp, I can tell you that. Then they had someone from the *Advertiser* snap a few pictures.

When I signed up my twenty-five men, I told them to go on up in the camp and make themselves at home. Bill Hatcher would oversee things for me. I had to get back to Ruth and make peace with her.

Well sir, she had some supper cooked for me. Chicken and gravy, salt meat, cabbage, pease puddin' . . . all the vegetables. She'd even made a figgy duff.

When I went in the door, I didn't know if it was best to speak or not. So I went and washed up. When I came out to sit down, she came over and put her arms around me. I put my arms around her too, glad to have harmony restored to my house.

We had a little cuddle for a few minutes. She murmured, "Oh, Rod. We can't be mad with each other. We have to stick together."

Well, it was time for me to climb down off my high horse. Twenty-five years of marriage to Ruth was too important to throw away.

"Yes, my dear. I'm sorry I bawled at you this morning. I've been thinking about it all afternoon. Maid, we're going to have to go in to St. John's and work things out."

Ruth kissed me again. "I was hoping you'd say that, my dear. Come on and have your supper before it gets cold."

$$\wp$$

The last two weeks of March brought about a change in the residents of the town.

The three churches had prayer services as the young constable lay in Grand Falls Hospital and, then, on March 12, when he passed away, there were more prayers. I thought to myself that the Badger people were carrying the burden of guilt for what had happened, although surely everyone knew they were in no way responsible.

I watched on my little black and white television as the Smallwood Government, which was responsible, treated his death like a circus as they paraded the coffin across the province by train, stopping in each community. Then, when they reached St. John's, the procession went through the streets. It seemed to me as though the government was trying to hide its guilt behind an ostentatious display of false grief.

I wrote to Jonathan and mailed it. I also posted one to the Pentecostal Assembly office, asking to be relieved of my post for a period of time. I cited that I didn't feel able to perform my job at the moment because of what I had witnessed. I told them I knew it would take time to bring in a replacement and I was willing to wait it out until the new pastor arrived.

March 13, 1959

Jonathan, my friend:

I received your letter three days ago, on what I have to say was the most awful, traumatic day of my life.

Oh Jonathan, I witnessed a riot and a killing! I know you can hardly believe what you are reading, and I can hardly credit that I am telling it.

Since I last wrote you, this community has become embroiled in a loggers' strike, officially called on December 31, 1958. It isn't just Badger, but almost the whole province. Newfoundlanders can be passionate people.

Our provincial government actually intervened, and decertified the union. Over a short period of recent days, loggers amassed here, because of Badger's geographic location, which is the centre of the A.N.D. Company woods operations. Police were imported into the town as well. We are so small that we do not have a local detachment in Badger. Outside God's and my church, roads converge. It was here that the loggers made their last stand.

I watched from my church window as police and loggers came together. My mind reeled in shock. I cried, I tore my hair. It was dreadful!

Then, even through the windowpane, I heard a crack that I'll never forget. A police officer was struck in the skull and went down. As I watched in horror, the blood seeped from his head onto the snow.

I am sure that God put wings to my feet at that moment as I fled to my house, grabbed towels and ran around the corner of the church to the scene. I knew my life had been leading up to that moment. Jesus had been preparing me since I was born. I was put there to offer aid to an injured man.

I have to believe that God has a bigger plan for all this. I am praying and hope to receive answers – for the community and for myself.

I think I might apply for a sabbatical. I need to go away and meditate. Right now I feel that I cannot stay here. The spot out by the church where it happened seems to still hold the horror. At first the police said that I would have to testify in court. They tried to get me to name the striker who struck the policeman. I said that I wasn't sure. Perhaps I was, perhaps I wasn't. Anyway, it was a moot point in the end. I couldn't give evidence because I had viewed the incident through a windowpane. You know I was relieved.

One more thing. After these happenings, subsequent events saw me hiding fugitive strikers in my attic as the police tore apart the town, searching. I am a disgrace to my profession. I cannot write any more.

Please forgive me for pouring out my grief to you. I have no one here that I can confide in.

Yours, always.
Damian

My friendship with Virtue had remained the same, as I took no steps to take it further. I wondered if I should do that and ask her to be my wife after my leave was over. I was unable to contemplate any kind of future. I longed to hear from Jonathan.

By April, the IWA Strike and the Badger Riot was old news and had disappeared entirely from the newspapers. I continued with my duties for the church, but my heart wasn't into it. My prayers felt hollow and useless. I felt as though I had aged ten years.

𝄢

Constable Moss died. Now it was murder.

My God, Madeline and I, and my brothers, David and Thomas, are only kids, and all of us had seen a murder! We've been whispering among ourselves. A man from over Bonne Bay way was arrested. We're well aware that we must keep quiet to outsiders. We're scared. The town's turned inward on itself. People are careful of what they say. The reporter from the *Toronto Star* stayed around for awhile, but no one would tell him anything. He was at the scene of the riot. Perhaps he saw for himself. Perhaps not.

I've been feeling sick ever since the riot. My parents said it was the trauma of the event. Dad told me that I could stay home from school, but I had to go. I might have missed something if I stayed home.

One week later, I awoke one morning with a sticky, itchy feeling between my legs. I threw back the covers and saw the sheet stained with blood. Instantly my mind had a flashback to the last blood I had seen, around the policeman's head. I screamed as loud as I could. "Mom!" She came running up the stairs. I started to cry. "Mom, I think I'm starting to menstruate."

Some time later, when life was calmer, Mom and I had a talk about womanhood, periods and stuff. It was hard for us to get time alone in our house with my needy brothers underfoot all the time, but we managed it one day when she was doing her ironing and the baby was asleep. My mother had been preparing me since I was twelve, so I knew most things. However, Mom's thoughts on why it had happened at this particular time summed it up for me.

Looking at me with her steady grey eyes, she said, "When you think of this, years from now, you'll realize that the shock of what you saw at the Badger Riot, the killing of a policeman, the blood on the snow, was what hastened you on your way to womanhood."

She finished ironing the last shirt and started to put away her flatiron. "Amanda, my child, you'll never forget this. None of us ever will."

Epilogue

I sat in the confessional box. The church was empty, but my parishioners knew I was there, as I was every Saturday evening, should they need to talk to their priest.

The conflict was over. Most of the loggers had joined up with Joey Smallwood's union, the Newfoundland Brotherhood of Wood Workers, and had gone back into the woods camps for the haul-off. Others had escaped back to their outport homes. Badger looked wartorn. There was a sense of unease in the air. The residents were still in shock. People talked to each other in low tones.

The door on the other side of the partition squeaked open. I heard someone kneel down. The box was dark. I slid open the grill between the penitent and myself.

"Bless me Father, for I have sinned," the voice rasped in the darkness. I knew most of my parishioners' voices, but not this one. Someone in disguise, or a stranger?

"What is your sin, my child?" I asked.

"Father, I . . . I . . . killed that police feller. I bashed his head in with me stick. I hit him three or four times, Father. It wudn't no accident. I did it on purpose. They should have left us alone. We was only loggers tryin' to make a decent living." The gruff voice broke, seeming to sob.

Before I could gather myself to speak, I heard the confessional door bang open. Running footsteps echoed down through the church, and the person was gone.

Afterword

When the A.N.D. Company and the IWA had not worked out a collective agreement in 1958, the IWA requested that the Smallwood Government convene a conciliation board. The board recommended a reduction in work hours, improved camp conditions, and a wage increase of $1.22 per hour.

These recommendations were accepted by the IWA but turned down by the A.N.D. Company. In response, loggers took to the picket lines.

Smallwood decertified the IWA and formed a government union to represent the loggers.

Two days after the Badger Riot, the A.N.D. Company signed an agreement with Smallwood's Newfoundland Brotherhood of Wood Workers – giving the loggers improved living conditions and a wage of $1.22 per hour.

Acknowledgements

This book would not have been possible without the help and encouragement of the following people.

My dear mother, Lucy Day, who at the age of eighty-seven delved into her wonderful memory, and made two trips to Badger with me opening doors into her generation – a generation who were young adults during the IWA conflict. Her love and her faith in me was a well of strength that I drew upon.

My brother H. Scott Day, a writer himself, who led me through his boyhood in Badger and explained technical things like tractors and undercarriages of cars. Scott, your patience with me was phenomenal.

My family: Carol and Bridget, my daughters, and Brian, my son, and their three spouses, who were rooting for me all the way. My grandchildren Katlynn Ballam, Brianna Ricketts, and Andrew Ballam, who knew their "Mugga" would someday write a book.

My daughter Bridget Ricketts started me on my writing journey with a gift certificate for my birthday to Gordon Rodgers's writing class at Memorial University. Bridget prodded me along with suggestions, profiles, timelines, and edits. Finally I was able to wing it on my own and she let me fly.

The people of Badger: Mary Card Killam – thanks for the www.newfoundwebbers.com thread and for your support in all things, from start to finish. For you who opened your homes, your hearts and your memories to me: Mike and Margaret (Patey) Murray,

Gordon and Margaret (Saunders) Patey, Ted Patey, for his video of the 2003 flood. Clyde and Marie (Gill) Loder, their daughter Lorna (Loder) Stuckless, Reg and Cora White, Mrs. Doris Burt, Fred and Hilda Wells, thank you for your hospitality and support. Earl Penney, who told me about the Company snowmobile and other stories, and his daughter Velda Penney Hewlett, Albert and Jean Loder Lush, for spending an evening talking, many thanks to you all.

Howard Noseworthy, who for four hours sat and introduced me to the wongers, the cable boat, the River, and who sang me a great song, *The Shores of Twin Lakes*, thank you.

Special mention must be made to Ms. Irene Matthews, my grade school teacher, who first showed me that it was possible to write and who, in my opinion, has a command of the written English language that is second to none. Her book, *Memories of Badger: An Anthology of Reminiscences*, O. I. Matthews 1991, was invaluable to me in recapturing the old-time feel of the town.

My gratitude and thanks to Gordon Butt for help with things past, Cyril Hannon, former Assistant CNR Agent at Badger, for help with train schedules and other matters, Frances MacDonald Newman for her advice, and Harry Hayden, for giving me his old books and notes. A special thank you to Matthew Aylward, who talked to me about burial practices in Bonavista Bay.

To those that have passed away while this was being written:

Ignatius Paul (1938–2005), Vice-Chief of the Exploits Valley Sple'tk First Nations Band, whose tales and stories of the Mi'kmaq community of Badger in the 1950s were wonderful and whose heart stone will stay with me always.

Marmaduke Noel (1914–2007), who, at ninety-four, still retained in his memory passionate views of the strike. Mrs. Elsie Loder (1914–2007), a lovely gentle lady, who related her memories of a terrible time seen through the eyes of a young woman.

To John Kitchen, author of *By the Sweat of my Brow*, with whom I spent many hours discussing the logging industry.

Although I consulted many articles and readings at the Newfoundland Studies at Memorial University and at the A.C.

Hunter Library, Newfoundland Room, the most definitive account was found at the Rooms by an archivist who came in on her day off to bring it to me. It is "We are only Loggers: Loggers and the Struggle for Development in Newfoundland, 1929–1959," Dufferin Sutherland (Ph.D. thesis, University of British Columbia, 1995) 183–87, 291–98.

A slim book called *The Savour of Things Past*, the Ongoing Book Committee, 1986, which I found in the most unlikely place, had a great article by Elmer Ball, a native of Badger, called "The Badger Drive," in which he describes the working life of a wonger, a word that has long dropped from use. Thank you to the Ball family for giving me permission to use it.

I also drew heavily on *A Class Act*, Bill Gillespie, 1986, Creative Printers, for the labour side of the dispute.

A video of Landon Ladd speaking to MUN students in 1983 brought the famous union leader to life for me once again in "Only the Strong are Free – the Newfoundland Logger's Strike of 1959," H. Landon Ladd CCLH Video Memorial University 1983.

Because the railway figured so largely in the 1950s, I drew on *The People's Road: on the trail of the Newfoundland Railway*, Wade Kearley, 1995, Harry Cuff Publications, and *Next Stop: Gaff Topsail*, Mont Lingard, 1996.

To the facilitators of the many writing classes: Gordon Rodgers, to whom the idea for this story was first pitched. His support and encouragement were the impetus that put me on this path. Also, Carmelita McGrath, JoAnne Soper Cook, and Paul Butler. By the time I reached Paul, I knew where I was going but didn't know how to get there. Thank you, Paul, for showing me the way. To all of you, your knowledge, patience, and expertise were invaluable.

Thank you to all the people who wrote me on the new-foundwebbers site with your stories:

Especially Madonna Piercey Mercer, Merlyn Dicks, Jerry Lush, Wallace Hoddinott. Others known only by their nicknames: Blue, Charity, Salty, river, Whammy, ocean, Diet Coke girl, Starve Gutted Gull, Viking, Pat, Dusty, Weezie, and many more.

My heartfelt gratitude goes to my publishers extraordinaire at Flanker Press – Garry, Margo, and Jerry Cranford – who gently led me through the editing process. From them I learned that it's one thing to write a story, but it's quite another thing to get it between two covers and onto the shelves.

A special thank you to Anne Hart for editing this book.

My late husband, Felix Ricketts, took great pride in everything that I wrote. His favourite comment was, "By the jumpin's, old girl, you can sure put it together." Even though it is sad that he is not here physically to see my book published, I always feel he is with me in spirit, encouraging me, pushing me along to the finish line.

Even though this story is woven around a true event, all characters are products of my imagination. Any errors in interpreting the logging operations during the 1950s are mine and mine alone. The eyewitness account of the riot is from my own memory of the event.

ABOUT THE AUTHOR

JUDY (DAY) RICKETTS was fourteen years old at the time of the International Woodworkers of America (IWA) Strike of 1959. A native of Badger, she, along with other schoolchildren, watched from the roadside as loggers and local authorities came together in a famous melee that effectively ended the strike. She believes that the children of the day never recovered from witnessing this terrible event in Newfoundland's history. Fifty years later, she knows that the emotions still run deep. Judy can be reached by email at jaricketts@nf.sympatico.ca. Her author website is www.jaricketts.com.

Marquis Book Printing Inc.

Québec, Canada
2009